A Mediocre Life

So far, the first.

A Mediocre Life

By Marvin Hill

A Mediocre Life

Names, characters, places, and happenings are the product of the author's imagination. Any resemblance to actual persons, living or dead, business establishments, events, or locales is purely coincidental.

ISBN-13:
978-1500706128

ISBN-10:
1500706124

For more information,
Visit the author's blog: www.marvhill.com

Dedicated to my late Father,
The Architect,
And the Bird,
Had it not been for your absence,
I would never have written a book.
Jerks.

A Mediocre Life

I often wake up mornings and figure that I am the loneliest person on the planet, if not the entire universe. At that exact moment, and hundreds of times over, billions of other people are thinking the same damned thing. We stand in front of mirrors, popping pimples or flexing in our underwear, trying to convince ourselves that we can be a happy people; that we are indeed lovable if anything in spite of our flaws. Vacantly we brush tartar from yellowed teeth. We grab at folds of flab and protruding unlovable handles. We stare across dirty houses and apartments run as amuck as our lives. We just haven't the strength to wash all those dishes and pick up all those clothes. We just haven't the wherewithal to live out our dreams and the lives that we do live, pale in comparison to anything worthwhile.

Some of us seek succor in pets. Some of us hoard things. Some of us sleep around. Some of us drink or smoke or take up other substances. Most of us do a combination of all or at least a few.

It's not healthy, but then again, most of us feel that we should be punished for some reason. That we deserve less of a life and less of the good things. As if it's largely ours to blame for being so miserably unfortunate and unfortunate looking. And, honestly, maybe it is. Surely no one told me to eat so poorly or drink so much or waste so much money.

But I still tried to find love. I still clung to this idea of Prince Charming. That after all the toads and frogs and murky underwater things, I could find someone that would help put my life together. Like many others, I scoured the Internet dating sites. I downloaded the apps. I'd "Grindr", I'd "Scruff", I'd Adam4Adam, but nothing. Zilp. Zilch. Nada. No bananas.

Maybe I was that ugly.

Then again, no one ever seemed interesting. The selection was little more than a slew of catty twinks, lackluster queens, and a few gym bunnies. Also, supposedly I looked too intimidating. A friend once told me that the latter was why the gays didn't like me. That, and I had a bad reputation. I just replied that I thought they all secretly wanted me. I had assumed for the longest time, that being bullied by the cliquish fags was as close as they could get to date me. He laughed and quickly changed the subject.

Because of all this, there was always a stretch of months wherein I had no love interest. For said months, I was like a leper. Not even with ten foot poles and all that shit would a man deign to have me associated with him. The only upside was that I became more productive. I made more art and even tended to lose weight. There's something about fooling yourself into believing that somebody loves you, which convinces you, that they'd love you for whoever you are: fat, ugly, drunk, unambitious... the works. I could grow a harelip and a humpback and still be assured of their affections. But that seldom lasts. And so, if anything, to spite said ex lovers, you drop a few tens of pounds and pretend you have a bevy of interesting hobbies you have only just recently *rediscovered*. Of course, said hobbies must be photogenic and catalogued. There's no point in doing anything these days unless you can instantly document it online. In fact, most people are too busy trying to prove that they're having a good time than actually enjoying the experience. That and they like making kissy faces.

"Babe, I finally have an Instagram! ... But I dunno how to use it..." I declared tentatively.

We had been drinking. That's about all I did back then, was drink. Beth snatched my phone from across the table of this 24-hour burger joint. She was a dark girl, one the color of a milky coffee, who had always been a bit plumper than even she had hoped for. Her nose was broad at the tip but her smile, that smile, ten times as wide and her laugh and humor as virulent as any I had ever known. Whataburger had always been one of my fav's even if only because I was addicted to ketchup and its various incarnations. They even had this thing called "Spicy Ketchup". I'm drooling as I write this. The place had these stiff booths, and bright fluorescent lights, which glared off the glass walls along with the reflections of many a lost soul. Everything was done up orange and white and beige and populated by mostly polite, if sometimes extroverted/drunk, clientele. It was our very own den of thieves, a throwback to the diner of old. After bars, people would line up and you'd run into old friends or friends who had a different plan that night. The seating arrangements were sometimes tricky but I've always found it comforting to eat beside strangers, make new friends, and have a good old chuckle.

Beth helped set up my account for yet another social network I'd abuse, as I so nimbly managed to make the meal in front of me look like a murder scene. I cannot stress how much I like ketchup. Seriously, it's like a good Christmas idea.

I've always thought that Social Networks are mainly what anti-social people use to trick themselves into thinking that they are popular. It's like: Hey, everybody likes my pizza picture… and yet I'm eating it all alone, and crying, with my ten cats, as I plead with Mittens the Second, to grab the gallon of Pistachio Almonds from the freezer.

"Babe! You don't even have any photos yet and you already have 117 followers!" Beth squealed out with joy.

For a second, I too felt a flutter and a blush. Was I popular??? Finally??? I had never felt particularly admired. I'd always spent my life lurking in the peripherals of society. Maybe it was some side consequence to growing up on the border. I neither felt here nor there. Not one of "them", much less "the other". But that aside, we then talked about everything and nothing in particular as she daintily nibbled on two potato and cheese *taquitos*, whilst I, ever the picture of decorum, ravaged a burger, fries, and some ambrosia like delicacy referred to as a "Honey Butter Biscuit Sandwich". I had ridden my bike to the bars, so after said carnage, I offered to walk her home.

In the dark cold, she smiled, step by step, "Man, that's so crazy that you found that ten dollar bill on the floor."

"I know, huh? We should totally walk Brooke to her car more often."

"Def'. But we should probably invite her to more fancy places. Maybe we can end up finding twenty-dollar bills or like some kind of jewelry that isn't rhinestones or a ring-pop." She laughed then kicked a pebble towards the curb as I mulled over the idea.

"So, we need to come up with these rules on dating if we're ever gonna even HOPE to get out of this fucking dry spell." I began, struggling to keep the bike balanced by my side.

The nights had started to get chilly, the first day of autumn a few days away, and those lonely god awful holidays looming in the distance.

I continued, "I've come up with one: No dating your exes." My bike quietly squeaked as the spokes and the chain and the gears went click click click click.

"Yea, THAT, and no dating anyone who's dated some one you know OR is friends with any of your friends." she added.

"So... basically... we can't date anyone." I thought aloud.

"Exactly!" She beamed then her smile turned sour after a moment.

Above, the stars twinkled just a bit dimmer as the cold wind brushed up behind us. Our feet dragging just a little bit more, our minds just a bit more cavernous, our hearts a similar depth. One of the main things we hated about our lives was that we had no one to date. We blamed it on our city, some chuckhole in the desert. We blamed it on the lack of potential mates. We figured that everyone worth his or her salt had long ago had the good sense to leave, to get the hell out of Dodge and dodge the endless boring nights. We also heavily gambled on the notion that big city folks would be more appreciative of our minds. That finally, somewhere, someone we'd never met, was out there wondering where we were.

I used to not have anything and then a friend gave me a dog towards the end of my college career and after that I took to collecting pets. There had always been dogs on the farm but it had been years since I had one of my own. When my mother was pregnant with me, my father bought them a chow-chow. I used to lay against her at night on the cold dinning room floor under this giant class cabinet with a brass frame. Her name was Fifi, something common for fu-fu dogs in the 80's. We would lay under silver plated tea sets and gold plated silverware and various knick-knacks. The sort of things families liked to display but never ever used. Sort of setting the scene for company that we were up and coming or keeping up with The Somebody's or Whowhat's. As a gay little boy, I of course delighted in polishing the silver. Although, in retrospect, I do not know whether the exposure to toxic household cleaning chemicals was detrimental to my "facilities" or just quite possibly the hallmark of negligent parenting. You don't even want to get me started on an eight year old I and an open flame, much less how I used to run around the house with chopsticks.

Anyhow, I broke the first rule. Went back with my ex. He was a beautiful and loving person but I was a louse. I felt like a louse. Like I let myself down for buckling under the pressure of "no options". Maybe he was the right option, but to be honest, he was basically the only option. What was a boy to do? I was just so insecure and indecisive. Then I was filled with a dreadful feeling as if I had sold myself short, that I had always sold myself short and that I had never given myself the opportunity to explore the world. Read: I felt guilty for not sleeping around more. I was such a coward. I was lonely but maybe I wanted to stay lonely. I knew nobody would want me because I was wrong... something in me was flawed if precious, "Fat girl but she's funny" sort of thing. And if anybody professed to adore me, I immediately suspected that there was something terribly wrong with THEM, and, truthfully, I couldn't have had that.

Sometimes we try and take on the world when we can't even tie our own shoelaces. Self-doubt can be debilitating: Either you're stuck on the floor, or running around in circles. Sometimes it makes you make really brash decisions. I looked at all the stuff I had accumulated throughout the years: Fancy things, antique items and forgotten oddities; Bowling pins instead of gaming stations; Birds and fish instead of children. Relics of my half assed pursuits: two trumpets; one bass; tubes and tubes of paint; a dust covered sewing machine; silkscreens; weights...Pots and pans from when I was pretending to be a grandmother. Everything went in boxes or was left out on the curb. I had read online that pawnshops wouldn't give you what your treasures were worth and what I had were indeed treasures. Old catalogues and magazines wondering if RFK would be the next president and even rare quarters and dimes hammered out of silver. I decided to sell anything that I hadn't inherited except for my pets and a few things I had planned to serve fancy dinners with, or cook on. That, and a fridge, an old and rusting Philco fridge from the fifties I had stolen from the university and fixed up from freezing its contents. My extra bed frames, bikes, dressers, shoes and those shirts I hadn't fit into for years... all for sale at a reasonable price.

I found myself standing with a book, one of many I had piled up by the corner outside my apartment. I was ready to start a new life, or, haphazardly, willing to give up an old one. As I stared back into the emptying three bedrooms, one bath, I mulled over the recent events that had come to change view on life entirely.

My father had died not too long ago. It was about a week before Thanksgiving and the day before my older brother's birthday. He was survived by my mother and three children, which we knew of. After the unsorted business of arranging for his body to be delivered across the border, back from Mexico to which he had been deported, and packing up his house, I was all but ready to escape somewhere, anywhere. The latter chore, which involved hastily rummaging through decades of HIS acquired crap, left me wanting to just get rid of all that I owned. Dad's three rooms, one bath, all stuffed practically to the ceiling with shit. Outdated computers. Books about theology and martial arts, long since needing revising. He had even kept a cabinet filled with the cardboard toilet paper cores. A friend helping us had found them and called out that he had discovered our secret inheritance.

The rosary and funeral actually weren't that difficult considering I had spent the both days chugging vodka and anything that would come my way. At the moment of my sidewalk sale, I was well into my third beer. Things at first had a price, some random nostalgic value that I had plucked from the air. Gradually those prices let way to negotiating and a sort of adrenaline rush most likely seeded by said spirits. By the end, I really didn't care. I was just so elated that no matter how little people wanted to pay, it seemed an okay price for something that had been sitting in my apartment just gathering moss, something just holding me back. It was like taking this really good shit after a really big meal. Besides, two dollars could buy me another tallboy.

There went my amp and my bass, my three electric organs. Some books on beatniks I never quite opened. Bye-bye boots, shirts, but not my toys, God forbid. I was saving those for my grandchildren. So long old typewriters, old desks, lamps and a ladder. Five cookbooks I'd only skimmed through. Buckets of screen-printing paint, acrylic paints, oil paints, my extra bottle openers (which were quite a few). More clothes, more antique cameras, another sewing machine. Desks. More dressers. Several chairs including the one I was sitting in, etc.

Everything, just about, found a happy home. And what I couldn't sell by the end of the day, I gave away to friends if they were willing to pick it up off the curb. If not, homeless loves thems shits. Tea party in the alley, whoop whoop. The more sentimental items, of course, were sent to my mother's where they'd stand a lonely and forgotten existence. But this was life. This was adventure, wasn't it? Everything you had, boxed up, shipped out. I told myself that I could afford new things, new treasures, and a life with exceedingly less anchors and replete with simple pleasures.

I was only fooling myself.

I stood in my all but empty apartment. It looked so much bigger. Maybe that's why I'd fallen in love with it all those years ago: that open space, its hardwood floors, these giant windows just letting all sorts of light in. There was an air of raw potential like cold morning. The type of cold morning you greeted before vacations or when you had something important to do like a job interview or the first day of classes.

Those cold mornings with vacant streets and light posts competing with the sun dawning.

"Wow! Babe! This place looks REALLY nice with out all that crap in here!" Beth laughed, a red bandana holding back her short blue hair that she had decided to dye on a whim. It fell just somewhere beneath her chin but the bangs kept getting in her face. I think she thought it looked like a moving-out outfit, an ensemble akin to Rosie the Riveter but after a half bottle of wine. She stood there, arms akimbo, with her knees bending in at the middle, reminders of when she had been heavier. In between packing boxes we joked about how going up and down the stairs counted as a workout and wondered if we should "check-in" and post selfies in front of the mirror for Instagram. But I didn't have a mirror anymore and we nixed the plan and opted instead for another bottle of cheap cabernet and a bag of vinegar and salt chips.

"I know," I hunched over a little as if the wind had been knocked out of me. "I remember when I first saw the place. I had brought some guy I was dating and immediately dropped 300 for the deposit. My landlord made us walk on paper or some kind of plastic runner or some shit like that." I laughed and nudged Beth, "She was afraid that we'd scuff up the newly 'finished' floors. But I think they had just covered them with brown paint. And now look at her... all scuffed up. Blinds busted. The windows cracked every winter a little bit more and more and... well... "

"Has she rented it out yet?" she asked.

"Na. I don't think so."

Beth pursed her lips and pointed out her chin, nodding ever so slightly, surveying the digs. My digs: So many good times; So many bad times. But there was just a plurality of the former, enough to have made me happy, really happy.

"I wonder how much she's asking for it..." she trailed off, imagining the place done up in her style. "It'd be a pretty tight setup and you could just leave this part open right here, for like dance parties or some shit." She waved her hand, drawing an invisible border around the second living room.

"Indoor jacuzzi." I suggested, raising an eyebrow and nodding my head.

"Indoor jacuzzi *slash* olympic size swimming pool." She smiled and sucked her teeth.

I laughed as I leaned over and braced myself for another heavy box. "Actually, that's the same thing Gloria used to say."

"Dayum, indoor pool?" She chuckled.

"Ha! No! About the dance party floor/open space, thingy." My gaze went distant for a moment. I was lost in the reverie of everything I had hoped for when I first moved out of my mother's house at 25, after college, and after a debilitating break up with my first boyfriend. I wondered for a second if that was my modus operandi, to just get up and go whenever things got tough.

Beth shook her head, "Oh... mmm dam, babe, why didn't we ever think of that?!"

"Please," I snickered, "You danced plenty of times by the table."

"Indoor jacuzzi *slash* indoor swimming pool *slash* floating table." She smiled wild eyed and broad, moving her head up and down, slowly and emphatically.

We both stared in opposite directions. Hands on her hips, mine around this big box of shit. She stared out the window and I towards the second living room. I put down the box to check my phone then ran a hand across the bumpy faced plaster on the walls. Those wrinkled drips where paintings had hung. Paintings I had been working on but never finished. These wrinkled walls that I'd fallen against, drunk at night, drunk during the day. These wrinkled walls that had smelled cigarettes at 4 in the morning as I sat staring at Netflix. These wrinkled walls that had heard me sing and sing terribly but never once complained. Those walls. That floor. Those windows. Le sigh....

I tossed an errant shoe on top of the box and braced myself once more. "Okay babe, let's take the rest of this shit then we can get the guys to help us with the fridge."

"Oh man, it's a shame you can't take it with you." she mused aloud.

"I know." I sighed. That fridge was one of my prized possessions. Really, something one of a kind, but, oh well.

Seeing remorse in my eyes, she tried comforting me with an old adage and a far fetched suggestion, "*C'est la vie*... OR like you could just pay rent to store it and all the rest of your stuff here." She looked back to the kitchen, "Shit looks heavier than a mother-fuck."

We laughed.

I said, "I know. Imagine?"

She pursed her lips, "Naw, on second thought, FUCK THAT SHIT! Then I'd have to help you move all that crap back in."

"Ready?"

"One... two... two and a half... Go!"

Seven of us were trying to negotiate an old lead fridge down two flights of stairs that had a landing midway, then led out in the opposite direction like a pair of open scissors. So, not only was it heavy as a "mother-fuck", but at some point we had to turn it around and manage not to get anyone accidentally crushed. I'd have paid movers if they had accepted hugs and kisses, but all I could afford was a 30 pack of beer and two five dollar pizzas from Little Caesar's. A chorus ensued of:

"Wait! Wait! Wait!"

"Put 'er down!"

"Aw! Fuck! My hand!"

"FUCK this shit's heavy!"

"Wait babe, lemme take out the racks and stuff." Beth opened the door and removed two steel racks and a couple of plastic baskets, one labeled "Meat", then slammed the door. A loud snap-thudded as the heavy latch closed. In reality she didn't slam the door but the thing was just SO heavy and the old mechanism to lock it SO massive that it made this heaving ruckus.

"Oh great, Beth, now I'm so sure it'll be lighter," her younger brother, Jeff, chimed in sarcastically. He was a wee bit of a thing. A stark contrast to the rest of his family who were large sideways, and his older brother, who was at least about a foot taller. For a second an image of him lying prostrate under this behemoth flashed through my head: Just a pair of tiny arms and tiny legs and a little red baseball hat strewn to the side.

"Shut up, Jeff-o!" She hissed then smiled and chuckled.

His friend David leaned over the top, smiled, and wiped a bead of sweat off his forehead. As it was, he was pretty pale for a Mexican, but I think the blood had actually rushed from his head and then all of a sudden it was back again in big, red, blotchy cheeks that spread all over until his whole face looked like some kind of allergic reaction. Mark and Paul hung back sweating, leaning against the wooden stairway rails. They were two cousins from the kitchen at work. Stocky little guys like light skinned Mexican Neanderthals with a farmer's tan. Mark was completely bald which for some reason reminded me about how cold it was getting outside and how inappropriate Paul's black wife beater looked in comparison to Jeff and David's denim jackets and jeans.

Later that evening, I had decided to try and describe the scene. I had taken to writing in public just to sort of soak up as much of the city that I was leaving behind. I never really did the pedestrian thing. I mostly stayed indoors, or if out, it was only ever to a bar. Never sat in a cafe or a coffee house until then. I tried hiking. Forgot how much I missed the stuff. How I used to like it when you'd get so high up that the birds would hop right along next to you. You could sit and eat a sandwich and the sparrows would just stare quizzically. No fear of humans. No real acquaintance with man. That was the mountain. A hike was a return to the land.

Also, the mall; I really liked the mall. I would order Chinese from this one place called Chinese Gourmet. I still swear that it's one of the better rice peddlers in town, even if it's cheapy and had no airs of being greater than a fast food joint. I'd ask for it in a to-go box because I never really finished what I ordered. But now, now I had nowhere to go. So I'd just sit and people watch. Stare at the children and mothers and the teenagers with more money than I would ever have. Everyone walked with something even if it was just an ice cream. Couples and families and loners like me would sit and chew and smack their lips and say something they thought was funny, but honestly, I didn't care who Jennifer was or how stupid her dress looked last week. Most people spent their time on their phones even in the presence of company. Some couples stared down at the table. Their married counterparts likewise only ever so often turning to feed a child or admonish a child or wonder where they had left said child. But it was alive and bustling. Retail workers would walk in and walk out and the youth of the city was so not the youth of the city I had grown up with. I swear every girl was pretty and every guy was handsome and they all were dressed like models. They say that this new generation has fashion trends at the tip of their fingers. You can keep up with Milan and order things online from Paris or the latest from New York. In my day, we had a handful of retailers and nothing close to an H&M or a Forever 21, etc. I think we had JCPenny and Montgomery Ward. Man, and when Sears hit the city, I think everyone was sportin' the softer side.

To tell you the truth, I did very little writing. I just carried around an expensive Moleskine notebook I later discovered was about 8 bucks cheaper at Target than at Barnes and Noble. In my mind was etched this image of the perennial hipster writing a novel at a Starbucks. In a vain attempt to not look so vain, I'd take an entry level math book and an old copy of Anthropological Theory so that it only ever looked like I was taking a break from studying to write in my diary about Dreamy Johnny or the sock-hop or some shit like that.

There were a few times I was approached by a random person, asking if I was in their class. I'd usually answer, "Nope. Guess I just have that kind of face. I swear my dad must've been busy back in his day. People always tell me I look like somebody they know."

One time this chick came up to me and asked:

"Really?" her voice squeaky like new shoes on linoleum floors, "I swear I have you for Daniel's, right?"

"Nope. I just carry these things to look smart. I don't even go to college."

She then made a funny face and awkwardly said goodbye. I just sat there sort of tapping my pen on the journal and rested my head in my hand.

"Now, where was I..."

"*Estoy muy emmoccionado!* I can't believe that you're actually going to come!! Aww, *bebe*, you make me so happy!!"

The Skype session had been dragging a little. Not so much the conversation but the "streaming" quality of the video left much to be desired. It was more so a series of stop motion images that didn't quite synch up to the audio.

"*Que tienes?* What's wrong?" Domi asked. A picture of his frozen stupid grin was stuck on the screen. He had a tiny head with a dark well-trimmed beard and 'stache. His pale face almost sallow like a wilting white flower which hung in front of an equally meticulous hair style that was shaved at the sides and left to grow about an inch higher at the top. His bare shoulders betrayed a long lanky body and a tattoo, which sat, right above his heart. It was a geometrically styled sparrow. Everyone had sparrows or triangles. They were the tramp stamps and tribals of those days.

I guess I thought my image had been frozen on his side as well, and that I could get away with letting my guard down but my unsure emotions must have shown.

"No. Nothing. Just tired," I muttered and dug a palm into my right eye.

"*Y tu mama?* What does my mother-in-law have to say?"

"Just, you know, that I don't know what I'm *doing*... She *seems* excited. Last night over coffee she asked the same things she's been asking since I moved back in: What am I going to *do* over there. How dangerous is it *really*. Is this *really* what I want..."

He laughed, "*Uy no. Mi suegra no me quiere!*"

It's not that my mother didn't like Domi. She honestly hadn't known much of him aside from a few photos I had shown her. It's just that she worried. But I think she was secretly rooting for me to do something with my life other than waste it away as a drunk and waiter at a restaurant. Actually, I don't think she realized how much I could, or did, really drink. Those last few days in El Paso, I had spent sneaking beer, hiding in my car in the parking lots of convenient stores and by the basketball courts down the street near the railroad tracks. That neighborhood was called the Lower Valley. It was essentially a system of narrow roads that led through farmland long since cut up into suburbia around the 1980s. There would be sizeable tracts of property with pecan trees and empty fields where cattle and horses grazed, right up next to a cul-de-sac. There was this one house near my old elementary that for a time even housed emus or quite possibly ostriches. As kids they'd drive us by there and we'd feed them breadcrumbs or dog food, then go home and watch cable or play Nintendo. It was both good and bad to be back home. I only ever hated it when I'd find myself alone in the house and inadvertently staring at old photos of my father and my mom and my siblings. The nights were worse and I often spent the time at bars and waking up in friends' apartments across town. I digress...

I smiled, musing on the subject, "But then she goes on and says that I better save her a room with a view of the beach. Is there even a beach down there?"

"*Si. Como tres horas de aqui ay Sayulito.* Two hours if I'm driving. You should invite her then. She can help us make *tortillas* and clean the house."

I crumpled my lips into a ball, squinted my eyes and stared off to the left. "Oh... I think she forgot how to do that years ago. I don't even think she can cook rice anymore. Like, seriously, last time we bought a box of instant rice and she put too much salt and a shit load of pepper in it for some reason. Oh, and butter. Like three huge scoops of butter."

He smiled then laughed, "*Jajaja mi pobre suegra!*"

"I know... I wish I could stay and cook for her but my brother is SO annoying and he just eats everything. Oh god, the other day I was making dinner and he kept saying something smelled funny and THEN started cooking something himself. So annoying. Who does that?! Like the stove is only so big. Like tiny. And then he just kept saying 'Something smells burnt, something smells burnt' but wouldn't move so I could check the fucking oven."

"*Pobre tu hermano joto. Solo quiere que lo pelas y que le das besos.* Mua mua mua."

"Ewoo..."

"*Andale! Dale besos para que se quede quieto! Jajajaja*"

"ANYway... Now that I'm moving away he keeps telling my mom that he's going back to New York. He pretends he has an agent or something."

"Se cree Madonna..."

"Latina Lady Gaga..."

"Gloria Trevi dos..."

"Scarlett Johansen..."

"Brit-eney Es-spears..."

"Something like that. He just keeps going on and on but I think he can't even afford it. He has no money and he doesn't have a job."

"*Y que hace? Por dinero, digo.*"

"I dunno. He sort of just wakes up after noon and starts chopping wood or digging stuff outside then goes shopping and comes back with random shit and tries to impress my sister. She just asks 'Where'd you get the money for that, *guey*?' I think he sells shit on ebay."

"*Oooo, esta rico?* I should probably marry him instead. *Jejejeje*"

"Na. He buys cheap little shit. I imagine him just walking around the mall with like gum packets in a fancy bag from Macy's or something, stealing Wi-Fi and pretending he's an actor. He probably just sits in the food court with that giant Shakespeare book he sometimes leaves in the restroom. That or he sits at the Starbucks playing Candy Crush. I dunno. He's *special*.

"*Y que cuenta tu hermana?* What does she have to say about all this?"

"She just sits there with the baby and says 'What you gonna do over there?'"

"Prostitute yourself. *No se, puedes vender tus pinturas o escribir ese libro*. Over here they love artists and there's a bunch of galleries you can exhibit in. *Puedes ser famoso! Facil!*"

"Mmmm... Yea... I said I was just gonna prostitute myself too."

"Ja ja, puto." he smiled, his eyes squinting into his laptop's camera.

"You knows-its. But she seems happy. Her and her husband kind of fight a lot more than I imagined. Well, like, 'I'm not talking to you' kinda fighting. I guess the kids are just stressful. The oldest one's SO annoying and like troubled or something. Plus, she shops a lot too. Like, serious hoarder status shopping; buying crap she has no room for or even needs."

"*Dale nalgadas.*"

"I slap and pinch her butt all the time."

"No, I meant your nephew! *Jajajaja Y porque le pelliscas sus pompis?* Now you like women or what?"

"Just... I think... it's funny."

"Well, you perv', *deberias aprender de eso y no pelear tanto conmigo.*"

"Meh. OR, you can just start practicing on telling the neighbors that you fell on the doorknob... again... repeatedly. And how that toaster's always stabbing you and shit. Oh gawwwwwwddd I need a cigarette or a drink."

A plane ticket from El Paso, Texas, to Guadalajara, Jalisco, on December 2nd would cost 744 dollars. From Juarez, Chihuahua, a hop and a skip away, you could cut the cost to a fraction of just about 136. There were calls to old friends, inquiries about taxis, etc. My mother had offered to drive me across the bridge but Ana was in town from D.C. so I just figured it'd be easier having her drop me off.

"No...Okay...Yea, I should be ready by then... Thanks again babe..." I hung up the phone after the last minute details had been arranged. I felt not all there, though, as if my judgment was cloudy and my sugar was low.

The morning wasn't particularly auspicious. It was a bit cold. The sky was purple and light blue for the moment as I smoked a cigarette for breakfast. I hadn't slept and instead repeatedly wiped the tired from my eyes with the palms of my hands. Palms to cheeks over closed little beady things. I walked back in and stood in my mother's small living room. In my mind I had imagined this day over and over: Me fretting and packing, excited and anxious and possibly a bit nauseous. But, really, I just stood there a lot, staring at five bags. Knowing I could only take 3. And when I got tired of standing and staring, I sat down and stared vacantly at whatever was on TV. I didn't really know how to work it. It had been ages since I had a television hooked up in the apartment. In my day things were simple: You clicked a fucking button and the channels went up and down. Now, there were these guides and collections of channels by themes and when I finally found something interesting, the fucking thing would change the channel to something it was preprogrammed to record. Because, apparently, they run old Law and Order: SVU episodes at six in the morning. Nothing like a little child rape to go with your coffee, am I right?

What am I gonna do??? Ana was going be at the bridge in nine hours. Nine hours turned to six and a half and six and a half hours turned into three and a half bags and then those hours whittled themselves down until there were exactly three bags, somewhat bulging, and a loot of extras just sort of littered about.

I tried convincing myself that they sold that particular soap everywhere. That if I bought generic shit here, would I really mind buying the generic Mexican version? Entire bottles of shampoo, those 3 rolls of toilet paper I thought might come in handy. For some reason, while folding a blanket, I came to the realization that I had been packing for a road trip all along instead of a 2-hour flight with no stops. And, I *actually* liked that blanket. I forgot where I got it. If whether or not I had inherited it from my mother's hallway closet or if I had picked it up at a thrift store.

My eyes traced over the green and white tartan pattern. I liked this side, green and vibrant. Its reverse was this sort of dark reddish brown plaid with white. Earthy like rusting iron bars on the windows of the home I grew up in, of this place. I looked around. It hadn't changed much. Fake wood paneled walls. Leaking roof. The carpet ripped up and never replaced, revealing ugly old linoleum in a weird black and yellow-white zigzag pattern. That side, the red side of the blanket, once looked so good on my green couch. The poor couch that had been ripped to shreds by my Great Dane, Lucy. The blankets served as a nice stopgap measure. And now, like my lovely lovely couch, I had to leave this blanket behind, this simple and precious thing. All those memories: Fucking my cheating ex boyfriend with it underneath; That couch, the one Ludvig and Josias helped me move from the old Popular Department Store Building downtown where it had sat outside the first floor elevator for some 30 odd years. And now, the couch, the blanket, my life, all left behind to whom knows what will. “29 years in three bags”, is what I kept telling myself. Twenty-nine motherfucking years summed up in a couple pairs of jeans, a bomber jacket, three fur hats, and two stuffed animals. One of which was supposed to be a dog toy to begin with. The dogs, geezus, what about the dogs?

I tried to tell myself that they'd be fine and as soon as we got things settled in Mexico, I would send for them. The words rang a little hollow even in my head. Like those promises to start going to the gym or calling your mother more. I sat down again, a bit more down hearted than before. I blamed it on sleep deprivation. I was leaving everything behind but because of who or what? Was it love? Was it because I had seen too many movies about someone running away to New York or California and having the time of their life? Had I really run into a sand trap here? Was El Paso really as bad as everyone kept telling me? I didn't know. My life there hadn't been all that bad. I made a ton of great friends over the years after starting out as a self-imposed pariah. Albeit, I had made a few mistakes, rancorous enemies abounded, but I never for a second thought that I wasn't liked. I never for a second felt deprived of good company. Well, at least not for very long. Even if we didn't have a fancy Metrorail or a Joe's Crab Shack, I had fun. I had bars and knew bartenders. The only thing haunting me was the idea of mortality, that of my father's and my family's and my friends'. I stopped for a second to think of everyone dying and choked back the tears. I couldn't let myself go. I couldn't let myself go into that big dark wonder without trying to be happy. I wanted less regrets. I felt those clammy frail hands of my cancer-ridden father in mine own, weakly begging to do things over again. Such worry. Such tired straining breaths against the no more hellos. Against the no more good-byes. Against the no more this hurts and this is exhausting.

I wiped the tears that were edging at my eyes.

I'd be lying if I said that my throat hadn't stung from something caught at the side, as if you'd been swallowing too much mucus or if you had smoked too many cigarettes. Though that was shortly remedied by my mother's alarm going off. It was a harsh buzz buzz buzz beep then a radio station with some annoying disc jockey wailing unfunny jokes in Spanish which were followed by a clap machine. How could anybody be that loud and that happy? Cocaine. I was sure of it. Two more hours and my mother would drop me by the bridge where' I'd trudge over my three fat children of bags into Ana's little SUV, and then off to start a grand ol' adventure.

"Wait, I *think* I forgot my charger...."

The contents of three bags:

The first suitcase was a large brown traveller with two side pockets running the height and dividing the length. It opened with a zipper that allowed the contraption to be accessed from the bottom if laid on its side. Within: two pairs of jeans and one jean short-shorts. Five pairs of underwear, 10 pairs of low profile socks with 3 long ones, striped and patterned like faux dress leggings.

I had so much money now from selling everything I owned that I could afford to buy a new everything. But that hadn't stopped me from clinging onto threadbare t-shirts and worn out stinky shoes.

"The fact of the matter is, I don't have to be particularly smart or attractive or witty or even smell like something that isn't shit..." I admitted to Ana as she took us nearer the Juarez airport.

"Baby, you were tellin' me about what you had packed." Ana drove less cautiously than I would assume someone would drive while NOT drunk in a city infamous for government corruption. The cops and *federalis* pulled you over for nothing and this, these 20 kilometers over the speed limit, THIS was definitely something.

"I'm just saying that I could get published for writing about what I was taking over there much less what I'm *GOING* to *DO* once I get there."

"Baby, I dunno. *Hijole*, why don't you come with me to D.C.? You'd love it! *Tienen* hot cocoa en *las* streets *y te puedes quedarte dormido en el metro*."

"Ugh, I don't want to fall asleep on the train... What if they rape me?"

A longer than expected silence ensued as we both mulled over exactly how unattractive I really was.

"Pero, bueno, no se. I don't know what you're going to be doing down there. At least you have some money you can live off of and I'm sure everything's gonna be really cheap. *Como que te puedes pasartela comiendo tacos del calle*."

"Yea, I could live off of *tortillas* or buy a mule and give children rides while tutoring them in conversational English. *Todo mal,* all wrong: 'The cow goes QUACK!'"

She broke out into laughter as she flipped the turn signal, narrowly escaping hitting a truck, and swerved to the left. "Baby, you can give drunk people mule rides home and sing to them, like, *serenatas*."

"Ugh, I can just imagine, you know: red vest, white button up, black pants, a dehydrated donkey, and me lip synching 'Oops I Did it Again' as it plays from a hand held radio."

She cackled, "No, baby, you have to do something romantic *como que...*"

"Katy Perry?"

"Ha Ha Ha! NO! *que asco!* Something like Kelly Clarkson *con marimbas*."

"Cha, Cha, Cha... cha-CHA!!"

I stared out the window. If this were a movie you could see the perplexed reflection of my face played by a twenty-pound lighter modelesque version of me.

"You know, I don't think I'll ever be back."

She scoffed. "*Yo dije lo mismo* but every chance I get, I fly back in. Like, hey, it's Christmas. Hey, it's Tuesday. Nothing's that far away anymore. You just jump on a plane and VABOOM."

"Ha Ha Ha, I don't think I want to be on any planes that go 'VABOOM'."

"*YA SE!* Jejejeje... *digo*, baby, you'll come back and you'll have more fun. You'll actually miss your family and appreciate the city. You don't know. I miss El Paso *un chorro,* like a lot, a lot. It's just such a nice place to live and I love it, just that there's no jobs *en lo que quiero hacer.* Like no opportunities whatsoever."

"Yea, my friend Gabe in San Antonio said the same thing. We're all convinced that THAT place is just like a bigger El Paso but with work."

"*Pero con Shamu.*"

"Ha Ha yea, but with Shamu and a Six Flags."

"Oo baby, we should open a Six Flags *aqui !* "

"Ha ha ha, *todo chafa,* with like one Ferris wheel *que se atorre* halfway, merry go round that only goes backwards with the horses all melted and shit."

"And the horses don't have heads."

"And the Ferris wheel only sits one person at a time."

"And our mascot would be a rat named Miguel Mouse. *Oye*, do you still talk to him?"

"*Quien*? Mikey? Na. Sometimes he randomly messages me on Facebook, but then again everybody does. I just assume that they're drunk or lonely or horny or something. *Cuando mi papa se murio,* he wanted to go have coffee *pero* I was all like whaaaat??? No way. *Y me dio mal espina*, like it seemed in poor taste of him to try and contact me during such a difficult time. Like he was trying to take advantage of a bad situation, just like always."

"Is that why you message me, baby? Cuz I make you horny??" she smiled and turned the steering wheel.

"*Si, claro, para hacerte el 'Es-skype Es-sex'.*"

She laughed, "*Jajajaja GUACATELA! No manches!* GROSS!"

There was a toll and a booth and a ticket was exchanged for entry into the airport parking lot. For some reason, I found it surprising that there should be so many people. I mean, I knew airports were busy but I guess it's like when I would see so many people waiting for a bus and automatically assume they were weird because I'd flying by in my car.

"*Bueno,* let me at least walk you." She was staring around, peeking over the dashboard for somewhere to park.

"No, baby, it's fine. You should've just left me at one of those drop off zones."

"*No, andale! No seas ridiculo.* I want it to be romantic *como en los* movies *y llego corriendo* up the escalator."

"Hahaha t*odo chafa!* The security guards stop you but I just tell them that you're retarded."

She made a face. Drew her lower teeth over her upper lip, crossed her eyes, and growled.

"I said I'd tell them that you're retarded, not Frankenstein."

"Ohhhhh ssshhhhcchhucks, *yo quieria ser el* Bride de Frankenstein."

"Hahahah no. You can be the wolf man. *Porque no te razurastes tus piernas*. No, wait, that's Maricarmen."

"Jajaja, porque? Ella tampoco se razura sus piernas?"

"Hahaha no. *Nunca haz visto su espalda?* Her back's all hairy like those newborn babies with black back carpets."

"*Guacala...*"

"I'm kidding. It's just 'cause she's dark and I ran out of 'Laura's a whore' jokes."

From there, there were a few hugs and kisses on cheeks and I love you's, and goodbyes. We sat for a little by the bookstore and flipped through a few magazines. I wanted to be Princess Diana. She said she wanted to see a naked Harry Potter. Then there was a boarding call and more hugs and kisses and a kind of sullen "I love you too, baby" then I went to stand in line to check in my bags and board the evening flight to my new home.

There were two rows of seats. Three blue chairs on either side. The ticket I had bought allowed me second choice in seating as I had opted to pay an extra seven dollars. As such, I was certain I would find a nice window seat, but to no avail, because I still got stuck by the aisle. I couldn't say that I *remembered* much of the flight other than that I felt under dressed and regretted not taking a shower before I left. I swore I could smell my crusty socks through my smelly, greased stained shoes. Whenever I'd try and get comfortable, rest an ankle on a knee or something, I'd get smacked with this whiff of boy and farm and dirt and stinky sour feet. The man to my left chose to do the opposite and basically drenched himself in cologne and something that smelled like baby powder, which he probably had applied to the insides of his thighs, *which* barely fit in the chair. His arms were massive and he managed to somehow stuff himself into a light gray suit with an almost silver sheen. It had probably fit him better a few months ago. The spaces between the buttons on his shirt wrinkled up beneath a black tie that looked like some kind of slide over his belly. His belt was tied somewhere around his navel but that belly kept going. I wondered for a second if he could still see his penis or when was the last time he had sex and was it with someone he loved or did he have to pay for it? I smiled, awkwardly perhaps. He just kind of leaned towards me and nodded when I sat down. Those giant arms, I felt their warmth and clamminess even from under his coat. They were pressed up against me like a muggy summer's evening. Now I am far from skinny or even a healthy weight, but oh my god, I felt like shoving a salad down his fucking throat. The seat by the window was vacant and remained vacant for the rest of the flight even though I had to basically lean the entire way on my right armrest. Like I know the rules in movie theaters and such, first person gets dibs on armrests, but, come on! There's an entire seat over there! Maybe he just couldn't make it in that far. Maybe he just sort of got stuck halfway or was afraid of heights or just really liked poultry and didn't want to be too tempted by the wandering migrating geese. I had no idea.

Why are so many people wearing sunglasses?

Oh gawd it's so cold!

Uggghhh this seat's too small!

Aggg I'm hungry now!

Where's my vodk-ey!

Everyone had tablets or computers or cell phones with bird games and although I brought a book of short stories and two thick novels, I found it difficult to concentrate on anything other than "I'm-really-doing-this, I'm-really-doing-this, I'm-really-doing-this..."

The adrenaline from the morning seemed to wear thin about twenty minutes in. Suddenly I felt the uncontrollable urge to cry over the dogs and imagined all sorts of horrible manners in which the birds would commit suicide: Them flying into a ceiling fan at my mom's... Out the window into one of those stray cats' claws... Them flying *into* a window. Them getting stepped on... There was also something about buckets of water and them drowning???

The list went on.

Then a "ding" brought me back from the precipice of a minor panic attack. Already in my mind I was asking myself "What if I only stayed like a week or two thennnn went-back-home?" It'd SHOW that I was committed to something with Domi even if at that very moment, every fiber in my being said NoNoNoNoNo god for fucking crissakes NO.

And then, the Ding again.

A flight attendant with an awful green vest went back and forth to a tiny Asian man three aisles down. I wondered if you get a discount for being diminutive? I mean, I'm pretty sure they charge larger people for two seats or that I had heard that somewhere. Eureka! The fat man next to me had bought two seats! But he was doing it all wrong... Anyhow, it was whiskey! I was sure of it! Dam you Mr. Miyagi! Either side of my tongue began to tingle. Whiskey sounded mighty fine right about now but at this point I'd settle for a double vodka and a side of water, hold the water.

It was so good. In a few minutes I was grateful I had not had lunch even if I was a bit terse with my mother when she offered we pick something up from McDonald's along the way.

She said, "Not even a coffee, *mijo*?"

"No." I was curt and annoyed and sleep deprived. Sitting with my arms crossed in the stifling air of her Mercury Mountaineer, plopped down in the passenger seat like some castrated child. I hate not driving. I just wanted to be on that plane, this plane, and gone already.

It hurt to think that my last few words with my mom were delivered so bratty and immaturely. But now I vowed to make it up to her shortly. What was going to be a forever in Mexico now would only be a short stint. Then I could go back and watch Lifetime Movies with Mumsy and talk about ice cream or vaginas or whatever it is women rattle on about.

By the time I ordered another, I had resigned myself not only in moving back to El Paso, but also in using this trip as a springboard to Austin or New York. This whole moving thing seemed so insanely easy. Easier now that I didn't have anything left but a few bags. All I could do was laugh at all those years wasted, vested in my tiny hovel, when I could totally just rent a brand new hovel elsewhere.

There were never any *real* goodbyes. Except, maybe death. But then again, God talks to me on the radio so I'm pretty sure there's some kind or afterlife or angels shooting good luck loogies at you from clouds up there. This could all just be one big vacation. Eventually I would settle down, but for now, I should be lost in the world. Or should I be finding myself in it? I didn't know. I just asked for another double and started imagining me in a slew of outfits, each varying, stylishly of course, with the climates of Russia, France, D.C., New York, Belgium, Cali', Las Cruces, etc. That got me thinking about the conversation I had with Domi about what I was packing.

"*Y que te vas a traer?*"

"My fur hats, of course, duh."

"Jajaja meco, si ni hace frio por aca. La clima esta bien suave y todo esta bien verde porque llueve cada dia."

"Well, anyhow, those were the first things I was certain I wanted to take."

Another sip. Why, oh god? What use would I have for fur hats in the tropics? Much less three of them! I totally could've taken like another pair of shoes! But I think I threw most of them away anyhow.

Another slurp.

By this time I had had about six shots of vodka and an itsy-bit of water. Oh god, another terrible idea. I shifted uneasily in my chair, my ears popping and my seat vibrating and that engine so god damned loud. I wasn't anywhere even near the window but my stomach could tell that we were way too high up for any of this sort of shit to be going down.

Just then, that business tycoon to my left, the fat one with too much cologne and not enough hair, decided to turn the page of his newspaper and give it a straightening out with shake fold shake. A warm draft of obnoxious air assaulted my senses. I gripped the armrest, dug my nails in deep and told myself, "You do this all the time, Marvin. You can handle it." That I've drank more than my share of doubles before. That I'd wake up hung-over as hell and the first fucking thing I'd do in the morning was walk the dogs and bag their putrid shit. Closed my eyes. Winced at the thought of... EYES TURNED AS BIG AS MOONS, reached for the blue bag... wait for it... wait for it...

Ding!

Saved by the bell. I turned around and saw this nice tanned lady with platinum blonde hair, somewhere in her 60's, hand like orange leather, give the stewardess something. Nothing's dizzying or unsettling anymore. That lady smiled and jiggled her head, which jiggled some gaudy large earrings. She laughed to the unseen person on her right. Oh man, I wish I had that seat so bad.

"You okay?" the fat man asked without even looking away from his paper.

"Yea, I'm good. Just for a second," I laughed, "I thought I was gonna make a scene."

He chuckled, flipped the page, shakes folds shakes the news again then said, "Well, if you think you're sick now, wait till you see the bill for all those damned doubles."

70-ish dollars later, the stewardess politely took a tip after I had asked if they were allowed to on this airline. She smiled and laughed and said, "Sure why not." About two visits to the piss room after that, my liver probably felt as relieved as I was when I was finally able to pass out. I wasn't actually planning on it, and I once or twice let my head bob then fall dangerously close to the fat man's shoulder before I bit the bullet and reclined my chair. At first I was slightly embarrassed to intrude on the person's space behind me. I never realized how small planes were. Hadn't been in one since high school when we took a trip to Nationals for Hi-Q: a trivia game show, like sports for nerds and highly competitive coaches. The latter of which is probably a very redundant thing to say and I think about the only thing I learned was that the answer is usually "-2" and you don't fuck with a six foot tall, perm'ed out goliath of a woman on hormone pills who taps her toes in her sandals like she would her fingers on a desk. But, well, the little bit of vodka still in me said, Fuck It, I paid my for my ticket in the sky, might as well ring all the bells and blow all whistles.

I later found myself trying to pack sweaters in a box. I hate sweaters. They're so unflattering on an over weight man with moobies like me. But there I was: folding, shoving, squishing, pinching, and rearranging this way and that way. My aunt came in the room and told me that if I *arranged* them by color, they'd fit better. So *I* did and *they* did. But the moment I went to pick up the box to put in the helicopter-car, everything fell out from the bottom... I flipped the box over and tried to reassemble the flaps. Folded them this way, folded them that way. Can't seem to.... get this... dam thing... I was filling it again but everything just kept falling out. Then the chopper's blades started whirling and sweaters started crawling over this dirt lawn with thorny patches of weeds. My aunt, apparently piloting the helicopter-car hollered out, "Hurry! We have to take your dead grandma to the groceries and then the movies! If we're late, the milk's gonna go bad and the popcorn's gonna get cold!" Zombie grandma just sat there, chewing gum and nodding her head side to side, disappointed.

"BUT THESE ARE MY FAVORITE SWEATERS!" I yelled back, waving my arms in the air.

"Great!" she shouted back, "Now you've lost your fingers!"

But I was so far away from the flying car... How could I lose my fingers? From there I was forced to limbo under the propellers to the back seat of what looked like my car and we took off. Once in the air, I stared down at these bloody little stumps at the ends of my hands.

"Don't be sucha baby, everything has blue tooth now. You can just talk into your phone and it'll type for your computer. What we really have to worry about is this traffic and whether or not we want to see a Romantic or a Scary Movie."

Ding!

Seats in upright position, trays folded in. The city approached as strings of lights in square grids as I wiped the sleep from my eye. The one thing I always worry about when I pass out in public is whether or not at one point had I farted. Everybody says I talk in my sleep. But I'm pretty sure I fart a lot too. The fat man stared out towards the tiny oval window. It reminded me of a thumbprint. I wondered whom was he going to see or what was he going to do in the city. Maybe we should've talked. I felt a little guilty I wasn't friendlier earlier and really that cologne didn't smell all that bad. I didn't have much time to ponder such things because pretty soon the only thing on my mind was how much I needed to pee. For about an eternity, or ten minutes, whatev', I debated whether or not it was permissible to unfasten my safety belt in lieu of what the sign read. Just as I had decided it'd be okay, a warm hand was on my shoulder and the stewardess said "*Por favor, mantienese es su asiento, Senor*"

"But.... But... dammit."

About fifteen minutes later, we were on the ground and I was skidding towards a new life possibly involving a new pair of pants and underwear from the gift shop. I told myself I could hold it in and managed to. I reminded myself about those 8-hour shifts at work with no piss break. Of course it's easier to reign in your bladder when you're running around. Much less so, though, sitting with a belt pressing against your tummy and the whole place vibrating.

Relief, finally.

While we were waiting to be taxied in, I made my way to the stall. Sometimes even I'm amazed at how awful my piss stinks. Smells like formaldehyde. After that it was a rush to gather up all your belongings. Check the overhead, under the seats, and make sure you're not forgetting anything. There was this mother who squeezed by me. Had this look on her face like she wished she could forget her kid, the one that kept screaming during a stint of turbulence. He kept yelling about how he didn't want to die. Maybe she was just mad at me because I had belted out laughing.

Maybe, just maybe.

We disembarked and it was a whole other world. You don't actually connect to a terminal but are let out on the tarmac then there's a walk towards the airport, which is really just a small building. I didn't know what I was doing. I was just following the guy ahead of me. We were going to pick up our bags. I was fucking wasted, unbelievably so. It was all just one big blur and I had immediately regretted bringing so many bags. But, honestly, after spending the last few hours cramped in a Pringle's tube, the fucking place looked like some awe inspiring cathedral sans the flying buttresses. Instead, there was a yogurt place, which, was closed. Well at least I think it was a yogurt place.

Spring in my step. I felt like a toddler who had just learned to use the potty, beaming with self-importance at my own minor accomplishments. The birds should have been out singing and fluttering to my fingers but instead I realized just how lackluster everything looked. Under the harsh fluorescent lights, everyone was tired and sweaty and their clothes were all wrinkled. Since that was basically how I looked all the time, it hadn't really caught me off guard until the arrivals were met by nicely pressed and fashionable huggers and kissers and laughter and a laudably loving cavalcade of family and friends.

Tippy toes, smiling and still beaming, I bit the side of my lip and stared out into the throng that was gradually thinning out. All along I had been rehearsing some line about "Look! How light I packed!" in the face of my reputation for hoarding. I was already running through my head this scenario in which I regaled Domi of the sweater dream and the fat man and that screaming kid in the back. There would surely be hugs and kisses and *maybe* someone was kind enough to have even brought a flask?

Beaming. Beaming. Beaming.

Five minutes turned to fifteen. I tapped at my watch the way they do in the movies as I sat in another uncomfortable plastic chair watching everybody and their mother take off either to the bus stop or to grab a taxi. About the only howdy-do I got was from the fat man who passed me by with his rolling little luggage carry on. He tipped an invisible hat on his head by tapping his right temple. It was way too early in my new life for all this to be going so wrong.

Stupid Hollywood.

Stupid Expectations.

Maybe I was back in a dream, some nightmare involving a lot of people in white shorts? I looked at my grimy shoes: Stained and stinky because I had had them forever. Had them so long that it hurt to walk in them. Made my ankles roll inward. I decided then and there to get new ones. Maybe boots? I stared at my watch again. Maybe loafers? I lost track of what time I had been trying to keep track from. I definitely couldn't pull off sandals. The drunken half of me was tempted to just jump on a shuttle that would take me to the central bus station. Yeah, I think I had overheard someone saying that that was cheaper than getting a taxi. But wait, I had to piss again. And, honestly, I had no idea where Domi lived.

So I got up with a sigh. Thought to myself, I should at least remember to bring my bags before somebody steals them and my collection of rags. Sat back down. Ten more minutes. Twiddled my thumbs and stared at my phone which said out of service. Got back up and walked toward the restroom where a weary *federali* in black riot gear eyed me suspiciously.

I dragged my feet more than I actually "walked". Every person who turned a corner, or turned around, was for a split second mistaken for a familiar face. God, everyone looked the same. All the guys were skinny with dark beards or dark and short or white and fat. I think I fell under the category of the "fat father" looking men: Big ol' beer bellies and nice shiny metal wristwatches at the ends of hairy forearms. After a while it kind of felt like I was walking through a Wal-Mart or one of those other big box stores where everyone just gives up on trying to impress anybody with what they're wearing. I thought back to that fat man sitting next to me. He at least wore a suit. Everyone else was basically in shorts or warm-ups or T-shirts and jeans. I was stuck in a red plaid button up. It was actually one of my nicer shirts but I must admit that it had fit better a while ago too. But I was SO hungry! The only problem was that everything was shut down and it was barely even ten or eleven or maybe it was midnight.

Wait, where was I? This wasn't where I had landed, and it suddenly dawned upon me that I had followed somebody out of the terminal we had arrived in, and into the main airport accidentally. Was that why they weren't here? Was Domi waiting for me at the tarmac with a giant poster board, staring into the high beam lights of a landing 747? It felt like that one time I arrived at 3 in the morning in Austin and the friend I was planning on staying with, wouldn't answer her phone. I drove around aimlessly on the Mopac, or whatever it is that they call that freeway, until I spotted a Wal-Mart glistening in the distance like the proverbial Star of Bethlehem. Then, I had to fucking spend another twenty minutes trying to figure out how the fuck to get off the freeway. My phone's screen was cracked and as it was, the navigation app never really worked with me, so much so, that I believe it thought we were mortal enemies. By the time I figured out which exit and which side road would lead me to the store, I resigned myself to just sleeping in the parking lot. But I was so hungry, so hungry and tired and stressed. No open arms to welcome. As it was, I didn't even want to be there. What a waste of a Spring Vacation. I just milled around the store. At that hour the staff was restocking. Everyone looked ethnic: Blacks, whites,

Indians from India. I picked up crackers, sardines, and a jar of chunky peanut butter then went back for a can of smoked oysters. This is what poor people eat, right? Poor, downtrodden souls? I should've just bought a can of beans and cooked it with my cigarette lighter. The plan had been to wander the aisles until morning, but my shopping took less than half an hour and dawn was still in another three.

I scanned my items at a self checkout, the bag of chips I picked up was twice the price advertised so I asked the attendant, this husky black woman with soft tight shiny curls, to help me. "Uhm, people just put 'em on those carts but they's really regular price." She smacked her gum then waddled off. I smiled. Just like now, back then I felt stinky and tired and reeked of alcohol from the two tall boys I chugged on the highway.

So tired.

So anxious.

So hungry.

As a social animal there is this other hunger, not for nourishment inasmuch as for the experience of belonging and being cared for. I wondered if Mexico had those yellow "safe place" signs somewhere like they did back in the states on firehouses and police stations. When you're plopped in the middle of unfamiliar terrain, it's easy to lose hope. Easy to let doubt wiggle it's way up into your brain. This place felt like limbo or like waiting in line at the DMV. It felt something like hell. So I just kept dragging my feet.

Walking. Walking. Walking.

Gradually the last ten minutes came into focus. People were actually friendly. There had been someone pointing in the direction of this terminal. Said something about me being able to get a taxi but that it'd be expensive. Was that where I had heard it from? Or had I read it somewhere? Did the stewardess mention it? Maybe the fat man? Everything was a blur and everyone seemed to pass me as if they were in time-lapse photography. I heard rolling luggage wheels in slow motion over the gaps between tiles going pop thud pop thud pop thud. I stared at my feet again, hoping that the end of the hall wasn't as far as it looked just a second ago. The facade: glass doors and giant windows. I swore that this technique worked when I ran and when those hills just looked way too intimidating. At least the floors were shiny if in a bit slippery from the wax. There was a man in the far left buffing the hell out of it. His face old and wrinkled. Light skin and sullen like lost in a reverie or trying to remember what his wife had told him to pick up from the groceries. Maybe he didn't even like his wife. Maybe he was trying to think of ways he could have her offed. He just winced into the distance beyond me and beyond the crowd of people.

Walking. Walking. Walking.

I looked back every so often. I looked up into the exposed ceiling lights, tubes that trailed off in lines. The place looked pretty modern. The sky outside, dark. Felt like I had stepped out of a movie theatre. Like those times when you walk into work during the day and by the time you're out, it's stars and quiet and no birds, no sun. I looked back again, nothing. I looked up again, more lights. I looked back again, nothing. I looked up...

After a bit more of me staring at my shoes, I heard loud laughter in the distance. I looked up and it was Domi and Elma running towards me with a folded sign beneath her arm that flapped in the breeze behind them. They were all smiles. Giant lanky dolls like those in a Chinese shadow puppet show. Basically sticks. I was sobering up and too tired to smile. Their shoes made this loud clapping sound as they approached. In the distance, a security guard blew his whistle and they slide to a stop about twenty feet away. They laughed to each other and approach regally, both radiating in joy. He was wearing a fitted black work suit and she was in a black dress with a low cut shoulder whose hem reached down just above her mid thigh. His shoes were shiny black leather and pointed at the end. Hers were ankle boots that folded over at the cuff like a pirate's.

"Marveen! Que emoccion!" she stretched out her arms, her short hair, in the style of Louise Brooks, bobbed at her display. *"Mire que te hicimos!"* She unfolded the sign. On it was written "*Bienvenido* a GDL Party City" and it had a Xeroxed cut out of Domi's head plastered over some body builder's who was wearing a red speedo.

Domi laughed then hugged me with two skinny arms. He was about my height but looked taller because he was so thin. The way long vertical lines can sometimes betray the eyes. *"Bebe! Estas aqui! No me lo puedo creer!"* I just went limp and sighed. Annoyed. Tired. Hungry. *"Que tienes?"* he went on. "What's wrong?"

"Nothing. I thought I was at the wrong airport."

I think they had been smoking weed before they came. They couldn't shut the fuck up or stop laughing. After struggling with my bags, we walked out the front of the airport. Behind us read *"Aeropuerto Internacional de Guadalajara"* in giant black letters with blue neon trim. The air smelled like gasoline fumes from the taxis mingled with wet dirt. The *taxistas* hollered at us that they'd take us anywhere. "Cheap ride, Cheap ride," but Domi and Elma just laughed. He could barely hold up my bag and was teetering to the right. I had given Elma my carry on which was less than 15 kilos and I took the heaviest. Wink, wink. Of course I gave Domi the fucking heaviest. Asshole left me waiting in the airport forever.

The walk to the car had been intermittent with, "What's wrong. What's the matter... I can't believe you're actually here!" Maybe I was just hung-over and didn't know it but I kept my head down and repeatedly assured them that I was fine.

When we got to the car, I ran my hand over the side of his black Jetta, early 2000's. The paint job was slick and shiny like patent leather, something like his shoes. *"Que haces?"* he asked me.

"I'm looking for the bullet holes." A year or two back, when we had first started talking, he had his car taken at gunpoint then it was later found riddled with bullet holes and filled with the dead bodies of *narcos*. He tried pointing out where the bullets had penetrated but I didn't see anything. He just mentioned that we should hurry because the *transito* were always stopping him when he drove at night.

It was tiny in the backseat but I insisted on riding there. I just wanted to stretch out long ways and fall asleep even if it was cramped and smelled like strawberry air freshener. He cranked the engine, which shuttered for a bit, then we jerked out in reverse as he almost hit a car parked behind us. He did a fake scream in high falsetto then they both laughed again. We then jerked forward and I rolled towards the front seats and got wedged near the floor. Jerked back and I was still trying to push my way up from the floor. Then jerked forward and we were in business and I rolled back onto the seat.

The house was about a half-hour's drive from the airport. He drove wildly and I was just sort of tossed around in the rear some more. I heard several cars honking and at lights he would honk too. Elma played with the radio and asked Domi to let her borrow his phone so she could put on a song they liked. He did. It sounded like electro disco jazz something or other. I think I hit my head a few times against the door when he'd take a sharp left. Finally I decided to just sit up. The city looked sprawling and a bit empty with a long curving road from the airport. As we got closer to the center, there were giant old homes, fancy big trees and fancy new stores. I saw signs for Wal-Mart and Home Depot, breathed a sigh of relief and felt a pang of homesickness. The streets were jammed with cars and busses but hardly any pedestrians from what I could tell. Maybe it was just too late for anybody to be out. We whizzed by. More honking. Crazy ass drivers with no turn signals turning like crazy. Elma and Domi just kept laughing. He stared at me through the rearview mirror, smiled and winked. "Oh god," I thought, "what have I gotten myself into..."

"Marveen... Marveen..." a woman's soft voice cooed and my leg slightly shook. I grumbled. At some point I had fallen asleep. The drive, this city; so long, so big.

"ANDALE MARVEEN!" Elma was violently shaking my leg by then. I think I had a boner but everyone was too polite to notice. I didn't realize Elma realized until we were getting off of the car and she whispered to Domi, *"Viste? Ya esta listo..."*

They giggled towards this gate that ran along the front of this two-story home. It was not as old as some of the colonial buildings we passed, but it looked like it had been around for a while. The facade was simple, just flat, a light tan, and the roof was vaulted at the edge with these terra-cotta shingles running the length of it. I stared up. It looked like a typical house you'd find in Juarez. These thin things that are built one right up next to the other. I thought to myself, guess this is home, then sighed a bit disappointed.

The street was narrow and I was trying to pull out my carry on, the one I had been using as a pillow in the backseat, when a car whizzed past almost knocking the back door to the Jetta off before disappearing down the street, honking and turning sharply at the corner. After that, a crew of three guys in sporty bicycle gear cling cling cling huff huff huffed by. It's so late, why are they out? I was half expecting a parade or marching band followed by a duck and some ducklings trailing after but all I got was Domi running over.

"Tienes que tener cuidado, bebe. Aqui te atropellan y te dejan en la calle. La vida no esta tan lento como en El Paso."

I rolled my eyes at him cautioning me to the big city life as he snuck in a kiss, grabbed my cheeks, and smooshed them together.

"Gracias por venir, cabron!" He laughed this weird little laugh he had and picked up my bag. It was like he was laughing through his nose like a fat kid would breathe: Heavy, but short, successive rhythms and blows. I shrugged him off. *"Ven, payaso,"* he said as he took my pinky in his hand and led me around the back end of the car towards the house. Another car bumbled by with loud thumping music and then a moped chimed with a bell and struggled down the opposite direction. I stopped behind the trunk and tried to get the hatch open, pulling repeatedly at the handle as if that would magically unlock the damned thing. But it refused, mocking me with this futile clicking sound. My shoulders were low and I was hunched over with my head thrown back towards the sky. Oh god, will this day ever end? WHY did I think that THIS would be a good idea?!

But I kept at it. My right arm outstretched as he held my pinky in his hand. He was already on the curb and had to turn around, then scolded me, *"Ahorita bajamos lo de mas! Vente! Tengo algo para enseñarte!"*

"It better be a return ticket home," I yelled back and reluctantly dragged my hand across the trunk as he pulled me towards the house.

"SURPRISE!!!"

A chorus of strangers. Geezus christ. Who the fuck? Ugh...

Would it make me seem like a horrible person if I said that the first thing I noticed after that, was a fold out table across the room, laden with bottles of booze? Hands being shaken. Introductions ending in, "Oh yea, that's nice..." as I slowly zigzagged through the crowd, eyeing the bar the entire time, over everybody's shoulders.

Almost... almost... almost...

A girl with dirty-blonde hair suddenly popped out of nowhere. She was all smiles and brought her hand up towards her face and held out her palm near her chin as if to shake. I smiled and raised my own hand but instead of shaking hers it took on a mind of its own and did this circular "dis" thing as it reached for the closest bottle. I smiled and apologized then tapped her cup with an apologetic “cheers”.

The setup wasn't fancy. There was white Jimador Tequila, the prerequisite "*wee-skee*", Jack Daniels, a cherry flavored Smirnoff, an Effen Cucumber, Jim Beam, Club Soda, Tonic Waters, Pineapple soft drink, Cranberry Juice, etc. Kid in a fucking candy store was I. I immediately went for the Passport scotch. I skipped the Crown Royal and Buchanan's. Let the fancy people have their cake. I poured the velvety yellow tea like liquid into a plastic disposable cup with a one... two... three... M-I-S-S-I-S-S-I-P-P-I... fourrrrrr... five. Done. The first drink always tastes like Dr. Pepper in the morning. Afterwards, the people seemed more bearable. I don't quite think it had been more than 15 minutes, but I was really annoyed there for a second, and then suddenly I felt very anxious about where Domi had left my bag. He'd been dotting around the crowd like a father with a cigar and a newborn baby. Smiling and hugging and slaps on his shoulders and slaps on his back. I tip toed over the crowd and waved him in towards me.

"*Que pasa, bebe? Todo bien*?” he asked.

"My bag!"

“*Tu que?*"

"*Mi mochila!* My bag!"

"*Ah, tu bolsa! Dejame lo busco.*" He spun around quick and gradually zigzagged back in-between the crowd towards where he thought he had left it. He looked around the floor but there was nothing, just three guys leaning against the wall to the right of the front door. It was this little green backpack I used to ride downtown with. Small like something a boy scout would wear but still large enough to haul a good sack of groceries. What I liked about it was that it kept out of your way as you coasted down the hills and struggled up the streets. Just then, I spotted it towards the left of the door by this big black trash bag where people were tossing their beer cans in. He looked back, raised both hands as if to say, "I dunno where it is," but I pointed in its direction. Yes there! By the door! So fucking near the door that anyone could've just swept it up and there would've gone all my papers and my passport. I cringed and took another sip. He stumbled back, confident and rigid like he'd already had to much to drink and was trying not to let anyone in on it. So that's why they were fucking late. Assholes. Drinking...WITHOUT ME???

"*Ten*, *bebe*," he smiled like a dog wagging its tail with a frisbee in its mouth. "*Vez, todo bien. Nada paso.*"

I shot him a sour look then whispered in his ear, "I don't want to alarm anybody... but I think the room's full of Mexicans..."

Who were these people? In the background Nu Disco boomed from somebody's iPod, which was connected to a DJ station in the corner. The TV was left mute on a random news station and the rest of the living room was dark save for the faint glow that trickled in as the lady on the screen pointed to a digital map of the weather. Around the music station were some guys and one girl flipping through their phones or mp3 players, comparing playlists and laughing then chugging cheap *Modelo Lite* beers from white cans. Maybe I was being a little bit snobbish or making some kind of face, but I had had the longest day ever in all eternity and the last thing I wanted was to play host to a bunch of *Guadalajaran* hipsters. Elma came up out of nowhere with her own cup and asked what was the matter this time. Domi made light of the situation and told her I had been afraid that someone had run off with my panties. She just laughed and slapped my arm then stumbled off into the mayhem. Just then, some guy came out from the right side of the living room and pushed through the crowd towards the DJs. There was this roar of, "*Eyyyy*!!" as if everyone was frustrated to have been shoved aside. The guy plugged in this plastic orb and set it atop the TV, flicked a switch with some difficulty, probably due to his drunken stupor, and then beams of multicolored lights shot out and the sphere started rotating. The crowd yelled, "*Eyyyy*!!" again, but this time joyfully enthused and a few even began to whistle loudly. Domi followed suit but he was so close to me, and the sound he made so piercing, that I back handed him on the shoulder and grimaced. This cloud of cigarette and pot smoke suddenly appeared looming over the crowd, catching the lights from the contraption. A poor man's fog machine, I guessed. Oh geezus, I thought and took another swig.

An hour or two into the party and my eyelids were heavy like cotton in water. I had been drinking all day. I was tired and crabby and came to the conclusion that these people were partying not in my honor, but because they liked to party at the drop of a hat. The door would open and more people would walk in from the street. Sometimes the door would open and some people would leave. But more often than not, they returned either more wasted or with more people. At some point a hot mess of a girl, petite and dark haired with a pixie cut, drunkenly leaned against me and told me she was so happy I was here. Fuck if I knew who she was, but she was trying to convince me that I would have so much fun. She slobbered out something about how the *Tapatio* way of life was awesome, that they had invented *tequila* and *mariachis*. I asked her if she had a piece of gum. She did, but she didn't get the joke.

Elma danced from one corner to the next. Like a *matachina* evoking some ancient Mayan gods. Sometimes she'd run into a person or a group of persons. Her being half ready to fall, they'd catch her and she'd straighten herself out, laughing then pretended to be insulted and slap the nearest one on the arm or squeeze someone's cheek. They of course would just laugh and raise their glasses then turn back into their circle and whisper something about how crazy that bitch is. People were huddled, rolling joints or having mini dance offs. I sat in a folding chair by the booze table, obviously, oh and Domi was like there holding my hand or something.

People passed us on their way to fill up and said hi or reiterated on how cool it was that I had come and that how cool the city was and how much of a good time I would have. I felt like a queen by my king holding court over a slew of lords and ladies.

"Hoo wad dat?" I would lean in and whisper to him. My pie hole, by that time, was mouthing words as if it'd been filled with peanut butter. He was so and so who did such and such in the art community. She was the daughter of some dude who owned a club and a shoe store at this mall where there was nothing but shoe stores. He organized events and brought in really cool DJs. He was a drug dealer. She was... well, he didn't quite know who she was, but she seemed nice.

I would rock back and forth in the folding chair. A bit more relaxed, the alcohol had begun to metabolize and given me that boost of energy I had come to expect from living a life of little sleep and much drinking. I began to bob my head. You know what? This isn't actually that bad. Oh hey, I love this song! I smiled wide and he leaned in to kiss me. I teetered back and forth some more. Slammed the back of the chair into this counter that divided the kitchen and the living room. It was filled with dirty cups and fresh cups and a box of crackers for some reason.

Teeter. Slam. Teeter. Slam. Smile... Teeter. Slam.

I had been double fisting a cup of scotch and a cup of Coca Cola for the last hour or so. I was convinced that that should keep me hydrated but I could feel the onset of a nagging migraine. I pressed my eyelids together and yawned. Maybe I was getting too old for this. Not even my first day in and I couldn't keep up with the natives? Stupid *Tapatios*. I liked you better when I thought you were just some kind of hot sauce. I stared into my cups. The least I could do was finish the scotch before I retired to the room I hadn't even seen yet. That room, the one I would be living the next few weeks in. Waste not, want not. I took a big swig as Elma clopped by and plopped herself onto Domi's lap. She pressed her face into the side of his head and hers got lost behind her short hair. She whispered something into his ear then bit his cheek and tottered off to the wall and motioned to another group as if asking for a stogie.

The corners of my eyes stung. I couldn't stop yawning and felt that perhaps if I just kept rocking back and forth, that I wouldn't pass out in my seat. I just wanted to run my hands through my hair and go to sleep and maybe take a poop somewhere in between. As the thought to put down my drinks crossed my mind, as I tried to teeter back forwards, the chair's rear legs slipped out from under and I went tumbling backwards. I hit the floor so hard that some of the cups from the counter vibrated off and a bottle or two toppled over from the fold out table.

Oh look, white marble tile. That's nice. "Ugh..." I whimpered out.

Domi turned to his right and just stared down at me smiling, as if not registering that I had fallen. He turned back to whomever he was talking to, then suddenly turned back, in shock, and got up to help me off the floor along with about four other people.

"Hey man, you okay?"

"Estas bien?"

"Que paso?"

"No mames, se vio bien culero eso!"

"Ya no mas tequila para ti, gringo."

Not sure if I was more embarrassed by the "me falling in front of everyone" or the fact that my belly was showing. I pulled down my shirtfronts and pulled up my pants as I made it to my feet. I mistakenly braced myself against the table and it almost folded under, but someone grabbed that, and the only casualty was an empty bottle, which didn't even break when it hit the floor.

"*Hay, bebe... ya estas pedo...*," Domi smiled and grabbed my face then planted a big smooch. "*Ven, ya es tiempo que te acuestas.*"

"But my scotch..." I pouted.

Elma stumbled over and mumbled, *"Ahora que hiciste, 'che gabacho..."* and stared me down. She raised her cup and attempted to take a swig but she was so drunk that it spilled down the front of her dress. *"No mames!"* she screamed, "*Este vestido me costo una quincena!*" She flicked at her top as if strumming a guitar, trying to wipe off the excess liquid from the dress that had cost her an entire paycheck. She then started for the restroom and I followed suit but stopped at the table to pour myself another drink. Domi snatched the bottle from my hand and tapped my belly.

"Ya no, bebe. Haz tomado bastante," he smiled and pretended to fall backwards screaming. I was not amused. He kissed my forehead and led me through a small kitchen where people raised their glasses towards me as one chick did a line of coke off of a wooden cutting board.

"Ooo, it's just like watching Rachael Ray!" I muttered, more pleased with myself than ever.

No response. I forgot that these heathens didn't speak the Queen's English! Perfect, an entire country that wasn't going to get any of my jokes.

We stepped into a dark hallway as a girl stepped out of a well-lit room. The dresses on some other girls, all who were leaning against the wall in a line, were illuminated for a second. Fine, fancy young things in pastels. Their faces remained lit by the phones they blankly stared at. I heard one of them say, "*Alguien que sabe el esclave del Wi-Fi?*" in a *fresa* tone and another said, *"No manches... ya me meo!"* and another one was just banging on the door screaming, "*Appurate pinche pendeja y dame una twalla!*" Someone wanted the Wi-Fi password, another was about to piss her pants, and the angriest just wanted a fucking towel.

Seconds later, the door scraped open and out walked this hefty spectacle of a gay man. I think I recognized him as Luis Raul. His head was humungous and his cheeks flat. He walked emphatically swaying his shoulders. The light from the restroom showed that it had been Elma banging on the door all along.

"Pinche puta!" she hissed at him as he patted his faux hawk hairdo.

"Callate, envidiosa!" he snarled back.

She slapped him on the ass and staggered-in to the dismay of the other five girls or so who had been waiting in line for god knows how long.

"Excuse me."

"Excuse me."

"Con permiso."

"Con permiso."

We walked past the line and Domi banged on the door. A collective sigh of discontent echoed from the girls in line again. From within the bathroom though:

"*Calme tu pinche pedo, Cristina! Ya mero salgo!"*

Domi laughed*, "Elma, es Beto."*

"Ah! Corazon!" she said delightfully inebriated.

From the first girl in line who I assumed was Cristina:

"*ElmaAAAA ... APURATEEEEE!!!* I need to pee!!!"

Domi:

"Vamos a estar en la recamara!"

Elma:

"Okay! Ya mero salgo! Tell Cristina to calm the fuck down and go suck a nut."

We walked away as Cristina banged on the door behind us and in the distance said:

"Pues sacalos de tu boca, pinche zorra!"

Just like Shakespeare.

We stood there in front of his bedroom at the end of the hallway. It was dark but I could see there was another entry to our right with a sliver of light emanating from beneath a white door where that first girl had walked out of. I heard unintelligible speaking and then a roar of laughter. He let go of my hand and fumbled in his front pockets.

"*No mames...*" he irately murmured then felt around in his back pockets and no ass, *"Ah! ahi esta!"*

He grabbed the doorknob and with quite a bit of frustration, fiddled with inserting the key. Click, Pop, Pop, then a shove with his shoulder and we were in.

"*Piense por un segundo que deje la llave adentro cuando meti a tu mochila. Si no lo hubiera encontrado, hubieramos tenido que hablar a los bomberos*," he said then kicked off his shoes and hopped on the bed, which was merely a mattress on the floor that sat length wise against the far wall.

"Firemen to the rescue? Oo la la... Yea let's do that instead!" I went to join him, hovering over his thin frame like some sexy drunk zeppelin. There were piles of clothes everywhere but piles of clothes that only an architect could design. Honestly, it looked as if he had barely arrived in the city himself. In spite of the stacks still teetering in their suitcases, the room looked sparse, sparse and small. Taking note of my expression, he apologized for the mess and pointed to a corner where he said he'd plan to make his closet.

"*Quitate los zapatos. Anda*," he went on then patted me on the ass as he avoided the kiss I tried to drunkenly plant on him. I fell to the right side of the bed and heaved out a sigh then flipped off my shoes with one toe against the heel. Repeat. I stared up at the ceiling. The fan twirled slowly and there was a faint light in the room from a lava lamp in the corner somewhere on top of something low that I naturally assumed might be a milk crate. Everything looked so cheap and neat. Not so much manicured, but sterile and almost clinical, as if the mess had been doctored or devised by a poorly skilled set designer. There were wrist watches on a low-lying nightstand which all faced the same direction towards the door, a bracelet, and a picture frame of him and Elma and some other friends from when they were even tinier and skinnier than they were now. I leaned over him to grab it. He moaned under my weight and sucked his teeth at the sound of one of the watches falling on the hard linoleum floor.

I playfully refused to move even over his protests, "Who are these people?"

A stifled huff, *"David, Elma, Freddy y yo. Anda, quitate, estas pero bien pesado..."* he wriggled beneath me and I sat up and propped myself on my right arm. The light from the lamp was yellow but the lava wasn't moving. It had just settled at the bottom. Clumped down there like goopy pieces of play dough. I laughed, "What's wrong with your lamp?"

He had since sat up himself and was trying to rearrange the watches and put the picture frame back just so, "*Hay estado quebrado por anos. Mire,*" it had been broken for years he said as he stood and walked two steps towards the lamp. He turned it upside down then right side up twice, like mixing some incandescent martini.

"Oh... so *that's* the trick," I smiled, feigning to be impressed by the little light show.

He smiled, pleased with himself, and said, *"Si. Cuando nos ponemos bien grifos, eso hago, y nos tripeamos por un buen rato,"* then he feigned sparking up a doobie.

I recalled, "I've always wanted one. But they always seemed too expensive. Then again, I was like twelve and had like no money whatsoever. Fuck, I had to save up for McDonalds. Mmmm ... mouth watering nuggets...."

He laughed and looked down at the lamp then leaned to his right and tried to carefully set it back near the foot of his bed, "*Si, pues si son muy carros. Era de un tio por lado de mi mama. Me lo regalo cuando yo estaba en la prepa.*"

"Your uncle? Well that was nice of him. Was he a big druggy too?" I asked.

He laughed, "I think... maybe. He studied in the States and then went to live in London."

"Ah, well, one time... I went to Las Cruces," I joked.

He looked at me puzzled.

"It's a city... near El Paso... El Paso, like, where I'm from? Like forty minutes away; it's a shit hole, never mind."

He laughed again then leaned over and kissed me. I felt the bristles of his mustache and then the ever so faint scrape of teeth and then tongue and...I pushed him away. A burp was coming. I held out an arm.

"Estas bien?" he said very uneasy, *"Espera, no vomites!"*

"BBBBBBBBUUUUUUUUUUURRRRRRRRPPPPP."

He was at the ready with a plastic white trash bin. I smiled, "Why is everything white?"

Domi chuckled, relieved that I hadn't turned his bedroom into the splash zone at SeaWorld, and then sat on the bed. He squeezed my leg and we both faced each other with the window behind us. Two silhouettes framed by white curtains. He grabbed my hand and started slapping it between the two of his as if he were tossing around a mini pizza dough.

"Porque esta sincillo y de moda. Cuando tengo casa, voy a tener todo en blanco. Pero te hago un cuarto atras para tu estudio. Haci para que no me ensucias todo," he laughed, *"Eres bien sucio, la neta, verdad?"*

"ME? DIRTY? NEVER!" I said pretending to be shocked, "Besides, an all white house would be hella stupid hard to keep clean. I mean the dogs alone would..."

He kissed me and said, *"Si eres, no te hagas, y no es tan deficil. Ash, no mames, hueles a perro."*

"It's called: Eau de Saint Bernardé. Jerk."

That night I had dreamt about moving back into my mother's house but then had decided to move back to my apartment in Sunset Heights near downtown El Paso. I told my mother in the dream that it wasn't her, it was me. I was just tired of being blamed for the hair clogs in the tub.

"But you have three dogs, Marvin!" she flung her arms up then dropped them dramatically.

"Mom, I just got here. The dogs haven't even been inside the house. My fridge is still in the car!"

"But your sister washed them this morning!"

"Mom! We've been driving all day!"

"Well then if you're so smart, who has *that* many dirty dogs?!"

"I dunno, maybe your other son's shedding."

"Oh please! He's in New York!" Then my brother sauntered out in a towel with my toothbrush in his hand and whined in this valley girl accent, "Uh, the tub's clogged again guys."

"MOM! HE'S GONNA USE MY TOOTH BRUSH!"

She took a deep breath and her eyes began to water then said, in a pithy manner, "I. Am. Sick. And tired... of you guys fighting over stupid things!"

"MOM! BUT THAT'S MY TOOTH BRUSH!"

She then turned and walked towards her keys and purse she had left somewhere on some table I had never seen, "I'll be in the van until you two learn to grow up!"

"BUT, MOM?! MOM! MOM! IT'S MY TOOOOOOOTTTTTHHHH BRRUUUUUUUSSSHHHHH!!!"

I came to, a bit disorientated. Was I at my mother's? My place? That fan shouldn't be there. I turned my head to the right. YIKES! Two big black eyes, rimmed in thick dark eyelashes, laid there just staring back at me. Wide like moons. Wide like a serial killer's or a crazy's or like two big cups of coffee from an aerial view.

He laughed then said, *"Estabas llorando por tu mama. Jejeje, meco."* He stared down at my lips and tried to kiss me but I pressed my mouth together tight and pulled the white comforter over my head. A glow from the window seeped in. It was like being trapped in a snake's egg; soft and leathery. The glow like that light from a thumb pressed against a bulb but less orange and more yellow. He struggled for a bit to get under. Shaking his head side to side violently as he breached my little cocoon. Then his neck, then shoulders, and with his arms he flipped up the far end of the blanket and let it roll out like a wave then he wrapped his right leg between my knees. He bounced his head once on the pillow then smiled. Said there was no getting away from him. That he had tossed out my passport. He stared at my lips then my eyes then my lips again.

I moaned as I stretched. Pointed my toes and my fingers towards the foot of the bed. Arms straight, knees unbent. It's how I imagine skydivers form their bodies into bullets when they wish to go faster. Faster down into the inevitable, hard, and boring. The plummet is like sleep and the sky like your bed. A stretch is only inviting the possibility that you'll leave the sanctuary of it.

He was still staring at me, his nose almost touching mine. It was pointed but wide at the end, flaring up to the sides like a bull's. His eyes, now squinting, a bit happy, a bit mischievous, like a child who knows he always gets what he wants.

My right shoulder was sore from not moving enough in my slumber. Like from a dead sleep. The kind when you're so tired you forget that you're supposed to toss and turn a little. He just stared. I poked him in the ribs.

"Don’t start!” he grabbed my hands, "Then there you’re gonna be, crying for your mommy, and she’s not here to save your punk as.” He tried kissing me again but I pursed my lips and wiggled my head out from under the blanket.

"What time is it?" I asked.

He popped his head out, “Like nine. *Ven. Besame. Andaaaa... bebe, besameeeee...*" he whined like a little brat, puckering his lips, eyes closed, still holding my hands with one of his. I looked at him. That tousled black hair. Long on the top with the side’s shaven down close to the skin. Thick black eye brows that pointed at the ends. His mustache and beard, neat. Trim. Hipster. Chic. It belied the fact that he had no real chin and worked wonders to help his profile.

Why was I so lucky? The thought had crossed my mind several times before. In the hotel rooms where we had shared our first few days, when at night, back home, I would stare blankly into the pictures he had on his profile and smile to myself at the messages he'd leave on my phone.

The blanket was up around his face like a hood of clouds, "*Hace frio*, *Brrrr...*," he said and shivered a bit then stretched the same way I had, "*Me duele un poco la cabeza*," he laughed again through his nose then grinned as he rubbed the sides of his temples. Crooked flat teeth and a snaggle tooth the size of a baby's that grew over another on his right. He had the habit of trying to only smile on his left by raising his lips that way. When he talked I could see his silver fillings. His smile was whiter than mine but it looked British somehow. My teeth may have been yellow but they were pretty straight. Also I spoke English and he spoke that heathen speak which might well have been a succession of clicks and whistles. Even his thoughts came out crooked. Ugh, I didn't know if I wanted to hit him or kiss him.

He loosened his grip and I punched him in the belly. "No," he said curtly and smiled, *"Eres como niño. Pegando y gritando por tu mami. Uy mami mami, me ensucie mis huggies..."* I tried punching him again. He took hold of my hands with one of his and then pulled the cover over both our heads. He tried kissing me again and this time I let his tongue between my lips. He let go of my hands and I played with his right ear with my left hand. I farted, pulled the covers over his head and popped my own out from under. He struggled then started tickling me. I let him out from under. He turned his head away and began to fan out the stench as best he could with the blanket.

"Eres un cochino!" he hissed

"No, baby, no *cochino.* You meant to say 'sexy'. Com'n, kiss me! Mua mua mua!" I implored with eyes straining against the light. There was a curtain drawn over the window but it might as well have not been there. So thin and pale was the fabric, like flour bags or those cloths you use to dry dishes.

Like cheese cloth, like a gossamer wing. Like your mother's stockings you would pull over your heads and pretend to rob banks with back when a handful of pennies made you feel rich.

The room looked even smaller than it had a few hours ago. His head was so tiny. The pillows were a pale yellow like washed out sunflower; orange juice in a good screwdriver. They matched a stain on the wall, cut through by a thin crooked brown line. His arms were so thin. The thin brown line looked like a river on a map. His arms like paddles for a canoe. "What's that?" I asked squeezing his biceps, the muscles all but not there. He turned to look at the corner with the stain. He said that the water came through there sometimes. He had told the landlord but the man had yet done anything about it.

"*Uy no*. I'm going to drown," I told myself out loud.

"In kisses, maybe..." he started pummeling me with morning-after breath. Ashtray and whiskey and beer and stale saliva like strong coffee with sour milk. I figured mine might possibly have tasted worst but now we had one. One spit, one saliva, and we'd have practically had one tongue if our tongues weren't so awkward. Months since we had kissed. It reminded me of all and every handshake I had ever gotten wrong. Like trying to impress an older man with a firm howdy-do, but instead giving him a limp wrist. This time it felt as if Domi had forgotten how to kiss. And, let me just say, a limp anything is nothing to be desired. I felt as if I was dancing in a middle school auditorium when the lights dim darker and the music goes from happy shake shake to something sappy. Hands on hips? Or is it hands on shoulder? OR is it hands on ass? How close do we stand? P.S. Earth Science rocks! Get it?!

He unbuckled my belt. Well he tried to anyhow. The thing was like a puzzle for two hands that were way too eager. Thin, frail, fingers. Thick knuckles in the middle but thin tips like his wiener. His nails were bitten down little jagged things. Edges scratched my belly. He had the habit, when nervous or bored or not thinking, to chew them. Half of my ass was already hanging out of my boxers but he was still fumbling at the front. All I could think of was: Where is my other sock? More kisses then our dicks were out. He was stroking mine and I flicked his. He winced and crumpled into a ball. No, he said, as if reprimanding a child. We kept kissing. He kept tugging and then asked me how do they let me put that thing in them? I shrugged. My dick wasn't that big, I said, but he said it was thick. I sighed. Outside we heard footsteps, someone coughed, and then the door from the restroom closed. The person outside had struggled with it too. Like the wood was too saturated from humidity. Swollen. Too big.

"Come on, try it," I pleaded a little half inspired, half still sleepy. I kissed his eyes. They closed. They opened. So big like pools of tar you could get stuck in. Like Zooey Deschanel or Betty Boop.

"Come on..."

He laughed again through his nose, "*No, me va a doler.*"

"No it won't. Promise I'll be gentle. Just the tip. But I love you! I swear I'll call tomorrow! PINKY PROMISE!!!"

The toilet flushed then a second later the restroom door thud thuds open. Footsteps.

We both lay there quiet. Necks barely above the blanket then a BANG BANG BANG.

"GET UP ALREADY YOU FUCKING FILTHY FAGGOTS!" Elma's voice thundered, bassy and muffled like a gangster gorilla. Domi tossed the covers back with a, "*Ya callate puta!*".

I whispered to him, "I don't think she even washed her hands".

He yelled, after a pause, "*Y ni te lavastes los manos, pinche sucia!*"

BANG BANG BANG BANG

"I did! With my own piss and the blood from my period!" she asserted.

We laughed.

He sat up. I stared at him in the beautiful glow of that late morning. The kind of late morning after the mailman has come and gone. The kind of late morning when mimosas are served. The kind of late morning when by the time you roll out of bed, you might as well be ordering lunch instead. It was somewhere between ten thirty and eleven. You don't feel as guilty because you woke up before twelve. But you know you've missed the birds singing at dawn. At least you missed traffic and that cold morning air. He was so rail thin. He hadn't a shirt. Just moles on his back and inward his stomach curved. Two, three big ones. You could connect them like dots, like a constellation on some pale firmament. I see a... I see a... He was checking his phone that he had picked up off the bedside table by the two watches and bracelet that I now recognized as something I had given him. Chrome chain. Something semi-gothic/rocker-ish. Something a kid in high school who liked Harley's might wear at a punk show. Maybe a cholo. I know that I found it, that I hadn't bought it. But one of the last times, the few times, we met in Juarez, he said he had a present for me so either leaving the apartment, or waiting in the car, I found it. Repackaged. Repurposed. He liked it. Or maybe he kept it hidden. Squirreled away in a shoe box or at the bottom of a drawer and he only took it out because he knew my presence was to be expected. I can't remember what he gave me. I think it was a string bracelet that since we had broken up and got together, I had lost. Maybe it was that cookbook. That notebook he made out of hand and of paper he had stitched together and then sprayed with cologne. The kind of cologne, the previous time, he'd worn. I had mentioned how I adored it. But you never really do adore the perfume. You adore your face in the armpit. That shadow of a person left by scent. That person as they get up from the couch next to you to go to the restroom, and this thing, this invisible cloud of essence, lingers, instilling an instant longing. Then again, I was drunk.

He swiftly turned back into bed then under the covers we both went. The glow was around us again. Back inside our snake's egg. Back inside a tent made of longing for kisses and blow jobs and handskies and naked flesh. In the clouds it felt like again. Again skydiving. Or like when you're in a foam party and the bubbles give way. There is this cavernous something only big enough for two heads. Kisses. More kisses and tugging and touching and twirling ones finger around belly hairs that near the pelvis right under the navel. Soft, then hard, then biting of lips. A laugh. Then more. Lather, repeat.

Legs intertwined. Lips on the neck. His naked belly, warm, a bit furry. He begged me to get naked. I said it was too cold and he assured me that it wouldn't be so for too long. *"Te caliento, no te precupes,"* he said as he started popping my buttons. More kisses. More neck. Dicks being felt. Noses in the way. Noses get kisses. Breathing, loud breathing. Hot and sticky hung-over breath. Palms over penis heads. Rubbing like that controller on Centipede. Shafts being tugged and pulled and yanked.

BANG BANG BANG!

An effeminate male voice: *"Osea, se van a quedar jalandoselas o que?!"*

We kissed, both oblivious to the world without and Luis Raul's insinuations. A sweet and tender kiss like a goodbye in front of friends or in front of family or at least in front of the police. I could hear the TV and someone laughing at it. Then the smell of bacon and it smelled yummy. I guessed the whole house was up and about. Guessed we should get up although I still wanted to stick stuff into other stuff and suck on other things.

Moments later, our door creaked open. Domi headed straight for the restroom. He shuffled in barefoot while I spent the next five minutes trying to find my right sock. Then I stood by the bathroom door. Elma walked up with a frying pan and spatula in hand. "Does this look burnt to you?" She had a wide mouth, lips like the Joker's, from one side to the other, from ear to ear. She wore this perplexed emotion, her lips pouting and big. Puffy like pillows of rouge wrinkles, almost as if they were sad that they were not still as red as they were the night before. I tried to put her face somewhere. Like somebody famous, but she just stared at me a bit bewildered as my gaze went past her and beyond. I leaned my head to the right, flipping channels in my mind. She smiled and then kissed my cheek. The hot spatula now precariously over my shoulder, dripping some grease.

She then banged on the bathroom door. "Quit being so rude, you louse! You left poor Marvin out here, by himself, on this, his very own honeymoon!"

From within the restroom, a strained fart noise, then a laugh.

The digs were small from what I gathered. As you walked to the front, there was the back room, which was Domi's, then, a bathroom to the right. Another bedroom was opposite the bathroom, which was Elma's, or some kind of municipal dumping ground. Then a short hallway, like five steps, and a corner, where there was a doorway to the left that led to the kitchen. It was about the size of a bedroom where the first thing you passed was a big brown fridge to the left. There was a small table in the middle with four mismatched chairs and a ceiling fan right above it. A counter and a sink and another counter and cabinets hanging over on the same side where the big brown fridge sat humming. They ran into a windowless wall, perpendicular, which ran into another right angle wall cut through with a rectangle from the ceiling to about four feet above the floor. Therein a counter that served as a bar. It divided the kitchen from the living room. From the living room, to the right, was another den fashioned into a room with dressing dividers, their folding screens, and dangling beads like those found in hippie stores with no doors. One screen was of an Asian wood block nature. Silhouettes of black cranes and of steep rock faces with trees that were hanging, heavy with age. The other dressing divider was fashioned out of 4 inch white squares, framed in light brown wood. Luis Raul sat on the other side of the counter table. That was his room behind him and to the right, a sanctuary somewhat haphazard. I was surprised that no one had knocked over the screens last night. He sat there, hair pressed down on his scalp except for a single clump pointing out to his right as if he had slept on one side more than the other. He chewed, disinterested, on something then rolled his eyes and swiveled back in his chair towards the TV in the corner with that disco ball light.

The place was a mess but the kind of mess that didn't really matter. There was no furniture in the living room except for the empty fold out drink table, The folding chairs had even been nicely put against the wall. "That bitch," he cattishly blurted at the TV where some reporter, blonde and busty, read from a teleprompter.

Elma struggled at the stove, this tiny thing with two burners, one large and one small, radial electric pieces of crap. Depressing. I thought, you'd have to cut a pizza in half just to make it fit. Whenever I see electric stoves I think of things burning or getting too crisp. My mind doesn't register "levels" on the knob. My mind only seems to register "more fire" with "less fire" although I always seem to cook on a high heat. Years ago, some little Asian man told me to do so. It was an old stove though. Nice little art deco clock/timer in the middle under a glass face and pale pea green enamel. Maybe it was more of an avocado hue. Not sure, but I was already looking forward to asking Domi for a gas stove if not a real wood burning one. I played it over in my head, "I moved five gazillion miles, gimme gimme gimme!"

Elma was humming something like a techno melody then started popping her lips frenetically. It sounded like bubbling water or water draining down into an almost clogged sink. The grease on the pan accompanied her with a hiss as the bacon burned in one skillet and little squares of potatoes fried in another. I took a seat at the table behind her. My head a bit woozy from the smell of food and my sugar levels dropping. My stomach felt more vacuous than ever. I watched her bony shoulder blades move under a big white t-shirt as she bobbed her head, her hair pulled back into a short pony tail. Domi came out from the hallway. So skinny, such an Adonis. He walked with the kind of swagger a nerd might have. The kind of nerds who get all those Math teacher jokes about cosigns and square carrot somethings. He sat down to my left then half got up, leaned over the table and planted one on my face, sat back down then grabbed my hand and started fondling it. I quickly pulled it away and gave him a “foochie caca face” then pushed my chair back and walked to the sink. I stared at the mess befuddled.

"*Que buscas?*" Elma asked as I daintily rummaged through this pile of multicolored plastic tumblers. I hate plastic cups. She pulled a pink one out and assured me that it was clean, that she had just washed it but hadn't the time to put it away and apologized for them not having a rack to let them dry on or something.

I leaned against the doorframe by the fridge whose motor kept singing then tink tink tinked to an end. Elma swiveled towards it, opened the door, revealing how basically empty it was. I peeked in for a second and then SLAM!

"We're making omelets in your honor!" she announced gaily and self-satisfied.

"Eggs are very expensive around here," added Domi.

I retorted with a "Don't you mean they're *eggs-spensive??*" but they didn't get the joke because they were stupid and spoke another language or something. My vote goes for: they were just stupid.

I made another face at Domi, crossed my eyes and stuck out my tongue then beat a limp hand against my chest. He laughed, sipped something out of a mug and called me *estupido* under his breath. I guess Elma caught me with the corner of her eye, she laughed and said something like “You've never looked more handsome.” I gave her the stink eye. Luis Raul yelled at the TV some more, cursing the talk show host. Mexicans are such a colorful people, I thought, then, started singing the Star Spangled Banner and Elma gave me another uncertain look.

"What's up with you, *gabacho*?" she laughed.

"*Se cree muy Americano con su pinche cara de nopal.*" Domi assured her, chuckled, and threw a wadded up paper napkin at me. He would always make light of the fact that I thought I was so American in spite of my obviously Mexican features.

"See? I'm not even here two days and we already fightin'. P.S., where's the nearest Woman's Battered Shelter?"

"*Que's eso?*" Elma flipped the eggs and cut them sideways into fours with this gross looking plastic spatula. It wasn't necessarily dirty, but had been half melted at various points as if forgotten on the stove once or twice. Everything in the place was either Teflon or plastic or tin or something cheap and thin. Thing's easily replaceable but just as easily destroyed or dismissed. I already missed my heavy iron skillets. I already missed MY everything so I sighed and raised an eyebrow then walked towards the table but I didn't even make it there before the smoke alarm went off. It wailed for about ten seconds before Domi begrudgingly slid back his chair and walked over to pop it off of its place right above the hallway door. You'd think it was a fucking Rubik's cube. He messed with it for another few forevers. My head was pounding now. Sometimes I forget I'm hung-over until I lean down and get dizzy. Apparently piercing loud noises remind me as well.

"I thought you were smart?" I quipped.

He laughed and took his seat, "*Como?*"

"Forget it." I cupped my chin in hand and leaned down onto the table, tapped my fingers then drew an invisible circle with my nail. He leaned back in his chair and crossed his arms over and behind his head then kicked me from under the rickety square thing. Luis Raul yelled some more and flailed his arms in the air. Elma said the food was almost done then she dialed down the knobs on the stove and whispered some kind of profanity as she sucked at her thumb. She paced towards the cabinets and pulled out four mismatched plastic plates. They were something like melamine. Something you could drop and drop and toss out a car window but they'd never break. On them, designs long since faded or scoured off in lines and scratches from washing. A yellow one had a cartoon of some kind. That white one had a border of pink flowers on green stems. There was a blue one with a yellow Batman symbol in the middle and then there was a red one with Tony the Tiger. Fine china. Fine dining. Domi pulled out some forks, all from different sets as well, and some knives, some serrated and pointy, some just rounded butter ones.

Maybe I wasn't as hungry as I had imagined. I knew I hadn't eaten in awhile, maybe a day and a half or so. It felt like there was an empty pit at the bottom of my stomach. But, it wasn't food I was craving. It felt more like being home sick. Like the wind getting knocked out of me all over again. Like when you forget to smoke a cigarette and you get a bit blue. I forget my habits often. I constantly have to remind myself to drink water. I triple check to make sure I raised the car windows. I shake the doorknob to make sure the front door's locked. Well I used to. I used to have a car. I used to have an apartment. I used to... I used to…

"SHIT!" I stood abruptly, almost knocking over the chair and started banging my foot against the floor. "SHIT! SHIT! SHIT!!!"

"*Que le pasa?!*" Elma leaned back in her chair, a bit dismayed but still chewing. She covered her mouth with a knife in her left hand. God, do they do everything backwards here? She's barely had a few bites but reached over towards the center of the table, picked up a pack of Lucky Strikes, tapped the box on the tabletop, packing the tobacco, then pulled out a ciggie and lit it over the half eaten plate, her red lipstick adhering to the butt. Fork prongs up and knife by it's right, both on the left side of the plate. I then wondered if she had slept in her make up or if she had even slept at all.

"*Oooo....,*" Domi chimed in, "He didn't like your food…."

She exhaled, this long breath of smoke and chemicals and things that cause cancer from these lips that look like they're silently whistling. "*Callate, perra! A todos les encanta como cocino!*"

"No! FUCK! Food's good. I just forgot to call my mom! She's probably fucking crazy hellah worried."

"Ah," Domi said curtly then shoveled a heaping helping of omelet into his pie hole. A tiny yellow-white piece left dangling by the edge or his mustache. I squinted. Stupid no chin. He chewed on then said, "*No mames, que mal plan. Pobre tu mama. Dejando mi suegra aya toda preocupada. Te dije que lo dieras mi numero del telefono pero noooooo....*" But he didn't have to remind me of how terrible and negligent a son I was.

"Shut up. I don't even know where my stupid phone, that doesn't even work in this stupid country, IS!!! I don't get why you guys don't have Verizon!" I mocked in falsetto, "Meh-uhhh, we're Mexico... we only use walkie-talkies and cans with strings. Meh-uhhh."

Elma blew out another puff of smoke and tilted her head back, smiled then flicked the ashes into her plate. Domi bobbed his head side to side, chewing and asked if I had left it in my backpack under my soiled panties. They laughed.

Stink eye all around.

I hopped towards the bedroom. In the distance I could hear Elma telling Luis Raul to shut up and change the channel already. Some girl stepped out of Elma's bedroom in a pink oversized shirt. There was some kind of anime looking design on it, like a nerd jizzed out a cartoon cat. "*Hola buenos dias*," she said as she rubbed her hands over her face and brushed her shoulder length hair back behind her ears.

"Hola," I smiled politely then continued bouncing into Domi's room. "Bag? Where's my fucking bag? If I were a fuckin'..." I didn't know why, but I checked under the covers. Nope. I looked around hopelessly. I had checked all of ONE place and I was all out of ideas. My sugar must have been really low. So confused and running at full speed in neither

and every direction. I looked up and around the ceiling for some reason. Nope, not there either. How the hell can you lose something in a space so plain? It reminded me of when I used to lose my Saint Bernard, Hachi, in the apartment. I would walk through the entire place; fucker had some sort of camouflage or cloaking device. I finally admitted defeat and stomped back towards the kitchen, poked my head out from the hallway, "*Oye, Domi, no haz visto mi mochila?*" I asked.

He was laughing at something Elma was showing him on her phone. The other girl was pouring herself some milk into a bowl of cornflakes.

He looked up after a second, "*No seas mal educado, bebe. Saluda a Cristina*," he said, trying to reprimand me for seemingly being rude to cat jizz lady.

She said, "*Ya me...*"

As I said, "*Ya le...*"

"... *saludo.*" She popped the top back on the milk but left the carton on the counter by the sink and the dirty dishes.

"Domi..." I whined as I strangled the doorframe with my right hand. *"Andale!* Where's my bag?!"

In a mocking falsetto he said, *"Uy, mi bolsa!"*

"*JAjajaj... 'su. BOL-SA'*," Elma just HAD to put her two cents in as they both mocked the idea of me being so preoccupied by my missing "purse". I stomped back into the hallway. Domi slid his chair back, a long deep moan from its legs against the kitchen linoleum. Inside his room, I started throwing the sheets and blanket around again. Maybe... behind the pillows... hmmm...

"*Eit! Calmado!* We'll find it!" He grabbed me from behind and kissed the small of my neck. Swayed me side to side for a bit. He smelled like hair product and fancy cologne. I shrugged him off.

"Don't start! Where's my fuckin' phone, man? I can't fuck-in'-find-my-*phone.* You know? *telefono-no-no?"*

"*Uyyyyy siiiiii... calma tu pinche rollo. Pinche cara de nopal.*" he said sarcastically, again mocking my new found sense of American nationalism.

I went towards the window that was on the right. The curtains fell to the floor so I began thrashing them around. Right, then left, then right again. Mother fucking things kept falling back into place. Blind rage. Blind, unmitigated, rage. My arms were shaking. My sugar must have been uber crazy mind blowingly low. My head went a bit whoozy. FUCK-ITTY-FUCKING-MOTHER-FUCKING-FUCKTARD-CURTAINS!

All I found was an outlet with way too many cords and realized that the window had no view. There was just another wall about three feet from it. A skinny little walkway I imagined. Not sure why, but I stood there for a second. Fists like balls, I felt a little more homesick than angry. Why am I angry? Why do all of a sudden I feel trapped and suffocated? My head swooned again. I used to have a view. Even if it was only one of the gas station next door. And there were always people passing, sometimes strangers, sometimes friends. Now all I had was a wall. A mother-fucking wall of cinder blocks painted yellow.

Ugh, my stomach churned and it felt like I needed to take a shit. Like a messy shit. The kind where you wonder if they'll be enough toilet paper for it. I grabbed my belly and squeezed my ass cheeks.

"Mira, aqui esta. Quit being so dramatic," he handed me the bag and puffed air up into his mustache.

"Where was it?"

"*Atras de la puerta*," he said pointing to the door.

"Why'd you hide it?" I shoved a hand into the green backpack and felt around for the phone. Something sharp. A book. Something cold like a quarter... that felt like a penny... I find the phone! Still no service. No roaming, no nothing. Nada. Zilch. Capisce?

"Si. Claro. Te lo escondi. No seas ridiculo," he sighed at the idea of me scolding him for having had hid my things.

"Domi-robe-mochilas..." I laughed a little. The room didn't seem so hot all of a sudden but my armpits felt wet and on my brow I could feel the beads of sweat rolling down the sides near my temples. "There's no signal..." I frowned and my

right leg started shaking. My hands started shaking again. I smile. I smile. I smile. I'm going to be sick. "Lemme go to the restroom real quick...." I muttered out hastily.

I pushed past Domi and ran towards the bathroom. Luckily no one was in there but the damned thing was so small. A tiny sink, a pink plush toilet seat cover and a walk in shower which was beyond grimy and whose curtain pressed up right against the pooper. I cringed at the idea of what had been growing on that plastic sheet. The tile was the same pepto looking grossness and I suddenly found myself wishing I had brought some along. How do you pronounce “Pepto” in Spanish? Screw it. They cure everything with Sprite. Broken arm? Sprite. Liver failure? Two Sprites. Cancer? Two and a half. I turned on the faucet and leaned into the washbasin. I could barely hold my head up but I managed to stare into the mirror. You can do this, Marvin. You can do this. You've been through worst. Remember that one time... and then that other time... and then... all those days when the world seemed like it was crumbling in on itself and you were in the middle of that chasm? You can do this. You are strong. What would your comic book heroes do? What would Janeway do?

I adjusted the faucet from a stream into a trickle. As it was, the water pressure seemed to suck balls but the spout managed to make that delightful and comforting whistle. Like a valve barely open and water squeaking by. I started taking off my shirt. For some reason I’ve never liked shitting with a shirt on. I've always felt like it'd get in the way once you start wiping.

Where the fuck do I put my shirt? I tucked it into a flimsy towel rack with no towels. I supposed that it was just for show. Rusting chrome is very in this year. I sat down after debating for a second or two whether I should hover. I decided against it because I wasn't sure if this was going to be messy or not.

The seat was a chipped and swollen particle board. It swiveled awkwardly under my weight as though it was ready to fall the fuck off and now that dingy shower curtain had managed to wrap its cold, moist being around my leg. The sounds that followed were bassy popping then squirting then farting and water splashing. I tried turning the faucet on higher, leaned over to the right and just let the motherfucker hiss into the sink.

Tssssssss.

Immediately I did a courtesy flush. There was this centimeter wide line under the door where you could see into the hallway. I could only imagine what they heard much less what they smelled. There was also this weird rustling from the curtain as I pushed the annoying synthetic sheet to the other end of the...

BAM! CLINK! CLINK! CLANK!

Fucking thing came unhinged and fell into the shower's tiled floor but not before hitting the top of the toilet's water tank. I panicked and stood up hastily and my ass caught the edge of the tank's top and sent it flying to the floor. It shattered in two. Shit! I thought to myself: How do you say Super Glue in Spanish? The faucet started shaking and made this weird buzzing sound like the pipes were struggling. So there I was, standing with my pants around my ankles, diarrhea smeared between my ass cheeks, broken toilet and wouldn't you know, fucking *this much* of toilet paper left.

Why, oh god, why have you forsaken me?!

You have to be kidding me: So far from home, such a mess, more than a little stressed, and now no TP? I shuffled to one side then the next. Domi banged on the door and asked if everything was okay. "*Ocupado,*" I yelled out then shuffled to the other side. Under the sink? I opened the cabinet and a slew of half empty hair-product bottles tumbled out but no toilet paper in sight. Dammit. Mother fucking dammit. What is this? Am I on TV? Is this some kind of *Tapatio* hazing? I rummaged through the bottles. Half of these probably cost more than what they have in the fridge. Why do Mexicans need fake tan? Now this one's completely empty. What are they saving it for? Memories? But wait! Is that what I think it is?! YES! BABY WIPES! Take that *Guadalajara*! Marvin: 1; Life: 250,567.

Wipe. Wipe. They were a bit dry so I passed a sheet under the water. The package was full of dust and dirt. Poor little things, probably forgotten months ago. Wipe. Wipe. Wipe.

Well, you get the gist of it. After washing my hands I proceeded to look about the room for a towel. Still none. Out of second nature, I go to dry them on the shower curtain I have haphazardly put back on. Immediately I had forgotten how disgusting the thing was, much less how flimsy it had proven. The thing gives way again, of course. Another bang on the door. Am I still okay? Yes. Kinda... basically....

Great, now the door's jammed. I banged my forehead against the peeling paint. Why god why? Thud. Thud. Thud. Then a pull followed by another, this time a little stronger. Nothing. Maybe... this... time... SMACK. The door flies open and catches me right on my nose.

"Ah, perdon. Are you okay? We heard a shit load of ruckus," Domi stood on the other side of the door and laughed, "We thought you had fainted."

Domi. I hated Domi. I decided whole-heartedly, then and there, that he was the bane of existence.

With a hand over my face I mumbled, carefully emphasizing each half of the sentence, "You hit me.... on the nose..."

"Ooo! Fuchila!" he laughed, waving a hand in front of his face, and leaned down to open the cabinet beneath the sink. There was some kind of air freshener he pulled out and proceeded to spray this lavender like thing all up in my grill. If my eyes weren't already watering from the blow to my face, now they were also stinging in the midst of this fumigation. My lungs burnt a little. My sinuses cringed. He kissed me then closed the door and slid past towards the toilet and kicked up the seat with his bare foot. Daintily, he curled back his toes.

"Ewoo... lo ensusiaste todo, bay-bee," he laughed then let loose a stream of piss. "Hey... and what happened to the toilet top?"

I stared at his small flaccid dick and shit spatter on the under side of the seat. As he was putting his pipe away, he asked, *"No manches... que paso?"* he leaned down to in-between the toilet and the shower, *"Lo quebraste? No mames..."* He pulled back the curtain and reached down for the pieces and the thing comes tumbling down for a third time. "Ow," he said rubbing the back of his head and holding half of the tank top.

I rolled my eyes to the side and nervously laughed, averting his gaze. "Uhmm... *Domi Trap?* " He set down the shattered porcelain on the little counter surrounding the sink. Still rubbing the back of his head, he reached for the spray he'd left propped up on the towel rack and soaked the toilet.

"No mames, guey.... neta? You got to be kidding me," he sighed deeply. For a second I thought he might punch me so I flinched when he set the spray down on the sink. He laughed, *"Meco, que tienes?"*

I shrugged. He pulled out a new roll of toilet paper from a small medicine cabinet by the door. It was this thin thing, maybe half a foot wide but two feet tall. Not sure why I didn't check that before. Guess I figured it wasn't deep enough to hold anything but aspirins and those little tampons wrapped up to look like candies. He rolled a few squares out around his hand then used that wad to wipe down the bottom of the seat. He sprayed it again and rolled out more squares and repeated the process on the seat then the actual rim of the toilet bowl. He turned around and kissed me, *"Vez, para que no andas diciendo que no te quiero,"* then washed his hands diligently, twice, and then tried to open the door but it looked like it was stuck again.

One. Two. Three.... 'ee... 'eeeeee... YANK! It almost catches my forehead this time. We maneuvered out and I followed him into the kitchen.

"I had to clean him up like a baby," he beamed proudly to Elma and Cristina, a half captivated audience. Cristina sat opposite Luis Raul, both staring at the TV. She shoveling

cornflakes into her mouth. Him hunched over in his seat, his man boobs wrinkled unsightly beneath a white v-neck.

"Awww...," Elma smiled as she washed dishes, "*Y tu mama, Marveen?* Did you get a hold of her?"

"Nope. I don't have signal. Also, I don't want to point any fingers BUT," and the next half of the sentence I blurted out more as if it was one word than an actual slew of them, "Domi-broke-everything-in-the-restroom-and-pooped-everywhere," I sucked air through my teeth and smacked my lips.

Elma turned her head and asked a bit shocked, *"Que???"*

"That's what I said..." I raised my eyebrows and rocked back and forth on the balls of my feet.

"ASHHHHH! Como eres mentiroso!" Domi hissed and started towards me as if to pinch my sides. I ran off into the hallway towards the room but not before yelling, "Also he said breakfast sucked!"

He chased me and we fell over into the bed. Sheets rumpled. Everything a tidy mess. No wonder the guy had hemorrhoids. My asshole felt like a clenched fist just looking at everything "in it's right place". I get it, he's an architect. I get it that he's a bit anal and obsessive and a slight hypochondriac. But, com'n... give me a break. He tickled me. Wrestled my arms to the side then called me a big fat liar again. Said we would have to get the toilet fixed now. Said I ruin everything and have a Midas touch for making things go horribly awry. He kissed me. I struggled then farted. He called me disgusting and got off. Walked towards his phone that was charging on the bedside table, pinched his nose then asked me what the number to my mother's was. I wrangled my phone out of a front pocket from my jeans, "Lemme see...." I called out the numbers. Ten, but he told me to hold on a minute as he punched in another five or so. He put the phone to his ear. *"Esta sonando, ten,"* then passed me the phone.

"Hello?" a woman's voice on the other line.

"Ma'? It's me."

"Ay hijo, como llegaste? Estaba tan precupada! Porque no me hablaste cuando llegaste? Llegaste bien? How's the beach?"

"Mmmm... So far I fell off a chair and broke the toilet..."

"Ay, hijo, ya deja de tomar tanto..."

"Ay, it wasn't really my fault and I wasn't even THAT drunk. Shit just happened. Like, literally shit happened everywhere. I think I got that Montezuma's revenge or something. You can get that from whiskey, right?"

She laughed, *"Y Domi?"*

"Domi? Meh."

Domi yelled out, *"Hola suegra!"*

My mom laughed, "Is that him? *Saludamelo. Bueno,* tell me how was the flight and everything."

"Drinks are expensive and I thought it took forever but it was only like 3 hours. The city smells funny though. Like Juarez but wet. Like Wet Juarez," I farted again and Domi pinched his nose again then walked out of the room.

"Y como te sientes? Maria was asking about you. She says it's beautiful down there."

"Mmm... I'm like *whatever.* It's just like El Paso, I guess. But then again, I say that about everywhere. I could probably end up in Alaska and be all like 'Oh, hey, cold El Paso'. I dunno. It's nice though. They had a party last night. But I was soooooo tired."

"Te pusiste boracho, verdad?"

"Kinda... a little. I was just tired though. I haven't slept at all. I feel sick. My heart's racing and I just feel really anxious. Like I wanna cry at everything," my eyes watered just then at such an honest confession.

"Sounds like you're having an anxiety attack. Go outside and scream. As loud as you can, *mijo.* Or turn up the radio in the car as loud as it will go and sing along as loud as you can."

"I know... I'll try. It's just so... arg... err... it's just so much to deal with. So much to take in. How you doin' though? How's Virginia?"

"Good. I get sad a little. You know they're having a little prayer for your dad on Friday. *Pobre mija*, she was really close to your dad. She's takin' it hard...."

"Yea... I'll try and light a candle. *Bueno*. I was just calling to let you know that I got here safely. Say hi to Goya for me."

"Okay mijo. Bye."

"Bye."

"Alrighty, bye."

I hung up the phone and stared at the screen. It was cracked a little in the lower left hand corner and spread diagonally. For someone so anal about everything you'd think he'd have taken better care of his shit. Bullet hole ridden car. Cracked cell phone. Fat boyfriend. What. A. Loser. I sighed and wiped the screen with the edge of my shirt as it went dark. I heard the aerosol can from the restroom hiss. He came in from behind, my back facing the door. I turned and smiled but smiled faintly and wiped the corners of my eyes.

"Todavia huele," he laughed. *"Ah, bebe, no llores. Que cuenta tu mama?"*

"Nothing." I half sobbed, "She started talking about my dad. They're all bummed or something," I smiled and wiped a single tear from my right cheek. He walked up and rubbed my left upper arm with his right hand then squeezed my other elbow with his left.

He smiled, *"No llores."*

"I'm not crying!" I wiped another tear, "It's allergies. Also you smell funny."

"Aw, bebe..."

"Shut it!

"Fifi New Haven."

It looked like it had rained last night. There were some big bulbous gray clouds yet looming overhead. It didn't feel like December. It just felt nice. A little hot but by no means anything near to what I had come to know in El Paso. I felt like the world was breathing a warm breath on me, something akin to mother fucking halitosis. I fanned myself with a hand, the smell of sewer in the distance. I looked up at the sun peeking through the clouds. We were in the street outside of the house by Domi's car. Everything was moving but the leaves on the trees. They were still. Depressed, like heavy, in this sauna but hearty, thick, almost succulent looking things. Not limp like me who hadn't taken too kindly to the unfamiliar humidity. I had been awake for all of twenty minutes and I already I needed to take a nap.

"Suena bien," he approved of the name.

"And yours?" I asked.

"Mmm..." he pressed his lips together in deep thought as he heaved out my bags from the trunk. He seemed so frail that I expected him to topple over or snap in half. I would've taken all three but he insisted, chivalrously. Cars whizzed by. More people on bikes. One jogger. Two joggers. A lady texting as she dragged a small hapless white dog behind her. She was in a full on, skin tight, black and pink workout outfit with sunglasses and a hat but I doubt she was even breaking a sweat. I, on the other hand, wiped a few beads from my brow. God, I could be sitting in the shade with a fan and my feet in an ice bucket and the shit would just drip from me. I took a whiff from my armpit. Smells about right.

"*Que ves?"* he yelled back from the front gate after he had passed me. I was still standing by the car eyeing the lady and judging her silently.

"Do they have a hashtag for stupid pets being walked by stupid bitches?" I asked.

"Mmmm... no se. Sebastian Duro," he replied.

"What?"

"My porn name," he smiled back, sure of himself.

"No, no. You have to pick the first dog you ever had and then the street you grew up in or on. I'm not sure how it works if you lived on a farm or on the ocean. Are you a pirate? I'm a pirate. Arg, matey."

"Mmmm... pero me gusta Sebastian. Siempre me hay gustado ese nombre y claro que los pern-sterrs siempre tienen apeidos de doble sentido."

"No, no, no... ugh, why do you guys do everything wrong. Stupid Mexicans," I spat a loogey onto the pavement then ran my tongue over my teeth. They felt gritty. I *think* I had brushed them... sometime... that week... wasn't sure. The sidewalk was about three feet wide but it seemed narrower. It was at least clean. The constant showers had lent the place an air of neatness. He turned to the door, *"No mames,* what did you bring? Rocks?"

"Rocks? God no," I assured him, "Bodies. Mostly bodies. P.S., you have a shovel, right?"

He looked at me quizzically. Shovel? Ugh. Pearls before swine.

"Estan pero bien pesadas estas madres. Almenos trajiste my regalo de Navidad?" he inquired as I then totally realized that I hadn't even thought about Christmas.

I whistled out a, "Surrrreeeeeee...P.S. where's the nearest Wal-Mart???"

He laughed, *"Ooo... que mal marido. Ni me trajiste mi Chriss-mass."*

"I'm Jewish," I said curtly, "No, wait, I'm a crypto-jew. I think those are in this season. Shalom-ma-diddy-dang-dang!"

"Bueno. Pues tal vez tambien a mi se me olvido tu regalo," he playfully threatened.

"No, baby. Gimme my present! Mmmm... mua mua... Nintendo.... mua mua, Whiskey... mua mua, vodka... mua mua....mmmm... Puppy?"

"Puppy? Cual que puppy?" he stuck out his tongue as he laughed and accidentally slammed one of my duffle bags into the front door frame.

"Careful! Don't break my socks!" I closed the gates behind us. Looked up to the sky. I don't think I've ever liked the rain. Well, at least not since I had been out of high school. As a kid, I loved it. Then again, I had to walk everywhere and any respite from the blistering desert sun was welcomed. I stared out past the rod iron gates and wondered why I always used to wear black. I mean it's cool and all, but... it was never really slimming on me. I stared out through the bars to the sky and those ominous clouds, pressed my face against the warm metal, stared down to the pavement then the car and in the distance I could see the lady with the little white dog drag him across the floor, oblivious to its attempt to drop a deuce. I sighed. I thought then that maybe I had bitten off a bit more than I could chew... again. My breath quivered and I wanted to cry. I felt the city closing in around me like a tomb. It felt like graduation day all over again. What next? I took a big step. Where's my cookie and my gold star, god dammit?

I shut the front door and saw him waddle to his room, a bag hanging low at the end of each arm. I supposed it was now "our" room. I looked around. The place looked lonesome for a second. Dirty but not *lived in*. Is this paradise? I hoped this was love. It cost me a pretty penny and everything I owned. He still didn't have a chin though. His feet looked too long and narrow and he was circumcised. Why, god why, is there no freaking couch? I sighed. This is it. This *is* paradise. This is what all those comedic romances are about. Still, I couldn't help but feeling like I was running away from something instead of running towards open arms. From outside I heard a car screech to a halt then a loud whine, a falsetto bark and a woman screaming. I shrugged.

So, they tended to keep *Jimador* tequila in the freezer. I had never really taken to the stuff, tequila I mean. I sighed and closed the fridge door. There was a bottle shaped like a pineapple of mezcal on the counter and a mess of other cheap glassware, all empty. Trust me, I checked. Their labels sent me shivers. I gagged. Is that a cartoon donkey??? Elma and Cristina had been asleep all day. It was nearly four and Luis Raul was putting on a belt. He wore slacks under a trendy geometric sweater, brown and rusty red with tiny white diamonds. Every one here dressed better than me. Even Fatty McStinky Von Stupidface.

"*Que buscas, bebe?*" Domi asked as he was texting someone.

"Something... *anything* to drink. But there's only tequila," I pouted and rummaged through the row of bottles again, just in case.

"No, mira, tambien hay mezcal. Pero ese si esta muy fuerte," he winked at me as if challenging the integrity of my alcoholism.

"Is that what Elma drinks?" I replied coolly.

"Aveces. Porque?" he assured me and wondered why.

"Just. Her boobs... are like hairy. But, I mean she's really, really pretty... on the inside... with a bag over her face... and in a parka.... if she stands a hundred feet away... in the dark..."

He laughed, *"No seas ridiculo. Ella esta bien bonita. Todos la quieren cochar."*

"Gross. Straight people have low standards. It's like they're always drunk or in Vegas. This is Vegas right? Hey, hey, Domi, *mi muy guapo* etcetera, etcetera."

"Ash contigo. Juras que eres modelo."

"Shut it! REAL MEN HAVE CURVES! Besides is it really that strong?"

"Si, un poco," he laughed, "That's why there's always a bottle left after parties."

I rubbed my head. I felt sleepy but bored. Exhilarated by the novelty of the move and too excited to spend it in bed. "Mmm... then maybe... just... a little."

He laughed then reminded me of our chores and errands that day, *"No, bebe, es muy temprano y tenemos que ir a la tienda a comprar la tapadera del escusado."*

"I shop better when I'm drunk. Also, fun fact, if I drink before the gym I have a really good workout. Kinda... in theory. I've actually just done it enough times and *not* fallen on my face, so I considered it a victory."

He rubbed my belly unconvinced I had seen a day on the treadmill in my life, *"Si. Claro."*

"Hey... that's water... retention. Maybe a burger. But definitely a lot of water retention."

"No seas haci. Ahorita llega David. Quiere conocerte."

"He wasn't here last night?"

"No, tenia que tomar photos para un nuevo bar que abrieron por el nuevo centro."

"La-dee-freakin'-da. I broke a toilet. I think we know who get the crown."

"Como?"

"Nothing, never mind. Geezus it's so hot in here. Why don't you guys have an air conditioner?"

"No se usan por aqui. Solo tienes que anda desnudo," he winked and pinched my titty.

"Gross. Unless... hey does Luis Raul walk around naked?"

"No. Solo en playera. Una vez se despierto pedo con camisa y sin pantolones y sin chones. Lo vi su pene. Lo tiene

prieto," he mentioned a time wherein he had seen Luis Raul wake up with only a t-shirt on and how dark his dick was.

"'*Prieto*' you say? Hey, hey, Luis Raul, *ven aca*."

He laughed, *"Ya. Deja de ser tan puto."*

"But I *love* Pluto. Even if it's not a planet anymore."

"Que?"

"Nothing. So who's David dating now?"

"Unos tres chavos o algo haci. Sus amigos son muy guapos. Haci bien fresas, tipo hisster." Apparently David was some kind of player and his friends were all handsome, trendy, little rich kids. I always just sort of imagined him as a blonde oompa-loompa.

"Mmmm..."

"Mmmm que? Sabes que solo tengo ojos para ti, mi amor. Gordo. Anda, desnudate. Hace calor," he assured me of his devotion and told me to get naked to ward off the heat.

"No. Go with David and his friends."

"*Bueno. Almenos ellos tienen dinero,*" he laughed with a kiss placed softly on my lips.

"Dee-ney-hro? Pffft.. I got four dollars, American... in my shoes. How many haciendas does that buy me?"

"Callate."

"You shut up. In time Imma get sexy. Just you wait."

"Pero ya lo estas, bebe. Mi bebe, americano, secsy."

"Mhmm... I hate bar photos. It's always the same thing. People in a row smiling. Couple smiling. More people smiling and throwing up peace signs. So on and so forth."

"No. El si les saca buenos fotos. Almenos la gente esta mas estilero," he bragged as I inched my way towards the bottle, *"No. Marveen, la neta.* It's too early to start drinking."

"Pfft, you ain't the boss of me. You're just the only person I know in a strange, foreign country. So, basically, hmmm..." I acquiesced to being at a loss of independence.

"*Bueno*," he kissed me again, "*Dejame recogo un poco antes que vienen.*"

While he was tossing bottles and cans into a big white bag with a red tie string, I was opening and closing the cupboards. There had to be something here. Anything. I reached over and popped the top off of the mezcal. Gross. Smelled like strong, rotten tequila. Elma came out, sleep still in her eyes and her hair now down. She looked like a wet paper towel wrung out one too many times. She rubbed her hands down and across her face.

"How you feeling?" I asked.

She forced a smile, no teeth, eyes kept closed and pulled out a white bowl from the cupboard. In the background, you could hear bottles clinking and cans crumpling in Domi's trash bag. They'd hit the floor in the belly of that sack. Dull sounds. Hollow and fragile. Surprisingly they didn't break. She pressed a hand into her right eye socket. *"No mames, que pinche rido hace este guey.* Does he have to do this right now?"

"Hey!" I said defensively, " 'Este *pinche* guey hijo de su pinche madre."

She laughed then checked the fridge. Domi still banging the bottles, me slamming the cupboards, she winced at the impromptu cacophony. Still a wee bit annoyed she asked, "*Que buscas, Marveen?* Maybe I can help you find it?"

"Something to drink. I can't believe that they drank everything. Stupid Mexicans. Hate them. AND they smell like tacos but didn't leave me any."

"Tacos? Buscas tacos?" she asked wearily, her mind likely as unfocused as the visions from her encroaching migraine.

"Yes, tacos and vodka. But not necessarily in that order. Actually, let's skip the tacos, and just stick with the vodka? Carbs, you know."

"There's water and a little bit of juice."

"Where? I mean the juice. Where's that shit?"

"No se pero lo vi en la manana... estaba... por... aca. Mira! ve, cuenta como un regalo de bienvenida." she smiled and handed me a carton of Jumex pineapple juice that she snagged from the fold out on the other side of counter table and told me it counted as a welcoming present. I shook it. It

sounded lumpy. She stretched across the kitchen then quickly returned with a plastic orange tumbler. "*Ten*," she smiled then flinched and shut her eyes tight then yelled towards Domi, "Bitch, where did we leave the naproxen?"

"Mmmm... no se," he kicked a wad of paper towels towards the corner on the other side, *"Haz checado en el baño?"*

"No. Oye, hablando de eso, que pinche pedo paso con el escusado?" she asked, wondering what had happened to the toilet.

"Luis Ra-ooooL," I interjected.

Domi laughed then said not to worry, *"No te precupes, ahorita vamos a areglarlo despues que llega David."*

"Is he on his way or what?" she rubbed her right temple with closed eyes.

"Si. Quiere conocer a Marveen," Domi beamed again. Apparently I was the new It Girl.

I walked past the table counter. It was Formica or something that looked like the color of gritty vomit. It had been peeling at the edges. The fold out table in the living room was no better off and there was a stack of plastic cups: Transparent neon greens and reds and yellows that could almost be mistaken for brown. I found another box of juice but it was guayaba. Gross. Surprisingly it was almost empty. My esteem for our party guests sunk that much lower. Music played softly from Luis Raul's laptop. Peeking through the space between the dividers, I saw him laying in bed texting someone. He poked his nose and then stared at the finger to see what he had mined from his nostrils. I walked back towards the box of Jumex Pineapple, set my cup on the counter, poured out a heaping helping of mezcal, and then added the juice. Bits of ash then the butt of a cigarette poured out into the pale yellow liquid. Just my luck. However, I thought, Waste not, want not. Then I tugged my ear, as was my custom to do before drinking a shot, and swilled the liquor and soot.

It was December 3 and I had packed absolutely nothing that I could possibly pass off as an X-mas gift. I unfolded old underwear. I had no idea why I packed the ones with holes. God, they must have been about 8 years old. They had been through one ex, a handful of one-night stands, and a few dozen pets that had met a tragic and untimely end. I arranged everything out on the bed. Those undies, socks, wrinkled button up plaids, a few jeans with their crotches worn out. I had spent five minutes debating whether to put the yellow pillows under the white comforter or over the comforter and, instead, decided that I wasn't comfortable with just one drawer in Domi's room. He had tried setting one of the middle ones aside in this rickety pressed-wood dresser. Those kinds of dressers that are covered in a fake grain laminate. I was at least expecting half a closet space. To my chagrin, there was not even a stand-alone wardrobe and that middle drawer was a bit more shallow than I had realized. At least my stuffed animals survived the trip although my Daffy Duck looked a little jet lagged. I took him and the tiger that looked like Hobbs, put them in the middle between those two pillows that I had decided to leave under the blanket. There. Home. For the first time I noticed the apathetic stitching of their mouths. They just stared blankly and un-approving. Eyeing me as I at first tried to arrange my unmentionables in an orderly fashion, folded... fucking folded. Fucking won't fit! ARG! They watched me as I relinquished myself to stuffing in what I could and tossing the more worse for wear items back on the bed, a little pile of defeat. The tiger didn't seem too impressed by the closet situation either. There were a few plastic hangers in a cardboard box at the bottom tucked away next to a few pairs of tennis and a black leather belt that had fallen to the floor. It was something so thin it might as well have been a leather string. I looked back to the boys and raised an eyebrow then pulled out a few of those flimsy hangers and started putting away my button ups on a piece of rope Domi had strung from the end of the drawer, over the head of the bed, and tacked up to the corner.

I heard the doorbell in the distance but continued folding out things and hanging what I could. Ripped undershirts, antiperspirant stained everything, failed attempts at home tailoring, etc. In comparison to Domi's wardrobe, mine looked so drab in it's pathetic little corner. Practically all his things were new and in sizes that made them look like women's stockings instead of men's shirts. Shit, I counted three suits, all extra small and fitted, beside them, my sad parade of size L flannels and plaids and tartans. I had one “nice” black button up: short sleeved and in a western style cut with pearl clasps but the damned thing had grease stains from work. It was faded to an almost grayish blue and the white rim around the pits was much more prevalent than in the others. I sighed.

"Marveen..." a knock at the door frame. Domi stepped into the room, behind him David, a small, pale creature in shorts that looked like dress slacks hemmed up to right under his ball sack. His oversized sweater with tiny triangles matched his beanie under which you could barely tell that his ears were taped in white gauze, like a puppy Doberman. He was just as snarky with his hello and didn't even bother to take off his sunglasses. He just stared around the room and pursed his lips in contemplation. No doubt he was taking in me more than my new quarters. In the back of my mind, I had always felt unimpressive in comparison to Domi's friends. As if they were all secretly egging him on to upgrade. As if the group mentality was begging him not to let their standards droop so low. I mean, as the saying goes, birds of a feather...

"Hola, Marvino," he extended a limp hand to shake or was it to kiss? I wasn't sure which. "I brought you a little something," he smiled peevishly. In his other hand, a tiny black box. Not small enough for a ring but just about the right size for a pastry. Maybe I was just hungry and thinking about donuts or *pan dulce*. It even had a little pink ribbon around it with a bow on the top. I only thought that it'd fitting that he should bring the new fat kid a snack.

"Oh... thank you," I smiled and bobbed my head side to side like a little kid playing hot potato.

"*Andale, abrelo.* It's not much but I think that you're going to like it," David said rather nonchalantly, assured in his own gift giving abilities.

Domi's eyes widened and he tucked his lips in between his teeth, *"Si, anda! Bebe abrelo."* he said excitedly. I'm sure a part of him had already decided that half of whatever mine was his but bitch be cra'y if he thought I was gonna share this donut.

I laughed nervously. I hate opening gifts in front of people. I always feel like my reaction isn't up to par and that my disappointment is always so transparent. Oh... you shouldn't have... I mean... really... what... the... fuck...were you thinking?

Just then, in walked Elma with a bowl of cereal, snooping around like a younger sibling. "*Que traen? Que hacen aca? DEJAMEN VERRRRR...*" she said as she tried to tip toe over Domi's shoulder.

Domi said with his goofy smile, "David brought Marveen a gift."

"Ah... que chido..." she pretended to be interested but since the matter didn't really concern her or the idea of her getting a gift, she barely was. "But don't you forget, Marveen, that I made you the party... and I found you juice in the morning...and... mmm... here," she planted two lips on my cheek in protest to being upstaged by David's welcoming committee.

"I HELPED YOU GUYS OUT WITH THE SIGNNN!" hollered Luis Raul from his "room", not being one to be left out.

"MENTIROSOS LOS DOS! I organized the party and *I* made you the sign, baby," Domi laughed and tossed another beer can into the bag. He was damned if anybody else would take credit for making the gringo feel welcomed.

David rolled his eyes to the left then said,*"Callansen, perras!* Hurry!" he flicked a limp hand against my arm, where it rested, *"Abre tu regalo.* We're already running late."

I laughed nervously again as a chorus of "Do it! Do it!" ensued, then unwound the ribbon and popped open the box. David went on, "I didn't know what to get you and then I saw this at the supermarket and I said to myself, this, this is for Marveen."

Seed packets. For him not knowing what to get me, he was pretty spot on. Basil, tomato, chives, oregano, sunflowers. It was actually a really thoughtful gift. For a second I forgot him standing there, tapping his foot and smacking his gum. This wee bit of a little impatient man. I loved it.

"Now you can start yourself a new garden," he smiled then turned to Domi, *"Y tu?* Why aren't you ready?!" then turned back to me and pointed to the pack of sunflowers, *"Y son de buena marca, eh?* So you won't go saying that you have cheap friends with no clue as to what's organic and whatnot."

"Uh, actually really never cared ab'...", I was just about to tell him that I never really minded name brands or the idea of something being organic, but he cut me off.

"Bueno, now that you've opened your present," he clapped his hands, "hurry because they're waiting for us."

Domi, standing there half naked, popped his lips in a big 'O' then, *"Oooo... solo tengo que ponerme una playera,"* assuring us all that he only needed a shirt. Knowing him, however, I expected there to be some delay as we ran through a video montage of him trying on every single piece of clothing in arms' reach.

Me, puzzled, "Where are we going?" I accidentally dropped a seed packet and went to pick it up. Whoa, the morning after dizzies suddenly hit me. When I came up, David grabbed my arm with a, "Don't you worry. *Yoo... arrr... gonda... lubb... id.*" But even with such a guarantee, I was already expecting the worse.

I've always hated riding in the backseat when I'm sobering up. The shakes. The being unable to do anything but sit there. No focus. No fun cars or pedestrians to dodge. I tapped my sweaty hand against my pant leg then pulled on the cloth crucifix I wore. My father had sent a few to us as kids when he was in prison. It was a laced up lower case "t" in green, red, and white. The string that held it: candy cane red and white. One tree. Two trees. Three trees. Is that a tranny? So fucking boring...

Domi and David were up front dancing in their seats to some kind of Mexican rap techno shit. It was actually not that bad but I could only understand about a third of what they were saying. There was a lot of "*Putas*" and "*Mamens*" and *"OiOiOi!"*. I sighed, put my head back, and stared up at the roof. This tan dull thing like milked down coffee mixed with cement. I stared back outside, the city looked nice though. SO many pretty people. Stupid Pretty People... I've got it hard enough without having to deal with *Fernando,* the *modelo*, *Sasha,* the aspiring actress, or *Jesus,* the six-foot tall hipster with a beard on a powder baby blue moped. Dammit! Foiled again! At this rate, I'd never get discovered at a coffee shop and debut as the latest soap opera hunk.

Luckily, there were a slew of beggars and little dark native looking people too. Thems be my bitches. At the lights, some swallowed fire, some peddled bright souvenirs and umbrellas. There was a musician or two playing tiny toy accordions and child guitars.

"Ugh, whereeeee areeee weeeeee goinnnnnn???" I asked as they continued singing "*Mata tu mama y...*" David stopped long enough to answer *"No te precupes.* It's a surprise." But little did he know how much I despised surprises. Well, at the moment of an infringing bout of withdrawals and my sugar running so low, I despised everything.

Twenty minutes later we pulled up to a sentry kiosk and David mouthed out a name, which I forgot two minutes later. I was too preoccupied with already feeling under dressed in this city. Now I was left wondering if I still remembered which spoon to use and whether or not you snorted the coke with your right nostril or your left and was it customary to use rolled up American bills or Mexican pesos? Dammit.

We drove on a small road that curved to the right then passed these two big tropical trees. Behind them sat a huge white mansion with two columns in the front that ran to the top of the second story where the roof pointed up in a truss. In the middle was a tiny round window, the circumference of which was made up of emerald green glass squares, its middle, these red and orange jagged pieces. For a second I imagined myself up there looking down at me as I struggled to get out of the backseat. The house must've said to itself, Who are these people? Well, maybe it only said, "Who is THAT people" because the house is obviously Mexican with a poor grasp of English and *I* was the only one looking shabby. I wondered, was Hobo-chic still an option? Only a little later, after we walked to the left side of the house along this fifty foot white wall that ran parallel to the facade, did I realize that I had been over dressed all along.

After turning the corner and walking a few more feet, there was this gate. The smell of chlorine barely lingering in the midst of the muggy jungle air. That jungle that seemed to creep everywhere in the city, trying to claw it's way back onto the land that was stolen. But I guess coming from the desert, if I spotted a green weed, I would automatically equate that with the amazon taking its revenge. It was a pool party but the kind of pool parties *cool* people have. There was maybe one dude in the far corner, idling in the pool, flirting with these two girls at the water's edge. But, besides him and a few floating toys, the people were gathered around the lawn under canopies of tan cotton canvas. And it wasn't a simple get together. There had to be upwards 70 persons wandering around in either skimpy swimwear or posh black get ups. Everyone here liked tight black jeans and oversized geometric print shirts, rounded gaucho hats, and big black sunglasses. I stood out like a typical fat American tourist. Note to self: buy new clothes, take up bulimia, try not to punch somebody in the face. Whenever I see these hipster, fashion forward, slim, tanned and toned types, I get this irrational urge to trip them, or grab their glasses and crush those, or merely slap them silly. I know in my heart it's envy, but still, for fucks sake, smile a bit. Stop looking like everything is *so* boring and no, drinking wine neither makes you more intelligent or interesting. It just means that you're drinking fancy grape juice, idiot.

The people in trunks and bathing suits weren't anymore modest. Stylish one-piece bikinis like ones from the sixties or a James Bond movie. The men in tight little brightly colored swim trunks that looked more like girl's *boy* shorts than anything. I must admit, I couldn't help but stare. Domi slapped me on the arm, admonishing my wandering eye, "*Eit... ya te vi... puto.*" he laughed a little and pinched me playfully though perhaps a bit too hard. David made a faint whistling sound as we walked down some concrete steps, then tilted his head just so that his sunglasses slid down his nose, barely enough to get a better view.

There were a few in-betweeners: Hipsters in jean short shorts running barefoot along the length of the furthest side. They were at least laughing. Domi was wearing a black skull shirt with the sleeves cut off and his black jeans from last night. High top boots like old school Doc Martins, reddish brown, laces left undone. David stopped at the foot of the stairs and pulled out his cell phone from HIS short shorts. He looked around aimlessly as he dialed somebody and asked them "Bitch, where you at?" This definitely did NOT feel like December. Then again, back home the winters had been less like winters than infrequent cold fronts followed by nice sunny days. Here, everything was humid and hot and sticky like a gym shoe. He hung up the phone then grabbed me by the hand, *"Vente, Marveen,* I want to introduce you to someone," and led me away along the side of the sparkling translucent water.

He dragged me round the left corner of the pool as Domi stayed behind to snap a shot on his phone of the whole affair. I looked back for a second and my heart dropped to my stomach. I could never compete with these Adonis people. Everything here had a place and I looked more like the staff than any of the revelers. We approached a table in the middle, stacked with party favors and snacks. Cheese cubes displayed circularly on parchment paper over round silver-plated trays. Heck, they could have actually been real silver trays for all I knew. I imagined myself flinging the food over my shoulder and into the pool just to check the forged stamp at the bottom. But I didn't because that would just be "unclassy". A short husky dark lady stood behind the table under that tent, her hands behind her back, staring into the distance with a slight frown. She pursed her lips, oblivious to anything and didn't even blink as she handed me a small clear plastic plate with a white-gloved hand. I said thank you. She feigned a smile then walked to the left end of the table to meddle with some soft drinks in a tub of ice. David tapped me on the shoulder, brought me out of this reverie of imagining the lady's children in a humble home and her working a boring job in the midst of so much decadence. That empty pool. This mountain of food that the flies would probably eat before any of these too self-conscious anorexics would. All a waste. All a statement.

I turned around to find this frail little thing in a flower dress with knee high amber colored boots and a pixie hairdo behind giant fly-eyed sunglasses. *"Marveen, te presento a mi amiga Anabel!"* I sort of stood aback and waved my hand awkwardly in the air with a smile to match, like some retarded kindergartner.

"*Ven, ven*, Marveen. Don't be so uncouth." David waved me over, silently boiling at the idea of me being so offish and rude. "This is one of my very best friends."

"*Mucho gusto, Marveen!"* she smiled broadly and stuck out her hand so straight that it bent slightly backwards at the elbow. We shook. I wished I were as drunk as her right now. Wait... a ... minute.... That smell! She was high! As she leaned in to kiss me on the cheek, I got this whiff of skunk. Sweet but salty like when you're driving down a long road in the middle of a cool summer's night in Texas and you can smell Pepe le Pew in the distance. *"David me hay dicho que eres muy buen artista!"* she said. Apparently my reputation as some sort of creative creature had preceded me.

"Naw, I'm more of a writer these days. Like last week, I wrote TWO whole pages. So that counts, right?" I laughed coyly. Most days, I was the only one who laughed at my jokes anyway.

"Ah! How neat! I love poems! My friend, Cristofo, has published a few books of them. They're like so interesting," she smiled, making me feel less like a big fish in a little pond and more like a guppy in a tub of sharks.

"No, well, it's more like fiction. Kinda like *beat-ish,* or so they told me. But I think that was just my friend's way of saying that I don't know how to use grammar correctly. Also, I'm like drunk half the time so it comes out... mmm, *awesome?"* I laughed and looked around for a beer. Dammit! Stupid cheese! Priorities, people! Priorities!

"Ah," she nodded her head up and down several times and smacked her lips, slowly extending each one outward then resting her lower teeth on her upper lip for a second, *"Bueno,* right now I'm in a artist group. There are visual artists, musicians, poets— like yourself—AND we're always looking for people to exhibit their work."

"Ha, okay, but I left all my paintings back home. I mean, back at my mother's place. I mean, like El Paso or something. So I don't really have anything to show."

"Ah si! That's so true! You're from the U.S, right?" she shouted, forgetting for a second that I was an American uproot despite my horrible Spanish.

"Yup," I eyed around for alcohol once more. Where's the whiskey? Where's Domi to save me? Oh he's over there saying hello to somebody in sunglasses and not too much else on. Stupid Mexicans. Did everybody pirate a copy of P90x or something?

"*Bueno*," she went on, *"Mandame un mensaje.* Look, here's my card. If anything, you can send for your paintings and we can put them up in a gallery or a restaurant or something and maybe you can read your poems in the mean time when we have our jam sessions."

"Yea, but I'm really not a ..."

"Vez! Marveen! You're going to love Guadalajara!" interjected David as he slapped me on the back before him and Anabel went on about how some bitch looked stupid last night.

Domi came up, finally, "Have they introduced you to Anabel yet?"

"Yea, she's nice. Hey, I think David's leaking from his ear," I pointed to the back of his head where this clear pale yellow trickle rolled down the right side of his neck from under his beanie.

"Jaja uy no. He just had surgery so they wouldn't be so big. He plans to get into a soap opera or become a famous movie actor," he confided.

"Geezus! That sounds insane! I thought he had just fallen on his head or something. Like that one time I went to the restroom to take a piss and woke up under the toilet."

Domi looked at me suspiciously for a second. Winced, then turned around and waved at Anabel. She rushed over. "*Hola Domi! Mi Amorrrrr! Ternuda! Que haces? Como 'stas?!* I've already talked to Marveen and I assured him that in no *ta-ime* he's going to be a big artist and a famous poet!"

That hello was like watching a human firecracker flailing around the night sky.

"Bien, bien. Y tu? See, baby, you're going to be famous and we can retire to the Bahamas with *coronas* on the beach," he beamed with pride and the childish dreams of my inevitable success

"*Coronas* you say? Hmmmmmm...."I added. Success be damned, I needed a beer!

She jumped up and down excitedly, grinning ear to ear, "Yes! I can't wait to read one of his poems!"

Domi, relishing the novelty and his new American trophy, "Yes, he is a really good writer! Although I don't really understand much of what he's saying... because he writes mostly in English... and mostly when he's drunk."

I sighed, rolled my eyes and turned my attention to the fancy crackers and cheese. The dark lady asked if I'd care for something to drink. I inquired as to the alcohol selection and she sadly replied that there was none. Dr. Pepper? Dr. *Caca* more like it, I thought, then crossed my arms and pouted.

Sometimes you don't realize how hungry you are until you put that first piece of food in your mouth. I think that's just how you feel when you suddenly realize that you're stuck in a place full of people and you're entirely alone.

"*Hola*," a tall thin thing of a woman, about 5'8", came up to me, *"Eres amigo de David, verdad?"* She was pale skinned, round faced with long straight light brown hair that came down to just under her shoulders. Fuck, what is everybody here a model? Is this my intervention? Are those diet crackers? With my mouth full, I winced at her then puffed out a cloud of crumbs as I said hello. Way to keep things classy, boy, way to keep things classy...

I swallowed then followed up with, "Yeah, well, him and Domi. Domi is my... uh... roommate?" the last bit I said questioningly. I didn't really know how to introduce myself in the social circles down here. Back where I was from, the gay issue wasn't really an issue anymore. Well, at least I never thought of it as such. But down here, what if she was his coworker or his boss or some kind of anti-gay Gestapo?

"Ah, you don't look like you belong here... either," she laughed, graciously slipping into English, "I meant EITHER. Hi," she offered up a hand, "My name's Alice. I'm rooming with Anabel."

I extended a hand, dropped a piece of cheese in the salsa and said, "FUCKING FINALLY! Someone who speaks American!"

She laughed and said emphatically, " 'MERICA!" then followed coyly with, "Yeah, I teach Conversational English down at this school for rich kids," we both looked around, silently taking into account our situation, "Eh, it pays the bills," she said apathetically.

"Two questions: A) where's the fucking beer? 2) Are they hiring?"

She laughed, "They might be. I joined this program with a church back home then just had to get my TOEFL certification and bam, two year vacation in sunny Guadalajara. You should totally try and apply. Shit's super easy."

"But you have to wake up mornings?" my face wrinkled painfully at the thought.

"Uhm, yeah, but some schools have this weird rotating schedule where there's kids that go in from eight to twelve then another group of kids comes in from one to four."

"Do... they... have a four to midnight schedule? I can swing that."

"Haha no. But you'll get used to it. If you're really serious I can help you get better acquainted with the schools. There are about five public school systems and a ton of private ones. There's even this government-funded program that drives you out to the more rural areas to help teach farm kids in the jungle. It's so beautiful. Those rolling hills and everything. But the commute's like 40 minutes WHEN the bus doesn't break down and they don't really pay you any better. I actually think they pay you less. The best time to apply really is in August because a lot of spaces open up in September. But you might find a job in the summer."

"Love for the kids and all that crap?"

"Heheh, kinda. But my old roommate did that until she just decided to move down there. Said something like it was easier to just drive back on the weekends to party than to have to sit on an old stinky bus every morning at four or five am. But you can also teach adults. The way trade relations go between Mexico and the U.S., it's really almost necessary that you be bilingual."

"Dayummm, four or five?? She must really care about those kids! I bet they're made of gold or some kind of chocolate...." I looked side to side, mischievously

"Na', I think she just got suckered into it. But, honestly she was kinda weird. A lot of people in the program are like," she paused to laugh and shake her head, "like really weird."

"Like rejects from their own society so they had to move to a foreign country?" I offered.

"Exactly!" she laughed then self-consciously pushed a strand of hair behind her left ear.

I tip toed and looked over her left shoulder, "Don't tell me, you've got a tail back there or something, right?"

She put a beer to her mouth. The sides of my jaw felt like I had ingested something sour and my tongue began to water.

"Something like that. Hey, so how long are you guys planning on staying here?"

I shrugged, "Uhmm, I dunno. I sold everything and came here but on the plane I kept telling myself that it was too scary of an idea and that I should move back in a couple of weeks."

"Oh, no, I meant how long are you guys staying *here*?" she pointed down with both index fingers.

"Oh, I dunno. We just got here. Also they like literally never tell me anything. Or they do and I just think they're talking about tacos," I confided.

She laughed, "Allrighty then... Well, Anabel's always dragging me to these things."

I shoved a cube of cheese into my mouth, "Wal ah leaz dey haf food hare."

She giggled then tucked a strand of hair behind her right ear, "It's the only reason I come," she chuckled and took another swig of beer then stared at the watch on her left wrist. Domi came up from behind me and playfully knocked his pelvis into my butt.

"Hola Alice! Como estas?" he leaned in to kiss her cheek.

She lifted up her sunglasses into her hair, *"Hola Domi,"* she smiled, *"Bien bien y tu?"*

"*Muy bien!"* he kissed me on the cheek. The dark lady behind the table shot us this disapproving look but he just shrugged her off with a wave of a hand. Alice laughed as David cut in with a, " Ready guys? Oh hi, Alice," he half smiled as if more inclined to acknowledge her presence by custom than actual delight.

"Refry fo' wha'?" I chewed out the words with my mouth still full.

David half turned, *"Vamos ir a comer."*

I swallowed, "But they have food here... AND we just got here..."

Alice laughed, "We'll see you guys later."

In the car I asked what was that all about.

In the passenger seat, David fidgeted with the stereo and said, "It was a girl friend's birthday party."

Domi chimed in with a, *"Pero es bien buchõna.* She's really rich because she married a drug dealer's son. But the bitch is already 39 and all she does is party. I swear the last time she was popping pills with her sons at this rave and they're just about barely eighteen years old. They're kind of low class but with a lot of money."

"But she's really nice," added David.

"Si pues eso si," said Domi as he sucked at his right canine, "She's always buying me drinks and inviting me out to go shopping with her. When I used to work at Zara, she'd always ask for me to help her pick out ensembles and she'd always say that it was such a shame that I wasn't single. When I told her I was quitting, she seemed sad and even told my boss not to let me go. The only thing is that she drinks too much and gets super crazy. She's a very scandalous sort of person. Really hardcore."

"*...*Dancing on tables*...*"-David.

"*...*Yelling at cops*...*"-Domi.

"*...* Falling down in the street*...*"-David.

Me: "*OH...* so she's like *funnnnn?"* I had decided to toss in my two cents as they continued to play descriptive Ping-Pong about the old coot. I had come to know the type of creature they were illustrating. I remember hearing somewhere that your mind and personality set at the age of 22 or so. If you were a hellcat when you were younger, putting aside any particularly devastating epiphanies, you'd be basically the same 22 year-old the rest of your life. Mentally, speaking, of course.

Domi laughed, *"Marveen de señora."*

Me, "Oh please, that trash can came out of nowhere. Besides, the sidewalk was slippery."

"Si, bueno," David continued, "She's an older lady but she's a real vixen. I think she's had her nose done once or twice, but she's always been thin and savvy with fashion. Not to mention that she has these boobs out to here."

Domi laughed again, *"Marveen de senora,"* and I kicked the back of his seat.

"I didn't see anybody that looked like that," I frowned out the window and stared down at my nails that were in dire need of a trim. Did I even pack a pair of nail clippers? I had like three at home. Fuck. David pulled out a half-full ziploc bag and I immediately recognized the smell of marijuana again. He went on to say, *"No pues, ahorita estaba trabajando o algo."*

"Working? On her birthday? I saw the house, I sincerely doubt she couldn't afford to take a day off."

David, "Well, she has some sort of business. She's always on the phone and complaining about how incompetent everybody is. But her cousin was there. The party's going to get really cool though. Anabel told me that they're bringing in Buchetti."

"Who's Buchetti?" I asked.

"A DJ that plays really fucking cool," he said as he started packing a bowl, *"Pero nosotros, mis hijos, vamos ir a comer sue-chee!"* he then turned around and handed me the pipe and a tiny white bic lighter.

Oh well...

Twenty minutes more of gangsta-techno-bilingual crap-rap, accompanied by horrible accents later, we pulled into a tidy little strip mall. White washed with plain arches running the length of the facade and one as the entrance.

"Ten, ponte este espray," Domi handed me a little bottle of perfume after him and David had sufficiently doused themselves and half of Guadalajara. I was a little high but now hungrier than ever. I don't think the pot helped.

We walked into a den behind tinted windows and wooden blinds. Table for four please. The maître d', this short balding man, about five foot six with a thin waist and small black shiny shoes, led us to a table against a wall with a purple blue couch running the length of it. On one side of the table was this faux booth and on the other side some curvy wooden chairs with white cushions. The place was swank.

Typical Mexican trendy, as if they were trying to go for a European minimal twist with like a dragon every few feet.

Dragon!

Crane!

Plastic-Lotus-Blossom-floating-in-water!

Candle!

Crane!

Everything screamed "sue-chee" or the approximation of "sushi" that David could mouth. They kept laughing but I just smiled.

"Hey, who was that Alice chick?" I asked.

"Quien? Ah," David sipped water from a straw he pinched, *"Es roomie de Anabel. No te encanto?"*

"Yea, she seemed nice," I scratched at the top of my thighs, the cotton jean and the ripples made by how the textile wrinkled against my curves, were enticing.

"Es una de los TOP dawgs en el mundo de arte en Guadalajara," he went on, informing me that she was something of a big deal in the art scene.

"Wait, what? She told me she was a teacher?" I asked confused. Wrinkle. Wrinkle. Wrinkle.

"Que? Quien?" his features crumpled together into a frown, he looked just about as bewildered as I.

"Alice?"

"Ahhhhhh Alice... no, no, no, amiga," he laughed, "I meant Anabel! Alice is just sort of always around. I think she works at some restaurant or some convenient store on the weekends," he sipped again the same way, a bit preening, shaking/dancing side to side impatiently in his seat.

Domi laughed, "En *Gual-Marr*. [Wal-Mart]."

I pouted, "Don't be mean, guys. She seemed cool. And she teaches kids in the jungle or something."

"Ni sabes, amiga," David went on, *"Ella es BIEN desmadrosa!"*

At that moment in walked Elma clomping towards us in heels, arms outstretched, *"Hola, Perras!* You guys order already?"

Domi and David got up to hug her hello but I stayed seated, a little discouraged by their cattiness. Eventually I came to a "half get up" to *saludad* her from behind the table. It shook a bit as my knee caught the edge and the water in the four glasses that were set out, rocked back and forth. Mini oceans. Mini islands. Fish out of sea. I couldn't help but stare.

"So, Marveen, conociste a Anabel?" she asked as the waiter tucked her chair in behind her and she thanked him.

"Yea, she seemed nice. I also met that chick named Alice," I pursed my lips in a fake half smile.

Elma laughed, "Eeee careful with that one. She could give ME a run for my money."

Domi, proudly, "*Si, y le dijo que en tiempo le va a dejar exhibiccionar sus pinturas y cantar sus poemas,*" he rubbed his hands together briskly under the table, likely plotting some manner in which he could ride my coat tails or otherwise extort me.

Elma took a swallow from her own water, opened the menu, looked as if she was staring at hieroglyphics for a second, tried to focus her eyes, then asked, "Marveen, you write poems too? I had no clue."

I raised my eyebrows, "Nopes, strictly Sci-Fi... I kept trying to..."

Then Domi mouthed out slowly, "*Eh-sky-figh*," and laughed.

David sipped again from his straw and nudged Domi then whispered, *"Es como cuando van a casar elefantes y girafas en Africa*," he nodded sagaciously, assured that I had indeed focused the majority of my literary work on Safaris. The three erupted into laughter even if Elma was a bit more demure than the rest. She looked up from the menu with these Louise Brooks eyes: big bulbous dark things with a mile wide line of mascara, *"Que... es... eso?* You're kidding me right? Giraffes? Are you all high or what?"

I rolled my eyes then raised my hand, "Waiter, what kind of beer do you have?"

It was seven days till Christmas and I still couldn't figure out what to get Domi. They took me to the mall the day before, but unless I figured on blowing my savings on a sterling silver Givenchy telephone dialer, I had better start thinking of something creative. Can you gold-glitter a penis? What's worse was now I felt I *had* to buy Elma and David something. Maybe not Luis Raul. Well, maybe I could get him a pack of gum. Lord knows he needed it. I was there sitting across from him at the table counter trying my darnedest to weasel my way out of having to buy anyone anything. Maybe I could say I was Jewish? I had the nose for it. Like, literally, everyone says I have a penis nose. Question two: can you gold-glitter a nose?

Maybe I could buy the house some groceries or like a group present that was sort of thoughtful, but kind of generic, but more importantly was necessary. It would be the epitome of a yellow sweater or underwear present, but, hey, everyone needs sweaters and *chones.* All we basically lived off of was cereal and 1 percent skim milk. That's like not even milk at all. It's basically bath water. Note to self: bottle bath water, sell as Premium Milk, make loads of *pesos*. Well, maybe I was being a little harsh. We also ate a lot of potato chips, sodas, and I made it a point to drink plenty of beer. We hardly went to the market. Most of our sundries and supplies were purchased at the little corner store down the street which made it that much more convenient for me to pick up four rolls of forty-six grit, one-ply Toilet Paper, and two *caguamas.* It got to the point that I would splurge on *Charmin Basico* and hid those rolls under Domi's "closet" (a duffle bag) or in my bag. Maybe I could buy them something from there. Do Mexicans consider Twizzlers and emery boards traditional *Navidad* stocking stuffers? Or, should I stick with cherry flavored generic chapstick and cartoon-rip-off stickers? Scooby-doo is apparently blue somewhere in China. Well at least I had Luis Raul's gift nailed down. Everybody loves gum. Cigarettes! Ta-freakin'-da! Eureka moment here! They all smoked like the devil who's been shoved in the microwave and after somebody's pushed that damned Popcorn Button. On second thought, nothing for poor little-big Luis Raul who now annoyingly slurped from that damned spoon of his. All he did was watch TV or message people on his phone. All freakin' day, you'd hear his cellphone vibrate viscously on whatever stupid surface he'd leave it on. He'd pick it up, smile into the screen, then compose some kind of ingenious, awe inspiring message akin to, "Nothing. Just here. Ya know?"

I hated him so much.

Between the slits of the dividers, which cordoned off his *room*, you could see him lying on his bed in "various" (read: two) positions. Text. Text. Text. He had a garden of course, in the form of a series of varying plants in an equally as hodgepodge set of plastic pots. I never liked plastic pots. My grandmother's garden was basically the same. Multicolored, plastic, dirt buckets gradually accumulated from gifts or dollar stores or that aisle in the market next to plungers and mops. He, god bless his stupid wide fat face, lent me one to plant the seeds David had given me. The dirt wasn't bad but it looked full of perlite--those tiny white styrofoam looking balls. It was an okay size though, about eleven inches wide and a foot deep. Though the color was a weird muddy kind of green. As if drawn out by the sun into something more like a brown. Like a caca-yellow-pea green?

"Thank you, Luis," I said, forcing a smile.

"*De nada*," he rubbed some dirt off his hands and continued to fill up a small bright yellow watering "can", also plastic, from a green rubber hose with two long white stripes which ran it's length. Outside, the sun was on my face as I stared at the back wall. It felt nice. No clouds, less humid. The birds were cat calling in the distance, more angry than happily singing. Cars sped by honking intermittently as children walked behind the alley, laughing and egging each other on. It looked so bizarre, this big hefty tall guy going pot to pot with a dainty little spout. Reminded me of a few dicks I'd seen on those beefy muscle heads.

He began in a sort of husky effeminate voice, *"Que emoccion!* Now they're going to have TWO garden aficionados in the house," his eyes widened as he grinned and tucked his chin to the right shoulder and looked back towards me. I have to say that the patio got good light. The house seemed to face north so that the sun trailed over all day, but the harsh evening light was abated by the tall cement walls that blocked off the setting sun. In the middle, a fountain filled with stray grass and some cigarettes. Looked like some cats had been at it too. Tiny clumps of feces and paw prints near the butts of Benson Hedges and *Delicados*. Luis Raul kept his pots along the east wall wherein a dark, dilapidated wooden fence had been propped up. It hovered a foot or two above the paved-in floor that covered the yard and had these pink flowered vines trailing over. It wasn't a structural fence by any means. More like merely something someone had long ago found and decided to nail into it. The neighbors must have had a nice yard, I thought, one with a patio set or a gazebo or something like that. A working fountain, not an ashtray filled with dirt, cat piss, and weeds. They might have even had a swing set or an outdoor bar. Oh, the possibilities. Over the wall, over the rainbow, were various other homes, about three stories high, which had their roofs transformed into little gardens. Everything was so green and structured but chill. The city tended to grow up carelessly in squares but with style. Yards were replaced by roof top patios with lawn chairs, under tarps, that scraped the sky.

I decided to put my pot on the west wall under another low hanging vine. This one barely had any leaves and was basically a canopy of knotted brown tentacles, but a spray of pink-violet petals yet remained. Something like Bougainvilleas. I guessed that the sun hit too hard there, but under its shade, I hoped my plants would do fine.

"I don't think that they're going to get enough light over there," he said, filling up his watering can again. Why he didn't just walk around the yard with the hose escaped me and was quietly frustrating. Not heeding his worries about the low light under the mass of vines, I shoved the pot all the way back up against the wall. The sand caught between its bottom and the cement, giving a bit of protest.

I clapped the dirt off my hands and confessed, "Well, we'll see. Honestly I've barely learned how to *not* kill cactuses, I mean cacti, this last year."

"What happened to you having a garden and that you would make bonsai and all of that?" he asked. Apparently my reputation as a "Master Gardner" had preceded me too. I could only imagine what other lies Domi had told them about me but treasured the idea of slowly unraveling them all. In my mind, "No, no, no... I never said I cut hair professionally. What I said was that one time I shaved my dog entirely."

I went on, "Yea, well I tried. I also tried losing 80 pounds, becoming a famous painter, starting my own band, opening up a restaurant, buying a house..." I shrugged my shoulders, "Eh," the litany of failed pursuits in my head suddenly dogging me.

He laughed, "Yes, well, Domi would always go on about how you had bonsai, and that you wouldn't answer his messages because you were at the gym, and that you were taking some kind of home buyer's class, hahaha."

I stuck an index finger into the dirt, by then my mind a bit elsewhere. It was dry, well as dry as anything could be in this forever moist, sweaty air. I wiggled out two small holes about a knuckle deep. Luis Raul went on about something but I had gotten so used to him walking around the house with his blue tooth that it didn't faze me. Half the time I couldn't decide whether he was trying to have a conversation with me, or was gossiping with *sancho.* Now I couldn't decide whether tomatoes or sunflowers would be better. I had about six packets of seeds and all their spacing requirements were in metric. Needless to say, I was at a loss.

"Y pues porque no compraste casa?" he asked.

"Didn't have the money for a down payment. Besides, after my dad died, I didn't want to stay in El Paso forever. A thirty year mortgage seemed like forever," I dusted my off my hands again, "Also I decided NOT to have any kids and that I would never get married or..."

Sunflowers....

Tomatoes...

Basil?...

"...you know, do a bunch of other stuff I had been doing or thinking about doing before. They all just seemed stupid. Like, Hey, life's too short, kinda crap," I stood, the blood rushing a bit to my brain, I felt nauseous like my sugar was low. When was the last time I had a drink? When was the last time I ate something? Do cigarettes count as carbs?

"*Pues*," he leaned over to pour water on some giant agave looking thing, "Maybe it was for the best. El Paso didn't sound all that interesting. I mean I know they had stores but..."

I sighed, kneeled over again, my neck hurt and my thighs were starting to ache a little. "Well no, I do suppose a lot of people say that, but I liked it. It changed a lot in the time I was there: More things to do, a better music scene. Pretty safe too. I guess if the guys were hotter or at least interesting, or, just, you know, had like lower standards or something, I would've stayed. But they were mostly idiots with a Britney Spears or Beyoncé obsession."

He asked, *"No habia guapos?"*

"Sure, a few cute ones. But they never gave me the time of day. And when they did, if they opened their mouth, trust me, you weren't sticking a dick in it 'cause you were horny," I stood back up. The day suddenly felt hotter and the cicadas in the background were booming and buzzing and booming and buzzing. I rubbed my temples and pushed my hands into my eyes. A wee bit of dirt made them water and I laughed to myself, "I always find a way of not liking something. Especially people."

"Y pues que con Domi?" he stared quizzically at me, his weight on one leg, from across the fountain scape.

"Well, Domi, he's different, I guess, or whatever. And I guess after my dad died and he came down it made me realize like *wow*, here's this dude that's really into you, Marvin. Besides, there's this line in Breakfast at Tiffany's where they quote Lula Mae as saying something like, 'Well, I've never been married before'."

"I freaking LOVE that movie. So you are planning on marrying him?"

"Mmmm...," I looked at the pot, past the pot, pursed my lips in an upside down U, "I guess so. I'm not getting any younger," then I rubbed my belly, "OR any skinnier."

He laughed, "Don't you worry, gurlfriend, what's in now is big cheeks, scruffy beards, and bears. RAWR!"

"I guess so..." I laughed to myself at his histrionic display then held out two seed packets, one in either hand, "Hey, which do you think is better? Tomatoes or Sunflowers?"

"Sunflowers! Definitely! And you've got to be kidding me about the tomatoes. They are so cheap at the market. Sunflowers, on the other hand, are way cooler, they're very pretty, and they grow really tall."

"Ah... okay..." I smiled and opened the packet of tomatoes.

Later that night, in bed, the sound of the TV being carried in from the living room where Luis was entertaining a "guest", I laid with my head propped up in a hand and stared at Domi as he took off his shirt, then the painted gold watch that didn't work, then his shoes, black dress pants, and finally socks.

"Very sexy underwear," I said as he stood in the corner and arranged the watch just so on the bedside table. He leaned down and kissed my neck.

"Ewoo, gross, cooties!" I yelled.

He laughed, *"Cual* que *'e-oo, groz'? Porque no te quitas la camisa?"*

"No, 'cause you'll see my *chi-chis.*"

"But I like your boobs! Boobs with a big dick... mmmm...yum."

I smiled, "Besides, I have a headache. My car won't start. The dog ate my homework and the toaster's been making fun of me. But, seriously, ouch, my head. I quit drinking... as much. It's probably just my sinuses going ape shit over all the green. Hey, Luis asked me earlier if we were gonna get married."

He sat on the bed with his back to me as he scratched the space between his toes then picked up his foot towards his face to smell it. I counted the constellations on his back. Little dipper. Big dipper. One, two, three, four, five, six moles. *"Y que lo dijiste?"*

"That I wasn't sure how much money you had in the bank. I checked the mattress but all I found was a set of spare keys for your stupid, tiny, baby, clown car," I stared at my nails. I thought to myself how everything grew quicker down in the tropics.

He looked over his left shoulder, *"Cero. Pero tengo milliones en besos y amor."*

"Kisses and Love? Pfft! Fine. I'll start packing tomorrow."

He flung himself backwards onto the bed and hugged me and drove his tiny head into my armpit, "No," he whined in a high voice, *"No te vayas bebe.* I'll get a second job; I'll buy you a mansion."

"No. I want a McDonalds. And I mean a REAL one.... with a play place.... and a ball-room. No, wait! TWO ball-rooms in case I get messy drunk and poo in the first."

He kissed then tickled me and then I was on my back laughing, his face a few inches from mine but it might as well have been an infinite expanse between us. Big dark brown eyes, black almost, like the chasm of space. Thick lashes and brows with just the hint of hair in the middle; I ran a finger above and through the bridge of his nose, "Do you pluck your eyebrows?"

"No, I shave them," he laughed a little and kissed me on the nose, "You have a dick nose," he said then bit the tip of it.

"Yuck!"

"Y tu? Porque no te quites el pelo ni te cortes los pubes?" he asked. Why I never manscaped being a particular subject often discussed.

"Mmmm... I dunno."

Then serious, like a child trying to explain the world to a parent, "No, baby... Well, you should at least trim your hairs a bit. You know, a little upkeep."

"Ba!" I huffed out. I had no intention of anytime soon taking a machete to the amazon below my belly button, "It's a crotch, not a topiary. Besides, you're lucky I even brush my teeth. The whole point of being in a relationship is that I can finally let myself go. I mean, go further."

"Ahora resulta! Pero, si, bebe, hazlo! They get into my mouth and I don't like it!" he laughed again, pretending to pluck imaginary hairs from his lips, *"Anda, quitate la camisa.* Let's sleep naked like if we were lost in the wilderness."

"No. What if Elma walks in and gets jealous."

"Por los boobis? Jajaja."

"No, not my boobs. What if she sees my penis and is all like: Hey, hey, Marvin... and then I'd have to be all like: Hey, hey, Mezcal Buyer... and then there'd be a hairy baby nine months later and you'd start crying..."

"Then I'll just have to beat that bitch down and run her out of the house! *Pinche zorra...*" He sat up and pretended to throw a shoe at the door then plopped back down, *"Segun su morro lo tiene bien grande."*

"Oh, really? Hey, hey, *morro de Elma,* come here."

He pinched me, *"Lo sabia! Zorra!* All you think about is penises!"

"Maybe... Actually I think mostly about pizza, but you were close. Seriously though," I wiped my right hand over my mustache and pinched my goatee, "You think we gonna get married? I'll trade you my hand for a large pie with everything."

Him, now lying on his side with his own head propped up in his left hand, looked down into my eyes as I stared at the ceiling. He closed his, laughed a little and patted my belly.

"Si pues, si," he assured me then kissed me politely on the lips. I sighed and looked back up at the ceiling fan that didn't work.

"Luis also gave me a pot to put the seeds that David gave me."

"Pero ni es tiempo!"

"I figured anything would grow anytime in the jungle."

"Plantame rosas para el dia de San Valentin."

"Roses? Valentine's? Better yet, I can plant you a *caca* tree."

"No, baby, those don't grow in the soil of love," he kissed my ear, then my right eye, then my nose, *"Siempre tienes cara de puchero."*

"What does that mean?"

"Like the face of a discontented child. Like you're always pouting or pooping or something."

"Well you don't even want to marry me and I moved all the way down to wherever this is. Can we drive to Australia tomorrow?"

"Si. Si quiero... But, everything in time. Like when I have a good job and you're famous... When we can afford to buy a house or at least rent our own apartment. *Si sabes como?* Like when we're a bit more established."

"Mmmm... so then never. I hate that you're never spontaneous. Sometimes it feels like I'm dating a calculator. You're always like, 'Stop taking out you penis,' here, and, ' Pull your pants back up,' there, and, 'Quit drinking/passing out on the toilet,' etc."

"Ay, pero te sales! Siempre quieres andar de grosero! Pero, si, bebe," he pushed his hips into mine, "*Todo en su propio tiempo.* We'll start a business making furniture and you can have your art studio. You'll see. Right now I'm just really trying to focus on making a good name for myself at the company."

"Ay, you and your stupid company. All you do is worry about work. You put in long hours and they're always bothering you at home. Besides, screw a furniture shop, I want a restaurant instead. For twenty-five grand we can open a Texas Roadhouse down here."

"Yea, I've always wanted to open up a restaurant too," he laughed, "I used to always watch that show with the two girls who are waitresses. I'd always imagine you as the snarky one."

"Oh please, I was always super nice to the customers... maybe not so much with the rest of the employees, but it was either smile at the tables, or smile at my coworkers. And, god, you've seen me sobering up, I just get cranky and my coordination goes right out the window."

Now we were lying on one pillow, facing each other and twiddling each other's fingers. I tried to bend his backwards then went on, "I suppose I can just have a garden and sell tomatoes."

"Don't be silly," he scoffed, "they're so cheap at the supermarket. That and they're organic. No Monsanto down here."

I sighed then admitted defeat with, "So then prostitution it is!"

He pinched my side.

"Ouch!"

"No seas puta. Vende tu arte. Ya te comunicaste con Anabel?"

"No, but I'm not sure Ana knows what she's doing. Besides, I don't have any of my paintings here to sell."

"Uy no, she hates it when they call her Ana."

I furrowed my brow, "Why?"

"No idea. Supposedly she thinks it's so common."

"Well *ANA* seems like every other artsy fartsy person I've ever met. Full of themselves. More interested in hearing themselves talk than in what others have to say."

"No, but she's really nice," he planted a peck on my lips, "And I know what you mean. I'm familiar with this one guy who just goes on and on and on about nothing..."

"Oh please! I have a lot of interesting stuff to say! It's just that most of it is lost in translation. And, for gods sakes, she thinks I write songs for the DIxie Chicks!"

He furrowed his brow then smiled, *"Quienes son los Discy-Sheeks?"*

"Ugh, forget it. She thinks I write poetry but I freakin' hate poetry! I always used to skip over it in books or in the Paris Review. Bleh, stupid, just stupid."

"Bianca's brother is a poet and he's famous. He's been published in several books. I think I showed it to you once."

"Yea, I remember. And I also remember just pretending to check out the link like when you'd send me romantic music videos while I was watching Netflix. But, hey, everyone's *famous* these days. Amazon will publish anybody. Trust me, I could write a book and call myself famous. I have the furs for it. Do... you... think.... I'd look crazy wearing fur in Guadalajara?"

He kissed my nose again, *"Ya deja de decir tantas pendejadas.* So then why don't you publish your poems? I mean,*"* he laughed, *"* your stories?"

"I dunno. I should. I just have nothing to say. I'm funny but I can't tell jokes, most of my adventures are a big drunken blur, and sitting too long gives me hemorrhoids."

*"*And so what happened to your author friend and that book you were writing?"

"Mmmm... I dunno. It's somewhere on my computer. I just didn't know where to go with it. Plus, he said it didn't have enough dialogue."

"Y tu amigo?"

"He's somewhere back in California. He keeps going from Cali to Tijuana, to El Paso, then Juarez. I think he really wants to end up in Puerto Rico though."

He kissed my right shoulder, the one touching the bed, *"Esta chido aya?"*

"Well, I guess. It's a tropical island or something. Plus he likes Latinos. Wait, well, he *is* some kind of Latino. No, wait, his family comes from Puerto Rico. You ever been? Do we still have beer in the fridge?"

"No. No lo conosco. Porque cerveza? Si ya te vas a dormir?"

"A duh, beer helps me sleep. Well, if there's enough of it. Anyhow, he's nice. Weird, but nice."

"No, bebe, ya no tomes tanto. Te lo pasas boracho. Bueno, a tu amigo no lo conosco muy bien, pero si, se me hace raro y bien puto."

"Ugh, but beer NEEDS me! But yeah, all he writes about is basically sex and heartache. Fucking and love loss, then more fucking to compensate for said love loss. Also he sprinkles in some really bad addictions to meth and shit. Have you ever tried meth? Do we still have meth in the fridge?"

"So was that what your book was about too? Tell me! *Pinche puta!"* he laughed and pinched me again. I shoved him off the bed like a rag doll with my feet. He was so tiny, it was cute, like Ethiopian kind of cute. As he slid off the side, his eyes widened like moons. Big white circles of oh no oh no as he tried to cling to the sheets which slid from under the comforter as well.

People in the living room were laughing at the TV. He got up and again, like a serious child, *"No, bebe, me lastimas. Porque eres tan brusco? No te ensenarron como portarse con tu pareja, verdad?"*

"Shut up. What's the point in dating a guy if you can't punch him or kick him or toss a toaster into his bath water? Eh? Eh? And you call yourself a romantic...."

He sat back down on the bed, after gathering up the sheet and tossing it at my face, then said, "No. That's just not how you do it. You should be sweet with your boyfriend and buy him chocolates and give him kisses and caress his hand," he grabbed my hand. I was just laying there, my face in that ball of cotton. It was soft, probably high thread count. The world was like a cocoon again. I would've stay there forever if my breathing hadn't made it so hot. I tossed back the linen.

"So then... we're not getting married?"

"No", he stared at my face wrapped in the sheet like some white lion's mane, "Because you'll probably just end up throwing me from our bed on the Honeymoon," he looked up at the ceiling, *"Enverdad te quieres casar?"*

"Well... mmm... we could always get a divorce if it doesn't work out. Baby, I want a divorce! *Anda, no seas culo!"*

He leaned back down and pulled his legs onto the bed, snuggled up to my face in the pool of white. "No. Marriage means forever."

"Or, until one of us dies... Baby! Let's get married, Life Insurance, and a toaster!"

He laughed then chanted, *"Yea! Ea! Ea!"*

"Yes?"

"Sure. I'm betting that with your diet, the way you drink, and your lack of anything remotely considered exercise... *no mames,* I'll be in the Bahamas by the time I'm 35."

I opened my mouth in shock, "What part of potato chips soaked in vodka, being the base of the food pyramid, don't you Mexicans understand?! Besides, there's nothing to eat around here other than fucking cereal. You know who eats cereal? Retarded thirty-year olds and basketball players. And, I'm just saying, I'm not seeing anybody slam dunkin'..."

He kissed me and said tenderly, "YA, SHUT UP, PLEASE. Seriously, all you do is talk out of your ass. Tomorrow we'll head to the groceries after I get out of work."

"Good. I need a vegetable in my life. I don't think tobacco counts and the last thing I saw green was shoved into a bong."

"Cuantos cigaros haz fumado hoy?" his eyes moving from my eyes then my lips then my brow then back up to meet my gaze.

"I dunno. Maybe four or five. I was thinking about maybe switching to cigars. I just feel really stressed. I worry about my mom and my family and my dogs and my plants and all that other fucking shit I left behind. Sometimes I tell myself that it's okay. God has some kind of plan. But I know it's not true. We make our own messes. I just hope this one was worth it. You should've seen my apartment. Shit was HUGE. Like twice the size of this place. But I left it. I ran away and left everything," I crossed my eyes and tried to get a look at my nose. For a second that creeping anxious feeling crawled from over my shoulders and something in my stomach curdled. I started shaking my leg. I felt nauseous and wished I had bought more beer. I wished I hadn't drunk all the vodka in the morning. I wished I was ordering shots and shots and shots in the din of some stink hole cantina. I wished I was back home. That I could walk across the street into my own apartment and greet the parakeets and that cockatiel that couldn't fly. Take my dogs out for a walk. Have lunch with my mother and her sisters. Fucking have one mother fucking fucking fuck fuckitty fucking conversation in English. I just wished I was home.

“See, you’re going to die way before me,” he brushed some hair out my face, “I’m guessing heart attack or liver failure.”

"Pffft, my liver’s a champ. How many have you smoked?"

“One, during my lunch with the guys from work. They were talking about girls and I told them that mine had come down from the States. But I know one of them is a faggot. He’s friends with David.”

"I'm sure they know you're gay. When you say *friends,* you mean he slept with David?"

"No," he stared curiously down at his nose, "Just that they hang out every so often. David is really popular. He knows about half the city. Well, he was more like good friends with David’s ex and that’s how I met him. I’ve told you about him. How he doesn’t have good taste in music but he dresses nice,” he laughed, “When he first came to the office, he was singing Beyoncé’s Drunk in Love. Come to think of it, I even think he came to your welcoming party but left because David never showed up,” he stopped ranting and kissed me, *"Sabes que te quiero, verdad, pinché puto?”*

"Oh please, you say that, but when I ask you to marry me and leave me a widow it’s all like ‘Everything in good time, mehhh…’ But I dunno. I don't remember much from that night. Besides everyone here looks alike. It's like back home and people in plaid and fat. We all wear it. You all wear tight black things and oversized, overly printed shirts. But, I mean, com'n how could they *not* know you are gay?"

"Well, I don’t think that they know. A girl from work did ask me about who was my friend who I was always taking photos with. I think she might suspect something,” he laughed, "We talk about clothes and fashion designers.”

“Blue; water. Faggot; Fag Hag."

He laughed some more, “Well, babe, I guess since you don’t want to kiss me, I’m going to turn off the lights,” he then leaned back to turn off the table lamp. It was one of those long V-necked things with a green glass cover. The kind you could imagine in a fancy study. While he was at it, he set the alarm on his iPhone and answered a message, a faint blue glow coming over his shoulders. You could barely make out the biggest of moles on his back but I knew they were there. Like stars in the daylight. Hidden things but things only forgotten for a few hours. Secrets intrinsic to a being, to life. That firmament of a being. Details like scars on wood or the layered rings that make up the years. Stuff you'd glance over. Stuff you chose to dismiss in the shadow of the gestalt of a composition. He laid back down and asked about my mother.

"No, well I haven't talked to her but I messaged my sister on Facebook. Her daughter's so fat. Like a little Michelin Man. She seems kinda sad. Talks a lot about my dad and what's going on with the head stone. Those shits are expensive. Like three grand or some crap."

"Oh, yeah, those things cost a lot. Hehehe so she's fat like her uncle?"

"I am not fat! Anyhow, she takes after her great grandmother. Yeah, like they're super pricey. I think it's a big scam though. This entire industry based on taking advantage of grieving people. Like when my grandmother died, or maybe it was my grandfather, they started passing out golden crucifixes to the daughters and anybody else who wanted one, then charged them fifteen bucks a pop. Maybe it was more. I dunno, it was just weird, like some kind of morbid memento, and like how are you NOT gonna be persuaded to buy one? I mean, there's the, 'Everyone is doing it,' factor, and then you're bummed out and wanting to grasp onto anything that will remind you of the person you lost. I wish you could just burry people in your backyard still. When I die I just want to be cremated and tossed in someone's garden or in the garden I dream of making."

"More like I'll toss your ashes in a bar."

"Or that. As long as I can either come back haunting your tomatoes or your Budweiser, I don't care. But, backtracking, she said my mom's going to this new church thingy. Well, it's not *really* a church but some new age kind of deal where they talk about accepting all religions and about working through loss or something. I think my mom's still bummed. Last time we talked, she mentioned how she still had a lot to deal with. Like, that she had lost her best friend. But I think we're all dealing with stuff. Just, fuck, she was there for most of it. She was the only one there when my dad died I think."

"Que triste."

"Yea I know. Whenever I think about it I want to cry. But, oh well. Whatya gonna do?" My heart sank again for a moment, "And, hey, I'm not fat. I'm just bulking up for cutting season."

“Que es eso?”

"Forget about it. It's a gym thing."

“Oh please. You swear. I like how you’re always trying to give people diet or exercise advice but you never take it yourself,” he said then pinched my love handles, “In fact, tomorrow I’m going to the gym. You should totally come with me.”

“Ay, I’ve seen a lot of TV and I listened to a lot of radio in my day. But what time?"

“Like six in the morning.”

"Fuck dat shit. How come you can wake up an hour earlier to go to the gym, but when I ask for pancakes, all of a sudden…"

“Anda,” he slapped my ass, “We can shower in the locker room together.”

"Ewoo..."

"Como que ‘Ewoo?’ "

I giggled, "Maybe I should've planted the sunflowers instead. My mom loves sunflowers."

“I like them too. When I was little, my mother would plant some near the house and I’d always watch them follow the sun.”

“ ‘Watch them follow the sun?’ Didn’t you guys have the Disney Channel or something? Stupid Mexicans. Anyhow, but you can't really EAT sunflowers. Their seeds aren't really, you know, *substantial.*"

"Hehe, you think like a fatty...of what's gonna give you more food. And, no, *pues,* we were kind of poor. I remember you showing me pictures of all the toys you had. I would've killed to have so many toys when I was little. But I spent most of my time just running around barefoot in the sun like a crazy Indian. I was so dark, you wouldn't believe it if you saw me now."

"Following it like the flowers?"

"Something like that. That and trying to convince my friends to let me stick my penis in their butts."

"Ewoo. Geezus! So THAT'S what happens when you don't have cable... But didn't it hurt them?"

"No, well, we were little. Our dicks were little. It didn't hurt. Just sort of *ploop*, and you were in, like a pinky, just slides in. No problem. One time I convinced my neighbor to get naked under the covers with me and then her mom walked in on us and we just laid there, scared and naked, with the blanket pulled up to our necks. I got into so much trouble and wasn't invited to ever go back."

"Ay, you're such a perv'. That's probably why your mother had your foreskin taken off when you were nine or whatever."

"No, bebe, no digas eso. She had to have done it for some health purposes. She was a nurse back then and I don't think she would've done it for just whatever reason."

"I remember reading that Brave New World thingy and about the kids that would play around naked in the bushes. Like, for children, sex is mostly a curious thing. But still, I have to say, your stories are extreme."

"Uy si!" he jeered playfully, "You never did anything like that when you were little?"

"Mmmm... I used to play with dogs' boobs. But I never like tried to hook up with a priest, and honestly, I think I just kept to myself. I never really had any friends that stuck around. I remember my first best friend in Pre-K... I never got to say good-bye because he got the chicken pox or the measles like two weeks before the school year ended."

"Ay, I never intended to hook up with the priest. I was just intrigued by the idea and I wanted to meet him. We used to talk on Messenger but he turned out to be ugly and old. Was your Pre-K friend cute?" he laughed.

"Mmmm... *puto.* I think the only reason we decided to be friends was because we had the same bowl haircut. That and there were these two girls who would always be bugging us and trying to kiss us. I guess we were the cute boys."

"Ay, y que te paso?"

"Shut up, I'm still cute... kinda. It's just that I'm more of an acquired taste. But maybe that's why I didn't really have friends growing up. I always held onto this thing, this feeling of being abandoned or not being able to say so long, farewell."

"Pues, I remember when we first started talking, people said that they knew you. So you must've had at least a few friends. *Almenos los Engres, no?"*

"Oh, that's another story entirely. But yeah, they were always nice to me. It's funny how we started hanging out. There was this one bitch who was a whore, who thought I was friends with this one guy, who she wanted to fuck, but who I hardly ever talked to... hey, are you even listening?"

By then his eyes were closed and he muttered, "Yes, yes, chicken pox. I'm just tired. I have to get up early tomorrow."

"Ay, you never want to stay up."

"Tu!. Tu nunca te duermes. Eres como enano o algo."

"Ay, what's that even supposed to mean?"

"Pues, supposedly gnomes only work at night because they don't like to be seen. That and they sometimes sit on your chest and whisper nightmares into your ears."

"Ohhhhhh....pleeeeeheaseeeeee. That was one time! And I thought it'd be funny to wake you up with my dick slapping your face."

"Ay! Ya callate por favor!" he said a bit frustrated but ever more sleepy.

"Stupid calculator," I pouted.

"Ya, go to bed. Tomorrow you can tell me more."

"Mmmm..."

"Tu y tus 'Mmmm's'. Well, good night, *marido*," he said then tucked his legs between mine, and an arm between mine, and his head under my chin. I pulled at his hair with my teeth and he slapped me on the back with a, "Quit it. Ya, go to sleep."

"*Buenas noches*, future ex-*marido*," I said as I felt his dick harden up against my thigh. I pushed my body closer to his, my own member getting stiffer. I stared out toward the window with its pale curtains and the soft yellow light from a street lamp filtering in. There was the hum of the TV and some quiet banter from the other room followed by a loud laugh. I realized that there were no crickets, just the occasional car pulling past the house on that narrow street. I closed my eyes, imagined cars swiping side view mirrors in the dark. Those crimes people commit under the anonymity of no witness but the stars above the haze of an over crowded city. I opened them again. I felt his breath on my clavicle. He readjusted his legs and I looked up past the walls into the garden. Those tomatoes in the cool night air should be fine. I'll plant the sunflowers in the fountain though. Yes. The sunflowers in the fountain then I can plant some beans and some jalapeños in between their stalks. I think that's what grandma said to do once. No, wait, that was with corn. No, I'll plant a weenie tree instead.

I laughed.

He mumbled, *"Que traes loco?"*

"Nothing. I was just thinking about Homer Simpson."

Six days to Christmas and I had planted the basil in with the tomatoes, the sunflowers in the fountain, along with some chives, and I even struck up a conversation with a little old lady living three doors down the street. I was on my way to buy more Coca-Cola and chips when she apologized for sweeping water at my feet.

"*Ah perdoname*, *hijo*," she said fanning herself with a paper plate.

"Don't worry," I smiled and stepped in between the cars, into the street, then back in between the cars and back onto the sidewalk. On my way back, she was just finishing sweeping and pulled up a milk crate to sit on against the wall. She fanned herself some more as I noticed she wore a thick plastic flower apron that hugged her like a lead vest. There were pink petals against a pale yellow background with the edges lined in a deep red seam. Like lipstick. Jungle Red. The shallow neck was squared and the straps wide, maybe three of four inches. Her sandals, not new but a well kept polished brown. A semblance of laces like Miami Vice or some kind of gladiator. The skin on her feet, dry and cracked white against coffee colored flesh.

"Do you live around here?" she asked.

"Yes," I smiled, "A few houses down," I swung the plastic white bag of groceries in the direction of Domi's house.

"Ah," she leaned her head back, pointed her chin up towards me and said, "You're not from around here," then squinted. Looking past me and into my accent and horrible Spanish.

I laughed, "Nopes. I'm from El Paso, it's near Juarez on the American side."

"Ah, I have some cousins around them parts. Their son lives in Denver though and another lives in San Diego."

"Ah, I've never been... Well, I don't think I have," I took a bite off of a piece of *carne seca*, the Mexican version of beef jerky, and offered her some.

"Ah. No thank you," she pointed to her cheek, "Bad teeth. I always see you walking to the store."

"Yea, we don't really have much money for groceries. I just sort of grab snacks or anything I can."

She laughed, slapped her hands on her knees then made a drinky-drink motion with her right hand, her thumb and her pinky extended, *"Pero para la cerveza si tienen."* Yes for beer we had plenty. She smacked her gums then stared down the street into the distance, beyond the tiny corner store and the kids playing soccer in the street, *"Pero haci es. Haci son los jovenes.* Well that's how I used to be, anyhow," then she chuckled and wiped her mouth.

I started slowly walking backwards and waved goodbye, "Well, *vecina*, see you later then," I smiled.

The gate to the front patio always seemed to stick. A part of me felt the old woman's eyes boring into the back of my head. I wondered what she thought of me. Did she really think we, does she really think I, drink so much? Do I really drink so much? Was I really such a sore thumb in this city? Were my rounded shoes and tattered clothes such a dead give away? Did I smell *too* American? Suddenly self-conscious, I hurried with a huff and heavy push against the gate. It whined open then pretty soon I was fumbling with the keys at the front door. My head suddenly itched. Felt like the hair follicles were on fire. My forehead broke out in a sweat. My vision blurred in the dark of the living room. There. Safe. Home... -ish. Luis Raul was in his "room" on the phone with someone laughing and basically saying nothing much more than, "Nuh uh?", "I don't believe it!", "That bitch!".

Why is he always laughing and talking? Maybe I had gotten so used to living in silence with the dogs back home that any trifle disturbance became, for a second, immediately infuriating. Gradually that feeling subsided. But the smell of people would linger. Sour feet and armpits and ass.

I didn't know if it was rude but I accidentally slammed the door to Domi's room. I winced and stood still behind it for a second, leaning against it as if to steal from it a bit of fortitude. But Luis Raul just went on laughing in the distance, oblivious and fat.

The bed wasn't made.

The other day Domi had made an offhand remark about that. Implying that I was always leaving such a mess. That if I hadn't a job, the least I could do was clean a little, or, try to not make matters worse. He sighed deeply as he had made it himself after a long shift at work. He said he didn't really mind but Elma just rolled her eyes as she stood in the doorway and spooned yogurt into her mouth. At times I envied their almost psychic connection. Like the way I could tell when one of the dogs needed to take a piss. All I could do was kick a bottle cap towards the corner of the room, hoping that he hadn't noticed it fall from the covers.

The day before, she had spent a good five minutes looking for a raspberry yogurt, her bony, triangular ass sticking out the fridge. I just hid my head behind the newspaper someone had left on the table counter and vowed to buy her a replacement.

"It's just that... I swear... I had left one..." she mused to herself as if pondering the mysteries of the Great Pyramids or the Lost City of Atlantis. Luckily, everyone in the house smoked so much weed that things going missing, or time being lost, was pretty much normal and expected. I would often playfully admonish them with a sarcastic "And *I'm* the one with the drinking problem..."

Most of my days were spent with Luis Raul, or I should say in the proximity of Luis Raul. That man had no qualms about being messy as long as his shirts were pressed. We were always only a few feet away but never in the same room. I thought it funny that when he took a shit he would raise the volume of his radio, that radio that was near his bed. And when I would take a shit, I'd just run the faucet. I mean, we both knew what the other was doing even if sometimes he took longer in the restroom and I suspected other things transpiring. In the beginning I felt some sort of resentment on his part. I think my staying there robbed him of his previous liberties. Images of him strolling naked through the house, while Domi and Elma were on the clock, passed through my head every now and then. God knows I'd do it.

Dinners, luncheons, and breakfasts were largely cereal which didn't mix so well with all the quarts of beer I'd down. I couldn't tell if I was losing weight or if Domi's slim wall mirror was playing some optical illusion on me. The scene from Clueless stuck out in my head about how the main character, Cher, didn't trust mirrors so she'd just take polaroids of herself.

I should get a camera for Luis Raul.

He watered his garden about every two days and sometimes I'd just sit there writing in my journal. Watching him walk around with a mobile glued to the side of his face. We'd share cigarette breaks, or, more so, ours would overlap. The house rule was no tobacco inside. Weed was okay because NASA had proved that the odor dissipated or something like that. But they swore tobacco just clung to the walls and furniture.

I would sure hate for their plastic kitchen chairs to reek like an ashtray.

The Internet connection was shitty at best. I think I would've done better with two cans, a string, and a slingshot. And, because my MacBook didn't have a battery on account that it had swollen up a few months back, I was confined to the bedroom if ever I wanted to browse or watch a movie. My phone had no service but was still Wi-Fi capable, though it was just as slow to load porn. Half the time I left it by the bedside table, acquiesced to owning a very expensive Alarm Clock/calculator apparatus.

Four days before Christmas, I found myself contemplating traditional fried sweet bread recipes with that little old lady down the street. I had since forgotten her name and our relationship was to the point that we were so familiar that it seemed rude to ask for it again. And so, we simply referred to each other as *vecina* and *vecino.* Neighbor, neighbor.

"No, *mijo*, what you have to do is put the husks of *tomatillos,* boil them, and use that same water to make the *bueñuelos*. If you do, you can roll them out larger and they won't tear."

"Ah... well it doesn't really matter. I left all my cooking stuff back home. Well, back at my mom's anyway," I laughed, a little drunk, "But the funny thing is that my mom doesn't even cook. One time we argued over her buying boxed *bueñuelo* mix instead of making it from scratch."

She laughed, "*Bueno, haci son las cosas*," she furrowed her brows, "When I was a little girl, we'd wake up at 5:30 every morning to make *tortillas.* Now I just go down to the store. I used to know this really good recipe that my grandmother taught me but since I stopped doing it every day, I've long since forgotten it. Maybe they just tasted better because it was a family thing. Now all I have to cook for is Ronaldo. And I don't like him very much," she laughed and wiped a hand over her mouth, over the beads of sweat which would gather like dew on the tiny hairs of her elderly mustache. Ronaldo was her husband whom I had seen working on the car every now and then. He was this tall, balding white man who walked with a slouch and was always in a white wife beater. On the sides of his head were patches of white puffy hair, which he refused to shave, as if he were clinging to some misguided semblance of youth.

She went on to ask about our plans for Christmas. I said I had no clue. I couldn't even think of what gift to get my "friend". She laughed and drew her right wrist across her damp forehead. The air was always thick. Sometimes it felt as if I was swimming in butter.

"Well," she went on, "when I was a kid. Ooh *years* ago," she raised her right arm emphatically, "we didn't have money for much. We had one set of clothes for the week, and one set of clothes for Church on Sunday and Holidays. Usually we'd get new outfits for Easter and wear that all year long. But for toys on Christmas? Hmmpf! You were lucky if someone gave you a hand me down. Anyhow, well my mother didn't have money for presents. My dad worked at a nearby mine but he'd drink away his paycheck before he even got home. Mom used to do laundry for the neighbors to make some extra loot but it still wasn't very much. So, from there sprung this tradition of her roasting pinion nuts and placing them by the stove. Back then everybody had a wood burning stove," she leaned over and nodded knowingly.

I smiled, "Ah, that's really nice!" a little buzzed, a little dreamy, imagining the whole affair in a rustic sepia fashion. A glow of a wood burning stove and little if any light but a few shadows against the wood walls.

"Well," she wiped her mouth with her right hand the way a man would wipe his mustache, "Being so poor, anything was a treat and Pinion Nuts were absolutely delicious. We'd wake up early in the morning, outside, the sky was still blue dark, and in the slight glow from a dying fire, we'd compare bags. One with the other. Five children in total. Sometimes we'd fight because this one had a little more than that one," she laughed and cocked her head to the right, "One year I cried so much. I must've been about six or seven. My bag was always the smallest and I guess I just expected something different that year."

She laughed.

I laughed.

Shit my beer's getting warm.

She went on, "And what would you know? My mom, standing by the stove, watching with weary eyes as my father snored loudly on the bed behind her, she leaned over, hugged me, then picked me up and sat me on her lap at the table. In those days we only had one room. The house was small. We all slept in one bed or on the floor. So she leaned in and whispers to me, 'Maribel, don't cry. Why are you crying?' And so I tell her, I tell my mother that Santa Claus doesn't like me because he gave me the smallest bag. And she, I remember it so vividly, she starts to tear up. Ah, my poor mother, *dios la bendiga*. She said she was going to tell me a secret. That there isn't any Santa, nor reindeer that fly. And me, being so young, what do you expect I thought? But my mother, my dear, dear mother, she goes on to say that my brothers and sisters still believe in him but that now I was a big girl and I should know what was what. That although I was the youngest, I was the smartest. I should know that there was no elves or workshops or north poles. That it was her and my father who'd buy us toys and clothes and, well, this year was harder than most. She says, she tells me, that I shouldn't cry because I was the only one mature enough to understand that. That she was pretty sure I had already figured it out because I was the only one who looked for hidden presents in the cupboard yesterday. And she was pretty sure that I could understand that she didn't have enough to give everyone the same quantity."

She smiled, tearing up, looked into the distance, the sun bouncing off the beige walls across the street and glittering off shiny metal cars onto her face, "And what do you think? I stopped crying and I smiled. She smiled and kissed me then pressed her forehead against mine. I felt so happy to have her confide in me *big girl* things. My sisters never told me anything and I was always left out of the loop when they'd gossip about boys. They just said I was too stupid and I was a baby and that I wouldn't understand. But my mother, she knew that I was upset all along because I wanted to belong. I wanted people to stop treating me like an infant. That's why I cried. Because my bag wasn't the same as everyone else's. Because I wasn't the same as everyone else. But my mother, my momma, she goes on and she tells me to open my hand. She told me that my hand was as big as my belly and to see how nicely the bag of nuts covered almost all my fingers to the tips. Then she took the bag, placed her hand next to mine and put the nuts in her palm, which barely filled that. 'See,' she said, 'This bag is big for you but not enough for me. Now imagine your brother Andresito's stomach and his big stinky feet?' we both laughed. That was the best gift my mother ever gave me. This confidence. This secret. This understanding between what we think we want and what we really need. It made me feel real *chingona.* Like I could take on the world. Like I understood the world a little better. I may have been the smallest but I was the only one who knew the truth: That not all things are meant for everybody. And although things may seem unfair, they are given to us in doses we can take and because we are meant to understand these differences and appreciate them."

All I could say was "Wow" before I finished the last bit or my warm *caguama*. On that note I left, a little less burdened by the ever-looming holiday. That I should not have the perfect gift weighed less heavily on my shoulders. I was here. Was that not enough? I had left everything I'd ever known behind. I had opened my eyes a little bit to the world. And as I walked back home, I wondered what time Wal-Mart closed deep down in Mexico.

Christmas Eve. All day Elma, Luis and Domi seemed to have spent on their phones. I sat at the table counter smoking a cigarette. David sat to my right with his own stogie. He'd been texting some guy(s) he met on Grindr. It was the holidays and rules could be bent with the advent of company who themselves chain-smoked religiously. We'd just left the door open. The weather warm and sticky. No snowmen this year. I sighed to myself. I was always one of those people who got blue around the season. Walking through stores, that music which played the same 15 songs every half hour, people excited by thinking of just the right gift. All that made for this low sinking feeling. Compounding that familiar sentiment was this nagging homesickness. One of the only bright specks in the season was getting to visit with my mother's family. I had grown up more so close to them than my father's side. We all had a good sense of humor. Or maybe I just enjoyed the audience of persons who had seen me grow up awkwardly, and then into something of a charming character. That sinking feeling in the back of my throat crept up. I thought about my poor dead father, lying in the ground somewhere, under two layers of metal. I emailed my mother that morning, but I didn't think there'd be much reception six feet down so I didn't bother with him. This, I thought as I cupped my chin in hand, this would be the first Christmas without dad, without my family.

I tapped my pen against the counter. What was I trying to draw? I never did like going over to Juarez, where my dad was deported, where he had grown up as a child and into his teens. I always tried to find the silver lining. No more Dad meant no more three-hour lines to cross back. My mind wandered like my pen on the paper. Circles and shapes like ovals, then faces, then limbs of things in varying positions. I did some doodles of phones and Santa and a little old lady sweeping away elves. Everyone's families were hours away and although one or two could afford the flight, they stayed in the city as an act of solidarity. I had asked Domi why we hadn't gone to his parents. He said we couldn't afford it. That they were in Vegas with his sister. When I asked why hadn't we gone to his aunt's, the one he had been staying with prior, he said that they were very conservative. David's parents were on their way into the city from the coast. Elma's were in *Cuauhtémoc* making snowmen and *tamales*. Luis Raul's were... I dunno, eating bacon somewhere.

Last night we had set up lights against the wall in the shape of a zig zag spruce. There were presents on the floor by it but none were from me. The packages were small but finely wrapped in ribbon and bows. It was a house full of pacing and me eating cheap cereal from a bowl. The doorbell rang and it was some dude Luis was dating or possibly contemplating cannibalizing. He was about 5'9", slim, not ugly but not anything special. He looked young and his clothes fit baggy. I was so used to seeing everyone in fitted apparel that his baggy slacks stood out in my mind as belonging to someone of a less experienced level or means. Like he was wearing a Sunday outfit his mother had picked out.

I kept doodling.

There seemed to be a pit in my tummy, a hole in the back of my throat. My shoulders felt heavy and my chin now rested against the page on the counter. I stroked my beard often and thought again about my dad missing his first X-mas. I thought of my sister and my mother and how annoying my older brother could be but how much my nephew and niece loved him.

I'd never have children. Since everything went down in November, I swore off marriage and family. What Domi and I had was nice, but in the back of my head, I knew, I was just using him and this move as a stopgap measure. In the back of my head I always thought that things would end. That everything ends. So when he walked up and hugged me from behind, it was almost a knee jerk reaction that I should put my hand on his face push him away.

"*Payaso.* Now for that you get no Christmas," he said and clopped past the kitchen into his room.

The day before we had gotten high then began talking about our previous Christmases. For god knows what reason, that conversation had lead to a discourse about our previous relationships. I think one of us might've mentioned a terrible holiday with an ex or something. Anyhow, he had recounted a time in which he was single around the holidays and was invited to a party wherein he suspected someone had spiked his drink with a pill. By the end of the night, him and a few other boys had their pants down and were whacking off in a circle. In another instance, he recalled, he had been dating some boy back in Chihuahua, but then that his ex had visited the city from Cuauhtémoc for a few days in the season. Now he took to great pains to express to me that the boy he had been dating at the time was somewhat of a liberal minded person. That that boy, himself, had previously been visited by his own ex a few weeks prior and Domi had been certain that the two had slept together because the "friend" had stayed at his then boyfriend's house. Trust me, it took me a few seconds to grasp the convoluted scenario myself. Anyhow, Domi had arranged for a sexual meeting with the boy from Cuauhtémoc and that then snowballed into a fiasco and a scene.

Domi assured me, "It's just that things were different back then. I was young and my boyfriend and me were really open-minded. And when I heard that my ex was coming into town, well, it just brought up all these old feelings. Besides, it didn't really matter. I knew that I wasn't going to be dating that guy forever. And after that, honestly, we had a few threesomes and stuff."

I, in shock, disillusioned to a degree, just sat there on the fountain outside in the dark. In front of me, Domi's silhouette, an antumbra of a figure before the porch light behind him. Who was this man I was living with? Who was the person I had become? What of my former self had I lost?

That's what family was for: An anchor. A solid rock. A lighthouse. A beacon. A reminder of the things you once were.

I thought of my aunts and cousins. I drew more loopdy-loops and pointy corners. First tiny triangles then larger triangles which ran across the page. I started with eyes then ears then faces frowning and mad. Some were distraught. There were robots and ducks in a line and a plant that seemed to leaf out in vines up towards the edge of the page then settling at the corner. I drew a dog. Then two dogs and a fish. I drew a penis then a pen and a man with glasses in a hat. I drew pots and a garden and a bonsai with a stone beneath the roots and a low hanging branch. I drew my old fridge and people laughing. I drew. I drew. I doodled, then I drew, and I wrote some captions of carols I knew.

"God rest ye merry gentlemen..."

No real tree, no family. Not even a dog. Oh god, my dogs! I never bought them presents! I wondered if my aunt or mom had? A family portrait with them in ugly sweaters would have been nice.

A tap at my shoulder. I turned around, drearily, sleepy eyed and tired like the kind of tired I get from being sober and when my sugar goes low.

"*Hola!*" A broad smile like a child's. Luis' date was beaming, proud of himself for nothing. I hate him so I smile like I've learned to smile at work.

Luis Raul went on, "*Marvensito,* let me present to you my good friend Jose Luis!" he then smiled broadly too. Geessuz sometimes it felt like Mexicans had about ten names to choose from when it came to their children. From there they picked four and called each other by the first two. Idiots. I hated that country. I hated being away from home. I was always away from home and holidays meant I could peaceably spend it with family. It was a treasure after a long absence from their weekly get togethers which, because I had always worked Fridays, had tended to miss.

I pursed my lips, "A pleasure," and shook his hand, "Name's Marv."

"*Mucho gusto!*"

"Marveen is from the United States," Luis Raul chimed in and his friend told me that he had a cousin who lived in Kansas and asked if I had ever been.

"Nope," I sat up, "I'm from Texas. Well, the part of Texas that's basically Mexico. We're right across from Juarez."

"Ooh," he coed again, "Isn't it very dangerous around there?"

"Uhmm, I guess. One time the cops like stole my iPod or something." I laughed and remembered an ex.

At some point Domi walked back into the living room, phone in hand, staring at the screen and smiling, "No", he butted in, "It's VERY dangerous."

"Not as dangerous as where these guys are from," I pointed a backwards thumb towards David then twirled my hand, index finger out, including the entire house. I leaned in and whispered to Jose, "I hear they have *bears*." He laughed. "Besides, the first week I started chatting with Domi, he had his car stolen and was mugged. The day before he had been trying to convince me to make a trip down there for spring break or something. Yeah, wasn't gonna happen."

David looked up from his phone, "Nope. We don't have bears, *estupido,*" text text text, "We have drug lords, mountain lions and old men with rifles who can't aim."

"Ah..." Jose Luis rocked back and forth on his heels, nodding his head ever so slightly.

"Well," Luis Raul said checking his phone, "We'll be back in a minute, boys."

"Where ya'll going going?" Elma, taking out the mini ham from the oven called over her shoulder as she kicked the old stove's door shut.

With no discernible jawline, Luis Raul responded, "To visit some friends..."

Text Text Text. David looked up, "He means he's reservations for that orgy."

Nervously the two laughed, looked at each other then to either side of the room and shuffled out in geometric scarves with tassels at the ends."

"Mexicans are so nice. I mean *polite,*" I flipped to a new page and smoothed out the kinks near the corners.

Text Text Text. David staring at his phone, "Well I have to say that they show us, early on, how to be courteous. How to greet people and how to say adieu."

"How boring," I slumped back in my stool, "If I ever have to write a book about them, about you guys, Imma totally leave that part out. That'd take up half a chapter. And what do you mean by 'that orgy'?"

"*Mal educado...*" Domi said laughing as he swept the kitchen with a plastic yellow broom. Maybe I was poorly educated in etiquette but those affairs of hellos and good byes were so formal and tedious. I remember hating them as a child. Touching grimy old hands and wrinkled old skin. Why couldn't you just wave to everybody goodbye? I can understand the forever line of hello's to satiate people's egos. But seriously? Again? Ba! Hogwash!

"Bad boy. The term is Bad Boy," I mocked him, citing a point early on in our relationship where he implied I was some sort of James Dean miscreant.

Text Text Text, "Oh, I got an invite for that too. There's something about the holidays and everyone coming home that makes gays want to have marathon sex. There's like six profiles on Grindr right now that just say 'party' and give directions... mmm well, more like the general neighborhood. Actually, I think there's one down the street but it says something about leather. "

"Buuu," I said then yelled back to Domi, "Where's my divorce?! The last time I was in an 'orgy', I basically just sat back and drank everyone's booze. Also like the guys that go to those things aren't ever really hot. I think it's something akin to how you'd imagine nudist beaches to be all like 'hey sexy people' but it's really just gross people and you're all like 'ewoo, get off me grandpa'."

Text Text Text, "Mmm... not these ones. I've been... I've *heard*, I mean, that there's always sexy guys. People down here are picky. Maybe not Domi, but the rest of us have standards."

"Buuuu... he's just marrying me for his papers. Also, like I'm a total catch. Grade A Trophy Husband here. None of that boring teetotalers crap. I'm like a black belt in drinking and making people laugh. Or at least I used to be... back when everyone spoke English."

Text Text Text, "I speak English."

"So do parrots, but I don't think that there's a lot going on upstairs with them either. Besides, it's totally different being funny in English and being funny in Spanish. I can be cute in Spanish. How do you think I snagged me ol' Ichabod Crane over there? But the jokes? Eh, it's all like 'he said donut but meant vagina' and then something about tacos."

Elma took a saucepan off the stove. I drew the faintest whisper of an oval. The outline of a jaw and two eyes. I called out to her, "And you Elma? I never figured you for a cook. What's with the nice spread? Also, where are the *tamales?"*

She laughed slow and hard, "Fuck that shit! Too much trouble. *This* year we're having an American *Crissmass!* We got ham, mashed potatoes," she gently dipped her finger in the pan, turned around to get a spoon, and continued, "Corn, gravy and something *very* special..." she spun back, smiled and stuck the thing in the pot with the spoon. She raised the tiny shovel and let this syrupy chocolate creep-creep down back into the pot.

I threw myself on the counter table and whined, "Ugh! I HATE Mexican corn! I wish we had yellow corn. Sweet, sweet yellow corn."

"Shut it!" she laughed, "And GROSS! It's too sweet! American corn is like candy. Disgusting! *Guacala!*."

"I know!" I hollered back in delighted agreement and closed my sketchbook, placed it on my lap as I slouched even more, "It's soooo good though... Mexican corn is just like little flavorless starch squares," I sighed, "What are you making now?"

She was filling an ice tray with the chocolaty molasses."Lolli-pops," she smiled, head down, but eyes looking up from under her bangs and winked. She took out a roll of saran wrap and stretched it tightly across the top of the tray. She then proceeded to skewer each and every square with a tooth pick, did a 180 then with a, "Now, twenty minutes and we're set!" she slammed the freezer door and voila!

"Are we getting high again?" I moaned and flung my head back.

She leaned against the flimsy kitchen fold out table, laughed and took a sip of water from an old mason jar. Mockingly, she sighed and mouthed out in a heavy accent, "*Our wee gonda git hay agin...*"

I rolled my eyes. I didn't understand why they wouldn't let me drink before four. A part of me was already running through an imaginary scenario where Domi hadn't really bought liquor and the whole *we're hiding it till everyone gets here* was just a bunch of bull-crap. I mean, he apparently wasn't the person I thought he had been: Freakin' whoring it around Chihuahua and shit. So how was I to trust that he had remembered my medicine?

I tapped my pen against my gaping mouth, "Now you're sure you guys bought the vodka, right?"

Text Text Text, "Ugh, Domi, just give it to him already."

"No!" Domi laughed, "Then he's going to drink it all and make a scene. *Pinche boracho.*"

"ME?! MAKE A SCENE?!" I retorted then gave a deep throaty moan and rolled my eyes so far back into my head that I think I could have seen my brain stem. I slammed my head down on the counter. Elma laughed as David was taken aback. Startled, he leaned to the opposite side, clutching his phone to his chest. I think he had the vapors.

I muffled out as my head remained on the counter, "This is the WORST Christmas, ever... of all time..."

Domi, still sweeping the trash into a dustpan, "Stop being so rude," he laughed, "Or Imma send you to your room without *Crissmass*."

Text Text Text, "And your mother, Marveen?"

"Mmm.... I talked to her yesterday. I'll probably call her tomorrow."

Text Text, "How strange. I mean, it's your mom and you won't even call her for *Crissmass*."

"Maybe... if I had a, I dunno, A DRINK, I'd be more inclined to."

Domi, washing his hands in the kitchen sink just across the way with his back turned to us said curtly, "No."

"UGGGGHHHHHHHHHH...." I swirled around in the swivel chair and hit my knee against the lower wall. "Ow."

Text Text Text, "Just do it already, Domi! He's resorted to hurting himself! In a little while he'll be slitting his wrists."

"Goood riddance!" Domi blurted out from behind a smile, now facing us and leaning against the sink, his lips hidden by a colorful novelty mug. I squinted my eyes, suddenly suspicious that those *waters* had all along been something else. I was annoyed by then and my right leg started shaking uncontrollably, nervously almost. Why did nobody want me to NOT get sick? I knew that if I didn't get a drink pretty soon, I'd be cranky and vomiting and my eyes would fall from their sockets and roll around the floor and the entire universe would collapse in on itself.

Elma said, jokingly referring to my suicidal tendencies, "Well, at least red goes with the holiday decor," and then laughed into her own drink.

Is it whiskey? That was all they drank but I couldn't smell it from where I was sitting. Mezcal maybe?

I stared at her viciously. I winced my eyes, hunched my back and said accusingly, "Is... THAT... the vodka???"

Domi, a little annoyed, "Ya, Marveen, just a little longer. All we're waiting on is for the mashed potatoes," his phone rang and he pulled it out, smiled at the screen then responded in good Holiday cheer, bobbing his head as he typed out the message. I hate him. I hated him vehemently. If I could've I would've shoved that phone down his throat but I needed it to call my mom sometime tomorrow or at least by the end of that week.

"Uuuughhhhhhhhhh... now I want potato vodka!" I tossed my head back dramatically again.

Text Text Text, "That, girlfriend, is really expensive."

"Marveen!," Elma hollered out from the kitchen, "Say *carro*!" I couldn't roll my "r's" so Elma liked to tease me.

"Elma," I yelled back, "You say *Third World Country."*

She laughed back into her jar sipping Mexican Moonshine for all I knew.

"ENOUGH! Children! Behave!" Domi laughed and turned down the stove, "I'm going to send both of you to your rooms without *Crissmass* AND without dinner."

"Good! That whale could afford to skip a meal!" Elma interjected, pointing her chin at me.

Domi went on, "AND without presents!"

I stuck my tongue out at her and looked at my watch. "For crissakes, at least put some music on! All I hear is *ding ding* from David's phone!"

Elma, "Ah yes, I heard tell that whales like to sing. *Roooooo...waaaa... yeee, yeee."*

I flipped her off.

Text Text Text, "What the hell was that? And shut up Marveen. Don't get me involved."

Domi laughed quietly to himself, savoring his own wit, "Actually, if anything he sounds more like a cat in heat."

Elma laughed, took the tray of lollipops from the freezer, "Well, love, that IS more accurate."

They all laughed.

Bastards.

Domi began to pour himself some water into a small blue plastic tumbler from a thin water cooler that was hidden between the pistachio green fridge and the sink counter. It was never plugged in. Something or other about wasting too much electricity. I just knew he was smiling from behind the rim of his cup. His eyes were squinty, beady little black things with mischievous one liners in a row behind them. I just rolled my eyes and swiveled right to left, to right to left, as David lit another cigarette. Elma peeled back the saran wrap, bent the plastic ice tray one way then the next with both hands.

"Ready whores?" she smiled, propping up the goodies as if it were a turkey and this were Thanksgiving.

"Remember, Marveen," Domi said like an admonishing mother, "Just one because we have to leave enough for our guests." I picked out a toothpick towards the center of the ice tray and stared at it for a second. In less than that, Domi snatched the one I had in hand and traded it for a smaller one he had in his. I was left with a dark brown uneven cube about half an inch thick.

"Here, baby," he said, this one is better," he smiled, narrowed his eyes, then popped the one he'd taken from me into his mouth before I had a chance to protest. Gross! Domi spit! HE COULD KEEP IT!

David daintily licked his chocolate rectangle. Elma had hers in her left cheek just as the doorbell rang. It was Orel and Bianca. Him: a frail sliver of a macho man with a Freddie Mercury mustache and no ass. Her: a posh pale version of a model in Cat Power bangs. I hadn't seen them since my welcome-to ho'e down. Well, at least I thought they were there. A shit load of *Holas* and hugs later...

"Here, my love", Orel handed Bianca a lolli and in a few minutes, I felt a light euphoric curtain cascade over my eyelids. There was a lot of talk about nothing. Domi had promised that once the food was ready, I could start drinking. Then even after everything was done cooking, he still said we had to wait for our guests. Damned guests had been there a good twenty minutes and I was still without a glass in hand. And so, utilizing my GT skills, I put my thinking hat on and found myself a spot near Bianca against the kitchen wall that led to the hallway.

"Hey," I coquettishly squinted and leaned in towards her, savoring the coffee like sweetness of the intoxicating candy, "Did you get a new haircut? That dress looks SO cute on you! Ugh, I wish you'd tell me your secret. I've been trying to lose weight since forever. Hey, you don't maybe want a drink or something?"

She giggled and smiled politely, turning to me then leaning her right shoulder against the wall, "Uhmm, no. I haven't cut it in months. Drink? Well, sure, why not?" Teeth like diamonds. Pearly white row between two jungle red leaves of lips. She stuck the lollipop back in her mouth, that bright, deep red lipstick glistening against a pale face and almond eyes. She was wearing a black jumper with a red sweater beneath. Black leggings and high heel shoes with a thick strap. They were like platforms or something that a Brady would wear or like a more stylish Frankenstein boot.

I casually looked around, "Why I could've sworn we had some... right over... You know what? Why don't you ask Domi?" I pointed my chin to her and nudged my head towards the kitchen where Orel was an inspiring center of attention, "I was helping cook earlier while he was cleaning. He must've moved it somewhere. I swear, if my head weren't screwed onto my neck..."

She slowly pushed herself off against the wall, her long hair streaming over her arm as she held her head sideways. She walked up to Domi, who laughed, covering his mouth and arching his shoulders down in response to whatever double entendre joke Orel had just mentioned. Her hands caressed his biceps or where his biceps would've been if he had any. She whispered something into his ear like a voodoo priestess blowing white powder into the eyes of an unsuspecting victim. He looked at me from across the way. His head bowed down and his eyebrows furrowed then he whispered something in her ear. She looked over at me, smiled coyly, then laughed and slapped him on the arm. She then covered her smile with a hand like a geisha. He mouthed something else to her then she bowed halfway, her head bobbing to the side, and he squeezed her arm and led her into Elma's bedroom. She turned to my direction, kicked back the heel of her shoe, winked, and gave me the thumbs up.

"And well I said, *No mames!"* Orel threw up his hands as Bianca giggled into her right palm, holding her drink in her left, a pink plastic tumbler, down by her thigh. We all sat around that flimsy kitchen table. You couldn't put your elbow down without evoking the San Andreas Fault, which I suppose helped to keep my manners in check. Elma stuffed her face. David leaned back in his chair, sipping on a whiskey water that was more rocks than anything (pussy). Domi squeezed my right knee with his left hand as we sat watching the entire affair unfold. Our backs to the kitchen sink, I looked out into the dark living room imagining people knocking or walking in but there really wasn't anybody. He then whispered behind my ear, "Babe, eat something," I smiled mischievously. Food was too filling. Drink was more satisfying.

I took a swig from the drink in my left hand, took my right arm from around his back and placed a square of ham from my plate into my mouth. The thing didn't taste half as bad as I'd expected. It might have been a little dry but in Elma's defense, it had been sitting there, judging me, on a paper plate for a good half hour. Everything at that point was dry and cold, yet somehow awesomely appetizing. I just had no more room. My belly was so full up on liquor and the weed made me feel as if I was aware of every tube and orifice: The sensation of my saliva trickling down the back of my throat, my belly bloated. I wasn't sure if I needed to poop or fart so I held them both in. I had tried drinking a beer to hydrate myself, but the burping that ensued was for a split second mistaken, by me, as the precursor to vomiting. My palette satiated by cigarettes and the biting of nails. Wait, I wasn't biting my nails. It was Domi. But for another split second I had imagined myself through his eyes. I stared intensely at him, "DUDE! I was totally in your fucking head right now!"

He paid me no mind. All night long it seemed as if I couldn't get a word in edgewise. I'd start to comment but would get cut off. Peevishly I'd smile and take another sip. I hate weed. It always makes me so awkward. What was worst was that I really had these funny things to say but by the time I could add something, the topic of conversation had already turned. As it was, I understood maybe a third of the jokes but I've learned, long since when, that there is a cue for laughter. So I laughed when they laughed. I leaned forward and slapped my knee. I'd rock back and forth in my chair and sometimes pounded the table, forgetting how precisely precariously the drinks stood. Towers like in Asia. Hong Kong doing the shimmy.

Honestly the whole thing wasn't that bad. I didn't have to drive anywhere, the company was good, and the drinks were plenty. I only ever felt out of place when one or another of our friends would check their phone. They'd be these breaks of silence and everyone including Domi would tap tap tap out a holiday hello to somebody somewhere. But I hadn't anybody to talk to. More so, I hadn't had a working phone. At one point David stood up and said that we should take a photo for Instagram. He set the timer and we leaned in as a half circle around the table in our chairs. When I looked at the photos later, after he had posted it and Elma was ridiculing his faces, I noticed how exactly out of place I looked. Not smiling. Not happy. Not skinny. Not anything. Just a greasy faced blob, second from the left.

I heard the door knock again. It felt as if I had been going back and forth between it and them. This had to be the third time at least or maybe it had been the tenth. But no, nobody was there.

"Who the hell are you expecting, Marveen?" Orel yelled over his shoulder, snuggling up to Bianca, his back towards the door.

"Santa Claus, *pinche meco*," laughed Elma as she wiped her plate with a piece of bread.

Out in the street, past the front gate, I couldn't see anything. I couldn't hear that common whizzing of cars. Quiet as a mouse indeed. I looked back towards the kitchen. Domi was on his phone again. David crossed his legs on the tall bar stool he had been sitting in, lit a cigarette and blew out a Marlene Dietrich kind of plume.

I looked back outside, sighed, and then shut the door. I walked over to the table from out of the darkness of the empty living room and from the chill of a quiet night. "Well, a duh," I smiled, "You people don't even have a chimney! How the hell else is Santa gonna get in if we don't open the door?"

Everyone smiled politely then looked away.

Silence.

Maybe I wasn’t as charming as I had thought.

Just then the door flew open, startling even David from his ice queen reverie. In walked Luis Raul and I said, "Well, it may not be Santa, but I sure got the fat guy part right."

"*Bebe*, wake up."

Hazy, blurry, sleepy, shoulder aching, I could barely make out the faint whisper of Domi's voice.

"Mmmmm..." I slammed my head into the pillow. It smelled, something awful but I didn't care. It reeked of cologne and sweaty ass. I was tired from a whole day of doing nothing. He laughed through his nose and slapped me on the butt.

"Hurry! See, that's why I didn't want you to start drinking so early."

"Mmmmm..." I moaned again into the stinky pillow. Why the fuck does he spray everything like it's Sephora?

Sarcastically he said, "Do you want another shot?"

The words hadn't even finished coming out his mouth, but I was up like a shark's fin from the water. A spark, immediately aware. Propped up on both arms, I had been laying on my stomach, grinding a boner into the mattress, fully aware that my bladder was about to burst.

"I thought you said we ran out last night?!" a look of hurt and betrayal veiled my annoyance and a slight headache from a stuffy nose, "Fuck!" I blinked my eyes rapidly then started stumbling out from under the covers, fully dressed save for one missing black low cut sock, "I really needa take a piss," I wiped and rubbed my eyes with my right hand, "Like REALLY need to take a piss. Like a man who really needs to take a piss for a pissing contest in Piss-to-chec-vecs-slovakia."

He stared at me perplexed. I knew he hardly understood English, much less my bastardization of it. I smiled and went in to kiss him but he turned his head.

"No," he said, "Go brush your teeth first. You reek of alcohol and cigarettes."

"ALCOHOL?! CIGARETTES?! WHERE?!" I shot up again.

He didn't find that funny either. I sat back down on the bed, completely unaware of the time or place or era I was even in. The room spun for a second as I closed tight my eyes.

"Bring me water?" I pleaded, "And a double!" I raised my right index finger valiantly.

He patted my cheek, a little harder than would be considered lovingly, then left and returned with a plastic green cup. Bianca poked her head in from behind the bedroom door then tip toed in on her heels, "Marveen..." she leaned over the bed and shook my back. By then I had my face back in the pillow but my body remained contorted, half sitting, half lying into the bed, "Marveen... we have to go."

I propped myself up again and mumbled out a, "Fanks fer cummin', I'd love yous," then gave her a half hug.

"No," she smiled then laughed, a warm glow over her face from the light of the table lamp and the din of a few whiskies, "We're going, all of us. Hurry, get up."

I slammed my head back into the pillow, eyes wide open, I professed, "I hate sitting down when I drink. It sneaks up on ya."

"What?" She smiled and rubbed my shoulders.

"I always get sleepy. Ugh, maybe it was the weed. Stupid gateway something something something..."

From a distance David yelled, "*Andales amigas!* We're gonna be late!"

Elma stepped in, rolling her back over the open doorframe, licking her fingers and laughing quietly she said, "*Amiga*, don't be such a dumb slut! Get up!"

Bianca, now sitting on the bed beside me, rolled her eyes and rubbed her cold hands behind my neck, "You okay?"

Muffled by the pillow I whined, "Domi..."

She tilted her head to the side and frowned then called out, "Domi, come here! Aw, *bebe,* you miss your boyfriend. How precious."

Orel was in the background trying to tell David a joke but David was too preoccupied texting. Domi rushed over, clipping on that golden watch with no battery he said, "What's up, *bebe?"* then rubbed my back, "You feeling okay?" he cooed.

I whiffled out from under the pillow, "Wher'f my double?"

To my credit, I did not vomit on the drive over, although, the sensation to do so had passed over me once or twice. I was foolishly under the assumption that it had been morning but I had only blacked out for about an hour or two. David sped through the night as if he were playing space invaders. A hard rock to the left then the right and a tight turn here and another there. I blamed my queasiness entirely on him when I leaned over and sullied Domi's shoes as we finally stepped out of the car.

"Kisses?" I smiled as the Irish in me came out. He was not amused and proceeded to wipe his shiny black pointy tipped shoe on my pants, "Hey..." I furrowed my brows, "No fair!"

He laughed nervously as Elma wrapped her shawl and arm around me then walked us towards the house. It was small like ours but built right into the neighbors' on either side. The windows were these dull yellow rectangles of light with shadowy figures that brushed the curtains now and then.

David pursed his lips, "Marveen, are you done making a mess? Because we're going inside now and I swear to god that if you start puking in front of all my friends from work, I will positively die of embarrassment and NEVER, EVER, talk to you again."

I ran my tongue across the front of my teeth, "Uhmmm... sure. That is to say.... I think... Woo! PARTY!" I then raised my arms, pushed past everyone, and ran into house. David stood behind in the street, slapped a hand into his face and shook his head side to side.

Two minutes later, Domi walked in on me standing in the kitchen as I, to Anabel, said, "No, no, no. I really shouldn't. I can't take shots right ... Oh well, maybe just this one..."

His eyes were like slits, like knives disapproving. I smiled but in one fell swoop he managed to wrestle the tequila from out my hand.

"What the hell, Domi?!" Anabel laughed.

"*Hola,* Anabel!" he smiled then raised a brow annoyed at my behavior. He kissed her on the cheek and continued, "No more for him. He's had plenty."

"Who?" She laughed, probably high herself, and slapped her right hand against his left shoulder.

His brows made another V then he quickly looked to either side, did a 360, but I was long gone by then. From down the hallway, one could hear me yell, "WOO, SPRING BREAK!"

I found myself standing in the middle of this living room that had been made into an impromptu dance floor. I was just doing my thing, minding my own business, when Domi rudely pulled me aside and breathed hot and heavy into my ear, "Hey, man. What the fuck? You come here alone or what?"

I giggled, "Ah man, that was TOTES my song!" then I started doing the robot again.

He grabbed me by both shoulders then gave me a tiny slap on the face, "Hey! Listen! Don't get lost! Come with me. Let's find Elma and David."

"Bianca too?" I said blithely, "I like Bianca. She's pretty."

He sighed, "Yes, Bianca too!"

I raised both arms again and yelled, "Alright! SPRING BREAK!!!"

As we walked away, in unison, the hoighty toighty people on the dance floor breathed sigh of relief.

We caught up with everyone in the kitchen. Bianca smiled at me from behind a disposable red cup. Her right elbow resting in her left hand. Beside her, Orel said, "What's up, Marveen? You feeling okay?" he smiled and patted me on the shoulder.

Domi, tapping his foot, said imperatively, "You need water."

I leaned in too close and countered with a, "You're not my mom, Domi!"

He rolled his eyes with a, "Don't start," and stared off to the side. Everyone happy and euphoric and him there having to babysit a drunk.

I let these words roll out of my tongue and rounded my lips: "Mommy… Domi… Domingo… Mingo… Mom-go..." I laughed, incredibly amused with myself. Why wasn't I writing for Leno?

Annoyed, he bit the lower right side of his lips and said, "Yes, yes, 'Mom-go'," then puffed a breath through his nose.

I tapped the tip of it, "You… *you're* cute," I smiled.

"Ay," he sighed, "We should've left you at the *casa*."

At that moment I decided to practice my Spanish. "*Casa?... quilobasa!* And you should've! I could've watched that black angels movie?"

Bianca laughed and leaned in, "Which black angels movie?"

"That one," I brought my arm against my chest, pointed up to the ceiling, and said each word deliberately, struggling to annunciate, "The one where the baby puts talcum powder all over herself 'cause she's too dark or something."

Bianca, "Ah, now I know which one you're talking about."

Domi leaned in, now less angry than before and kissed my nose, "I'm so sure. Knowing you, you'd have spent the entire time masturbating in front of Santa Claus."

I pressed my index finger against his lips, “Shhh…Quiet! *Mom-go…*”

Orel laughed, "Behave yourself, Marveen, or else they're going to run you out of the party." He then motioned with his cup to across the room where David was standing by Anabel and another girl, rolling his eyes in my direction.

My head bobbled and I swayed, "PFFFT! Like I care... FUCK DAT BITCH!" then I started to throw gang signs at Bianca. She laughed. Finally my thoughts began to coalesce as the THC ran out my system and the old familiar alcohol claimed it's rightful place.

From behind, a woman's voice cut sharp through the booming music that pervaded the place, "What's this I hear about *bitch fucking*?" An arm hung itself across my shoulders. I looked up to find Alice leaning against me. I covered my mouth with my left hand and hugged her.

"Hey! Alice! Sorry I'm all stinky. I just threw up everywhere," I couldn’t help but smile.

Domi rolled his eyes and blew a tuft of hair out of his face. Alice just laughed and said, "No worries," then winked at Bianca and yelled out to her, "I like your outfit. I tried finding something red to wear but I haven't done laundry in forever." Bianca curtsied and said thank you.

I yelled, "SPRING BREAK!!!" with my arms up once more.

Alice laughed and told me, "Marvin, not so loud!" then she sipped from her own disposable red cup and said to Domi, "I take it you guys have been drinking all day?"

He was on my right now, bowing under my weight as I leaned more on him, my arm over his shoulders. He sucked his teeth then said, "No. SOMEBODY just doesn't know how to drink. Americans *never* know how to drink."

Shocked, I said, again, each word deliberate, "I do too so know how to drink!" Out of nowhere I had apparently found a cup of whiskey, and proclaimed, "Look," then downed the whole thing.

Domi yelled, "Noooooo!!!!" like Kirk yelled Kahn but I had chugged it before he had the chance to take it away. Bianca laughed and Alice slapped me on the back with a, "That's the spirit!"

I cocked my head to the side and stared at her, "You know what? You...*you're* pretty..." I cooed.

The physical ramifications of a hangover are never quite as bad as the moral ones. As far as I was concerned, if you couldn't remember it, it never happened. That is of course unless it comes to cheating on someone or running someone over. Those two definitely count.

For me, Christmas day was met in a dim room beside a pile of jackets and an empty bucket and the sun barely humming behind sheer curtains. I suppose the bucket was for “just in case” and at least the pile of leather and denim served as an impromptu blanket. It had been a bit chilly. I recalled that every so often, a few times at least, someone had opened the door into the pitch black room, turned on and off the lights, then rolled me to one side or the other in search of their precious coats. There was a tiny square window at the edge of the room. The kind of window you'd expect in a basement or a restroom but no, I was surely lying on a bed that smelled of *Suavitel* and various perfumes.

Ooo the headache. It was the kind of headache you get from drinking too much wine too quickly. The kind, that if you stay awake long enough, you can keep it at bay with another then another, until you're just altogether drunk again.

I sat up, rubbed my eyes. Looked right, then left. The music was still blaring but it was different now. It was Mexican Country, *Rancherias,* and a live chorus was singing along like some misguided bunch of carolers.

The door creaked open and the shadow of a head peeked in.

"You fine?" It was Domi. I could smell him from four feet away.

"Yea," I said. My temples felt like there was a clamp hitched to either side of my head, "Where are we?" For a second I thought we were back home. Back at *his* home. For a split second before that, I had thought I was back in my old apartment number three.

The door creaked fully open. That light. Oh god that light from the kitchen. So bright. So unwavering and unforgiving. His shadow casted over me as I winced up to meet his gaze then found it missing in the contrast.

"There," he said with an outstretched arm. "Drink that."

"Vodka?" my voice's pitch rising towards the end. Me still thinking I was funny.

"No. It's water," he tried to appear in good spirits but his voice echoed with annoyance. Had I really been so bad? Immediate moral hangover. He said he left me some.

"Where?" My right eye was killing me. That sinus cavity always gave me trouble. I think it was because I always fell asleep on that side. The boogers pooling up and drying, leaving me with only one nostril to breathe.

That light, again, from beyond the door, those mocking waves of laughter.

"There. On the table," he took his left hand that he'd been using to clutch the doorknob and pointed to a little dresser to my right. There sat a glass. An actual glass-glass. The people who owned that place must've been really fancy. I had grown so accustomed to nothing but plastic and that taste of BP-something. I downed it like it was rumplemintz. It was only eight ounces. I was used to mason jars back home. Gotta keep hydrated right?

"You want some more?" the shadow of Domi asked, the bright light behind him, a halo of sorts. His head was so small. Why is it so small? Lanky, tiny man. His arms for miles and the pants of his legs were so well fitted it looked like two thin rods with hinges. I tried to make out his features but all I could see were the outlines of his beard and mustache. Everything so nice and neat. We'd been visited by aliens from the land of "a big head's not fashionable anymore. Have you seen my Louis Vuitton luggage?"

"Yes... please. Do they have bigger glasses? Why is your head so small?" I managed, trying to stretch the muscles on my face through various expressions.

He let out an amused huff from his nose, "My dad used to call me *cabezita*. Little head."

"Maybe you're *special?"*

"MAYBE you're just a drunk that has to make a scene everywhere we go."

"Quite possible. Did I make a scene?" I pouted, my eyes drawn down at the corners. Had I really made another scene? My friends sometimes joked about how much trouble I got into. When we'd go out drinking, there'd be an instant when I'd transform into a giant drunk baby. At least they portrayed me kindly as a giant drunk BUT entertaining baby. About the worst thing I ever did was disappear into the night or take my pants off and whip out my dick. But there, in Guadalajara, where could I run to? Who could I show my penis to? Everything seemed so far. I was still a bit shell shocked from the flight over and the drive into the center of city. If I got lost, I'd get lost forever. The last thought echoed in my ear. Inviting.

He drew closer. He smelled so nice. Always. Even after the gym, or before, he'd spritz on some cologne. It was never really the same cologne. He had a slew of them. A whimsical chemistry lab for each and every occasion. For a split second I remembered being afraid he would hit me. I don't know why the thought had entered my head but I flinched. He laughed and pulled my throbbing head into his belly as he stood there. We rocked side to side.

"Eres un cabron," he whispered as he kissed the top of my head, then pulled it back by my hair and planted a smooch on my lips. I kept mine pursed as the faint sliver of his tongue graced them.

"Why don't you want to kiss me?" he asked still holding my head back by the hair: this mangy, long, unruly thing.

"Because you smell like caca."

"No YOU smell like caca. Caca and vomit."

"Elma lent me her perfume," I countered, "And why am I a *cabron?"*

He laughed, "*Menso*, you tried kissing her.... and Alice... and Anabel...."

"Oh god, please don't tell me I tried kissing Luis Raul."

"Jejeje, no. But you kept slapping David's ass."

"Did you get jealous?" I winced my eyes mischievously.

"No. *Te conosco*, I know you didn't mean anything by it. BUT if it had been anyone else, I would've punched you in the face."

"Good. Besides, I don't like David. He makes too many faces."

"And what about Elma and Alice? Anabel? Do you like them?"

"Do they have money?"

"Jejejej, no. Not one *peso*. Ay, Elma still owes me for dinner last week. She never pays me back though."

"You know what they say: Money lent to friends is best considered a gift never seen again... or something like that. Ow, my head. Do they still have whiskey? Can I have whiskey? Are you made out of whiskey? Come kiss me, Whiskey."

"No," he flicked back my head and I fell down into the coats.

"Buu... I want a divorce."

"*Bueno*, tomorrow I'll leave your things out by the front door."

"With whiskey?"

"No."

"Buuuu... *bueno,* we can stay married then."

He was standing with his legs between my thighs. I squeezed my knees. I could've broken him if I tried. I felt my dick get hard with pre cum. We swayed some more in the dark. I wanted to fuck him right then and there. We hadn't really ever fucked. Never. No penetration. He always said I was too thick. Ah fooey. But, it being *Crissmass* and all... I sat up and tried unbuckling his belt. The thing was like a fucking Rubik's cube. Thin and slender like him, almost just a rope. He just stood there and laughed at me. Said I was too drunk. I said no, baby, please. He laughed again.

He smiled, "Now? With the door wide open?"

"Yes. It's about time Elma learned that we're not really *just* friends."

He scoffed, "Oh please, every morning she tells me you fart too loud."

"I do not," and then I farted really loud.

He pinched his nose with his left hand and attempted unsuccessfully to wave away the stench of no food in my belly but lots and lots of gas gas gas. From outside, Elma laughed then shouted, "*No mames*, what the fuck was that?"

I yelled back as Domi was calling me a *cochino,* "Something died up Domi's ass!"

I then tried getting up off of the bed. The room spun for a second but not the kind of second that lasts forever. It was a wee bit of a moment but just long enough for Domi to take notice.

"Careful, don't fall again," he said.

"Again?" I smiled and shuffled towards the door.

"Yes, you fell in the kitchen. In front of these really pretty girls. One of their boyfriends was gonna fuck you up."

"And where were you? Mister *till death do us part?"*

"WELL," his eyebrows rose, "I was pouring you a glass of water. Turned my back for a second and you were about to fight with the biggest guy in the room. I'm not lying. He was all muscle, no neck."

"Is... he.... single?" I smiled and hunched over, the weight of my shoulders suddenly sending me a little off balance.

He laughed, "Not anymore. I gave him my number."

"Whore," I winced at him threateningly

"*Puta* wanna fight everyone," he parried.

"Touché," I laughed then "strutted" into a kitchen, which was larger than the one back at Domi's, where everyone was sitting at a square pale wooden table. White marbled floor tile, white washed cabinets and drawers, and ceramic counters of a pale almost peach color whose squares were about two inches. They had fancy cutlery displayed around it. That kind of knife holder made out of wood. There were ladles and spatulas in a white pottery. A small wooden cutting board was left out next to a Santa themed red towel, on it, the remnants of limes. I even remember thinking that the blender looked fancy.

"Hey Marveen!" Elma sang out then patted the seat of a white wooden chair beside her. Inviting and friendly, she commented on how nice it was to see me alive, "How'd you sleep?" she giggled mockingly.

I rubbed the right side of my face, "My head hurts and Domi farted on me." He sat down across from us and said *"Sure,"* smacked his lips then stared out into the dark and dimly lit living room behind me.

"Hey! Marv! You doing okay? Want another drink?" Alice, perpendicular to my right, inquired, saying the last part jokingly as she shuffled a deck of cards.

"Yes. Please and thank you," I responded.

"Really?" astonished, she had Domi cut the deck, "If I were you, I'd cut back on the drinky-drink for a few."

"Ugh, and if I were you... I'd mind my own freakin' business, Mom. Fucks shit sake I need a beer," I laughed as my eyes widened then squinted. I was thinking of what would be the closest thing to throw at her.

Domi, "Don't start," he forced a laugh of his own then picked out a card from the top as Alice proffered the set then set it down on the table.

"Where is everybody?" I wondered out loud.

Alice laughed, "They all left. After you passed out, there was a fight outside and Lencho here told everyone to go home."

"What was the fight about?" I asked, not really caring but carrying on the conversation.

"Who knows?" Domi shrugged and Elma clicked her tongue then picked a card from the deck after the other four people had. I didn't recognize them or faintly recalled maybe having had said hi at some point in the evening. They all seemed tired but wired on something and chained smoked incessantly. There was a guy I'm guessing was Lencho, who owned the place. He had short cropped, blondish hair. To his left was a slim fellow with long dark hair done up like a rooster. Beside that guy was a dude in a baseball hat who stared wide eyed at the screen of his phone, scrolling then laughing intermittently. Behind the three stood a girl with the sides of her head shaven down and the top of her hair combed low to a point. She smiled at me, turned her chin up then walked to the sink to put out her cigarette.

"Marveen, it's your turn," Domi handed over the deck then leaned back into his chair. I started to reach over for a card, Alice sipped at her drink then raised a brow.

"Wait," I pulled my hand back, "What are we playing?"

Lencho smiled then tapped his card on the table, "Highest card wins."

"Oh," my shoulders dropped and I looked around for a clock. Kitchens have clocks, right? I suddenly remembered that I always wore a watch. It was either 6:30 am in El Paso or 7:30 am, next Tuesday, in Guadalajara.

"Hurry," Domi said, holding up his card against his nose. Elma did the same but crossed her eyes and they broke into this sort of deep, low laughter. The dark haired guy tapped the cherry off his cigarette and into an ashtray that lay hidden somewhere in the middle of that table behind napkins and plastic disposable cups.

"Hurry, dude," the guy in the hat slowly traced his card along the O of his mouth.

I sighed, picked out a card then flipped it over: Seven of hearts.

"Buuuu" a chorus from the peanut gallery. Lencho slammed his card down on the table, a Queen of Diamonds.

"Hurry, fuckers!" he grinned then leaned back in his chair. He was a bit plump but not bad looking. His nose, small like a button. His face was red and the blood tended to gather in his cheeks. He put his hands behind his head, elbows outstretched.

"BAAAAAA," Elma and Domi laughed then each took a sip from their respective cups. Alice cut the deck and smiled. I leaned in towards her.

"So what's next?"

She dropped the deck on the table, "How do you like *mezcal?"*

"Depends. Ashtray chaser or straight up?"

She grinned, a bit puzzled.

"Never mind. I'm just saying... *deja vu....*"

She narrowed her lips, made this sort of smiling frown then opened her mouth and her teeth like a row of pearls. She slapped my shoulder. The dark haired guy cleared a path in the middle of the table, lined up several shot glasses, then poured out a liquor from some yellow tinted bottle about seven inches high. It was wrapped in twine up to the shoulder, right before the neck. He smiled like a boy holding a spider, creeping right up from behind his unsuspecting sister. The cork went ploop.

Six shots, seven people. I suppose highest card gets spared. Happy Christmas. Raise a glass, wish you were here, hoped they liked "chunks".

"What are you up to, Marveen?" Elma asked, her shoulders hung low and inward as she walked into the kitchen, opened the fridge and leaned into it, staring blankly as the dull yellow light emphasized her puffy eyes.

"I couldn't sleep," I shrugged and finished sweeping the floor by the furthest wall. It was about 2 am and I leaned the broom against a corner then started to wipe the counter table. The living room was dark, the only window at the front of the house being in Luis Raul's "chamber", where every so often, you could see the headlights from a car beam through. The Christmas lights he had tacked on the wall around a Lana Del Rey poster, casting another faint glow.

Elma pulled out a half gallon of milk, set it on the table, then hunted down a tumbler from the cabinets by the sink. She popped the top, poured herself some half ways into a pink plastic cup, took a drink, slow, like the cold was too much for her teeth or maybe it was too abrasive to the roof of her mouth. She smacked her lips and sighed like a child actor in a TV commercial and put her weight against the table with one arm.

Wipe. Wipe. Wipe. Scrub, "You know, you shouldn't drink milk before bed."

She furrowed her brows then looked distantly into the ether between tomorrows and todays. She ignored my comment and said, "I couldn't sleep either."

I folded the dishcloth that I had been using to wipe everything and their mother, twice, then folded it again into fours and attacked the uneven grooves on the counter table.

"Yea, damn...whatever... the fuck... this ... is... But it'll give you phlegm," I sighed and wiped some sweat from my brow. It was the real sweat too. Not the fake movie sweat. Why was I sweating so much? Why do these people not have air conditioning? I missed vodka, "They say you shouldn't give babies a bottle before bed. Something about how they can choke on their own spit."

Her eyes rolled to the side and she took a seat and another sip defiantly.

I sighed. She laughed and said, "I love it when you sigh. You're always sighing. What's wrong?"

I turned around and leaned my back into the counter table, "Nothing", I sighed, "I guess my circadian rhythm is just set to the bar schedule. Then again, when I was little, I used to stay up all night cleaning the kitchen. Listening to the radio. Blaring it while everyone was just hush. Hush and asleep. Every so often someone would stumble into the bathroom. I'd hear a toilet flush and then go back to scrubbing with some black man singing soul and a wall of sound and a hey Mr. Postman. Also, I dunno, Domi's weird. He's like a grandpa. All he ever says is that he has to work in the morning."

She hunched over onto the table, rested her body on her elbows and used a free hand to rub the back of her neck. She popped up her head and blew a puff of hair from her face. Such pronounced features: An almost ruddy brown sheet of skin. Worn lines and mascara that she never seemed able to wash away. Her long straight nose that bulged out at the end. Her large oval eyes that became sweet almonds at the edges. She almost looked like a man. Like some glamorous transvestite who could barely pull it off.

"Really?" she blurted out like a child who's refused bed. Hyper, interested in everything but not entirely aware of what was exactly happening. Her gaze drifted nervously every now and then, almost coquettishly, "You have any cigarettes?"

"Yes," I said as I was about to grab the broom again, "Hold up, lemme get them from the..."

She raised her hand, elbows still on the table, her head now down, "No, wait," and after a pause, lifted her head, pointed out her chin, eyes still closed she bathed in the warm glow of the ceiling light. It was this tiny thing. Looked like a spike. Like a super charged tinsel light or the type of bulbs they use for cars. Why is everything so weird in Mexico? She went on, "I have some in the room too. Anyway, I don't want you disturbing Grandpa's beauty sleep," she laughed then stood up, then dragged her feet into the hallway.

I pulled out a chair. The one that was heavy. It rubbed this deep sound out of the linoleum floor. I hated the floors. Everything was either dirty old linoleum or dirty old tile. Not once had I been invited into a home with wood floors. All the houses or apartments were grimy and old but the kind of old that didn't very well seem "lived in", just sort of abused and uncared for. Nobody had real furniture. Me and Domi slept on a mattress, on the floor, in the corner of a room with no closet. He had lent me this one dresser drawer that barely fit anything of mine. For the most part, I just lived out of my luggage that he stared at discontentedly every now and then. We fought often about the space and messes and how I smelled or that I didn't wash my penis enough. Fuck, we didn't even have hot water.

A minute later, she was back. I heard a wisp of music as she opened and closed her door. I said, "We should get a radio for the kitchen," my eyes said I should start sleeping more than three hours a night. I ran a hand through my hair, more rubbing my scalp than anything. She sat down, tapped the cigarette box on the table then took out a ciggie and lit it. She turned the half gallon of milk around and began examining the nutrient label, winced and took another drag, stretched out her hand and offered me a puff but I waved it away politely with a No thank you.

She laughed, "It's basically all fat. Fat and calcium," then leaned back in her chair which gave a quiet squeak in nod to her slender frame. Her arms now crossed with the one that held the cigarette up in the air, she began to examine me, "Why didn't you turn on the TV?"

"I didn't want to wake Luis Raul."

She scoffed, "No worries. That dude sleeps through the smoke detector," then she hunched over towards me as if to tap the cigarette in an ashtray but there was none.

"Shit," she said before pouring a splash of milk into her cup and ashing it there, "Voila!"

I smiled and scratched the side of my head behind my ear, "When I started cleaning I thought I was making too much noise, but the fucker hasn't stopped snoring. Like seriously. I'm worried. People die of sleep apnea, right?"

We both chuckled a bit. I leaned in and stretched out my right arm, "Here, gimmie some," then took a drag and passed it back.

She took a puff then smiled. Big old wide mouth, horse like teeth. Just ear-to-ear kind of genuine sleepy eyed grin. Cheshire and Alice in the woods.

She tapped the ciggie over the cup and I asked, "How's work?"

To which she responded after biting a lip: "Shitty. I have to go in tomorrow at eight. But at least I got Saturday off so life's just peachy keen. And how are things with you?"

"Fine, fine," I tapped my fingers on the table then rubbed my hands into my face, took a good stretch with my elbows out. Breathed out under the strain, "Every thing's good. I think Domi's gets annoyed because I sleep in so much. But I mean, I hardly sleep at all. It's usually just naps. And he's not even fucking here. I think Luis Raul has been snitching on me."

She laughed and tapped then ashed again and said, "My poor Domi. I think he thought that you'd ride in on a white horse and become a famous *poeta*," still laughing, she took another drag then passed what was barely the butt of a cigarette. She exhaled, lips drawn tight now, "But that, *amiga*, is pretty hard."

I turned right in my seat, smiled, rested my right elbow on the back of the chair, cupping my head and rubbing my hair. I stared at the filter then reluctantly decided to get up and over to the sink, ran a little water over it then tossed it in the bin.

I reached over for the milk and opened the fridge whose door stuck a little, or maybe just my strength had long since dissipated between the dust bunnies and the stains. I put it back in between the mustard and Sriracha sauce then stared vacantly into the abyss of yellowing broccoli and a mysterious tupperware that had been there for at least two weeks. For some reason it felt as if I was beginning to mirror the house. Its lack of amenities, the simple poverty of decor, or more aptly, the haphazardly strewn together design, was beginning to weigh heavily on me. The place began to almost mock me. It screamed NO SUBSTANCE, that I'M JUST A SPACE. The idea of transience pervading everything, like we were one step up from lying on soiled futons with beer cans littered about us in piles and pissing in corners. I was surprised they hadn't thought to drag an oil drum to the center and grill squirrels on a side turned shopping cart.

Sarcastically she said, "I don't think I've ever seen the fridge so full," then rubbed the back of her head.

I smiled, "I know. It WOULD take a fatty to make you guys' buy, quote-unquote, groceries. When I first got here, I think you people had a packet of ketchup. And, seriously, like it was an opened packet of ketchup. Like, who does that?" then I accidentally slammed the door shut. I did a quick 180 and we both just stared at each other in silence. Like children after having had shattered a priceless family heirloom. Oh no, the Ming Vase...The absence of Luis Raul's snore precipitating Domi opening and slamming his door because that's just what he did sometimes when we were too loud.

A tense second later, a snort, then a snore. There was no slamming of doors and we, in the clear, stared away from each other and silently gave ourselves benedictions. I leaned against the sink, something so tiny with the caulking long since gone from around its edges. When you live with people, the messes seem to become that much more apparent. Why we had spaghetti sauce stains on the tile behind the faucet? No clue. Nobody cooked. You ate ramen that you microwaved because nobody wanted to up the gas bill. Most of us smoked rather than ate and when we were hungry it was so much easier to just walk down the street, and grab twenty tacos for a dollar or a bag of chips. I missed home. I missed dinner parties and conversations that didn't revolve around the latest Nylon magazine or how high up in the social ladder your one friend or a friend of a friend was. I missed the nothing and the big wide open and having a horizon with a sunset. I missed the bells not tolling every few minutes after seven in the morning. I missed so much and felt that the city had given me so little. Granted there were a ton of pretty people and most were genuinely nice. The only thing was that the manner of friends I had made seemed to all stem from the same place, Chihuahua, and half the time, I felt that they only talked to me because I was dating their friend. The few locals I had met, we had taken to fabulously but I never got to hang around them. I never got to do the really local kind of things because my dance card had been written for this tight circle with little avenue for social mobility. To this day, I'll never understand why people move away just to hang around the same fucking folk they hung around with in their home towns.

These people lived these lives where they worked like dogs forever to just party or drink or get high. Although the cost of living was low, the pay was even lower. Your jobs wanted you there long hours. Long shifts with no real in between time save for maybe a Sunday. But everything, everything was just sort of up in the air. You had no furniture. You could move in and out of other people's homes with ease but, in reality, it spoke more so to the fact that nobody had a real home. Nobody had a real place. You were mired in some routine, but everybody was just as expendable as the cheap plastic everything which permeated our lives. Everybody had nice and fashionable looking clothes, but the colors would run, the fabrics would stretch, and the seams themselves would come undone after the second or third wash. Everybody was just wandering around trying to make it in a city where ambition was little more than what you wore and the *"aft-errrs"* you were invited to.

Elma shifted left in her seat and propped an arm against the backrest just as I had. She nestled her chin in it then stretched out her legs and said, "But don't worry, *amiga*. Don't lose faith. *Hechale ganas.* In no time, you'll have us stocking TWO packets of ketchup. If you really get lucky, we might even splurge and go in for some mayo. And if you do get famous, we could probably afford a bag of apples or something."

I smiled and then accidentally blew out some boogers, laughed then wiped my upper lip with my sleeve, "That was random," I said then stared at my right hand as if I could discern the amount of veins and vessels in a second. Must've been thousands upon thousands of itty-bitty boulevards. I confessed, "I knew this was gonna happen. I mean I have no real marketable skills besides dropping off food at peoples tables and speaking English."

She frowned thoughtfully, "Well why don't you do that? Teach English?"

I smiled, " Just imagine me, 'be-eer'-- '*cerveza*'."

She smiled and traced invisible lines into the table, "Or you could get a job in a restaurant. Just walk down *Chapultepec*. They're always hiring. AND you can get us the hook up."

"No. Because none of you put out," then I whispered, "Dude, it's been like forever since I got laid. Like, seriously, it's just hand jobs and BJ's. I'm just all like, what the fuck?"

She averted my gaze and rolled her shoulders.

I went on, "I mean, I get it. He works long hours and he has to sleep or something. But I can't even stick a finger to the first knuckle up his hole without some bullshit. I dunno. Maybe I shouldn't be telling you these things but, JESUS, why the fuck did I move down here then?"

She pursed her lips, "Well, do you try and be the... uhm... the girl sometimes?"

"I've tried but it's not the same. I have to be super horny. But, I mean, is that normal? I feel like we skipped the honeymoon and went straight to the 'I secretly hate you but we bought matching cemetery plots' phase."

She just shrugged again and was about to take a sip from the cup we'd been ashing in. She stopped herself just before, and started laughing, "I'm so stupid", she confessed.

I loved her. I knew I loved her the moment we met. Well, the second time, at least. Maybe sleep deprivation had just made me delirious, but if I was straight, I'd totally hit that. Oh my god, I thought to myself, had I been so sex deprived that the thought of sticking it in a girl seemed palpable. For a second I humored the notion. In my mind's eye I saw us kissing. That was nice. Then underwear and rubbing. That was nice. Then, ewooo, that looks like the desert monster from Star Wars with the big teeth! And finally me crying, huddled in the corner of the shower, rocking back and forth.

I stepped back into the moment, "I don't think my Spanish is good enough. Also, Mexicans tip like shit."

She nodded in agreement. Every time we went out it seemed almost customary to NOT tip. Things that are lost in translation... A culture of people who expected everything but rarely ever left a monetary thank you note.

She slanted her head to the left, the length of her black hair coming to a point just above the clavicle, "Maybe you could sell your art?"

I smacked my lips, "It's all back in El Paso. Besides, there's no room to paint here. Maybe I should move out. I've never really lived with anybody. Even when I was back at my mom's, for the longest time, I had like my own door and I would even go outside to take a piss. And, hey, listen, I know I smell; you know I smell. But, seriously, I swear I can smell everybody up in this place. It just smells like PEOPLE. Even when it's perfume or cologne, it's just weird and nauseating.

And most of the time it just smells like feet and farts and butt sweat. I just don't think I was meant to cohabitate."

She went mmm then said, "Ay, you swear. YOU'RE the one who stinks up everything. I honestly don't even know how you still smell like dogs. But you have this aroma of mutt and hangover. I mean it's not bad... You just sort of smell like an old man. Like mothballs or something. You just sort of smell like, I don't know, 'Marveen'. Anyhow, what about Anabel? You haven't talked to her about maybe renting a space or something?"

"She messaged me the other day but I don't know. She's a bit annoying. The art scene seems so pretentious. I guess it's like that everywhere, though. Just here the kids have their daddy's money. I mean, well, I think. Domi says I need new clothes," I laughed to myself then continued, "The other day, I tried on one of his shirts and it ripped where he had sewn it. Like where he had had it tailored to fit better. I hid it at the bottom of the laundry pile. Today in the morning he was looking for it but I just pretended to be asleep."

We both laughed and she quietly slapped the table before reaching for another cigarette. I went on, "Anyway, they're just so full of themselves. It's more about dressing the part than actually making anything. About dressing well or intentionally not dressing well to prove you're something. That and they're like always high. I mean, I get it, I know I drink a lot but, GEEZUS. I mean you all just come home from work for lunch and hit the bowl. Dude, the other day Anabel was showing me some art some dude she knows makes. It's like screen-printing designer labels but he puts Indians on it. It just looks like he picked up a copy of Nylon and decided that what Chanel needed was a *Tarahumara* holding a baby. I guess it means something. Maybe I should do more things like that. Maybe I should smoke more, but, I dunno... "

She seemed interested, "*Neta?* Actually that kind of sounds like a good idea. What's the guys name?"

"Martin something but he has like a nick name that means lizard or something. Why does every Mexican have a nickname? I mean I'm pretty sure that they've given me one by now but it's *probably* not flattering. Anabel calls me *pinche gringo* all the time. Does that count? Does that mean that I'm *in?* "

She laughed softly, mouth just open and barely breathing out a whisper with the smoke she exhaled. She ashed then said, "Ah, I think I know who you're talking about. His name is *La Lagartija*. And yeah, his parents are big shots somewhere down in *Chihuahua.* I think they have some kind of trucking business. Import/export."

I smiled then motioned over for the cigarette, "So what you're saying is: 'drugs'."

She yawned then smiled, "Something like that. And yeah, I buy weed from him sometimes. But hey, you're right: You're always drunk. So why are you being such a hypocrite? I can smoke and do my job. If anything, I do a better job high than when I'm sober."

"Yeah but it's not the same. I'm telling you! I don't like drinking and drawing. There's this different kind of high you get. Like in the *zone* type of shit. You just get lost in the painting or the sketching or the lines and the drips."

"Ah," she stretched out her arms and clasped her hands, "Well maybe you should take your own advice and quit drinking so much. I haven't seen you paint or draw since you showed up. I thought you artists just drew all the time, like in coffee shops, or in the park, or something like that."

"No, well, I need to write more. Drinking brings that out. Besides, I'll get sick if I don't. I just need to finish this book and then I can hopefully get some money out of it. Take Domi on vacation, buy you cigarettes, buy Luis Raul some gum, etcetera."

She smiled while the cigarette ash fell onto the table. I could tell she was tired and about ready to call it a night as she tried unsuccessfully to scoop it off the surface and into her hand, "That'd be nice. You know, I've never been partial to flowers. But the men who buy me cigarettes, I usually suck their dick. And," she yawned, "what have you written so far, anyway?"

I bit the bottom of my mouth and tugged with my teeth at a sliver of flesh from my parched lips, "Hmmm... well, some stuff about my dad's funeral. About how like when we were getting things all squared away, my mom's car wouldn't stop beeping and funny shit like that which happened. I wish I had been more sober though. Stuff's kind of a blur. I was thinking about writing a fake account of my mother on vacation around the world. But, I dunno, I just don't know anything about the world, ya' know?"

She tossed the butt of the ciggie in the cup of milk and leaned back in her chair. Another slight protesting squeak. She smiled and crossed her arms, "Write about her visiting *Guadalajara* then."

I blew out a puff of air from my nose in protest, "Ewoo, gross. *I* don't even want to be here."

She pursed her lips and then, "Now what? *Te quejas de todo*. Also, don't let Domi hear you say that."

I stared up at the ceiling in desperation. Stains running tiny rivers in the roof, "I don't know. I'm starting to think that this entire thing was a bad idea. Like I don't even want to drink. That's how stressed out I am about not doing anything right with my life," I bit my lip again, "Besides, honestly, I don't think he'd be too upset about me moving back. He's different. I'm different. I guess it's just different being in the same room with someone all the time and, like, you know, when I was over there, we wanted to see each other. Like we missed each other. Now I just imagine that he's bored with me. Like he feels he has to talk to me instead of WANTING to talk to me, which just makes me NOT want to talk to him at all. And then he gets mad and says I'm being snobby and offish. He says that I swear that my time is so precious. Ay, dude, sometimes, I swear, and you're gonna think I'm lying but there'll be times when I catch him just staring at me. Like I can feel his eyes boring holes into my head and I turn around. For a split second I can see him hating me. Like he's imagining throwing a shoe at the back of my head as I leave the room. His eyes are just wild. Like crazy big all consuming orbs with that white at the edges. Last time he asked why I always walk backwards into the hallway. I just winced at him and kept shuffling in reverse. Maybe I'm just going crazy. Maybe I'm just paranoid. I dunno."

She scrunched her face in disbelief, a bit troubled by the outpouring of neuroses, "Wait, what do you mean? And what do you mean about not drinking? You had like four of those orange juice shits at dinner."

In protest, "Yea, but I mean, like right now, when I woke up, I didn't want to drink. I felt I needed to do something. Some thing sober. Like I needed to clear my head."

She stretched again, this time just a wee bit longer, "*No mames*, so then sit down and draw. Sit down and write," her palms now up in the air, as if reiterating how simple the process was.

"No," I had walked over to the freezer and pulled out the vodka then pulled up a chair next to hers. I took a swig then said, "It's not that easy. I know they say 'Just write'. That inspiration is the crutch of the novice. But," another swig, "honestly", I tapped my fingers on the table, "I feel like I have nothing to say," I bit my lip, "All I do is get drunk and pass out on Domi's bed. I mean, FUCK, it's not even MY bed. It's HIS blankets and this is HIS milk!" I flicked a finger against the cup and heard my nail pop on the plastic, "This house, these things, and now I don't even feel like he's mine. Ag! I just don't know what to do. I had everything and I gave it all up for this! For some one else's dream," I frowned, my eyes suddenly heavy and a bit watery from frustration.

She raised the right corner of her mouth and stared off into the table then tapped my knee, "That's life. That's love. That's how things go. That's how you just feel sometimes."

I shook my head. She laughed.

"Marveen, well then why did you move? Why did you sell everything and come down here if you were so happy over there? You left because you weren't. And things come and go.

People, come and go. You can't be living your life afraid of that. IT'S ONE OF THE FEW THINGS YOU CAN BE SURE OF. It's like that, death, and taxes."

"No, that's just it. I WAS happy. Well, I think I was. The whole my dad dying sent me for a loop but I was coping. I've spent so many years being depressed and bullied but I had a nice apartment. I had this awesome fridge. I had a garden, I had fish, my birds, my dogs. I had this really good group of friends and a decent job. I gave it all up just to do the same thing I was doing over there, here: nothing. Absolutely. Fucking. Nothing."

She leaned in on her left arm, elbow on the table and cupped her chin in her hand. With her right, she traced some more imaginary lines on the metal surface, "Well, I don't know what to tell you. Only that change is good. It's good to expand your horizons. It's good to get out of your comfort zone. You only live once. And if you're worried that you're doing the same thing here that you were doing over there, then the problem's really not your location. The problem's you. I think you think that things are going to define you. That where you live is somehow going to make or break you. But they don't and it's not. You always talk about your stuff. You're not that boring, Marveen. You don't need objects to impress people. Have you seen my room? That shit's a mess! But I still get laid."

"Pffft! What 'horizons'? And I know. I've always said that you take heaven and hell with you no matter where you go. I just feel stuck in a rut and sort of adrift at the same time. THAT and we don't even have Netflix! My GOD why don't we have Netflix?!"

She laughed then patted my knee again then stood up to stretch, "Well, kiddo, save the rest for next week's session. I'm off to bed."

"Okay," I said a bit downtrodden.

"Good night. Don't stay up too late, you hear?" she looked back, biting her own lip in contemplation.

"Good night and don't worry, I won't."

She walked out past the fridge and into the dark. A second later, her head peeked out from the doorway as she held onto the frame, "Hey, Marveen", I looked up from the bottle, still tapping my fingers on the table, "We'll see about getting you that radio for the kitchen," then she smiled benevolently and pointed a finger, warning, "But if Domi starts complaining about the noise, that shit's all on you," then she receded back into the dark.

I pulled a paper napkin from the holder in the middle of the table. There was a blue pen randomly lying there, I picked it up. I loved blue pens. I wrote, "So, there was this one time..." Ugh! I chucked the pen back to the center of the table. The ink was black.

I leaned in, rubbed my hands through my hair then began to fold the napkin into fours until it was just this thick, squarish ball. In my head, words resonated, "Dear Diary..."

"Here, *bebe*," Domi walked into the room as I was standing by the bed, folding a blanket. He kissed my lips, sweetly, with a peck and grinned, "I got you something. Ta-da!" from behind his back, he pulled out a small white canvas about two feet high and a foot and a half wide. Some pre-fab number, wrapped in plastic with a triangular label at the bottom corner, which had splashes of color and a cartoon palette.

Pleased with himself, he proclaimed, "Now you can get back to painting!" he smiled broadly and stood there with a foolish look on his face.

I just rolled my eyes and threw myself, face down, onto the bed then muffled out, "Budd ah wan-ed ah ray-dee-oh!"

I turned my head in time to catch his joy whither as fast as his arms, and the canvas, swung down to his sides. Defeated and annoyed, he said, "*No mames,* what the fuck? Are you serious?" his eyes narrowed, his lips curled incredulously.

I got up quickly then grabbed him by both shoulders, "I'm just kidding, man," but he wouldn't look me in the face. With my right hand, I began to pull his chin up but he shook me off.

"Get away from me!" he hissed then sat down on the mattress. Naturally, I turned, sat down beside him, and tried wrapping my arm over his shoulders but he wasn't having any of it.

I sighed then grabbed his hand, "Hey, I'm sorry. I was really just kidding. What's the big deal?"

He looked off into the other direction then turned back at me and sullenly said, “Don’t worry, I’m over it."

I took a deep breath, "Oh. No. You. Don't. You say that now, and then two days later, I get some angry email while you're at work, after you've been chit-chatting with your gal-pals, and they suddenly convince you, that there's something you need to get off your chest that's been festering for like a gazillion years. Dude, I still have that screenshot from that essay you sent me about how I need to start leaving the toilet seat down because there's a woman who lives in our house. And I showed it to Elma, and she said she didn't fucking care!"

"Ay, you know it's just polite. I hate having guests over and them thinking we live like animals. But no, it's fine."

"BULLSHIT. I ain't falling for that crap again!"

"I swear! It's fine! It's just that you're so rude sometimes. You don't know how to act and it's like living with a child. A big, fat, retarded child," he laughed, now a bit less cross, composed himself, then grabbed my face with both hands and smooshed it in then flicked my head back, "Ah..." he went dreamy eyed, "And all day long, I was really looking forward to giving you this. I spent like an hour at the store wondering which one to get, or what to get, and it was so hard trying to find anybody to help me too. And then when I finally found somebody, they asked me what kind of paint you use and I couldn't remember so I had to ask for their Wi-Fi password so I could check out your website, which took forever to load, and just had a bunch of half naked photos of you and some other dudes... So just imagine..." and after suspiring at the last two thoughts, he continued, "*Esque... eres un malcreado.* You don't know how to appreciate things or the things people do for you and sometimes it just gets too much. And I am so over it right now. I mean, what else would I expect from someone like you? You're just always ungrateful and bratty."

"Ugh! Name once!"

He then started counting off on his fingers, "Tuesday, I brought you leftovers from work, you didn't even say thank you, and I caught you giving them to that stupid alley cat!"

I gasped, "He's my only friend!..."

"... Wednesday, we went grocery shopping and instead of getting my cookies, we got yours...."

"Ah! Dude! You totally said you didn't care which! BESIDES, if I recall correctly, you said you weren't having carbs that week because since I moved in, you've supposedly gained two pounds or something..."

"...Thursday, I cooked you a fancy dinner and you just got drunk, gorged yourself, then threw it up because you said you felt too full..."

"Ugh! I'm lactose intolerant, Domi! Do you want me to die of stomach cramps?!"

"...IT WAS SALMON, MARVEEN! Yesterday, instead of going out with David to this opening, I stayed home with you to watch movies because you said you have nothing to wear..."

"Ugh! They don't sell anything in my size here! The last thing I found that fit me was a RAIN poncho! I can't even find boots larger than a size 9! All I have are tennis shoes! And remember, you're the one who gets all uppity if I don't borrow Luis Raul's slacks when we go out for dinner..."

"...You see, all you do is make excuses! I sacrifice so much for you, practically do everything you want, give you everything you need, and you turn around and act so UNGRATEFUL."

"Geezus! I WAS JUST KIDDING!" I threw my arms up and accidentally hit his nose in the process. He winced in pain and fell away. I covered my mouth in shock and he mumbled out, "Fuck, you're fucking kidding me," then punched me in the arm really hard.

He went on, still cradling his nose, his eyes red and watery, "No you weren't. Or you always are. You're never serious about anything! You may not realize it but you're crude and you treat people like shit. You don't respect anybody, not even yourself. You swear your time is so precious; you swear it's fucking gold. I've never met anyone like you who thinks so highly of themselves and doesn't do shit! You just sit around getting drunk and daydreaming. You live a fucking mediocre life, doing mediocre things, waiting for, I don't know, some magic fairy man, or gnome, or whatever it is you think is going to fall from the sky and save you."

I was still rubbing my arm but the bruises developing in my mind seemed like they needed better attention. I said, shaking my head in disbelief, "Oh god, really? Then why the fuck would you buy somebody who does nothing but 'day dream', a fucking cheap ass canvas? That's like buying a heroin addict a set of diabetic needles. And gnome? Really? 'MAGIC GNOMES? That's the best you could come up with? It couldn't have been Prince Charming or the winning Lotto Numbers? It had to be fairy people? You know what? No, never mind. You're just always like this: crabby and over sensitive."

He stood up and with derisive laughter, "Why do you always have to be the victim? Every fucking time! It's always the fucking Marvin Show, staring Marvin, written by Marvin, and sponsored by Marvin. I got you a fucking gift, man, and you couldn't even just say thank you. You can't even fucking pretend to look happy when I come home. You can't even say

Good Morning. You can't even say Goodnight because you're too busy bungling around in the kitchen till god knows what hours. You can't respect the fact that I have to wake up early. You don't have a fucking job, Marvin. You can go to sleep at the same time I do or at least not be making a fucking racket in the other room till the sun comes up! Because, god forbid that you should be holding your boyfriend at night instead of watching videos on the Internet and banging pans. You're so spoiled! Seriously, no respect for anybody! I guess your parents just didn't raise you with any sense of decorum!"

Mouth agape, I said, "Oh please! Don't lecture me on parenting. At least my father didn't go off and have a fucking other kid and all these other fucking mistresses!" and then, aside to myself, I whispered, "At least, I don't think he did..." then aloud again, "You Mexicans are the worst! All this 'machismo' crap and 'screwing over your neighbors' shit because if you don't do it first, then they're obviously gonna do it to you. And THEN you guys have the nerve to cite social protocol if I don't fucking kiss everybody on the cheek or shake everybody's hand or say Good Morning? Dude, like seriously, you just finished telling me the other day that you cheated on your old boyfriend because you were pretty sure he had done the same or was GOING to do the same damned thing. How fucked up is that? Where was your high horse then, bitch?"

Domi spit out, "What the fuck do you know about Mexicans? You're a real piece of work, you know that, Marveen? You can't even fucking roll your R's. *Por tan culero cara de nopal, ni sabes nada de tu pinche cultura!* You've lived here a few weeks and then suddenly you're an expert? And where the fuck do you get off talking shit about me and my past relationships? I may be no saint, but if you want to tally up the scores, I'm pretty sure you're going to come out losing. Mister I slept with all of El Paso and Juarez..." he then laughed angrily and began to search through the top drawer where he kept every random thing. He pulled out a watch and some gum, popped the gum in his mouth then began taking off the watch he was wearing. Seething, he put on the other watch and calmly said, "And you know what? Don't ever fucking talk about my family again unless you want to go there. Because at least my dad's not dead and AT LEAST I would NEVER use that as an excuse like you do for your little maudlin displays and lack of ambition!" then he did a quick left, walked out the room, and slammed the door behind him.

I just stood there and then yelled something stupid about his hair. It was one of those times when you just didn't have an appropriate response but felt it necessary to comment, to have the last word. I threw myself back on the bed and stared up at the ceiling. Outside, birds were singing or maybe it was just the traffic lights letting blind people know that it was okay to cross. What was I thinking? What was I doing here? My head spun and I reached for my cigarettes but the pack was empty. I threw it at the door but missed and hit the wall. So I sat up and stared at the floor. Ugly tile. I missed my wood floors. And there, by the bed, lay that stupid piece of canvas, mocking me.

I hadn't known what to do and I was too angry to drink so I just took a shot to calm my nerves and stepped out into the street. The sun was just about to set so I turned right, outside the gate, and walked in the opposite direction towards the store for a new pack of cigs. I just didn't get it. I just didn't get why I couldn't be happy or nice even when I WASN'T trying to be mean or spiteful. I was honestly just joking, but maybe people weren't always in on my jokes. By the time I doubled back, the sun had gone and I reluctantly climbed up the front steps like a child who had disappointed their favorite teacher. I walked past the kitchen where Elma was glancing at a big copy of Bazaar but I didn't say hi. I felt too ashamed at the thought that she had probably heard everything. When I walked in the room, Domi was sitting there on the mattress mulling over something. Was this it? Was this the way our relationship would peter out? His hands were clasped over his nose and mouth, his index fingers the only things pointing up, likely chanting one of his stupid mantras, and then he started:

"Listen, sit down," he patted the bedside to his left and I sighed and followed his instructions, "I know," he grabbed my right hand, "that you don't want to be here, but you could at least make a little more of an effort. Nothing's going to fall in your lap. I'm not sure if you're expecting me to just support you forever, or that one-day your dream job will fall out of the blue, but it's not going to happen. You have to go out there and look for it. You have to actually *do* something, Marveen. Relationships have to be fifty-fifty. And you should actually try and enjoy the city instead of complaining about every single, last, thing. You're not even trying to make the best of your time here and right here is where I'm trying to build a life."

I couldn't look him in the face so I just stared at his thin fingers and played with his hand, "What do you mean?" I asked, "I like it here. They have mezcal."

"Elma told me about how you've been having second thoughts..." he sighed and slapped my hand when I started to twist his thumb backwards.

I yelled out into the hallway, "Fucking Elma! *Pinche puta!"*

Elma, in the distance, yelled back, "Your mother, *guey!"*

He laughed then grabbed my knees, "Baby, it's just that I feel like I'm giving it my all, and you're just not meeting me halfway."

"YOU'VE GOT TO BE KIDDING ME!" I shot up onto my legs and began pacing the tiny room then started counting off on my own fingers: "One, look at this," I pointed to the dresser, "I have like half a drawer for my shit and I don't complain because you say that you have to have your socks folded this way and your panties folded that way and your white shirts can't touch your darks shirts..."

He sighed, cupped his chin in his right hand, and breathily said, "But, baby, you have no clothes."

"Two, we didn't even watch the movie I wanted to on Friday."

"Ay, *bebe*, but that dinosaur one seemed really stupid."

"C, I cook all the time. Like, literally, if it wasn't for me, Luis Raul would've lost those twenty pounds by now..."

"And," he waved a hand graciously, "I always tell you how good your food is."

"Duh, I'm a fatty. I know what tastes good. But I don't cook to hear you say Thank You or for some kind of praise."

He raised his right index finger, as if to make a point, "But I do it anyways because it's just proper etiquette."

I sighed and sat back down besides him, "But that's not the point," I slapped the back of my right hand into the palm of my other, "The point is... wait, where was I going with this?" I stared up at the ceiling and he just laughed then he said, "The point is that you don't even know what you're saying."

"No," I shook my head, "The point is that I am grateful for everything, and all the things that you've done for me, and the things that you do, but I don't always, like, maybe...," I ran my hands in a circle, trying to conjure the words from the air, "... like always show it because I don't expect people to always show it. It's like, I know my friends like me so I don't invent these tests for them. Like I cannot hear from them or talk to them for years, and we can just pick up right where we left off. I'm not there holding a grudge because they never sent me a Happy Veteran's Day card. I don't expect people I love to be one way or another, just as long as they're not intentionally trying to be mean to me, or like, if they at least don't smoke all my cigarettes. I used to hate when people would tell me that they loved me because after the fact, they'd just stand there with their stupid faces waiting for a response. Yeah, like that face that you're making right now. I'll say it when I say it.

Because if I say, it I mean it. Well I used to. Since then, I've learned that it's just an easy way to get what you want. And, seriously, why do you get mad if I don't tell you Good Morning in the kitchen after I've spent the last fifteen minutes touching your ding dong? I think the issue is that you're more preoccupied by the way things look than by the way things actually are."

He laughed, "No, I think the issue is that you are so spoiled, uneducated and spoiled. Every other day Elma or Luis Raul ask me if something's wrong with us because you never say hi to me. You just wake up and say something stupid then hide in the room. And then you only come out when you need a refill. Don't you see that it's like living with a ghost? The truth is, you're worrying everybody. But I just don't want to fight anymore. Forget everything and just give me a kiss already. I have the feeling that you're not going to remember any of this tomorrow anyhow."

"Four! I let you kiss me all the freakin' time! Also i remember plenty!"

He laughed then patted his knee a few times, "You don't remember shit because you're always drunk. The other night Elma woke me up because you had passed out on the floor next to her bed. Marveen, not only didn't you make it to the right bedroom, but you didn't even make it to the bed. *Pero basta! Siento que nunca vas a cambiar. Pero bueno,"* he smiled, "Come here and give daddy some sugar."

I leaned away and stared at his face. His eyes were closed and his tiny head was coming at me in slow motion, "Sugar? More like caca. No, wait, I mean you're caca."

He leaned away then fell back onto the bed rubbing his eyes with both hands. When he stopped, his face was ruddy with frustration, "See! I can never have a serious talk with you! Even when I try to make things right, you always have to come up with something stupid to say!"

"Pffft! And *I* can never talk to you in English! Five! I always talk to you in Spanish!"

He tucked a finger from his left hand into one of my belt straps and said, "Oh please, don't start. You don't even talk *real* Spanish. *Hables como puro pinché pocho*."

I slapped his hand away with a, "No. I'm still mad. You always try and solve everything with touching my penis. This is elementary school and that janitor with the keys to the soda machine all over again. Aw I miss those free Dr. Peppers. Wait a minute... those weren't free Dr. Peppers... THOSE WEREN'T FREE DR. PEPPERS AT ALL!"

He laughed. "Come on... I'll buy you a *caguama,"* then he winked and scratched his mustache with his right pinky.

I puckered my lips and swayed my head side to side, taking into consideration the prospect, "A quart you say? Well at least I'm moving on up. Take that! Every school guidance counselor ever..."

Just then Elma thudded down the hall and peeked her head in, "What's going on in here? Did Domi slap you yet?"

I kicked a sock towards her, "I said RADIO, jerk! NOT GET ME DIVORCED! Stupid whore."

She laughed, her eyes a bit glazed over from the pot she'd been smoking whose fumes drifted in alongside her. Like Mary had lambs with this one, I swear. "No," she blurted out, "Domi said no radio because you never let him sleep!"

"Ugh," I rolled my eyes and crossed my arms, "Just for that, I'm telling Luis Raul that you've been switching his diet soda for regular soda and pouring Splenda packets in it!"

She contorted her face then declared, "I haven't even touched Luis' soda!"

I turned away from her then back to Domi, "Whatever, I was bored and thought it'd be funny but now you're taking the rap for it. Also, Domi, baby, she's the one that came up with the whole RADIO idea. I just asked her if she had any extra headphones."

Domi laughed then tossed a pencil he had found by the bed at her. She screamed, "AH!" then clonked back down the hall and into the kitchen where I heard the fridge door slam.

"Bitch better not be drinking my vodka..." I hissed.

Domi laid back down and then ran his hand under my shirt and along my back, "*Bebe,* come on... kisses," he pleaded, stretched out his other arm, and motioned with all his fingers as if he was trying to do a one handed clap.

"No!" I pouted, crossed my arms tighter, then stomped my foot and adamantly said, "RADIO!" then turned my head away and stared out the window.

Officiously he said, "Well then, now really forget about that *ray-dee-do.*"

Without turning to look at him, I snorted back, "It's fine. I can just sing all night. Also I know where you keep your vitamins."

I could feel him roll his eyes as he cattishly breathed in and out deeply, then took the bait, "What's that supposed to mean?"

I raised a brow and half turned around in his direction, "What? Oh no, I just want to make sure that you're taking all your supplements. You said that you're allergic to penicillin, right?"

"Ay, don't you dare threaten me," he smiled then pinched my muffin top.

"You swear!" I laughed, "As if I knew where to get cheap medicine without a prescription, down the street, or where you hide you B-12's, next to those Snickers bars, under that Backstreet Boys cd in the top drawer."

His leg twitched nervously, "No, I meant with your singing."

"WHAT...EVER! I sing beautifully!"

"Si, bebe, claro. You're the best! *Mi cantante favorito!"*

"Okay, fine, better," I nodded my head, "Also, thank you and you're welcome," however my efforts to be more polite fell on deaf ears. He just scratched his nose and sucked his teeth then said:

"Well then, I guess that's settled. You don't want to kiss and make up so I'm going out to buy myself a *caguama* AND just ME a *caguama,*" he stood, neatly pulled down the tails of his shirt then ran a hand through his hair. I immediately wrapped my arms around his waist and emphatically said, "No! Domi! *Te quiero!* mua mua mua! Plu-heasssseeee buy me a *caguama!* I'll love you forever!"

It was New Year's Eve and I was just sitting on the toilet, staring at Elma putting on lipstick. I wasn't pooping or anything, but I felt a little like crap. I had decided not to take my afternoon cocktail (Read "cocktail" as two doubles of vodka). She popped her lips together then snapped the lid back on her Jungle Red tube.

She glanced coquettishly at me and said, "What are you looking at?"

I smiled and said slyly, "Nothing. You look nice."

She reached for a towel and tried whipping me but I dodged it.

"Tell me! You always have something stupid to say!" she screamed low and raspy, her throat mellow and deep from the apple we had just smoked. I just laughed some more and said:

"Are you almost finished?"

She ran her pinky around the right lower edge of her eyes. Under the lashes, wiping off the excess eyeliner, "No, why?"

I retorted, " 'Cause I have to poo."

She laughed and powdered her nose again, "*Cochino.* Don't be gross! And I know you just went," she shifted to her right side and leaned her hip into the sink as she fluffed out her bangs, "Every time you fart it smells like rubbing alcohol," she stretched her torso back and tucked in her chin. Just then,

Domi walked in with a long sleeved white button up. A thin row of ruffles ran down the middle, but the kind of ruffles that weren't all that "ostentatious". He was busy stringing his black leather belt between the loops of his trousers and whistled a song.

"Marveen! I thought you said you were almost ready?!" he huffed as he tucked his chin into his chest, eyeing the catches on the buckle as he fumbled with the clasps. I looked over, stood up straight, crossed my arms and said, "I am. Almost... kind of..."

He looked over, under a tussle of hair, raised an eyebrow, then said, "We're going to be late! What the fuck? This stupid belt! I'd hit you with it if I could only figure out how... arg!"

Elma laughed, took a step back and hunched over. She was so thin. I could break her with a breath. She stepped back towards the sink and leaned against its counter and said, "Marveen, you're never, ever ready," then to Domi, as she applied mascara, "I don't even think he wants to go," she fluffed back her hair once more then blew a kiss into the mirror and zipped up her make-up bag, "*Bueno*, boys, I'm ready."

I rolled my eyes, "About freaking time. All that effort and for what? Meemaw always said, You can dress up a donkey to look like a horse, but a gator's always gonna have scaly skin."

She tapped the tip of my nose with her right index, smiled and said, "You know what? You, you roll your eyes way too much," then pushed past Domi and into the hall.

I uncrossed my arms and stepped towards the doorway to watch her silhouette disappear into her room where the music played from a PC laptop computer. I turned around then put my shoulder against the doorframe. Domi, so nice, so clean, so well put together and me just there like a fly on the wall watching all these pretty people get ready. Even though he had picked out a new shirt for me, I still felt like a mule in a horse's outfit. Maybe Meemaw had a point there. I looked over my shoulder for a split second and, suddenly, Domi pushed me through and slammed the door.

I banged on the door and hollered back, "Hey! No fair! I was next!"

From inside I heard the toilet seat drop and him singing *Lero, lero,* the equivalent to a childhood Na-nana-na-na. Then there was a wee bit of a fart noise. Like some dainty anorexic passing gas.

I put my back against the hall in the dark, "Ugh, I'm never gonna get to poop," then banged the back of my head into the wall.

Elma screamed, "Marveen!"

"What!?" I yelled back, disheartened.

"Come!" she heaved out like an old witch in a cookie house.

I yelled back, "What?! Why?!"

She pleaded, "COMEEE."

I lazily yelled, "No!"

Again, from in her room, in the distance, like siren in the midst, "Come!" then she cackled, "Help me pick out something!"

"No! Besides! Everything you have looks ugly!" I assured her.

She laughed and I heard the fridge close from the kitchen then Luis Raul yelled back at us to hush down.

Maybe I should've drank some more mezcal. All morning long it had been an event, even before Domi and Elma had got back from work. I felt more high than drunk. Everything was some sort of an amber colored high. Nothing like the alcohol I had come to know and love. This was easy and chill. Like a lover who slips in under the covers when you're half asleep. Not to mention that a bottle of mezcal cost us less than two dollars! “Swept me off my feet” is an understatement. But, at least, I didn't have any vodka. Mezcal didn’t count as “cocktails”. Why I was practically a teetotaler.

I walked the few steps into Elma's room. Looked like a hurricane hit a hooker then passed her onto a tornado, that flew through a Mexican H&M. It was a stereotypical Guadalajaran room. Her mattress was angled in the corner with a string of hipster artifacts strung over the bed on a line with clothespins. Little knick-knacks and wood block printed cartoon animals. Piles of clothes everywhere, and a duffle bag full of heels, flats, and I think there was one or two stilettos. I stood by the door, let my back rest on the frame, crossed my arms and dryly said:

"Yes. Those. Wear those. They bring out the blue in your eyes," her eyes being coffee brown.

She wheezed out a laugh and said, "Shut up!" then peeled off some glittery silver ballerina shoes, turned around and quickly grabbed something from a milk crate that had been turned upside down. It served as an impromptu nightstand with the addition of a heavy fashion magazine as a tabletop. I moved towards the bed and tried to find a space to sit. It was about the size of a twin but half of it, that half that she hadn't dug out a sliver of space to sleep in, was still filled with clothes. On the floor, by my foot, was another fashion magazine on top of which were the remnants of marijuana seeds and ash from bowls, a yellow lighter, not Bic, and a piece of paper with a number on it. I pushed some of the clothes towards the head and sat with my back to her, stared at the bathroom door, and hissed out a voodoo curse to its occupant under my breath. I then plopped down backwards and stared at the ceiling, fingering the buttons on my shirt and listlessly smiled at the idea of me doing a horrible strip tease. She hovered over my head, her face upside down and asked, "Which do you think?" as two different earrings hung from either side of her.

The toilet flushed.

"Hurry! Which?!" she insisted and smiled. Her red lipstick already staining her two front buck teeth.

"The red one," I pointed.

"Shut up! Quick! Silver or Gold?!"

The restroom door opened and I bolted out of the bed and pushed past Domi who was zipping up his pants. Before I slammed the door I yelled: "Elma's-trying-to-make-out-with-me-and-Luis-Raul-is-eating-all-the-food-in-the-fridge!!!"

SLAM

In the restroom I stared into the mirror for about half a minute. It was the kind of half of a minute that seems to go on like an eternity. A millennium or two later, I finally turned on the faucet. The plastic knob gave that familiar squeak as Nicolas Jaar hummed out in the hallway. Then the water whistled and I sighed. Closer to the mirror, I perused my face in search of a blemish to pop. I've always found popping pimples to be therapeutic, or at least a very handy friend to those who procrastinate. But no such luck. I tried anyway to squeeze an invisible black head or two from my nose.

BANG BANG BANG

From behind the door, Domi threatened, "*Appurrate!* Marveen! Are you listening to me?! If not, we're going to leave you here!"

"GOOD," I yelled back then sprayed the toilet seat with generic Lysol and wiped it with a few squares of one ply toilet paper.

Finally, a breath of relief. But there was nothing that came out. I felt so bloated but I hadn't eaten much all day. I almost had half a banana, but, for some reason, the look of Luis Raul crawling out of bed gave me the heebie geebies. I was standing in the kitchen when he rolled out. His eyes were still closed, his hair up in a mess to one side, and a five o'clock shadow cascaded over his double chin. Maybe it was the spittle dried on the side of his cheek. Maybe it was that I was going through my morning withdrawals. Maybe I just saw in him the fat and unattractive me that I pictured in my head.

I sat there, telling myself it was just gas. Then, after a second, decided that it had been because I hadn't had my vodka. That in all my wisdom, I had interrupted the metabolism I had cultivated. But the mezcal... why!? WHY HAVE YOU FORSAKEN ME AGAIN, MEXICO?!

BANG BANG BANG

Domi yelled, "Marveen! *Ya bebe!* Hurry up! I'm not kidding!"

Elma chimed in, "Hurry the fuck up, Pooper-ella!"

Ugh, I didn't even want to go out. My stomach was a jumble of nerves and I was so tired. So very, very tired. Exhausted by the prospect of having to mingle with the young glitterati of the city. Most of which hailed from Chihuahua and who brought with them the same kind of catty closed-minded society I had come to know from up north. These people were cliquish, entitled, and skinny. The latter of which was the most abhorrent quality. Half the time I went unnoticed and pushed out of a conversational circle. The other half of the time, I was ignored in a corner, trying to decipher what people were yelling about and playing this game where I counted how many of them had the same "designer" shirt from C&N or Zara.

I finally gave up, stood and looked into the toilet bowl. Nada, nothing; but I flushed it anyhow. I then proceeded to pout in the mirror and turn sideways. In profile, I didn't look *that* big. I turned off the faucet then walked out into the world where Luis Raul and some dude were laughing at the TV. They had decided to stay in and watch the Ball drop in New York. Over canned, strawberry margaritas, they mused on about life in that big city. How glamorous. How cold. How hard it would be to live there. Three jobs for a shitty apartment. I just looked around and pursed my lips in quiet contemplation. Sometimes I wished Domi was more of a homebody on weekends.

I walked into his room, "You think Luis Raul is single?"

He was putting on some dressy black loafers, no socks. His thin hobbit feet barely squeezing in, "Not sure," he struggled, "Why?"

"Just wondering. He's always bringing home a different guy."

He fumbled with his finger caught between the heel of his foot and the back end of the shoe, "That's not true. They're... ugh...mostly.... just... his friends. There. *Listo.*"

"Yea, sure, 'FRIENDS'. Like how I'm on a 'DIET'."

He laughed and said, "I like you just the way you are, *gordibueno.* Don't change a thing."

I grabbed my belly and stared into his cheap full length mirror, "But nothing fits. Not even Luis' suit."

He got up off the bed, walked over and said, "My shoes don't fit either. But you have to suffer for fashion," then he kissed me on the cheek and turned me sideways so as to get a better view of us both in the mirror, "*Mira que guapos.* A more handsome set of men has yet to be seen!"

I hurled him out of view and pretended to fix my tie and said, "There. Much better."

He rushed back, tackled me into the wall then turned me around and shoved me onto the bed.

"No," I giggled, "Domi! WE'RE GONNA BE LATE!"

They had reserved a table at this bar on *Chapultepec,* one of the main fairways in the city, where David's new beau was bartending. Well, at least I thought he was a bartender, but it turned out that he was some sort of cocktail waiter who looked better dressed than me.

"Pssst," I leaned into Domi, "You think they hiring?" then motioned to this quaffed young man and winked. He pinched me and called me a slut.

We had a bottle of Absolut with an assortment of juice mixers in small pitchers laid out on the table. There was a bucket of ice, some highball glasses, and the table was decorated with two cloths, lain one over the other, so that you could see the white under the red square. I always felt guilty when they'd order bottle service. I knew the price of alcohol. I knew that buying the actual bottle would cost a fraction of what they charged. I knew that the juices were sub par. Also, I knew that the good juices always went first. One pitcher was grape, one was pineapple, and one was orange juice. I hated grape, but by the end of the hour, I was pouring it like purple was my best friend. We were sitting in this half booth with shiny leather seats when Domi tapped my knee:

"*Bebe,* slow down. It's barely ten."

I looked at my watch, trying to catch enough light from the flashing lasers to make out the time. Stupid thing went blurry on me but I muttered out, "Itsa almo' twelvvvvvveee," then I raised my glass and toasted nobody but the air.

I smiled, full of myself, but he just feigned a grin and turned to tell David something after which they both laughed and slapped each other on their chests with the back of their hands.

Ah, what a world, I mused to myself.

"HEY!" Somebody tapped my shoulder and I turned around slightly.

"HEY!", I was all smiles even if I didn't recognize the shadowy figure looming before me. The iridescent lights playing a symphony on their face. After a second I recognized the figure as Alice, all dolled up. She was looking a bit uncomfortable but dressed to the nines with a hairdo straight out of a New Jersey 1980's yearbook. Her hair so up high. Those bangs, so teased.

I blurted out, "What's with the bangs? I mean," I stopped myself to take another sip, for composure of course, "I love them! So awesome!"

She shifted uneasily in her high heels and tugged at the corners of her dress. She was wearing a short, skin tight, neon pink thing that came down to her mid thigh. She laughed and tossed her hair back with a glittery clutch purse that she held in her left hand, "Anabel made me. This was actually an old Halloween costume but she said I couldn't come in jeans and a fedora, so, it was either this or stay home eating *tamales* we bought off the corner."

I danced in my seat then toppled over to the right towards her, "Ha! I love it! Where is she anyhow? It's almost midnight!" I then slapped her on the arm a bit harder than intended and chugged a little more. She stared down at her thin tennis wrist watch and said:

"Uhhm, it's like ten till eleven and oh, she's on her way."

I yelled over my glass, "WHAT?!" with a hand held over my ear, as if that would negate the blaring techno.

She leaned down and hollered back, "I SAID, SHE'S GETTING US SOME DRINKS!"

"Drinks?! You want a drink?!" I motioned to the table and she shrugged an okay. I did a 180 and bumped into Domi.

"Careful, babe," he said.

"What?!" I cupped my ear again.

He grabbed my other hand between both of his and placed a tiny half pill of ecstasy into my palm, "Here, take this," he giggled then grabbed my head with both hands and planted a big old wet one. Scratchy beard and mustaches making sparks on my face.

"Oh... so that's why..." I came to the conclusion that everyone was high but me. I couldn't put my finger on it prior, but they all had been acting a bit weird since we arrived. I shrugged an Oh well, then tossed back the drug with a sip of my cocktail.

Drink! Alice! I had almost forgotten!

I turned about and handed her my drink. She looked questioningly at the half empty glass, this thin tube of euphoria and confidence with a slim black straw. In the little time it took me to fix one of her own, I had turned about in time to see her shrug again, take a sip from the rim then wince. Snatching the first drink from her hand I said:

"Hey! I told'ya to hold it! Not drink it all!" then grimaced and stared brokenhearted into the wee bit of liquid left. She pinched the straw in the new drink and winced again.

I smiled, "Good, huh?" then she handed it forward and said:

"Put a little more juice in it", then laughed.

Disappointed, I mumbled out, "Pussy."

Just then Anabel scooted in with eight-inch high heels or some shit like that, and a puffy purple ballerina dress. She was almost as tall as me. She screamed:

"Howdy Marveen!" then leaned in to kiss my cheek but I slammed her with my chin instead.

Head down, apologetically, I said, "Hey there! Sorry! ... I always do that."

She simply laughed and asked, rubbing the side of her face with the back of her hand, "What time did you guys get here?"

I responded with a, "I dunno. About four of these things ago," in my hand, I rattled the ice left in my glass at her.

She laughed again, "Good," smiled, stood up straight and popped out her chest, "Let me say hi to these bitches," then she tapped me on the shoulder and squeezed by the table, and a few strangers who had been standing in front of us, towards David and Domi.

Our crescent booth was littered with coats and scarves. I had no idea why scarves and wondered such things as I pushed every article to the side, patted the seat and motioned for Alice to join me.

She flicked out the straw from her drink and asked, "And Elma?" then lightly pressed her lipstick against the glass.

I slightly shook my head and said, "I dunno. She said something about going for a 'walk around'. I think she got stood up. Dumb bitch."

She laughed as a portly fellow in a red sweater walked up to us, clutching his phone close to his face. The glow from it was not at all that flattering on him. He wore large seventies' styled glasses. His cheeks were a bit puffy and his hair was shaved close to the scalp. He looked like a pedophile, to tell you the truth, but the kind of pedophile that didn't get much action. He stood there texting. His lack of social skills betrayed by the "textual" nonchalance he was attempting to portray. The proverbial hugging yourself in the corner to have it look like you are making out with somebody. Apparently he was really popular. Probably was the tweetering or something. Possibly too busy hashtagging the world to look up and say hi.

Alice flailed her right arm and hollered out, "RUBEN!" with a big old smile.

He looked up to right and then to the left with the vaguest resemblance to a molting parrot. His head was cocked back, chin pointed out, and his eyes were wide and magnified by those spectacular spectacles. Behind him, a waiter in a red and black vest poked his head out. Ruben pointed a stubby finger to the table and then the man walked around and towards us. The waiter leaned in with a tray of drinks as Alice jumped up to hug Ruben, her dress coming up from behind and showing half an ass cheek. The poor waiter seemed distracted for an instant then returned to business. The notion of finding a spot on the table to set the drinks, however, seemed more daunting than he had expected.

I couldn't get over Ruben's thick-rimmed glasses. Part of me was jealous that I hadn't thought of it before. That SO totally could've been MY conversational piece. Then again, Domi rarely let me go anywhere wearing anything I thought was interesting. I imagined getting ready with him was like being a toddler arguing with his mother about how very necessary a towel cape and swimming goggles were to the entire ensemble. Half the time, Domi would just set out a shirt and tell me for godssake not to wear those boots again. I could tell, in that very instant, that we were going to be friends.

He finally put away his phone in time to side hug Anabel who tip toed back to greet him. Poor thing. Those heels must've been tortuous. Most nights out, people shifted uncomfortably in their attires. Their only solace was when a friend would compliment the outfit. Two seconds later, a doppelganger would stroll by and everyone would just sort of look to the ground then turn their heads to either side and change the subject. When everybody reads the same magazines and shops at the same stores...

The waiter stood politely by the side to let them finish saying hello. Anabel then turned to the him, "whispered" something in his ear, he nodded, then with a flair, twirled around as he flipped the tray in the air then under his arm and walked away. I wondered how many times he had accidentally hit a tweeny socialite in the nose doing that number. They shuffled over like a set of penguins and Anabel flicked her wrist and told me to scoot over. She nestled in between me and Alice then grabbed my knee and said, "Don't let me forget my card," she winked then pulled out a cigarette.

I felt the world get warmer and imagined that where she had set her hand was a puddle of sweat but it was completely dry. The faces in crowd looked like blurry ovals of pale flesh upon which specs of light blinked as if everyone was wearing a mask of Christmas bulbs. I think the drugs kicked in right about then.

I laughed to myself. Covered my mouth and swayed back and forth to the music. Ruben was back on his phone. His eyes were like moons now and I just stared. Domi walked around the table and behind him, tapped his shoulder and they hugged. Anabel bowed towards the edge of the table elegantly with the cigarette in one hand and her elbow in the other. Ruben dipped over the table and extended a hand. I shook it and wiggled my drink in hello. He yelled over, "Why so happy?" he smiled. I immediately thought he and everyone else in the room suspected I was on drugs. How had they known? Dammit, there went my reelection next year.

Before I had a chance to confess THAT, and my entire childhood, Alice jumped in with a, "We got jaeger bombs bitches!" she winked. Oh no, I didn't want Alice, of all people, to think I was some sort of druggy. But her face was stuck in that wink even as she continued to talk and hand out the drinks.

I tried reclining with my back straight as a board. I figured that if I acted "naturally", everyone would forget the stream of heroin coursing through my system. Of course, that move had the opposite affect and Anabel whispered into my ear, "Are you okay? That doesn't look very comfortable."

I tightened my lips impishly as Alice began to hand out pint glasses half filled with amber colored red bull. One to me and one to Anabel, who motioned to leave it on the table, then one to Domi. Ruben grabbed his own and a little shot glass of dark liquor. I held the glass tightly then felt it slipping so I put it down. I couldn't. I absolutely couldn't take one more drop. I could feel my saliva crawling down my esophagus and something bubbling underneath. Anabel, still leaning against the table, looked over at me and shot out a puff of smoke. More Christmas lights flashing in the midst of that nicotine cloud. Then all of a sudden her face was two inches from mine. She made a curious face then pointed with her chin to the pint glass as Alice handed her one shot glass of jaeger. For a second I thought I was going to vomit all over her. I stared down at my feet and shook my head vigorously. She grabbed my knee again. Oh god, that puddle. Was that puddle my puke? Had I already vomited and then forgotten?

She whispered heavy and in slow motion, her breath smelling like perfume:

"WHAAAAAT'S... WROOOONGGGGG...???"

Suddenly the music brought the world back into focus, back into tempo. I turned to her and said, "No. I can't. I really can't. I drank way too much. I swear I just drank too much. No one gave me anything. Are you calling me a liar?" still shaking my head, I stared up at Domi with such contempt. It was the kind of contempt women in movies who are going through labor use to crush their husband's hands. But Domi was on his own trip, biting his lower lip and starring at the stage far in the distance. I took a look. This place must be huge. I thought we were in an empty stadium and then the people came in and out of focus. For a split second they just looked like floating hands and heads and then I realized it was because everybody was wearing black. Everybody but me!

Still in shock at this epiphany, Anabel, with her pint glass now in her left hand, backhanded my shoulder and nodded again to the red bull. I refused again but then she said, "Just do it!" and I honestly couldn't refuse after that. Like she was some mystical puppeteer. So I leaned in to grab the shot glass of jaeger from her right hand and she pulled it away, laughing, then pointed with her nose to the table. Apparently I or somebody, or maybe some kind of gnome creature, had already placed one in front of me.

At that precise moment, I noticed Ruben was staring at me incredulously. His head was low to the right side and going lower. For a moment I thought he might topple down to the floor then I realized I was the one leaning further and further into the pile of light coats and shawls. He just smiled, raised the jaeger then dropped it into the red bull. We all followed suit. The light blinded me for a second. The shot glass hit the front of my teeth. The fizz reminded me I was nauseous. I lifted my left hand daintily over my lips. If I was going down, I was going down like a lady. Oh my god, I just imagined my mother giving head.

Alice hissed out a refreshing sigh, Anabel laughed and laughed and asked if I was alright.

"Yes," I shrieked, suddenly seeing the world for what it was, "Oh my god, babe, everybody's just a bunch of floating heads and arms and we're trapped in this gooey mess of civilization and expectation!"

She propped herself against Alice and gave me a funny look and smiled. Domi behind her was now getting his James Brown on as Ruben sat contently, eyeing the stage, which decided to intermittently disappear then reappear. Behind me, David was asking his friends if it had hit them. God, was everybody on this shit? Who was going to take care of me? For a second I was back on the dark streets of El Paso trying to make my way home, dragging my body against the rock walls and stumbling where the pavement was uneven.

"Did it hit you?" The world came back into focus. David's face was looming over my shoulder. He had been speaking to me all the while.

I, of course, said nervously, "No. What hit me? Anabel? No. She didn't mean to. She was just trying to get me to take the shot."

He smiled, stood straight and rubbed my right shoulder. I wasn't sure if I should tell Domi then or later that his best friend was making the moves on me.

Then there was this creeping euphoria. A tingling from under my spine that made its way up to my neck and I could feel my ears sag, then down over my shoulders and into my tummy. I closed my eyes and pushed my lips together and tasted the sweet mango flavor of my Burt's bees wax. When I re-opened them, I smacked my lips and my eyelids seemed to soar into the ceiling then sink into the floor. Domi winked at me from beside Ruben and over the table. He smiled this beaming smile, his teeth crooked. He always had trouble with his teeth.

Oh my freakin' god! His teeth just fell out!

I covered my mouth with my left hand in horror then back handedly slapped Anabel, who was now Alice, on the side arm, "Babe! Domi! His teeth just fucking fell out!" All I could see was the back of her head and that teased hair. But she told me to calm down. I could hear her laughing and she shook me a little. Then her face was four inches from mine and she swept a lock of hair from my forehead.

"Here, drink this," she pinched a black straw then maneuvered it into my mouth. I swayed back and forth like a cobra in front of a turban headed charmer.

"Oh my god! We're all just puppets!" I screamed and she laughed then stuck the straw in my mouth and told me to suck on it. I wasn't sure if I should tell Domi then or later that me and Alice were planning on getting married.

I sucked down the entire drink and said, "Thank you, I really needed some water."

Alice smiled, "Babe, that was your drink. I think that was, like, all vodka."

I raised a fist and yelled, "DAMMIT!"

I caught Domi's gaze again and winked at him. He was so pretty in spite of his no chin and lack of foreskin. So very, very pretty. I was the luckiest guy in the world. He blew a kiss at me and I crossed my eyes at him. We both broke out into laughter as invisible glitter fell from the rafters on everybody if everybody was me and him under a spotlight. He reached over Ruben and Alice, shook my knee then kissed me on the forehead and asked, *"Que tienes, loco?"*

I smiled blithely, "Nothing," then tried to take a drink from my hand but there wasn't one so I reached over to the table and grabbed a glass. The straw eluded me for a few moments before I comprehended, somewhat disappointed, that it was just full of ice. I turned around and saw David flirting with some guy. I wasn't sure if I should tell Domi then or later that he was cheating on the bartender AND me. I shrugged it off then poured myself another. "Unfortunately", there wasn't any juice left so I bit the bullet and chugged the vodka as the waiter returned with a bottle of scotch and a pitcher of club soda.

Secretly I hoped Luis Raul wouldn't catch on to all the stains his precious sports coat had taken. I confided this to Domi and he simply joked, "Eeee, *te van a pegar!"* Horizontally I shook an open hand and yelled back after sucking my teeth, "You can't tell him! He'll smother me in my sleep!... with his butt and stinky feet!"

I couldn't stop laughing. Why was I so clever? I immediately convinced myself that I should go home and start a YouTube channel. Just then I took note that Anabel was standing before us arguing with the waiter. I stood up, shook the table accidentally and was about ready to rumble when Domi pushed me down with one hand. Anabel asked what was wrong, a cigarette sensitively in her hand.

"What the fuck was his problem?!" I felt like a bull ready to charge.

She laughed, "No babe, he was asking if we needed another round of drinks."

I sat myself back down with a knowing, "Ohhhhh..." then tilted towards Domi and asked, "Hey, hasn't Elma been gone a while? Should I go look for her? Let's go look for her. Wait here, I'll be right back," I began to get up again but he pushed me back down into my seat.

He said, "She should be fine. Stop acting crazy."

"Crazy?! Me?! Pafaw!"

David ran his hand through my hair and smiled. Told me that she'd be back in a bit. I suddenly felt so pretty and dainty and smiled at everybody in the room. Yes you. And you. And you. And you too. And hey, where do you think you're going?

BANG. Smile bullet.

Anabel turned to me, "What's wrong, babe?" she smiled and rubbed my back.

I beamed back, "Nothing," sat up straight and wiggled my bottom in the seat. She laughed some more then wiped the top of her lip with a finger.

She sat beside me and confided, "You really need to come down and check out the gallery my friend Gilbert has," then she panned her head and with both arms elaborated, "It's huge. The size of that entire wall..."

That entire wall? The one that went on forever?

I smiled into my drink, held it close to my nose. She tapped me on the leg, then with her right arm into her chest, like a debutante, "Seriously, Marveen, I saw your stuff online. You're really good. Why I was," she turned to Alice, "Why I was telling Alice, wasn't I telling you Alice? I was telling Alice that you have a lot of potential."

I stretched and hovered my feet under the table and accidentally hit the bottom of it. The drinks did a little shimmy with me. Oh my god did I just almost float the fuck away?!

Alice veered in and bit her lip, "What? What's happening?"

Anabel turned her head slightly in Alice's direction then gracefully back again, placed a hand on her knee then, "I was saying that I was telling you how good Marveen's art was."

Alice nodded as she took a sip, "Oh yeah, it's really good, babe. Like I was trying to figure out what you were trying to say with it but there was just so much underneath. Like these hidden faces. Like all these stories going on. Like I think I saw some guys in the back seat and then I saw some hugging and then I saw someone crying. I really liked the..."

Hopping in my seat I blurted out, "I LOVE THIS SONG! Who sings it?!"

Anabel interjected, "Well yeah. It has SO many layers. Do you paint in oils or acrylics? I usually paint in acrylics," she slapped her left hand on her chest then dramatically rolled her eyes, "Like I could totally see you on a magazine or in New York living in a loft or something."

By then I was fist pumping the air violently to the song. I wasn't so far gone that I'd been spilling my drink but the table took a few more beatings. I laughed and simply said, "It's way too expensive over there!"

She smiled cordially, "No, but seriously. Next week I'm picking you up and we're going to Gilberto's. You'll absolutely adore him!"

I cocked my head to the side, "Does he drink?"

Ruben, then standing by the table, and after infinite silence, tossed in his catty two cents, "Cheap wine, maybe."

I laughed.

Anabel gasped, "STOP! RUBEN!" then she laughed and nodded her head in agreement, "He's super sweet though."

Ruben shifted his weight to one leg, "Yea, if by super sweet you mean stupid. Hashtag: full of himself. Hashtag: street art. Hashtag: Live painting. Hashtag: poor little rich kid."

I bursted out into laughter. Wherein before, Ruben's eyes were moons, now they had looked like tiny brown marbles in the distance. "Now him," I motioned to Ruben then nudged the ladies, "Him I like!"

Ruben smiled and Domi whispered something into his ear. He put his phone away, "Hey guys, it's almost twelve. Do you want to stay here or go down to the dance floor?"

We all looked at each other then Domi raised his arms and said, "*VAMONOS!* "

I think I yelled "Woo" and the girls followed suit.

I tilted my head back towards the jackets. My neck felt rubbery as if I could touch my toes with my nose, "But what about the stuff?"

Ruben smiled then cocked his head back, "Please, gurl, that's what we have bottle service for," he then strutted over to one of the waiters standing by the fenced ledge, they exchanged a few words and he strutted back, "There. Now that's all settled," he grabbed a drink from the table, took a neat little sip, smacked his lips, "Com'n, ladies, the New Year ain't gonna wait for us."

As we walked down the stairs which led from the raised portion of the restaurant into a pit that separated the tables from the main stage, I snuggled up to Domi, smuggled a kiss, then said, "Hey, happy New Year, jerk."

He smiled and brushed something off my forehead, "*Feliz año nuevo, marido.*"

I contorted my face in disgust, "Hubby? Pffft! This is an entirely platonic arrangement."

"*Que?* Quit being such a clown. I got you alcohol and drugs. Per our agreement, that entitles me to your hand in marriage."

With a straight face I said, "No. I got me a new man," then I pointed my chin at Ruben who was leading the cavalcade.

Domi just laughed, tucked in his no-chin, which made it look as if he had a double chin, and said, "*Wacala!*"

I winced, and bobbed to the music, "What are you talking about? The likes of such an Adonis has yet been seen! Besides, I never signed the papers. Also, that lawyer you got was beyond incompetent. Fifty heads of cattle? Pffft, you could've had fifty two if you had stuck to your guns."

He scrunched his nose, "But he's fat, short, AND bald!"

I grabbed his arm closer and confided, "Just how I like 'em," then rested my head on his right shoulder for a second.

He kissed my forehead and asked, "Did it hit you?"

"The pill? No. Well, like for a second I thought I was gonna be sick."

He pinched me with a, "A huh. Sure. Right now I'll give you more. We bought seven between me, David, and Elma."

I beamed tenderly, content with everything. Happy with the world and just the way things were. Heaven on my shoulders and tiny angels caressing firefly lanterns. I wondered, "And them? Where did everyone go?"

We finally made it down and he said, "To whore it around, I'm sure," laughed then whispered, "But the suckers left me the pills", winked and wagged a finger with a *"Lero lero"*.

NUEVE!!!

OCHO!!!

SIETE!!!

SOMETHING!!!

FOUR!!!

TWO!!!

UNO!!!

"GAH-APP-EE NU-YARRR!!!"

As Auld Lang Syne played in the background, Domi and I embraced in the middle of the dance floor where Ruben had pushed and shoved us all the way through. I remember flashes and confetti catching the dancing lights. Noisemakers making what they do best. We all hugged each other and Ruben took pictures on his phone. Champagne was everywhere. People were smiling, grabbing each other by the shoulders and dancing in circles like posh merry go-rounds. And while everyone was laughing, under the spray of bubbly and good will, Domi and I popped another pill. In the distance I imagined a set of red glowing eyes on an expressionless face but I later attributed that to the to the exit sign, by the door on the far left.

We stepped out of the restaurant at around 3:30. I believe the shindig was going to go on until four, or maybe until sunrise, but the night seemed enchanted and in need of adventure. I suppose a high enough dosage of heroin and MDMA could do that to a person. Along the way we had lost David but we had found Elma. She walked beside me, shawl over her bare shoulders, with glittering gold, dangling earrings about five inches long, brazing the bottom of her neck every now and then. I put my left arm over her as I held Domi with my right. We were all sweaty but I'm sure I was more than my share of damp.

I asserted, "I'm so glad I came down here, guys. I love you all so much. God this is just where I wanted to be all my life. I know it. I know it. Like I can feel it in my bones. Like my bones were always here somehow and my skin was off like just floating around elsewhere. Like a sheet in the wind that fell off a clothesline!"

Elma tucked out from under my arm and bawled out in laughter. We were on Chapultepec and nearing the intersection with Lopez Cotillas. There was an OXXO convenient store on the corner. I turned back, "Hey! What's so funny?! I'm being serious here, guys!" Other party revelers passed us in swarms. Elma couldn't stop laughing and slapping her right knee. Domi smiled and said:

"And, supposedly, they didn't hit him."

Elma finally stood up straight, her right arm akimbo, and her left hand still covering her mouth as she attempted to compose herself, "Didn't hit him my ass! Did you fucking see him jumping around, fist pumping?!" she broke out into laughter again then said, "There, there. I'm fine now", then sighed and giggled once more," Ay, Marveen, *te pasas.*"

Domi was somewhere between being drugged and annoyed, "Hey, let me get some juice, I'll be right back." He disappeared into the store as more throngs of people passed us by. The nicer ones said Happy New Year. Elma irreverently mocked them then bawled back into laughter. I walked up to her. Wanted to kiss her so much but thought that damned red lipstick would give me away. I imagined Domi walking out of the store and catching us in the act. I'd turn around looking like Bozo and he'd drop the juice then go off running into the night crying.

I put my right index finger over her lips, "Shhh... I know what you're thinking. But we can't. We can't let Domi go running."

She slapped my hand away and looked at me amusingly perplexed, then broke out into laughter again, "What the fuck? What the fuck are you talking about? Domi doesn't run. Domi swims!"

I put my finger again over her lips, "Shhh... I know. He'll be swimming in tears. That's why we can't."

From behind, I caught a shadow and did a quick 180, slapped my hand against my chest, "Jesus christ, Domi! I thought you were that devil guy from the club!"

Domi was taking a drink from a big plastic bottle of orange something, furrowed his brow then asked, "What?"

Quick on my feet, I said, "Nothing. We weren't doing anything!" then over my shoulder, winked at Elma. She just laughed and walked towards us, then said:

"Hurry. My feet are killing me," she placed a hand on my left shoulder and walked in between me and Domi. She turned to him and smiled, "Domi, Marveen really doesn't want you to go running."

I interjected, "Unless it's from that devil dude. Guy totally looked like he wasn't having any sort of fun."

At the end of the street, we walked a few more blocks towards this place where there was supposedly an after for that after party that had got cancelled at the last minute. They were friends of friends. Domi had always said that our part of town, Santa Tere, was more "Mexican", if that made any sense. He said it was more dangerous at night but I never really got the feeling until at that precise moment when I remembered the conversation.

"Guys," I started, "Do you think that was really the devil back there?"

Elma laughed again and said, "Yes. He bought me a drink. He's actually very nice. He said he likes cats."

I shook my arms and fists, jumped in the air and turned around to stop them, "I KNEW IT! CAT PEOPLE ARE BORING!"

Domi just chewed gum as Elma pulled me by the arm, "Com'n, let's go *mee-ster* cat people are boring."

A street or two after Garibaldi, we took a quick left and soon found ourselves standing outside of a gated set of houses which ran perpendicular to the street. Domi whipped out his phone. Geezus, I thought he was holding a ball of blue fire. Elma just stared at me, "What now, *loco?"*

I stared at my feet, "No. Nothing. I'm fine. I'm just tripping," I reached for my cigarettes but couldn't find them. I checked every pocket about three times, "Fuck! I lost my ciggies guys. Do you have one?"

Elma smiled, "Here," she reached over with a lighter. Why was everyone holding balls of fire? I dodged her hand. "What the fuck, Marveen," she laughed and insisted, "Here!"

I winced at her, "No, I said if you have a cigarette."

She smiled and turned to Domi who was still on the phone, "*Que le pasa a tu morrito?*" then to me, "Marveen, look. You have a cigarette in your mouth."

And, just like that, out of nowhere, I had a cigarette in my mouth. I checked my pockets again for my pack and out of nowhere, just like that, it turned out that I had my pack in my hand all the while.

The gate opened and a dark figure with a beer waved us in and walked us to the front door of the first house to our left, which was under some kind of carport. It felt as if we were being ferried through the River Styx. At the door, thinking of good manners, I asked the guy who was wearing a baseball cap, t-shirt, and some jeans, "Hey, is it fine if we smoke in here?" He said not in the house but upstairs on the patio was fine. I turned quickly and kneeled down to put out my ciggie on the doorstep only to find that it had never been lit. Domi raised me by the arm and told me to behave.

I don't know why but I just felt like he didn't like me anymore. That thought kept bouncing through my head as we walked up a winding stairwell to the third floor. I just stared at his ass as he walked ahead. I really didn't want to disappoint him. Why was I always disappointing him? The air hit me nicely though and I came to the conclusion that he didn't really have much of a bum.

There wasn't that many people. Maybe about twenty or so who inhabited the patio and a room adjacent. There was a cute girl sitting on a washer machine that was placed in an alcove right outside the door to the stairs. She smiled at me and I smiled back. She was so pretty, I thought. There was a rod iron ladder set into the wall at the right. Elma scooted ahead of me and began to climb it. It looked so daunting that I shook my head. Dizzy. Swooning. Domi grabbed me by the arm:

"Are you okay?"

Insinuatingly I smirked and retorted, "NO, are YOU okay?"

Annoyed he said, "What's THAT supposed to mean?"

I swayed once more, "No. Nothing. I just can't climb anything right now. I don't even think I could go back downstairs. I'm like a cow or something. GEEZUS, is that why you don't like me? 'Cause I'm fat like a cow?"

He sighed angrily, "Ay, Marveen, don't start. Don't ruin this for me."

I smiled. Inside I was dying but I smiled. I smiled then flicked him on the shoulder, "Race ya!" I turned towards the ladder and flew up. Lord knows why I didn't fall off but I managed to make it to the fourth level, the rooftop. Elma was there talking to two guys in suits that I had never seen before. I swore she was winking at me. I swore that the moon fell upon her as if she were under a spotlight on stage. Seductive, white feather boa. Domi made it up soon after. I leaned back and whispered, "I think Elma's gonna have a threesome with those dudes..."

Domi pinched me, handed me the bottle of juice and told me to drink up. We both leaned against the wall. I thought there was another person behind us but it was just a water heater. Out before us lay the city and a church began toll in the distance. Domi smiled and looked my way then leaned on his right elbow and just stared at me. I was still ashamed for being such a cow so I pretended to be cold and buttoned up my coat, then, realizing it was too snug, unbuttoned it.

He smiled, "You're crazy. It's like you've never done this before."

In my minds eye I was 19 in a porno theatre sucking dick for the first time. I blurted out, "I've just seen a lot of movies," my lower jaw trembled and I sucked at my bottom lip to compensate.

He raised a brow then, "What? What movie? *De que hablas?*"

I laughed, "I dunno. I swear I was nineteen again doing sex stuff for the first time. Hey how was your first time? Hey, whose house is this? Hey, where'd Elma go?"

He grabbed my face with both hands and kissed me, "You taste like alcohol," he cooed, "Elma's right there."

"Hey, whatever happened to Anabel and Alice?"

He laughed, "Anabel was sitting on the washer machine. She said hi to you but you just walked off."

I stomped my foot with an enthused, "Dammit!"

He smiled, let go of me then leaned against the edge again. I was swaying side-to-side and bumped him then we were both swaying side to side. At first in unison and then syncopated the way signal lights on cars usually tend to do when you're waiting to turn at a stoplight.

My lip quivered again, "Hey, Domi, I'm sorry. I'm like really sorry. I really shouldn't be here."

Without turning he said, "Sorry? Why sorry? And where else would you be?"

"I dunno. Like I don't belong here. Like I should be back home taking care of my mom or hanging out with my mom or like walking my dogs and shit. I'm just sorry. This isn't my scene."

We stopped swaying and he spun to look at me, "Here, drink some more of this. Let's sit down."

"No. No I can't. If I sit down I'll be sick."

He sat down with his back to the ledge, patted the floor and said, "Sit, Marveen. I mean it."

I sat. People came up the ladder and walked over our knees as they now swayed with each other. Four knobby things, again at first in unison, then again in syncopation. Waves of euphoria mingled in with the possibility of having had drank too much.

"Domi, I'm sorry. I'm really sorry. Like from the bottom of my heart."

"Quit saying you're sorry," he grabbed my left knee, "Did you have fun tonight?"

The corners of my mouth lifted in delight, "Yeah," my entire jaw started clacking, "Do you have anymore gum?" he handed me an empty paper and said:

"No, you kept spitting it out. Here, just chew on this."

I laughed and mumbled to myself, "No, I've just seen a lot of movies... hahah fucking hilarious. Why was I such a dweeb?"

He stared up into the light blue sky, the stars now fading, the air a little cooler.

"Hey, Domi. I love you," I looked longingly at his profile: Still no chin and that same tiny head but whatever.

He turned to me, chewing something I suspected was gum, "I love you too, man."

"Hey, I thought you said you didn't have anymore gum?" to which he opened his mouth to reveal a wad of paper. "Okay. Anyhow, like I really like you, Domi. It's just that I don't think you love me." He grabbed my left hand and kissed it, his eyes rolling back into his head. I continued, "And like I think we should like break up."

He laughed, "Why should we break up?"

I started motioning with my right hand, as if conducting an orchestra, "I don't know. Like it's not going anywhere. Like I don't think we should get married if we're not in love-love. I mean you're young, and I'm young, and you have your whole life ahead of you. Like you're super cool and handsome and you shouldn't be held down by me. You know?"

He smiled then turned his head towards me, kissed my hand again, "You're crazy. Maybe we should break up. I don't want to date a crazy person."

I started to tear up, "I know. I'm super crazy and super wrong. Like there's something wrong with me. Like I was born wrong and that nobody could ever love me. Like nobody should ever HAVE to love me."

He tucked his head into my neck and told me not to cry then kissed my cheek. I wiped the tears, "Just like, if we break up we should still live together because I don't know anybody else in the city."

He laughed and slapped his left hand into his face, "You know Elma. You can move into her room."

I nodded in agreement, "But, you just can't bring boys home. That'll kill me."

He snickered, "Then what's the point of breaking up if I can't bring guys over? Na, better yet, I'll just move out and you could have my room."

"No, Domi, don't leave me..."

"Well you're the one who wants to break up."

"I just think we have to because I don't love you and you don't love me. Just don't leave me. Just don't bring boys over or get married or have kids or move out."

"Ay, Marveen, you're not making any sense."

"Love never made any sense."

"Ay, you just said that you're not in love with me."

"I'm not. Maybe I'm just obsessed."

"Ruben added me on Facebook."

Domi laid naked under the covers, "Oh? What does that whore want?" he laughed.

I was walking around the bed picking up socks, "Be nice. He just wanted to send me some of the photos from New Year's. He said he was going to tag us but wasn't sure if it'd be *appropriate*."

He reached over for his phone that he'd left on the floor, plugged into the wall. Distracted, he asked, "How?"

I picked up a light blue gingham shirt and tossed it at him, "Does this smell clean to you? Like if we were still in the closet or something. He just said he didn't know *Que pedo con tu y Domi*. I dunno."

The shirt remained strewn over his bare chest. He smiled into the screen of his phone, tapped a few keys and bit his lower lip then smiled again, "Ah, mmm..."

I kicked a pair of his pants to the corner by my bags, "'Ah, mmm' what?"

"*Nada*," he propped himself up on his right elbow and poked his nose with his left hand then pretended to flick a booger at me.

I folded a towel over my arm, "You don't like him, do you?"

He pitched his head back, a strand of black hair fell across his forehead and he stared up towards the ceiling seemingly trying to conjure the words from the clouds, “There’s just something about him. *Me da mal espina,*" he then proceeded to pick a tooth with the nail of his pinky.

I folded a pair of my jeans into the drawer and over my shoulder said, "Well he seemed nice to me."

Domi rolled his eyes, "Everyone seems nice to you. Everyone but the right people."

I furrowed my brow and tried to shove the drawer closed, "What's that supposed to mean?"

He checked his phone again, "Nothing. Forget it. It's just that he's always just talking shit about people. Very problematic. I hate people like that. The bad vibes mess with my chakras.”

I gave up on the dresser and smiled, turned to him then laughed, “Oh gawd, you and your damned chakras. I don’t think you can tote that around and still smoke pot AND still do hardcore drugs. Like, seriously, cocaine’s probably not that good for your chakras’ alignment either. And besides, I like that about him. It's like having a fat-girl friend. And you forget that I don’t really know anybody around here so whatever he has to say about people will fall on deaf ears.”

He sat up, then got to his knees on the mattress. The bed sheet fell, exposing a semi hard dick, "So, what now? You have a thing for fat guys? Fat guys with nothing better to do than stir up trouble?”

I grabbed another towel from the refuse in the corner, rolled my eyes, looked at him, "Ewoo, gross. Besides," I laid the towel over the foot of the bed, "You can't have TWO fat people in a relationship. I don’t care if he is the James Dean of the bunch.”

Still on his knees, he made his way closer to me, closer to the edge of the bed. His member bouncing and growing with each movement. I sat and he hugged me from behind then said, "That's why I like chubbies, because I'm so skinny," he laughed then kissed my forehead.

I sighed, "Skinny but ugly, maybe."

He laughed then proudly stated, "You wish! You'd be surprised how many guys are always checking me out. On Facebook they even asked if I wanted to make my profile a fan page because I was getting so many friend requests," then he pulled me down onto the bed with him. I was fully clothed, ready to go for a walk. I hated sleeping in after a night drinking. The best part of being kind of hung-over was enjoying the day and moving around.

I closed my eyes tight as he smothered me in *besos*, "Yea... well, Mexicans don't know what they're doing. Stupid backwards country. Hate it."

It was Saturday morning and we both just laid there in bed embracing. My head over his lower ribs, I stared at the remnant of dried sex on his belly and his dick that was still doing this stiff bobbing action.

I looked up to his face and asked, "Again?"

He laughed, "No. I'm tired and it hurts."

I looked back down to his member then past out towards the window and the light breeze which gently shifted the makeshift curtains. That lonely cactus still in its plastic square container with pistachio shells as mulch, "Mmmm, what a lemon you turned out to be."

"Shut up. Come, kiss me."

"No," I pouted, "My lips hurt... and I'm tired."

He tapped my shoulder, "Come on. Quit being a *yerk*."

"No."

"Ash... I'm sure if I was Ruben you'd be all up on me."

I shot my head up, my hair bouncing, and enthusiastically said, "Ruben?! Where!?"

"*Andale puto...*" he laughed then started tickling me. I grabbed his balls and squeezed them hard. He curled up in pain then moaned, "Owww... *no mames!*"

I sniffed my fingers, "Oh please. Quit being such a baby."

He smacked my head with the back of his left hand and I pleaded with him, "No, baby, stop. Kisses. Remember?" Then I smacked my lips and crawled over him. His dick rubbing against the buttons of my shirt, his scent from my fingers still in my nostrils.

He wheezed out, "Get off of me!"

"No, *bebe,* come on. Kissy kissy, romantic-snuggle time."

He reached back, grabbed a pillow, then buried his face under it then, with a muffled voice, "No!"

I laid down next to him, both now shoulder to shoulder, and placed my head on the pillow covering his face. His dick softening as mine grew harder. I started pinching him and he slapped my hand away. We laid there for a moment in pure silence. The TV maybe on in the living room or my hearing so shot that I imagined noise like a distant murmur. He reached over my torso, grabbed my left arm, then wrapped it over his belly and rolled over to his right, pulling me alongside with him. The faint hint of his shampoo still on the pillowcase or perhaps it was just so strong that it permeated from underneath. I tried to grab his junk but he pulled my hand back up to his belly where I began to fondle the soft black hairs that blanketed it. I tugged one or two and he back kicked me.

"*Puto,*" his sulking, muted, playful insinuation.

I said, "Shut it. Why I'm pure as the fresh fallen snow," then closed my eyes. The sun bouncing off the neighbor's wall and through our window. A bird chirped somewhere. A flutter. Then sleep.

"What are you doing?"

I was sitting on the bed, my back to the wall and my legs drawn close to my torso, just doodling. Domi, shirtless with tight dark blue jeans on, leaned over my legs but I clutched the sketchbook to my chest. "Nothing," I said roguishly and squinted my eyes menacingly. He just laughed and asked: "Penises?"

I brushed him off, "Penises? Ewoo, gross. I hate them."

He laughed again, "Yeah, sure, that's why there's always one in your mouth."

I shrugged, "Have to make rent somehow."

"Whore," he pushed my feet to the side then stretched himself beside me, "What are you listening to?"

"Lissie. I saw her in Austin that one time I almost died accidentally at Southby... again."

"What is *Southby?* And what do you mean you almost died? You've never told me you almost died."

"Some shitty music festival. Well, it used to be cool. They have all these free shows but like more and more douchey people started going. Also, uhmm, maybe I was just never really good at keeping up with music. Uhmm, I never told you about that one time I fell down the longest flight of stairs ever, then ninja kicked my way out of a taxi my friends had tried putting me in? I thought I did. It was that one time I woke up on cacti by the side of the road. Some girls found me and tried using my phone to call my friends but I ran away again and had to buy a new one."

He bit his nails and stared up into the ceiling pondering deep and pretty thoughts, possibly something about shoes or a new bolo tie or some kind of black gaucho hat, "She sounds like a lesbian. Why are you always running away when you're drunk?"

I laughed, "A little, I guess. She kind of reminds me of Melissa Etheridge. Uhmm, I dunno. I think the whole fact that I drink is me trying to run away from something. Plus I usually know when I'm gonna get too fucked up. I have like a fifteen minute window to get home before I do something stupid."

He dropped his hands over his chest then looked out the door, "Who's she?" then began to inspect at first his knuckles and then his digits, "I think you've just been drinking for attention. I'm always thinking, 'When is Marveen going to drop this act of his. Nobody can possibly like drinking THAT much.' Also I think you sometimes do things just to make me mad because you like pushing people's buttons."

"Mmmm, this one..." I YouTube'd Etheridge. That Come to My window song popped up, "You think? You seriously didn't believe me when I said I said I drank a lot, huh?"

"Ah, yes, now I know who. Well, I knew you were always posting stupid updates that were written all wrong. Your texts never made any sense. You practically speak your own language. But no, nobody can possibly drink this much. You would've been dead by now or you would've crashed your car or gone to jail. David says that you're just drinking a lot right now because it's like you're on vacation," he rolled over onto his belly and propped himself up on his elbows. I stared at his bare feet. So thin. So weird. He curled his toes as he sniffed his left armpit, "*Wacala,* I need a shower."

"You didn't shower before work?"

"Nope. I showered last night though."

"*Cochino.*"

He laughed through his nose then laid his head down again. His right arm all the way down and flat by his side. With his left, he tried rocking my knees side to side, "And you? Did you shower or no? Stinky boy," he laughed.

I drew a long thin line across the paper, "Pfft... I ain't got nobody to impress."

"*Ya quisiera...*"

"Mmmm... Me too. That's one of my top two if I ever meet a genie. It goes: wish for the winning lotto numbers, and wish to divorce Domi. Then there's something about getting super powers to shape-shift, or whatever, so I can look sexy."

He poked his nose with his left hand then stared at his finger and rubbed whatever he found on my pants, "And Ruben? What does that faggot have to say?"

I took a deep breath, "Nothing. Just that we're going to get married... in February... on Valentine's."

He smiled then jokingly whined, "No, *bebe*, don't leave me for that bitch. At least pick somebody more attractive."

I smiled to myself, "Hey, hey, Luis Raul... come here...." I laughed then ever so faintly began the outline of another figure.

"Draw me," he laughed, "Like one of your French girls."

Curtly I said, "No. You don't even have boobies."

He countered with, "Well, let me draw you then. Come on, pose."

I put my feet up near his hip and he flinched then rumbled, "DON'T START."

"What? I'm just trying to sit comfortably. You're the one who came to bother me. This is my room. I paid for it in hand jobs and blowjobs and something else that would make baby Jesus cry.

He bit his lip, looked up at me then back down at my feet, "You and your stinky feet. They remind me of *tortas*."

"And yours?"

He slightly turned over, looked back as he stretched out his left leg, rotating his foot at the ankle, "They're like fancy *fresa* women's feet."

"Oh," I rolled my eyes, "Definitely." I drew a straight line under the body as a border.

"One time, me, Elma, David and Patricio all tried walking around in heels. But I fell hard. Like really hard."

“Mmmm...”

He went back on his belly but tucked in both arms under his chest as if it was cold. As if we didn't need the fan on. As if he wasn't all too aware that I always complained about not having an AC.

He began, like a spoiled child, "*Bebe...*"

I retorted as if annoyed, "What."

"Kiss me..."

"No."

"Ash! Supposedly artists are supposed to be romantic. What a disappointment you turned out to be."

"Shut up. No refunds. Besides, supposedly architects are supposed to be rich. And here I am, paying the water bill and we don't even have hot water!"

He shivered then said, "*No mames,* You got to be kidding me! You waste a shit load of water," then he flipped his head to face the other direction and stared out the window. I flashed back to that time I tried filling the fountain but didn't realize that you had to close off the drainage pipe. Or that other time I left the toilet running all day. Or that one time I was so bored that I spent two hours trying to shoot down birds from the tree out back with the water hose.

"See," I replied, " Aren't you glad I don't take so many showers then?"

"No," he said as if he were drifting off to sleep, "Your penis always smells."

"I think it's all that pre-cum. Plus, I masturbate too much."

"What does that have to do with anything?"

"Well, I end up always smelling like sex. Isn't that some sort of *sexy?"*

"No. *Eres un cochino.*"

I shrugged, "Meh," then nudged him with a toe. He pushed my foot away.

"Hey, let me draw. I never bother you when you’re trying to meditate.”

He responded with, *"No chinges!* You're always passed out anyways."

"No, baby, that's how *I* meditate."

I kicked him. He turned around and said, "Hey, Marveen, ya, stop it."

"You're so spoiled."

Contemptuously he said, "Oh please, how? You're always with your:" now in high falsetto," 'Mom! Mom!' in the middle of the night."

"Leave me alone! I was dreaming about being stuck in the shower without a towel or shampoo."

"You should've just got out naked then."

"God forbid! Plus, it's always cold."

He laughed, "It's never cold around here!"

"Duh, I mean in my dream I was in El Paso. Over there it could be mid July and we'll get a snow storm one day and then the next it'll be 150 degrees or some stupid shit like that."

"You never dream about Guadalajara? Or Juarez for that matter?"

"Nope. Mexico is stupid. I wouldn't waste my time."

"I do. The other night I was dreaming that me and Elma were going to get you from the airport but you never came..." he stared off into the distance, "And I started to cry but Elma told me not to worry and took me to a gay club where I..." he stopped short and laughed.

I kicked him, "You were being a slut, right? Anyhow, imagine how I felt flying into the city and thinking I was going to have to take a taxi over here. I so totally imagined that you'd be waiting for me at the airport with flowers and a big sign. Instead I come home and find that you were partying. Jerk."

"It was supposed to be a surprise," he said coyly and laughed, "And what taxi? We did pick you up!" changing the subject, he went on, "Well I was at this club with some boys but I woke up really sad and for a second I thought I dreamt the whole thing. The whole you coming down here, I mean. When I opened my eyes, I was staring at the wall but then I rolled over and saw you. Then I think you farted," he laughed,

"I breathed it in deep, like breathing in roses, just to make sure that you were real. What's the matter? Don't give me that face!"

By the end of his, what I'm sure was to be a romantic confession, I was just staring at him like he was a retarded baby sniffing glue and eating paint chips, "Ay, Domi, *cochino*, Sometimes I wake up a little disorientated too. The other night I yelled out for Lucy, my Great Dane, because I heard someone moving around in the kitchen and thought it was her going through the trash."

He laughed, "Luis Raul eating cake from the fridge..."

I laughed too, "I wouldn't doubt it."

He turned his head towards me and began running a finger over the hem of my pant leg, closed his eyes and said, "I'm really happy you came, baby. *Bebe hediondo."*

"Mmmm..."

"Mmmmmmm... what? You're not glad you came?"

"I wonder sometimes. I miss Lucy... and Fuki, and Hachi and my half dead plants."

He laughed, "In time I'll get you a little Chihuahua. They're always selling them downtown."

"Ewoo..."

"Come on! He'll be just like *Mercedes*."

"I forgot you had that rat back home. Giant rats! That's all they are!"

"Jeje, of course not! They're cute and stay little all their lives."

"Small dogs just yap and yap and yap. I cringe at the thought. Hey, do you ever think about Rita? That cat they gave you that you basically left on the streets because she was too much trouble?"

He looked puzzled for a second.

I repeated, "Rita! The one you named after Rita Hayworth! That cat you had! The one you would leave in a shoe box when you'd go off to work!"

"AH, no," he giggled, "She was evil. Ask anybody. I mean she was really wicked. Like a bad seed. Like a street kid with nothing left to lose."

"Tisk, tisk..." I tapped my pen against the paper, "What if I don't turn out how you expected? I'm practically living in a shoebox. This room is so tiny. Would you leave me out in the street too?"

"Never, babe," he pinched my knee and said, "Then who's gonna pay the water bill?"

"And this, this is where we're thinking of putting the screen printing press," Gilberto, a yellow skinned, rail of a guy, a few inches shorter than me, pointed out to the corner of the roof where we were standing atop a house off of *16 De Septembre*. I stared out into the distance. On either side it seemed that you could see a cathedral or a park. The city was so beautiful and busy. People walking everywhere but with no real haste. Many simply laid on the lawns of public squares, barefoot, taking *siestas* or talking. Some, I imagined, waiting for a bus. Others, counting buses like they were sheep. Not too far away, I spotted some old kiddie carnival rides. A small merry go round with its sides covered in a black and white striped tarp. A miniature roller coaster which I was sure only traveled in a slightly undulating circle. In the center was a statue of a man dressed like a friar. He stared out onto a small row of tents selling touristy items: traditional Mexican dresses and brightly colored children's toys. Something like streamers or kites. I wondered for a second if ever there'd be a statue of me somewhere. Would it be flattering? Would I even garner a tombstone? I've always said that I wanted to be cremated. I thought then, for a second, back to my father and the tombstone my family had yet to afford.

"Is it fine if I smoke up here?" I asked.

"Sure, I'll get my pipe," Gilberto answered.

"No," I smiled and raised my pack of American Spirits like some foreign shield. Like some passport declaring I was some kind of pretentious. "I meant cigarettes. Is it fine if I smoke cigarettes?"

He laughed, "Oh yeah man, but still, let me get my pipe," then he scuttled off down the winding stairwell.

Anabel turned to me, raised her sunglasses so that they hung just above her hairline and asked quietly, though a tad hysterical, "So what do you think?! Awesome, right?!"

After two failed attempts, I finally got my ciggie lit, puffed out the first plume of smoke and said, "Yeah. It's a nice setup. I like the little courtyard downstairs. But so, like, is every room going to be turned into a gallery or something? Or are people going to live here? Like is it going to be some sort of hippie artist commune?"

Behind us, Ruben paced back and forth, trying to shield the screen of his phone with one hand. He hadn't stopped texting since we had arrived. He hadn't said a word besides curtly commenting on how "rustic" Gilberto's new digs were.

Anabel went on, "The neighbors are really cool too. Gilberto said that they're planning on maybe having a neighborhood show every first or last Friday of the month."

I took another puff as church bells tolled in medley from all over the city, "That's nice. I thought they already did that around here?"

She jutted out her chin and hunched over, adjusting the strap of her purse, "No well, it's not the same. Gilberto says that the few art movements by people our age are really just a bunch of snobs who stick to the mainstream. Most of them come from the University and think that this or that is art because some old man showed them a slide show in class. He says he's tired of somebody telling him what art is and what art isn't. Aside from them, there's this tourist racket. A bunch of Indian portraits and ladies dancing with tequila bottles or something."

I smiled then exclaimed, "DAMMIT! That was so totally my idea!"

From behind us Ruben suddenly broke his silence, "Hashtag: already happening. Hashtag: been there, done that. Hashtag: Downtown is cool."

I laughed as Anabel glared at him. From the stairs we heard Gilberto stomping up. The entire structure was adobe or some kind of concrete. With each step it sounded as if sand had been grating beneath rubber feet. He held out his arms. In one, a small pipe that had been packed, in the other, a lighter. I could tell he was fancy because the lighter was a Bic. Anabel laughed, bowed her head and graciously took the first hit. Gilberto said, "It's not the best, but my dealer's had trouble so this is all he can get," his eyes were already a little bit bloodshot. In my head I tried to calculate the time he had taken, and the time it would've taken, to smoke a bowl of the good stuff himself. He continued, "So, *Martin*, like I was saying, the point here would be to have a different market. Maybe something not so touristy."

Me and Ruben eyed each other questioningly then Ruben said: "Yea, *Martin,* doesn't it sound like a good idea?" I just smiled and nodded my head. I wondered how long had it been since we left the house and since I'd taken that last shot of mezcal? Ruben did a quick pivot on one foot, stared down at his phone then went on, "Hashtag: Awkward. Hashtag: gentrification. Hashtag: gringadera. Hashtag: Anything for Selenas." I tried to hold back my laughter but I was unsuccessful.

Unamused, Gilbert turned around and led us down the stairs. Anabel pinched Ruben as I walked behind them, trying to savor the last bit of my cigarette before tossing it out into the open air. She quietly hissed at him, "I told you to be nice!"

When we reached the second floor, Gilberto panned the room with his right arm dreamily, "And here, I'm planning on making some walls and just tossing a sleeping bag in it. I don't need much. Hardly sleep at all," he ended with a smile. I looked to the turntable, ipod dock, matching dresser/night stand, and came to my own conclusions. Of all the bedrooms I'd seen, his was already three times as furnished and the fucker hadn't even completely moved in. From the speakers drifted a low deep house set that was suddenly interrupted by a call. He leaned over a black speaker that said Bose, unplugged the device which rung out a loud pop and answered as he moved away towards the stairs and a wee bit of privacy.

I nudged Ruben, "Hey, you think he's single?"

He replied, "Hashtag: that lady is a tramp. Hashtag: insomniac. Hashtag: cocaine is a hellavuh drug."

A few moments later Gilberto returned with a, "Sorry about that. It was my friend from... who wanted to know if I had gotten settled in. I said not yet. But soon," then he pointed to the window, "I'm thinking of putting like that plastic, fake, stained glass right here. Like, you know, man? Like I think of the creative process as divine and like this should be a temple to it. Not like religious, but like, you know, just that sort of powerful love and safe haven."

Me and Ruben looked at each other again. Ruben shook his head, squinted his magnified eyes, and raised a hand as if to say, What the fuck?

Anabel laughed coyly, "That's so cool man! I'm so excited! And I, for one, know how silly that downtown market can be. It's just a bunch of old people and shit Indians make."

I pursed my lips, a bit astonished, "Well..."

Later that evening, in bed, I said to Domi, "Hey, have you noticed that all your friends are basically white?"

He was sitting up against the wall with a pillow below his lower back, going over some sort of paperwork "How so?"

I was propped up on my elbows in the opposite direction, flipping through one of his fashion magazines, coming to terms with the fact that I neither had a suit or such a skinny waist, "Yea, Anabel said something today and I realized that we, I mean, that you, don't really have any *dark* friends."

He laughed, "Ay, yes I do. There's... well, I mean to say... Well, you've met them before... Oh, well, there's *El Wookie."*

"He doesn't count. He's like your token hippie who's sunburned from spending too much time at the beach on daddy and mummy's money. Also, he's more like your drug dealer than your friend."

He laughed then flipped a sheet over at the corner where it had been collated. He creased the edges then continued to look perplexed. Honestly I thought he was doing word puzzles in Cantonese. I flipped my head to the side and tucked my chin into the corner of the magazine. I flipped through the pages rapidly, taking more pleasure from the breeze they produced than the actual photos which were mostly just ads for perfumes and expensive wrist watches that shot out at you from the ethers of some dark realm. Apparently "fashion" only existed in the mists of an abyss with Caravaggio like lighting.

I muttered out, unfazed by the labels, "I don't get this. Don't you have anything in English? I could've sworn..."

He looked down at his papers, tilted his lips to the right, annoyed by a query to whose answer the questioner already knew, "Nope," then he flipped another page, put the lid of a pen to his teeth, took off the top, then underlined something.

Four character word for Happy Young Girl Virgin.

"Ughhhh...." I moaned, "I hate this! English should be everywhere! It IS everywhere. Everywhere but this stupid room!" I kicked my legs up and down like a Willy Wonka character. The bad kind that got their come up ins.

He sighed.

"I'm better off reading the milk carton. Hey, did you know that it's mostly calcium and fat?"

He sighed, "YOU'RE mostly calcium and fat. Except, not so much calcium."

I brushed him off, "I'm just retaining water."

"Water? Water my ass! Don't think I haven't been checking the trash. There was like three bottles of mezcal there this morning."

I said curtly, "Elma had friends over!"

He said, like a know it all, "Elma hasn't been home since Tuesday."

I raised my brows, and then arrogantly, "Well then, I win. Elma's a prostitute," licked my finger then turned the page. Not one interesting thing. All the clothes looked like something out of a movie from the fifties, and the sixties, and the seventies, and, well, the eighties were just tailored poorly. Also, what the hell is a Givenchy? I dramatically rolled about, flung my right forearm over my eyes and said, "Christ! I'm going to rot down here. My vocabulary has been reduced to 'I'm American, From El Paso.' God how do you people live like this? Even the Chinese... Jesus, my brain feels like it's going to mush..."

"That's the vodka," he interjected.

"That's the 'I used your toothbrush to wipe my ass'!" I was lying of course. Only twice had I accidentally dropped his toothbrush in the toilet after having had taken it out of the top dresser drawer, after pretending his and my toothbrushes were orphan-style Barbies and that his was prince charming. Don't ask. I had a lot of free time in those days, "Ugh! It's all Spanish this! *Tacos* that! *Tortas* here!"

"*Cerveza* there..."

"Caca Domi here..."

"Oh please, caca your ass!"

"*Coca-lite*! *Hee-lo,* we are da res-rooms?"

"*Callate!"* he finally belted out and threw a pen at me. I wasn't sure if I should call the American Embassy or Mexico's equivalent to TMZ. He then, collectedly, flipped another page and asked, "And how did it go with Gilberto? Are you famous yet?"

I scratched my right canine tooth with my pinky, "Ugh, no. Never. Don't get me started. But Ruben's taking me on Thursday to see the art studios at the University," then excitedly, "I heard they have bears or some sort of yogurt stand..."

Uninterested he said, "Mmm," before reaching over for his phone which had begun to vibrate.

"Mmmm what? " I inquired.

He stared at his phone and said, absent minded, "Nothing."

"Who are you always texting?"

"It's from work. They want to know how far along I've gotten on the report."

"Why do you even have reports? I thought you designed display furniture for retail stores?"

"We do... but it all has to be exact. Basically we have to go through the measurements and make sure we got the centimeters and the millimeters and the meters right."

I turned the page onto a waif of a pale lady riding a stuffed lion in a thong that was selling shoes or some kind of chapstick, "Ay you stupid foreigners. How many times do we have to tell you? Go by the King's foot!"

He sighed, "Just don't go running around like a slut. Remember, he’s trouble. Always has been. Always will be.”

Flabbergasted, "Me? A slut?" then flattered, "You really think I could be a slut?” I looked back smiling but he was still staring into his phone. This, my friends, was not at all how I imagined married life. I assumed I'd have pearls and a house maid who only let me vacuum after she had vacuumed everything, but just in time for my hubby to walk in through the door and suspect I was being productive all day long instead of swilling back martinis and amphetamines.

I assured him, "The only one for me is Luis Raul."

He underlined something then said, “Oh, definitely."

I scratched my nose then said, "If I marry him, we're going to have tiny little, chubby, cute babies. How much do you think those go for on E-bay?"

He laughed, “If you say so."

I turned around again. Surveyed his thick eyebrows, that second chin, the way his nostrils flared when he was doing mental math. I said, "Domi, do you love me?"

He flipped a page, furrowed his brow, "Yes, yes. A lot."

Downhearted I commented, “That's what *you* say"

He smiled almost robotically, conscious that I was staring, "It's true."

“Mmm..."

He threw his papers to the side, "Mmmm! Enough with your 'Mmmms'! I HATE that that's your response for everything! You sound so retarded!"

I calmly replied, "Mmm," then flipped the page onto a sleek yellow Ferrari with a svelte brunette in a gold bond-girl bikini. They were apparently advertising sunglasses.

He began shaking his bare foot nervously, the sweat pooling at his forehead. He sucked at his teeth, raised a brow and flipped another page.

I looked back, "Domi?"

"..."

“Dommmmmmmmmmiiiiiiiiiiiiiiiiiiiiii.....”

"What?!"

"...mmmmm..." Apparently I was the only one who found it funny.

He pushed himself up off the bed with a, "I'm going to grab something to eat," then scurried haughtily out of the room.

I yelled out, "If there's still lobster, bring me some! ... jeje 'if there's still lobster'... where do I come up with this shit?” I confided the last part to myself.

After a few minutes I was bored so I decided to venture out into the kitchen as well. Domi was reclining on one of the chairs by the kitchen table. Beside him a cup of hot tea with the string and label cascading over the rim drearily. I opened and closed the cabinets. I looked back at him and noticed him shaking his feet again.

I sighed then walked behind him, put a hand on his shoulder but was quickly rebuffed as he flicked it away.

"Now what?" I said, myself getting a bit annoyed.

"Nothing. I'm just busy. Why don't you go bother Luis Raul?"

I leaned onto the seat's headrest and stared out into the dark hallway, trying to grasp the words to say. Something diplomatic and comforting. Close quarters had obviously strained our rapport. I hardly ever saw him and the few hours we spent together were usually just like this. Tense and awkward. Him tired, me barely stepping into my nightly groove.

After a few seconds I blurted out jovially, "I wish! But he left..."

After a few anxious seconds, Domi turned a page and, uninterested, said, "Who'd that slut go with now?"

"No idea. I can't keep track anymore," I mused then took a seat to the left of him."

"Don't rock the table," he sat up, placed the papers on the table then leaned in onto his elbows.

I rolled my eyes. He wasn't even using the table two seconds ago. Then all of a sudden I was Kitchen Table Godzilla.

Biting the end of his pen, he went on, "*Mmmno, te salio bien puto tu marido*."

Taking special care not to touch the table I replied, "I can change him. I know it. He's just a 'fixer upper'."

"If you say so..."

"You're just jealous."

"Yea, sure...."

I sighed, "In time you're going to be running down the church aisle objecting to the procession and professing your undying love for me. And I'm going to be all like..." I had, absentmindedly began to tap the table top with a finger which sent him into an uproar.

"I TOLD YOU NOT TO SHAKE THE FUCKING TABLE!!!"

I think we were both a bit taken aback. His eyes were still bulging but I could see that faint hint of regret that slinks in even before you finish a sentence.

"Geezus, sorry, man," I said as I began to get up.

He cupped his face into his left hand and rubbed back his hair, "No. I'm sorry. It's just that I have all these things to do and at work everybody's been bugging me. Half of the guys don't even do their fair share. The other half try but they're idiots."

I leaned in, "Hey, I'm sorry. You know what? I'm just gonna go back to bed. I could use the sleep anyhow," I smiled, rubbed his left knee, pushed back the chair and walked towards the hallway. At the doorframe, he called out to me, "And I wouldn't."

I looked over my right shoulder but not turning, "You wouldn't what?"

"I wouldn't object. I'd want you to be happy. I'd just show up with a model."

I couldn't tell if he was being passive aggressive or what but I just smiled and said, "Who? Ruben?"

He laughed, "Gross! Fucking baldy."

In the room I stretched out on the bed, half staring out the window, half lost in the ceiling fan. I wasn't sleepy but I was emotionally drained. I rolled over to one side and stared at the door. I wished it were morning already so I could get lost in the market. I wished I could just fall asleep and wake up after Domi had gone to work. I didn't want to deal with, well, I didn't know what I was dealing with. Although I had had boyfriends who basically lived with me, this was different. There wasn't each other's rooms or each other's friends. At times it felt like we were standing in a mud puddle watching the waters evaporate with every passing day.

Was this what I had come down for? Was this it?

I had imagined a whirlwind romance but instead got stuck with somebody who didn't like to stay up late and whose only ambition was to be a good little cog in the machine. With one finger I scratched at the sheet covering the mattress. For a city so big, for a house full of roommates, I couldn't have ever felt more alone. I sat up, stared out the window again. No breeze and the two fans we had on did little justice or gave little respite. I walked towards my bag and dug out a water bottle I had hidden. It was crinkled and old with the label torn off long ago. I twisted off the cap, tugged at my left ear and took a swig. Awful and warm. Took another swig, a slight cough but better. Took another swig; tasted like cherry.

I was pouring water from the hose into the pit of dirt-sand that was once a fountain. After having had realized that it could never be a pond again, I refilled it with dirt and set out to try and reclaim it as a garden. At some point Elma had snuck up behind me, "How are the sunflowers coming along?" she lit a cigarette and leaned against the only wall that had any sun on it. The evening was setting and the birds were in an uproar.

"Ahmm, I think they were duds," I honestly hadn't the heart to tell her I had uprooted everything in a drunken attempt at making a backyard Atlantis.

She laughed, "Don't lose faith, Marveen. Everything *in time*."

"Ugh, I hate waiting! I'm tired of waiting. It's always about waiting in this place! Tomorrow! Saturday! Wait for the weekend! Everything goes by so slowly here. Like there's no concept of immediacy. Everyone's just lying around in the sun on the lawn and smiling. Do you get how frustrating that is?!"

She flicked the cherry off her cigarette, smiled and looked away, "How are the paintings coming along?"

"What paintings? So far I've managed to master the art of poking my nose and masturbating at the same time. I tried showing Domi but he wasn't impressed."

She laughed out loud, "Don't be so gross! *Cochino!* I don't want to hear about that shit! Besides, I've seen your drawings. They're coming out good. I especially like the ones of Luis Raul sitting in front of the TV eating potato chips."

I laughed, pleased with myself, "He's my crush. My *muse.*"

She took a long drag off her cigarette then smiled, "Obviously. Hey, and what happened with Anabel and that Gilberto guy?"

"Ruben said that they started dating or fucking or some shit like that. Honestly, I think her introducing us to him was a ploy to get into his pants. Apparently she moved into the 'gallery' and now him and Alice spend all day smoking pot and painting, talking about how there are these reptilian creatures running the government."

She tossed the butt of the ciggie on the ground, mooted it under a pair of slip on black ballerinas, then asked, "Alice paints?"

"Kind of. I guess everyone's an artist these days. Besides, you get fucked up and four hours of finger Picasso-ing later, you're a bonafide prodigy."

She hugged herself, holding each elbow in either hand and said, broaching the subject tepidly, "And Domi? How things going with you guys?"

I shrugged and made a face, "Pfft... He's your friend. You tell me. I just sleep with him because I can't afford rent elsewhere."

She smiled, "Come on. I know you guys do nothing but pass the time sucking dick and fucking."

The water hose was streaming out, the dirt, a puddle of mud by then, "Mmmm..."

"Mmm.. what? You swear the walls aren't paper thin."

"I know, Luis farts SO loud in the morning!"

She reached for another cigarette, offered me one but I declined, "He eats too much junk food," she said, struggling with the lighter then looked out towards his wall of a lush green potted garden. I asked her, "Why don't you have any plants?"

She smiled, "I always forget to water them."

"Yea, I'm the same. Even with cactus," I noticed that her hair was getting longer. The lines of her face were getting deeper. She seemed a bit preoccupied with something but I summed it up to the long hours she had to work, "Are you going back to work right now?"

"Yea," she took a puff then rolled her shoulders, "It's life. It's a living. Right?"

"I guess. Still..."

She laughed, "We can't all enjoy the luxury of living like you. Besides, I'd die if I'd have to be a housewife."

"Hey! I earn my keep! See," I motioned to the fountain, "Gardener. Landscaping is my specialty."

She stared at me long and hard, squinted her eyes and took another puff before dropping half a ciggie on the floor and saying, "You sure you're okay?"

I laughed gently to myself, "Yeah, why?"

She pushed herself off the wall, "No, nothing. Just... just I have to get going. You hungry? Have you eaten?"

"Always. But Domi said he was bringing dinner. That he had to meet some investors or something and that he'd order me a plate," I smiled blithely, a shiver of warmth rising from the back of my spine. I felt safe and taken care of like people in the movies who talk about weddings and honeymoons.

She just looked to the floor, long and hard. I felt sorry for her. I didn't know much about what was going on in her life but I hadn't seen her with a boy in some time. My heart went out to her. I wanted to hug and hang out with a gallon of ice cream and a bowl of popcorn. Me, in my infinite egotism, often forgot how lucky I was to be with someone. To have something stable, and although not perfect, something healthy and binding.

Still averting my gaze, she smiled, "Street tacos, I'm sure. The way things are going you'll never lose weight!"

I laughed, still filling the fountain, "I know..."

Finally she looked up, her eyes like slits behind big lashes and mascara, "*Te quiero, Marveen.* You know that right?"

A bit taken aback, "Where'd that come from?"

"Nowhere. Just, you're funny. You make me laugh."

"Mmmm... I.... like... your... shoes. Also you make me want to vomit."

She laughed, "*Pinche meco.*"

"Shut up."

"You shut up, whore. Fucking fat stinky bitch."

I laughed. She laughed then told me I still smelled like dogs.

"Maybe dogs smell like me? Have you ever considered that?"

"Wouldn't surprise me."

"At least I'm not Mexican. Or I don't have fleas."

She smirked, "That remains to be seen..."

"Shut it."

She kicked the wall with her heel, "Well, I'm going to take a hit then make something to eat. Maybe a soup or something."

"Did we run out of cereal?" I said sarcastically.

She laughed, "Yes". A big broad smile. A big happy go lucky face.

I laughed, "Oh well..."

"Hey, how long are you going to be watering that shit?"

"I dunno. I thought maybe you and Luis Raul could jump in with bikinis and we could make a Tuesday out of it."

She smiled, said goodbye, then walked past the corner of the wall and headed to the side of the house. I stood there, surveying my mud. In light of everything green and gorgeous and growing, I had nothing. I'd be lying if I said that it wasn't to be expected. In the back of my mind I heard my father preaching about how superior he was when it came to gardening because I'd always tell him about my dead bonsai. He said he had this sixth sense. This intuition on how and when to water plants which had apparently skipped a generation. How he'd always had that gift. I thought about that last little tree I bought impulsively at the store while getting groceries. How it must be withering in my mom's yard under the cruel sun or hidden away in the dark dinning room. Then I thought back to my mother standing outside of my father's house. She had to leave the living room he laid in, on that couch, him moaning out. Him losing breath and screeching at the loss of oxygen. Her pacing in the front, choking back tears. She said it sounded like they were dragging him into hell.

I just kept pouring the water. Half hoping the seeds would drown. A little out of breath myself, my eyes a little dry at the corners. Dad, Grandma Meche, I hoped they were proud that I had left... that I was trying new things. But these things didn't seem so new or different. I felt stuck on a stair climber. Working hard to get nowhere.

I looked up to that deep pale purple sky. The clouds were settling at the edges. Somewhere in the distance was a storm. Often I wondered if the weather matched my mood or vice versa. That day might've been just "one of those days". A case of the Mondays on a Tuesday. Couldn't do anything right!

The water began to pop over the concrete edges. The sky... that sky.... A sky never to be seen again. Something close, perhaps, someday. But that same exact puff of white and gray and purple and teal and turquoise, never.

For a few days I didn't say much. At my old job, every job actually, they would say that I could influence the mood of an entire shift just by the way I walked in. If I stayed quiet, it was automatically assumed that I was grumpy. If everyone thought I was grumpy, then everyone automatically was upset. I was like some kind of emotional barometer. That's how it felt in the house. Domi and Elma argued incessantly about trivial things. Half the time me and Luis Raul just gave each other knowing looks. The other half of the time, him having a car, he left. I, however, was not so fortunate. It got so bad that Elma would make off handed remarks about me. It sounded like she was implying I was some kind of moocher. The high water bill, the food, even how long I spent in the restroom. Honestly, I didn't care. I was in my own little world and Domi took it upon himself to take us out to dinner on most nights. Anything to get out of the house, I imagined. During the meal we were pleasant but silent. Something akin to the dinning dead. He would broach the subject of his discontent and console the situation by telling me not to pay much mind to Elma. That she had a big mouth and didn't know what she was saying half the time. When we'd get back, he'd just slam open or close the windows to the house then we'd retreat to the room. Seconds later you could hear Elma storm out of her room and slam open or slam shut them again. He'd just roll his eyes then push his fists into his face and growl. I'd just raise a brow and fake a smile.

He'd say angrily, "She swears!!!"

If I were in the kitchen, she'd just bang things and smile passive aggressively. She'd invite over friends that I'd never met and they'd barricade themselves in her room. The smell of weed would permeate the place. The wall we shared would vibrate with loud and obnoxious music. I'd just lay in bed reading, roll my eyes and sigh every so often.

It was none of my business. Right now all I wanted to do was not hear myself think so I just kept reading or watching illegally uploaded movies online. The words on the page, or those mouthed by the actors, seemed to drown out my own thoughts. I'd cry every so often. Would get worked up by super heroes saving the world. I'd smile at people kissing in the rain on the streets on New York. I hardly even felt like drinking. My face just felt as if the corners of my eyes and mouth hung low. Low as if tiny fish hooks were dug in and anchored to bricks that swung at the ends of my arms.

I would wash the dishes. It didn't matter whose they were. We had early on established that if you used a plate, you washed the plate. That's just one of the things they fought about. I didn't mind, though. There wasn't much else I would do. If and when I decided to eat, I'd dirty a dish and a pan, have a bite or two then scrape the rest off into the bin. One time Elma caught me in the act. She was opening the fridge and just gave me a look. A look like, I could say something but you're not worth it.

I just smiled.

She rolled her eyes, stared into the cold cabinet then asked accusingly, "Did you leave any?"

"No, sorry. It went bad," I was lying, of course.

"Oh..."

"You know what?"

After a few seconds, after which I was convinced she'd just decided to ignore me altogether, she responded, "What?"

"Why don't we go get some beers or something?"

Tersely she replied, "I have no money," then dropped her jaw and rolled her eyes then left her mouth agape, her chin tucked into her neck.

I smiled diplomatically, "No worries. I'm buying. Just need a ride."

Curtly, "I don't have gas."

I sighed and shrugged my shoulders, "Fine," I leaned my back against the sink then suggested, "We can just walk or take the tram. Or we can just walk to the cantina down the street. How about that *pulque* bar? I could so totally go for one of those peanut flavored *taros*."

She still stared into our vast array of groceries: a rotten head of lettuce and two half eaten yogurts; bit her lip then said, "I don't feel like showering."

"So don't. I'm not gonna. Besides, it's not like it's freaking Christmas. And there's nobody to impress. Just a bunch of stinky hippies or toothless old men. You'll fit right in, baby."

I gave her a friendly slap on the arm with the back of my hand but she was neither in the mood or convinced and responded with, "I'll pass, but thanks."

"Come on. I'll buy you a *torta ahogada*."

"Gross."

"Fine." I sighed again and looked around the room unsure of what to do or say next. Things used to be so easy between us. Now I felt like a dirty dog. Unwanted, unloved and persecuted by everyone. She slammed the fridge door, smiled "politely", then walked away and shut herself off in her room. I, on the other hand, grabbed my tan cardigan that was hanging on the back of a kitchen chair and ventured out. I didn't really know where I was going or what I was about to do but I just felt that the absence of my presence could only mitigate matters in that house. Also, it was a Sunday, Domi had to put in overtime and, truthfully, I've always found Sunday's to be lonely and coming from Texas where they didn't sell liquor on that day, especially cruel. Thus, it was sort of a tradition to consider it a beer day and anything that reminded me of home was more than welcomed.

"Domi's looking for you," Elma plopped down in the barstool to the right of me. Its torn red leather and peaking cushion belying its age. I could only imagine how many stories it had seen, or heard, or listened to begrudgingly.

I took a drink from my *Negra Modelo*, smacked my lips then asked, "Why didn't you just tell him I was here?"

She pursed her lips, raised an eyebrow then said, "I don't know," then swiveled side to side in her seat whimsically, "Buy me a drink," she commanded coquettishly as if I had been sticking my dick in her pussy.

I laughed, "Bartender, two more!" I motioned with my fingers as I chugged half the bottle.

Two more beers and three shots of mezcal later, she was docile, all smiles and slap laughing my shoulder. I took another swig then asked, "What's been up with you two?"

She frowned, staring off into the mirror that ran the length of the bar behind the bottles and taps, "I don't know. We've known each other too long I guess. Sometimes we just get on each other's nerves. Some times you just get tired of a person and their bullshit."

I took another swig, "Yea, I know. You two are like brother and sister. I can't imagine. I can hardly stand a holiday with my siblings. It's like if it goes on for more than three hours, I'm done and ready to hit the bar. I mean, that is to say, that's how it used to feel. Now I dunno. I miss them and their stupid faces and theirs stupid jokes. Geezus, look at me? I'm all sappy. Stupid debilitating depression."

She smiled into the mouth of her beer bottle, "Aw, you're a baby! But na', me and Domi are more like sisters fighting over the same pair of shoes...," she laughed, "... who are on their periods... and have to share a car... and like the same boy at school..." she laughed again then took another swig.

"So... what you're saying... is that you like me? *Lero lero,* Elma's a chubby chaser! Ha! Ha! Loser!"

She took another drink, laughed then backhanded me on the right arm.

I leaned back, tapped the bar with one finger and said, “Hey, I’m sorry about the restroom thing. I just really had to take a shit."

She shrugged her shoulders, smiled, "It's fine. I should've started getting ready earlier. To tell you the truth, I just didn't want to go to work that day. I was just lying in bed, poking my ass all afternoon, and I guess it made me upset. This idea of having to go in and deal with a bunch of fuck-tards."

I laughed, "I know. That's what I told Domi. He just called you a stupid, irresponsible bitch who owed him forty dollars and spent all day smoking pot."

She punched me on the arm, took a drink then, "That fucking snake!"

We both laughed and reeled back in our seats. From the jukebox wailed this 1970’s tragic Mexican love ballad. I held the mouth of my bottle to my lips and played with the rind of the orange slice they had given us with the last round of mezcal. I looked out onto the far shelf of bottles. Browns, yellows, clears; Bourbons, Tequilas, Vodkas. The man staring back at me through the mirror didn't look half as bad. He wasn't all that uncouth even if every morning he stared back at me disapprovingly.

"Well," I confided, "I think you two should make up already. God, if not, me and Luis Raul decided to tie you two up and hose you down out back then leave you over night until you figured out how to undo my patented gypsy knot. By gypsy knot, I mean, of course, I was going to rope you guys together with zip-ties and call it a day."

She laughed and clinked her bottle into mine, "It'll do your *garden* good. Fucking stupid dirt buckets..."

"Hey... it's just not the right season."

She drank, "It's always spring around here! Maybe that's the problem. Everybody does whatever they want, whenever they want.”

"What do you mean? Problem with what?"

"I don't know. Never mind. Forget what I said. Just nobody takes anything seriously because it's always summer or something. It's like they think they can do whatever the fuck they want and it'll always be sunny and warm. When it's always spring...ugh... I dunno what I'm saying... Hey, I really have to go take a piss. I'll be right back," she swiveled off and headed to the restroom. I ordered three more shots of, this time of rumplemintz, and drank one by myself.

A few minutes later, she pulled out the chair and smiled impishly, "You're going to love this!" and in a full on baritone voice, she boomed out the lyrics to the song that came on next. She clutched her hands to her chest then waved around her beer and belted out something about love being a horrible burden but the best burden ever. I didn't recognize the song but I raised a glass and faked the extending chorus. We laughed and an old man, sitting by himself near the restroom at a small table for two, took a swig of his *Sol*. He smiled oblivious to the stink of piss, shit and vomit. Elma raised her shot glass to him, then down the hatch. She slapped her hand against her mouth, winced then burped. I shot mine with a, "I know, huh? Delicious! Just like Christmas in your mouth!"

She gagged a bit and I ordered another round then the tab.

We stumbled home through the streets, passing vendors shutting down for the night as children kicked balls and chased each other. The sun was setting and women stood by the doors to their homes. Some were smoking. Some, just gossiping and fanning themselves. A few teenagers sat on the trunks of cars, sharing chips and candy, drinking soda and courting each other's hormones. I tapped every trash bin along the way as if it were a magic marker or a pet's head.

"Careful," I confided to Elma, "I don't think that bitch with the poo'le picks up his shit."

She smiled and wrapped an arm under my pits and around my torso. I continued, "Hey, isn't this heaven? Like everything? Like people just happy being happy? Like no Xbox's or PlayStations and just kids running around on the streets. Like kids actually being kids?"

She laughed, "You're drunk," as we stumbled into a tree.

I laughed, "No, No YOU'RE drunk!" then laughed and stopped, reached for a ciggie, with some difficulty, then lit one as she walked on ahead.

I caught up to her, "Hey, thanks for coming. I still really don't know anybody here and like I don't care what happens between you and Domi. Like you can always count on me. And like we can have 'Sex and the City' dates and talk about penises or something. FYI, I don't like Domi's penis. It's ugly and he has no foreskin."

She hunched over, dying of laughter. The kind of laughter that's so funny it's basically silent wisps of air and toothy gums. She put her hands over her lips, her eyes slits with tears pooling at the edges.

Her knees buckled in and she began to lift her long black skirt.

Suddenly keen to the situation I yelled, "No babe! Don't!"

She gagged, "BUT! I!... But I!..." she couldn't stop laughing. A neighbor pulled back their curtains from a window. An orange glow escaped into the then dark street for a split second then disappeared as the street lights just hummed. Elma crab crawled to the door of a closed optical business and crouched.

She wouldn't stop laughing, "...I.... have... to..."

She just really wouldn't stop laughing, "...PEEEEE!!!..."

I leaned over, swaying myself. One wrong left foot and I would've gone tumbling down. I grabbed her by the arm, "Oh no you don't! I'm running for the board of the neighborhood association. Or, at least, I'm trying to convince *la vecina* that we're not all a bunch of drunk, drug addicts," I straightened her out and pulled her by the elbow down the three or so houses before we had to turn a corner. I felt like a principal escorting a troublesome child. I just prayed that this one was potty trained.

When we got in, she ran to the restroom and slammed the door behind her. From within you could hear a strong stream of urine escaping her vagina at warp speed. I cringed at the image that had just popped into my mind.

I tossed my cardigan on a stool in the living room by the counter table, "*Hola* Luis."

"*Hola*, Marveen," he said disinterested as he rested against the wall in his room beside the string of lights he'd strung up "fashionably".

I walked over, smiling, "Whatya doing?" I stretched myself alongside him to his dismay. His pillows smelled of face sweat and his sheets like unwashed feet. I laughed and thought again, "heaven". He flipped a page, sighed and rolled his eyes then licked a finger and turned another page and said:

"Oh, nothing. You know. Just here... reading."

I flipped over onto my back, put my hands behind my head and watched blissfully the shadows on the ceiling, "Oh," I looked out past his dividers and saw a shadow move in the kitchen. A bit elated, perhaps a bit hyper, I shimmied out of his bed, again to his slight annoyance, and made my way into the kitchen. In doing so I almost knocked over his entire haphazardly constructed wall.

In the kitchen, Elma was leaning on the table smiling into her plastic tumbler. It was a purple-pink, or just perhaps a pink, but below the water line it was a darker hue. It swished back and forth from her lips, to the bottom, to her lips.

I held out my arm, "Gimme some," and motioned my hand like a baby grasping at air.

A door opened from down the dark hall. Domi walked through the kitchen, shirtless in jeans and barefoot, past us and into Luis Raul's space. He asked him for a phone charger then basically stomped back into the din. Elma made a face and wagged her hand as if to silently say I was in for a spanking.

"Eeeee... somebody's gonna get it..." she laughed. I laughed, faking confidence, then took another gulp of water.

"You know," I told her, "I never got why you people don't just drink the tap water? I mean, you brush your teeth with it, right? Isn't it like the same thing?"

She swiped the cup from my hand, slurped it down, held it out, meditatively, then said, "I think, my friend, that you, sir, are in trouble and no amount of philosophizing is gonna get you out of it," her head swayed side to side a bit as she poked me three times with her left index finger on my shoulder.

"Great! That's all I need..." I rolled my eyes then stumbled towards the fridge. Hit the wall instead, then careened toward Domi's room.

The door was locked.

From inside he yelled curtly, "Who is it?"

I knocked with the middle knuckle of my right index finger, "Me!"

"Who?" he said, this time incredulously.

"Marveen! Hurry..." knock, knock, "Open up!"

"Wait..." there was a shuffling in the room. Noises. Books or magazines slapping against each other. The dresser drawer opening and closing. Silence. A few seconds then the door opened but just a sliver.

He poked his nose then his mouth out, "What?" he asked tepidly.

"Quit being such a buffoon. Open up," I tried to force my way in but he pushed back the door.

He stuck out his mustache again, "No."

"What? Are you serious? Come on... I'm tired... and I just want to lay down."

Shortly he said, "No. You run off without leaving any word."

"Ugh... But I told Elma!"

"Mmmm... well then why don't you go crash in *Elma's* room?" he accentuated her name, lengthening it as if he was rolling out a piece of rope, a noose on his tongue, for me to hang myself with.

I balled my hands into fists and punched the side of my legs, "Don't start! We just went down the street."

Calmly he said, "Ah..."

Me not quite composed, replied, "Ah? Ah what?!"

Nonchalantly, he continued, "Nothing. It's just like, what? You act as if you don't have a boyfriend or something?"

Astonished I asked, "Whatya mean?! You said you had to work and that then you were gonna stop by David's! I honestly was just gonna go for one drink and then Elma showed up!"

"Ah, so then Elma's your boyfriend now? I didn't know you two were dating. Is it serious? How long has it been? Have you set a date? Oh and if you said Elma JUST showed up I'm sure she told you that I was looking for you."

From the kitchen, a long and loud, "Oooooo," from Elma then Luis Raul hushing her. Suddenly embarrassed, frustratingly he said, "Get in!" and hurried me along. The room was dimly lit by the small lamp on top of the dresser.

I dropped my ass on the bed and was about to lay back but he pulled me up by the collar.

He said, inhibited, "No, you don't get off that easy! We're going to talk about this!" I probably shouldn't have rolled my eyes but he continued, the *picture* of composure, "You don't have any money for rent but you have plenty to go drinking?! And I'm pretty sure you spent half of that buying *that bitch* drinks too because she can't even afford to pay me back!" he turned away and began rearranging random items on his dresser then just put them back exactly how they were.

I moaned, "Ughhhh..." and slammed myself backwards

onto the bed, "Geezus! I was with Elma! We had a few beers! That's it!"

"A few beers my ass! You're fucking wasted! And you know very well that right now me and her aren't on the best of terms. But nooooo... *ay andas*... making a fool of yourself and not even giving me the common courtesy of leaving a note?! A fucking note, Marveen, that's all I ask. You don't have a phone... You say you can't afford one because you don't have any money... but then you come home reeking of alcohol and you can't even respect me enough to leave me a fucking note?!"

"Ay, you said that this morning! That's just how I always smell! It's glandular!"

He leaned against the far wall and crossed his arms, "So what?! What do you have to say for yourself?! Huh? Anything?" he walked up to the bed and kicked the mattress, "No! Don't you DARE fall asleep!"

I rubbed my eyes and rolled to my left then sat up, "What?! Domi?! What do you want me to say?! Fuck! Honestly it's not a big deal! You weren't here so I went for a freakin' drink! Elma showed up and we had a few more! What did you expect me to just lounge around the house reading coloring books with Luis?!"

He paced back and forth then rubbed his hands into his face, gave his back to me then said, "Ay! Forget it! If I have to explain it to you then there's no point!"

"Geezus! Take the tampon out already and just tell me!" I flopped back down and checked my watch then closed my eyes.

He kicked the mattress again and yelled, "DON'T FALL ASLEEP! And what do I expect?! What I expect is for you to fucking grow up. For you to, I dunno, maybe get up in the mornings and go looking for a job? Or, hey, maybe not spend money you 'supposedly' don't have? Or, hey, and this might sound crazy, maybe show some fucking solidarity for your boyfriend?!"

I groaned and tossed my left forearm over my eyes.

He turned off the lamp with a steaming, *"BUENO!"*

I'm not sure exactly how long I was asleep for but when I came to, it was basically pitch dark save for what little light hummed off the curtains. My head. Oh god my head! For a second my sinuses were killing me so I sat up until the pain subsided. I looked around to get my bearings. Domi was sitting at the head of the bed, shaking one leg and biting his nails. He craned his neck back, eyes closed, muttering something to himself. I pulled myself over the bed, closer to him and tried to untangle his arms but he violently propelled me in the opposite direction.

"Get away from me! You're so annoying!"

Still drunk, I hissed, "Ash!"

"ASH! ASH! ASH! ! THAT'S ALL YOU FUCKING KNOW HOW TO SAY!"

"Whoa... What did I do now?

"You know very well what!"

"Go out with Elma? Man, it's not my fucking fault you two are fighting. Next week you'll be best friends again. I'm not taking sides or anything, man."

He bit his nails again, his phone lighted up, he looked at it and I could see he was angry or hungry or something. I don't know, I'm really bad with expressions. He stopped shaking his leg then said, "No."

I moaned then said, "Then what?!" raised my hands in exasperation, "And who the fuck are you texting so late?!"

"It's not late. It's ten. You just got drunk and passed out early."

"It's called *napping*. Who the fuck do you always text?"

"David."

"Oh. Tell him I said hi."

"No, you get on his nerves."

"Well, then, good."

He began shaking his leg again, "I can't believe you! You just go out without leaving word. Not even a note. Nothing. *Haci si ni tuvieras dueño*. And what? Am I supposed to just wait here, with my thumb up my ass, until you so kindly decide to grace us with your stupid, drunk-ass presence? Well no! Next time, I'm just gonna go out with my friends too and get drunk. Let's see how you like it!"

"Ash."

"Hmpf."

"Domi! Enough! I was just going for a beer! I swear! I invited Elma but she was being all like, No this, no that, so I just went out by myself. She showed up eventually and we just hung around for a little."

"Oh, so she knew where you were at all along?!" and then to himself he whispered, "Fucking bitch...."

"No, well I told her that I'd maybe be there. I honestly didn't know where I was going to end up. I just got lazy and stopped by the nearest bar."

"Basta! Enough! I don't want to hear it!"

"Fine!" I started to get up, stumbled, and caught my head on the door.

He jumped to his feet, "Where in the hell do you think you're going?!"

"The couch!" I cautiously massaged my forehead then turned around.

He yelled, "We don't even have a couch!"

"Oh, that's right! I forgot we don't even have any fucking fuck furniture you fucking third world sonsabitches!" I reached in my pocket, grabbed the few coin pesos and a bill then tossed it at him, "Here. Go cray! Splurge on a bean bag!" Then turned back around. The fucking door was locked or stuck or glued to the wall. In an instant Domi rocketed to in between me and the exit then slammed his hand on the door, which I had still yet to figure out how to work. Shit was like a Rubik's cube!

"Where. Are. You. Going?!" his breath was hot and heavy into my face. I was half expecting him to hit me so I flinched then spat out, "Dranking!"

He yelled back, "No! You're not going anywhere!"

"Says who?" I brought my hand daintily to my chest in surprise, "You? Mister... you are no boss of me! I do what I fucking want!"

"Ni madres!"

"Papas con chorizo!" I hollered back and snapped my fingers like a catty drag queen.

He grabbed me by the face, squeezed my head. I tried pinching his rib cage but there was no meat to grab onto. He then rammed lips into mine. I resisted and when he tried to stick his tongue into my mouth, running it along my teeth, I responded by biting his lip before just drunkenly giving in.

The next day, as dawn was breaking, the church bells were tolling again, every few minutes, like incessant mothers before school. We were lying in bed naked. I think I might've had one sock on and my underwear loosely hung at my right ankle. My head. Oh god my head. I could hear my heart pounding in my head. I propped myself up on my elbows, massaged my eyes then the pain subsided. I blew out my nose the pressure that had built up, and soon it was entirely gone. I laid back down, massaged my forehead then turned to my right to kiss him. I aimed for the corner of his mouth where it wasn't quite the cheek but thereabouts.

At every ding dong ding he would mutter, "Leave me alone... five more minutes"... then when my lips grazed his he said, "Oww," then tenderly caressed the area with his left hand. I didn't think he was actually awake-awake but there he was, lightly tapping the bottom of his lip and moaning quietly as if to himself.

"What's the matter?" I cooed and hugged my head to his chest.

"You bit me! It fucking hurts a lot."

I giggled, "Sick day? Come on, call in. I do believe that you've come down with a case of Zombie Kisses..."

"*Cual que 'seek da-ee'*. One of us has to make a living."

"Mmm."

His phone buzzed on top of a pile of clothes by the bed so I leaned over to grab it for him. He got up with start and snatched it out of my hand almost viciously.

"Whoa, cowboy. I was just gonna get it for you."

He blinked his eyes open then squinted at the screen, "It's work. I have to go in now, now."

I laid back down, put my left hand behind my head and stared at the ceiling. I could see faces and a ship as if I was laying under the clouds in a park, "Well, hurry. You're gonna be late," I sighed, a part of me longing for romance but another part of me knowing what I signed on for. Architects were boring and anal about everything. He just laid there, clutching his phone as another set of bells rang.

I prodded him, "Hurry. Who's gonna pay rent then?"

Eyes still closed he said, "Leave me alone. Tell Elma, now that you two are such good friends."

"Pfft...I had to pay for everything last night."

His phone buzzed again and he sighed, "Ay, Marveen, *no mames*. As it is you hardly have any money..."

"A duh... What's the point of having a sugar daddy if I can't spend his money carelessly," I smiled and looked over but he just laid there motionless, probably concocting some other comment about how idly I passed my time.

He sighed, "I want a sugar daddy..."

I reached under the covers towards his dick, "No, *bebe,* you're too ugly."

He laughed, "If you only knew how many guys have tried to..."

I scoffed, "Pfft, then go. I'll marry Ruben and I'll occupy myself shopping with Alicia and Anabel."

He smiled, "Oh yeah? Whore," he began tickling me and wouldn't stop until I shoved him off the bed. He crawled back naked. From the waist down he was so hairy it was as if he were wearing a pair of black leggings.

I commented, "You're like a bear."

He retorted, "You're the fat one."

"No, *bebe*, you meant to say that I'm the one 'full of honey'," I winked and laughed.

"Yeah, sure," he raised his brow. I laughed then tried picking his nose but he said, "Don't start."

"Domiiiii.... Domiiiiiiiiiiii..." I hushed out in rhythm to the tapping of my finger on his bare chest.

He sang, "Marveeeeen... Marveeeeen..." he mimicked then kissed my forehead sheepishly with a wince, suddenly recalling that bruised orifice.

"Domi, *te hago el* like."

He laughed, "You, you're not so bad yourself."

Luis Raul's feet smelled so bad that I had to buy a can of Ajax and give him some sob story about how I too suffered a life long struggle with Athlete's foot. I cornered him and said, "See, just sprinkle some on the shower floor and rub your feet in it. Then take a brush or towel and scrub off all the dead skin. I mean, sprays help but whenever you shower, you're probably just reinfecting yourself with the fungus. And that fungus just lives off of dead skin and shit. Why do you think we all wear flip-flops? Also I got you this bag. See? I cut eyeholes. No more of that crying children running away from you in the streets nonsense," then I patted his chest and stumbled away.

Now that that was out of the way, I decided on exploring the city by myself. A few days ago I figured out where Domi had hid the bottle. I'd take a five count then head out the door. It was like being on the bridge of the Enterprise. I just pointed randomly and said "Engage!" Of course, I'd always been more partial to Janeway than Picard or Kirk so I spent half the time pretending I was a confident, self-empowered, hip chick.

Seemed legit.

There were so many things to do. Museums which I thought were free but weren't. Stores to window shop galore. They had entire streets selling the same item. This one was for glasses. This one was for shoes. This one was for books. That one was for pecans or some shit like that. Every few blocks was a square with a lawn you could just lay down in. Along the way you'd pass orange trees. I picked out one but it was rotten and full of worms. I thought, "Eee, just my luck," and tossed it over my shoulder where it rolled under some poor old lady's shoe and almost sent her flying.

My favorite thing to do was people watch, though. There were tons of parks littered with shoeless vagrants and children who should've been in school. I hardly saw anybody who looked suspicious. There were plenty of tourists and enough people giving tours where I could just hang back at the edges, smile, and smoke a cigarette. That's another thing: hardly anybody smoked there. Well at least they didn't smoke while walking. I felt like a sore thumb. I knew that there had to be people who smoked. Every few meters was a trash bin and atop the main receptacle was a little tray to put butts in. It was hard to come across a bar though. Most of the small pubs were on *Libertad,* which lay in between the main center and *Chapultepec*, the main fairway that led to Santa Tere where we lived. I rode the tram and the buses, which were 6 pesos each. Not too shabby. Most people our age were good looking and fashionable, which helped mitigate the fact that everything smelled like piss and sweat. I was hardly ever hungry but I enjoyed walking through the food markets. I would try and gauge which little mom and pop shop was the best by the amount of patrons circling the register. Even if every stand basically sold the same sorts of *tacos* and *tortas* and had the same slew of Coca-Cola products. At the front of the market were stacks of honey in varying sizes of jars. If you kept walking up a block you came to a street that sold nothing but fresh produce and ran along the same stretch as this old children's hospital which had been transformed into a museum. I walked in once and was unimpressed. The medieval looking images staring out as if themselves bored at being on display.

If ever I got turned around, there were these monoliths of directions pointing the wayward traveller to a sight seeing destination. If in that didn't help, everybody was but all too happy to help you find your way. The population was nothing like the Juarez or El Paso I had left behind. Back home, everyone looked upon each other with a large measure of distrust. In Guadalajara, life was chill, relaxed and basically without incident. Maybe I was just too drunk to notice.

Fridays were our movie nights. The Internet connection was slow but we managed. Dinners then largely constituted of chocolates and chips and eventually I had convinced them to invest in popcorn. We'd drink homemade limeade and smoke a bowl or two out of an apple. Then one by one, they'd all putter off to their respective rooms.

Saturdays were always party days. Once in a while we'd hit up a new club. Every week there'd be another or the same locale under different management. Most times we just hit up house parties and I'd make new friends. These new friends largely consisted of people whom I had met prior but had since forgotten in my drunken stupor.

The days were short because I slept so much while everyone was out at work. The nights, however, were long as I spent them in the kitchen writing. I could write most weeknights when Domi was in bed and Luis Raul had drifted off to sleep. Usually Luis Raul just watched videos on his phone then passed out, farting intermittently like the Bells of the churches. The weekends though were a different story. I was either too drunk or too busy tagging along behind Domi.

Also I felt it only polite to give Luis Raul some privacy with his guests.

Life was good. Nothing spectacular but nothing altogether bad. I always had food, a bed, and someone to lie with even if everyday it seemed as if Domi would get stuck later and later at work. Dinners were with Elma or Luis Raul and one of his friends. Sometimes I'd just have peanuts and chips at the bar. I'd stare across the counter at the mirror, smile to myself, then look on secretly to the patrons. Most of the time, the bartender spent it playing pinball. She was a petite but affable young lady about my age. There were hardly any customers. I got to recognize people peddling peyote infused snake oils, a small boy who sold candy for a school trip that never seemed to come, and a few townies. Most of the townies were older men who shuffled in with a toothless smile. No martini glasses and no matter how empty the place was, they'd all manage to find a seat next to me. One of the fellows was this 48-year-old taxi driver named Francisco Javier. I recall our first conversation revolving around beards and how for a time he used to dye it different colors. He said it grew out so white that he'd just one day decided, Hey, why not orange? Then it went to green, then to purple. He was a nice older man. The youngest of seven children, three boys, three girls, and himself. He talked often about his three children, two boys and one girl. We broached the subjects of finding work and how hard it was for an older gentleman. I was reminded of my father. But Francisco Javier was twice the size and with blue eyes. One time we spent a good half hour talking genetics and how he found out it was a recessive trait at the hospital. Apparently he had been taken into the emergency room and had his blood drawn and the nurse told the staff to pay special attention to him because people with colored eyes were lacking something. He said, when he was younger, those eyes helped with the ladies. Unfortunately none of his children were passed on that trait. In fact, his sons couldn't even grow a proper beard. To this he went on and told me about an old home remedy involving the juice of a "tender onion", the kind that are small and have a green stalk. Something like a green onion I imagined.

Francisco had a friend named Juan Carlos who smiled a lot but didn't say much. He was definitely toothless. A gummy old chap who always wore a baseball hat, loafers and white socks. Francisco would talk so much it'd be enough conversation for the two. Once or twice, Juan Carlos' wife would saunter in, ask for an ice cold Coca-Cola, wipe her forehead and say it was time for dinner. She always offered us a plate and sometimes Francisco would follow them down the street but I always politely refused. She was a nice lady. Portly with silver white hair. Her name was Martha and she worked at a hostel or hotel near the center of the city every other day. After five, she would take a bus to Chapultepec then walk up the avenue to Santa Tere. Their children were long gone but she sometimes watched her niece's little girl in the evenings. She mentioned how lonely a house would be without company. Said that's one of the reasons she worked and liked working where she was at. The place, even on a slow week, had people.

"You should stop by sometime! There's always foreigners. Young kids, your age, you'd like them. It'd beat hanging around these old crows," she laughed then kissed Juan Carlos who'd smile then wave his hand as if shushing a fly. She'd just slap him on his back and walk back out. I don't think I ever saw her finish a Coca-Cola, much less pay for one. Dafne, the waitress behind the bar, didn't seem to mind much. Sometimes she wouldn't even charge me for the peanuts. Often she offered me a free hand of *carne seca*. It felt like the Guadalajaran version of Cheers.

Sometimes kids would walk in from the street. They'd be sweaty from kicking a ball as cars whizzed by. They'd ask for water or a soda or some candy then swarm around the pinball machine. Once or twice when they'd run out of money, Dafne would walk behind the machine, reset a button, and they'd get a few free games.

If ever someone around my age walked in, they were usually tourists looking for directions. One time I met a couple of Europeans who were following a punk band around the world. At first they were offish. Sat at the end of the bar near a window drinking Indios and smoking a cigarette. Well, the girl smoked, her friend only ever so often protested with a slight cough. I was about to walk outside to have me my own nicotine fix but said, what the hey, and asked if they didn't mind me joining the table. It was this long bench of a thing that ran the length of the front wall. What else could they say but yes?

They had a bucket of beer and asked, reluctantly, if I'd want one. I suppose they were used to pan handlers and beggars. I lifted my glass and said no thank you, then offered them a sip of my drink. They looked at it suspiciously. I just responded with, "It's only vodka water."

The girl, lightly tanned with freckles, reached out her hand with an okay. Her hair was bound in a red kerchief around the top that held back a mane of sandy colored curls. Her friend was a thin, almost porcelain pale man with short yellow blonde hair. He wore Buddy Holly's, a black shirt and shorts.

She smiled, a bit afraid, took a sip then winced, "Wow," she said, "That's my first experience with vodka water."

I don't remember their names but she was French and it turned out that he was German. They had one day just decided to follow this band and had been riding with them ever since. The only thing was that Mexico was their last stop. Apparently the band was heading off to Europe next week and couldn't afford to fly them back.

In the short space of time it had taken for me to present myself as an alcoholic and for them to divulge their plans to travel the rest of Mexico, a good rapport had grown. We talked about nothing in particular. The German liked Star Trek and we went from there. He mentioned his first and only nerd convention, which was expensive to get in and then expensive to meet any of the actors. From there we went onto popular movies and the cinema culture we had all grown up with. Luckily, most popular movies from our youth were American. It was also a pleasure to speak "American". Sometimes it felt as if my English and vocabulary had gone down the shits. The German was a vegan, who didn't smoke. His French comrade didn't have much of a dietary preference besides beer. I mentioned that I had the same penchant but was trying to drop a few pounds. From there we argued the virtues of the American system versus the Metric.

It was a good time. About an hour later, a tall bearded young man with glasses walked in. He was wearing a red t-shirt and gray shorts with sneakers and was waved over by my company. Apparently he was Italian but lived in Tamaulipas. They were all supposed to meet for a drink but all got turned around. Frenchy's phone hadn't had signal. It was an old Nokia. I loved it. We were all immediately and simply lost. Strangers around a hearth at night. An exciting storm brewing outside. We spoke much about adventure and our future plans. We all came to the conclusion that all we really wanted to do *was* get lost. Frenchy of course said she had an itinerary of things she wanted to see before she died but admitted that some of the best times she had were when plans went awry.

"So if you guys are staying near downtown, why did you walk all the way over here?"

She laughed, "Our cleaning lady said that there was a *pulque* bar nearby."

I laughed, "Yeah, it's just up the street. About a block and to the left. It's a nice hole in the wall hewn out of an old house. You should so totally try the peanut flavored one. The oatmeal one's pretty dope too."

The German laughed and motioned to Frenchy, "I think you are allergic to peanuts no?"

Frenchy took a drink from her beer and nodded. The Italian didn't drink. He just leaned in and tried practicing his English. Every now and then he'd ask me to repeat something so I just repeated it in Spanish. About the only thing he contributed to the conversation was his trip that morning to a polluted lake that would burn your skin off or something. That and the fact that he had loved their hostel because it had hot running water. I, of course, was jealous. They all stayed at, what turned out to be, the place Martha worked at. I thought, how funny, what a small world.

We all took a bathroom break then went on about the kinds of luxuries you left behind when letting yourself out on the road. The little things became precious. The couple spoke of splurging and going for sushi later at a place near their hostel. I talked about missing my apartment and a working Google connection. I hadn't noticed how late it had gotten until Dafne walked over and said I had a phone call. I think I was as much surprised as the rest of the group. She led me behind the bar and near the register, stuck a piece of jerky in her mouth, offered me one, I shook my head with smile, then said:

"Hello?"

A man's voice responded playfully, "Hello..."

"Hello? Who's this?"

He laughed, "Well who do you think?"

"Domi?"

"Duh! You weren't answering my emails. I thought you were mad or something."

"No," I looked up to god, disappointed in my lack of responsibility, "No, I'm sorry, it's just that I forgot they have shitty Wi-Fi here. I was going to just have a drink or two then head back but I made some friends and we stayed talking by the window."

"Ah, well, so I'm almost out of work. I should be done in a few minutes and then it'll take me about 40 minutes to get home."

"Okay, we're still on for dinner right? I made... uhmm... ramen!"

Domi laughed, “Mmmm no, well, we can pick up something."

"Okay, see you then."

I handed back the phone to Dafne. She was still chewing on the piece of dried meat, reached over for the bottle of cheap vodka and began to pour me another drink.

"You know, you should really think about selling fruit around here. Like an apple or something," I proffered. She shrugged, handed me my newly refilled glass then smiled and did a quick about face towards an old man. She leaned against the bar, examining her cuticles and grinned as he regaled her of something involving dinosaurs or cavemen.

I walked back to the table and we talked some more. Within twenty minutes or so, Frenchy said that she was getting hungry and asked if I'd like to join them for dinner. She said she hadn't minded not being able to visit the *pulque* place but said she had fun anyway. The German told her to get my number and we exchanged digits. They reminded me that they wouldn't be in town for much longer but that they'd appreciate grabbing a drink later. The Italian said he was off to shower then meet up with some friends at a pub on *Libertad*. I graciously declined and told them that my handler was expecting me. I watched them pay their tab and walk out into the dark street. Silently I prayed that they'd have a safe journey home and enjoy the rest of their stay.

On my walk back, I looked up into the sky and thought, oh how pretty. I wasn't drunk-drunk but I'd be lying if I said that a blanket of euphoria hadn't crept over. It felt good to have an evening with friends. With MY friends or friends I had made. I spent few days like that. Sometimes I'd just meander about with my pocket journal but hadn't gotten much writing done. I always felt too self conscious or pretentious jotting down ideas. I decided that I was the type of writer who reflected at night, alone and in silence. At most, noise would well from the tiny speakers from my computer and even then, many nights I had to use head phones so as not to disturb Domi's drooling slumber. Any other time and there'd always be someone peering over my shoulder or someone with a joke they just heard which needed repeating.

I thought back to the dogs and felt guilty. I remembered yelling at the birds to stop chewing on the blinds or the sofa. Then I felt guilty for not having such said affection for the fish. When I walked past the front gate, I took one last look goodbye to the day. I told myself that I should email my mother more often. I told myself that it wasn't enough that I'd push "like" on the photos my sister posted of her kids. I told myself that I could surely take more than the two seconds it took to do that, and leave a little word or try a little harder. It'd surely be a better use of my time instead of lying awake for hours, staring at the ceiling and trying to hypnotize myself into sleep with the fan. Certainly, I could and should be more amicable to my family.

No one was home, of course. The house was dark save for the kitchen light. I made my way to the fridge. There was a rotting banana and some left over *salsas* from Luis Raul's tirade on the taco stand down the street. I sighed and took a seat at the kitchen table after pouring myself a glass from the giant blue jug of purified water. I eyeballed my watch every so often. Ten, then twenty, then thirty minutes. Domi should've been home by now but no dice. You could hear people walking past the front door and once or twice I swore it was Elma but it wasn't and the voices would just fade off into the distance. I walked into our room and looked for my water bottle of vodka only to find it empty and a note taped to it. In all caps, as is customary with architects, was written, DON'T EVEN THINK ABOUT IT. YOU OWE ME A SHIRT.

I shrugged it off and instead opted for a cigarette. I walked out into the garden. At least I could grow slices of grass and swore I had spotted a chive or two.

I thought, perhaps I could, as I was sometimes accustomed to doing, walk up and down the street, singing. I reminded myself to stick out my belly, to take full advantage of my diaphragm. I'd pick up rocks that were interesting. Nobody paid much mind. Only once or twice did a car zoom by heckling or whistling at me. One time a neighbor lady told me to keep on singing. That I sung beautifully. She then belted out in a traditional love ballad as she tossed a bucket of mop water into the street.

Those older neighbors were terribly nice. They waved and I waved twice or three times in their direction. I was petrified that they hadn't seen me being likewise polite. They smiled and I stumbled along smiling as they swept or rested on chairs in the shade of these giant tropical trees. Back home they sold them as indoor plants and you were lucky if they made it through the year. But these things here were massive on the main fairways. Their leaves were wide and waxy, about the size of my face.

My poor garden, trying its darndest in spite of me. I heard a car whizz by. I heard a car park and then a door slam after a minute. It must've been Domi. He was always in a rush not to be driving at night. He said that they had always stopped him because he drove a black car with bullet holes.

I just stood out there, a bit dizzy and staring out into nothing. I looked down and took a swig from my water. Domi walked out and said:

"Where did you find it?!"

"Find what?" I replied then took a drag from my cigarette. I was thinking about how much I missed MY cigarettes but had settled for harsh *Delicados* and Lucky Strikes.

"The vodka!"

I hadn't realized it, but I wasn't holding a cup of water anymore. I was staring out at the tree by the alley with a bottle in hand, "Actually, I honestly don't know. Where were you? I've been waiting for like an hour."

He held his coat jacket in his hand and rubbed the back of his neck, "I just had to finish something before I left. I sent you an email."

"Oh, I haven't checked my phone," I took another swig and smiled at the tree then turned around. I walked over to kiss him but he dodged my lips.

"No," he smiled peevishly, "My breath smells."

I smiled, "I don't care. Mine probably smells worse."

He averted my gaze, smiled, patted me on the chest lightly then turned around and began to walk towards the house. I took one last look at the tree then followed him into the kitchen where he was taking out a box of Jumex Pineapple juice. I sat down at the table, smiled and tucked my chin into my hand, looking on at him lovingly. My big ol' workingman. I asked, "So where do you feel like eating?"

He reached into the cupboard, pulled out a plastic red tumbler and placed it on the table. He sighed as he poured himself a drink then reached for my bottle and put a splash of vodka in it. As he was tightening the top he said, "Actually, I just ate."

I looked on, a bit confused, but didn't say anything.

He went on, "I was just going to ask you what you wanted. We can pick something up from wherever but I was pretty sure you'd just want tacos from down the street."

I looked down at the table, "When did you eat? I thought we were supposed to grab something?"

"Oh," he pulled out a chair, sat then bit the tip of his thumb and continued, "The guys at work, they bought some *tortas* downstairs because we had to stay late."

"Oh..."

"But hey, let's go grab you something."

"No... that's fine," I felt a little perplexed. I couldn't very well get upset with Domi for having to work late, but the feeling of our semi-romantic dinner plans being dashed left me wanting, "Actually, you know, I wasn't that hungry anyway. My stomach's been acting weird all week. Do you want to go grab a beer or something?"

"Ay, Marveen, you need to take better care of yourself. And no, I'm tired. And you, you need to quit drinking so much."

I smiled, "No, I can't. Vodka NEEDS me. It's my only..."

His phone vibrated and he answered immediately, "Yes?...Yes...a huh....Yes....No...Okay (he laughed)... See you tomorrow."

"Who was that?"

"Just some guy from work. Uhmm, he needed to know something about the new installation we're sending out tomorrow."

"He seemed funny."

"What do you mean?" he barked out a little guarded.

"Like I dunno. You laughed. He seemed funny."

He tapped the table with his finger, looked into his drink then took another swig.

I smiled and tapped the side of the bottle, "Oh, hey, I met some cool..."

He pushed back his chair and stood up, "Hey, I'm gonna go take a quick shower before bed."

My mouth agape, "... Oh... okay, I guess. Do you want to watch a movie or something after? I can make some popcorn and we could..."

He stretched out his arms, "No. You know I'm really beat. But you go on ahead. I can set up the laptop out here but I don't know if it has any battery."

"No, no that's fine. I'll snuggle up with you."

He laughed then tussled my hair, patted my head and walked away into the bedroom. I pushed my own chair back and followed him. I stood by the door as he undressed.

"Anyhow, so yeah, I met these folks around my age today at the bar. They're traveling through Mexico. One was a..."

"That's nice. It's nice that you're making friends. What do they do?"

"I don't think they *do* anything. They're just traveling through..."

"Ah, I see. Hey, have you talked to Anabel about Gilberto's gallery? Maybe you could show something there next month."

"Yeah, I should message her tomorrow. But, yeah, so like one was from..."

"You should really message her tonight. Why wait until tomorrow?"

"Uhmm, okay, I'll get online in a bit. But so like I was saying..."

He walked past me and tapped my belly, "Tell me more in a bit. I just really want to shower and get into bed."

"Okay..."

"So am I in your book?"

Anabel asked over a small aluminum cafe table. It was painted over with an old Corona logo. I always thought it a bit peculiar to eat outside.

I smiled and traced the beer logo with my finger, "Nope, it's all about people I used to know in El Paso. Turns out there's really nothing other than drinking we did. Some drugs, some parties. But most of it revolves around getting into trouble at a bar or after a bar."

She clasped her hands under the table and leaned in, "You should let me read it."

To her left, Ruben sat with his back to the street, sipping from his mimosa as I took a gulp from my Indio beer. Anabel reached for her paper coffee cup. Her arm like the neck of a swan.

I leaned my head back in dismay and stared up into the sky, "Ughhhh... I dunno. Nothing's typed up. It's all longhand in notebooks. I figured if I did it that way, I'd be forced to revise it at least once by having to type it out later. It's just frustrating sometimes."

She tore off a little piece of a bagel that sat on a paper plate by her coffee, "So it's like poems of you and your friends getting drunk?"

I sighed, Ruben laughed, then I said with a sarcastic smile, "Something like that..."

She was satisfied with the answer and looked out onto the street. It was a Wednesday and we were at the far end of Chapultepec. There's was plenty of traffic and pedestrians to keep us occupied whenever there'd be a lull in the conversation. Ruben flagged down the waiter, a short, pudgy, pale guy with attitude. He had sandy hair and freckles that cascaded over his developing second chin. Ruben rocked his champagne flute side to side and called out, "Another!" then gestured to me, "Do you need one too?"

I rolled my shoulders, "Sure," I could not get over how many bees there were everywhere we went. One had fluttered into one of my empty beer bottles whilst his cohorts gave Anabel plenty of opportunity to practice her Kung Fu. Ruben didn't much mind. He just said at the beginning, "I'm terribly allergic", smiled, then raised a hand by his mouth and whispered, "Just don't let THEM know that."

Anabel had been awfully quiet. I was so used to her running her mouth off, as if she was some sort of well versed five year old, that I figured something must be up. She sat there for long and longer periods just eyeing the birds and the people almost shyly. She picked at her bagel and when she decided to pop a piece in her mouth, instead of just ripping it apart on the plate, she'd chew with her head down.

I couldn't help but pry, "What's up with you, babe?"

Ruben set his flute down, smacked his lips then widened his eyes as if he was keeping a secret that he could finally let into the light. He said, "She's having troubles with Gilberto."

I dramatically frowned then said, "Oh no..."

Sarcastically, Ruben said, "He beats her," chuckled then grandiosely chugged the remaining cocktail. He ended with a, "How fucking hard is it to get a damned drink around here?!"

I eyed the table, trying to figure out what to say next. Instead, I leaned forward and snagged a piece of her bread, pinched it between my fingers, examining the tiny black seeds, then tossed it at her head, "Am I going to have to call Oprah?"

She laughed, reached for her own ammunition and got me square in the left eye, "No," she grinned, then reclined in her chair, arms crossed and continued, "He's just busy. Well, he says he's busy..."

Ruben snapped his fingers, "Girlfriend, Tyrone don't got no job."

She went on meekly, "It's just with the gallery and all.... Things haven't been working out so well. The guys he hired to fix the pipes and set up the walls want to charge him more than the estimate. And then the neighbors have been complaining about the noise at night. His friends NEVER leave. Ugh, it's just a bunch of stupid shit."

Ruben: "Hashtag: poor little rich boy. Hashtag: *mantenido.* Hashtag: send daddy the bill."

"Shut up bitch!" she slapped Ruben with the back of her left hand.

He winced, "Bitch!" as the waiter leaned in to set down the drinks.

After they had settled a bit, I smiled and said, "Personally, I think you moved in way too quickly."

Ruben scoffed, "That's rich!"

I furrowed my brows, "What's that supposed to mean?" then finished off the old beer and started on the new.

"You're fucking kidding me, right?" he uncrossed his legs and leaned forward, "You basically never met Domi before and you left everything behind and moved countries to shack up with some pixels on the internet."

I scrunched up my face then said, "That's different."

Anabel tore off another piece of the bagel and threw it in my direction, "How so?!" she laughed.

"We were dating for like a year or two... Like people do in prison. Those things turn out fine, right?"

Ruben took an orangey sip, "Hashtag: Second Life. Hashtag: my boyfriends a SIMs"

I slapped him with the back of my right hand to which he responded emphatically, "Ladies, ladies, ladies... chill pill. Since when did Wednesday become beat your Ruben day."

She grabbed another piece of bread and tossed it at him, "Bitch, please. You beat your Ruben every day."

"Hashtag: you don't use it you lose it. Hashtag: gotta keep the pipes clean."

At that moment I realized what they were saying was true. I hadn't really known the man I was living with. I laughed though as my heart sank at the idea of, I wonder if Domi knew what he was getting himself into.

"What about you Ruben?" I asked then affirmed, "Actually, I think Luis Raul gets more action than any of us."

"Hashtag: big girls need loving too. Well, if you must know," he smiled as he took a drink, "I've been *Grinding* with three boys."

"Ewoo," I said, a bit jealous and a bit longing for my single days until I realized that nobody ever really paid any attention to me on those gay dating apps. Anabel just smiled to herself, her spirits a bit more high.

He shifted his shoulders, "Not like that, silly," then slapped my knee, "I've been messaging three guys on Grindr, I mean."

"Why? They all look the same, don't they? Everybody's just this brooding six pack with a fairly well trimmed beard."

He smirked, "Fairly well trimmed beard but with just the right amount of effortless fashion and quaffed hair."

I sighed, wrapped both hands around my almost empty bottle, leaned in on my elbows and said, "David's always on it. He's always like, Hey, you think this guy's cute? And I'm all like, Ag, he looks just like the last one you showed me."

Ruben grabbed his phone that he had placed face down at the table. A few days ago we broached the subject of proper phone etiquette and since then he had been pretty good on complying, "No, no, no, silly. That's THOSE types of gay Guadalajarans. I like the more Mexican looking ones.

Here, like... this one," he tapped a few buttons and brought up some dude's profile.

I looked down disapprovingly, "Ewoo..."

Anabel leaned over, her interests now peaked, "Let me see!" She stole the phone away and scrolled down the page, "Gross! It says here that he's 5'4". That's like hobbit status or something."

Ruben bobbed his head up and down, "And??? I'm 5'7", 5'10" in heels. He's perfect."

"Hand it here," I reached my arm across the table, "What's his name?"

"Fernando."

I mused, "Ooh that sounds classy."

He went on, proudly, "He's a school teacher."

"Uy no," Ana rolled her eyes and slapped her forehead in dismay.

Defensively, Ruben retorted, "What?! It's better than what everyone else we know is doing. Everyone's either a bartender, waiter, or working in a call center. The other half of the people we know are just students..."

"Don't forget Drug peddlers and, hey, Domi's an architect... of sorts.... I think..."

"I guess," she acquiesced, "But he's so dark..."

"Hashtag: darker the cherry. Hashtag: sweeter the juice."

I shrugged, "WELL, what about the rest? The other two I mean."

He set his mimosa down on the table then, "They're all closeted."

I shook my head, "*No bueno*."

He went on, "But they all have nice dicks," and smiled.

Anabel almost choked on her bagel then spitted out, "Ewoo! *no mames!* That's how you guys say hello or what? Is it like, 'Hey, penis pic, how's your day going?' "

I mused out loud, "Kinda..." and rapped the top of the table with my fingers.

"Well", Ruben smiled to himself, "It's not a bad start."

We walked up a flight of stone stairs. Steps barely painted white. They were chipped and stained with black shoe scuffs. There was a door at the top to the right. Anabel knocked and we waited a few seconds for a response. A minute passed and she pulled her purse from behind her back, onto her belly, then stuck both hands in and riffled through it. It was this purple patent leather thing. She eventually pulled out a key. There was a window right across from the door and I peered out into the city from it. It wasn't paned in with glass. Just sort of a lookout post. A wide open square cut into the wall; the space like a semi indoor balcony. The neighborhood looked nice. Looked like any other and there was a park about two blocks down. I leaned with my hands on the ledge and looked out over it long enough to get a spell of vertigo. We were only one floor up but I was such a pussy when it came to heights. It was funny that I should move into a city wherein hardly anyone had a yard, but everyone relaxed on rooftops. Below, a man walked by with jug of purified water over his shoulders, oblivious to the fact that I was pinching off the tops buildings and squooshing his tiny head between my thumb and index finger.

She huffed as she pushed the door in, "That thing always sticks...." it was a blue metal door with tiny windows behind which a metal grate and been fastened. She was a little out of breath and put her keys down on a half moon of a table by the entrance. The place was dark and a bit stuffy. The hallway narrow and a bit claustrophobic. Its walls were littered with photo frames and posters of movie stars from an era long gone by.

I stared at one of them, a print of Audrey Hepburn. There was one of Bogart, one of Lauren Bacall, and one of Boris Karloff as Frankenstein.

"So this is where you used to live?" I asked.

Behind me, Ruben offered, “Hashtag: Bohemian. Hashtag: Rats nest."

"Yeah," she flipped a switch back and forth but there was no light. We walked towards the kitchen. It was tiny. Barely enough room for two people, much less three. Its window had been papered over in red tissue except for a four-inch space that ran the length of its bottom. Tiny plants in plastic rectangular black pots. The kind of pots you buy them in and the kind of pots young people forget to take them out of. Three cacti and one of something dead. Anabel went to the sink and ran water over her hand then over the back of her neck. The kitchen was about three feet wide with scarcely the room to open the fridge. Ruben tossed me a canned *Modelo Especia*l, took one for himself, then offered one to Anabel but she politely declined. They then slid past one another. She opened the fridge again and stared blankly for a second then took out a plastic pitcher with a pink lid and poured herself something that looked like limeade. She said, almost to herself, "I wonder where she's at?"

I wondered aloud, surveying the peeling ceiling, "Who else lives here?"

"Hashtag: stoners. Hashtag: Can I pay you the rent next week..."

I cringed, “I thought you were gonna move in?” I gestured to Ruben.

He disdainfully replied, "God no. I'm gonna ride the mom and pop train till I graduate. I do have a tooth brush here, though. But, honestly," he pinched out an empty Slim Jim wrapper from the sink full of week old dishes, "I don't think I'll be using it anytime soon."

Flies hovered above the plates that had been left soaking in gray water which bubbled at the edges. White puffs of something like cottage cheese floated in a blue bowl.

"Geezus!" I exclaimed, "And I thought Luis Raul was bad..."

Anabel shrugged, "It's probably all Alice. Why do you think I wanted to move out?"

I smiled, "You guys should've tried a chore wheel. Hey, so where are these guys?"

Ruben took his phone out and started snapping shots of some pictures on the fridge, "Probably out skateboarding or something. Hashtag: the thug life," he laughed to himself at one of the pictures, "Priceless!"

I leaned in over his shoulder to take a peek. There were a few photos of some guys in high school. There were a few more of them taking photos of themselves smoking out of bongs or rolling papers. There was even a pin up red head that was cut out and made into some sort of magnet. There was a bill marked past due and few other magnets holding everything together. One was of Godzilla and the other few were random cartoon character heads whose eyes had been painted blood shot.

Anabel said, "Come on, I'll show you to the living room," then she filled her cup again and led us out the kitchen, to the left, into a dark little room. Mismatched curtains ran behind the TV at the far end. It was a flat screen monitor but small and mounted to a table which had two shelves filled with books and DVDs. There were three couches, one on each of the other walls facing that window. We had to slide over the armrests of the two nearest the doorway. There was no table in the middle but there was an old skateboard with the remnants of somebody packing a bowl or rolling a cigarette. Empty orange zigzag boxes.

"Careful," she said and plopped down at the furthest couch. It was a dull peach, gray at the edges and armrests. Me and Ruben sat on the love seat directly across the TV. He clasped his hands: "So... what now, chickadees?"

Anabel was resting her head back and just stared across at the giant poster of Bob Marley that ran along the length of the empty couch. She snapped out of a daydream then scooted over towards the television and looked for the remote. Once she found it, she pressed a few buttons then after about a minute, the damned thing's screen went from black to a blue. Another few buttons and it was on a news station with scrolling numbers on the bottom. An old man with gray hair mouthed something. Big red pixelated letters spelled "MUTE" at the top left of the screen. She flipped the channel, "What do you want to watch?" and turned up the sound.

Me and Ruben shrugged and in unison, "Whatever." Just then the front door opened. We looked at one another in dreaded anticipation. Sleepy now, I sipped the beer and noticed that the rim of the can looked a little questionable itself.

From down the hall, Alice's voice, "Babe," she walked into the living room, "You shouldn't leave your purse lying around," then tossed Ana's giant bag at her and Anabel caught it on the side with a huff. She tucked it down further to her left. Alice plopped down backwards on the "Marley Couch" and continued to text someone.

"Where you guys coming from?" she said, more concerned with which emoticon to send than our response.

Ruben beamed, "Sunday Fun-day," and then rattled his beer can.

She kicked my arm, the one that was on the armrest nearest her, "And Domi?"

I shrugged, "He was going to have lunch with David and his parents. I think Elma was going to go too."

Alice flopped down her arm beside her and bit the bottom of her lip, "Why didn't you go?"

I tapped my foot, "I dunno. Sounded like it was a *Cuauhtémoc* kind of thing. Besides, I'm pretty sure they went somewhere snooty."

"Ah...." she brought the phone back up near her face then her arms flailed out and onto the carpet down beside her. She stared at me for a second then turned her chin upwards to stare at the TV upside down, "I don't think I've ever met David's parents."

Reluctantly I responded, "Well, neither have I. But it isn't David's parents that are visiting, it's Domi's."

You could hear a fucking pin drop in spite of the TV blaring nonsense. Ruben was the one to break the tension with a loud and effeminate, "Whaaaa' ?????"

I took another swig of my beer and tried to buy time by swishing the suds side to side in my mouth. Finally I buckled, "Well, he said he wasn't sure if they were like ready to meet me. They're just in town for the night anyhow. They're driving to the beach in the morning. He said he didn't want to ruin their vacation and like his dad has been having these mini-heart attacks or something about his sugar dropping a lot. I get it," I said, the words resonating oddly even before they left my mouth, "Domi's family is just different. Like they're not as open minded as mine, I guess."

Ruben furrowed his brow and plowed forward, "But, they have to know he's gay. And if not, they have to know David's gay. Couldn't you have just pretended to be HIS boyfriend or something?"

Anabel, staring at the skateboard, nodded silently in agreement.

I pushed myself to the edge of the seat, ready to take up arms, "No, but you don't get it. Like they don't like seeing gay shit or something. And besides, I get it. It's just like old friends getting together. Besides, Domi gave me drinking money," I smiled naively.

Ruben, "He paid you off so you wouldn't complain about not being able to meet his parents?"

Gesturing wildly with my hands, as if they could save me from the quicksand I was surely sinking into, "No, like so I could go to the bar while he showed his parents around the house."

Alice laughed, "No fucking way. No freakin' way are you telling us that YOUR boyfriend paid you off so you wouldn't be around when his parents came to visit?!"

"Oh please," I took a long chug, "You guys swear as if you don't know where my priorities lie," then, pretending my hands were a scale balancing my predispositions, I said, "Meeting Domi's parents... Free beer... Meeting Domi's parents... Free beer."

Ruben laughed, "It's not as if you wouldn't have gotten free drinks if you had gone to dinner."

They just weren't getting it, "No, that's another thing. He wanted to prove to them that he had his life together so that they might help him go back to school. He wants to join this interior design thingy at the University but he says he can't afford it at the moment. And he said that he'd know if I had gone then they would've been put off by like how much I drink and how much money I waste, or something. So, he just wanted to show them that he was financially responsible and not about to squander a loan on partying with his alcoholic... friend..."

Ruben wouldn't let up, "So... what you're *saying* is... that... your live in boyfriend wants to prove that he has his shit together by pretending he's not in a monogamous relationship and lying about being gay?"

"..." It had made so much more sense the way Domi had explained it to me that morning. Maybe I was just too eager to be pleasant and accommodating then to realize precisely how foolish all of it sounded out loud.

Alice, perhaps not so tactfully, followed with, "Change of subject. What you guys watching anyways?"

Ruben, "A Lifetime movie starring Marveen as a ghost wife who can't solve her own murder. 'I was murdered by my Husband but thought I had just forgot the safety word: The Marveen Heel Story'."

Anabel laughed then to Alice, "No clue. There's nothing on."

Alice kicked my leg this time, "I have the Star Wars box set?"

Ruben, "Hashtag: No."

She went on, "How about the new Wall Street one? I bought it at the *mercado* for a dollar."

I stared down into my beer. I didn't know what I was thinking or feeling, just that it wasn't something pleasant. Nothing to write home about. And if I had even tried to put it into words, all I could come up with was "A jumbled sensation of vomit-crying, punching-faces, light headed-ness". But feeling the eyes of the room upon me, I grinned and said, "Isn't it like 3 hours long?"

She stared into her phone, "Yup."

I stared back into my beer and ran a finger along the dirty rim, "I'd rather watch Gone with the Wind or something."

Ruben turned to his left and slapped the back of his left hand into my chest, "Hastag: OH MY GOD YES!"

Anabel shrugged, "Never seen it."

Alice wiggled her way off the couch, sank to the floor like a backwards spider, then pushed her hair out of her face and crawled towards the DVD collection. "Girl," she pointed to Anabel, "You're about to get schooled."

"Ugh, I wish we'd have barbecues like that," I stared enviously into the world of the wealthy and entitled plantation owner. We had turned off the lights. Our faces barely lit by the blues and yellows from the garish Technicolor. Ruben was slumped in the couch next to me, resting the beer he had been nursing for the last fifteen minutes or so on his arms he had crossed, "Hashtag: big girl problems." I punched his arm and he let out an "Ow!".

Anabel was chewing something and said, "That dress... I'd die if I had to always wear something like that..."

From the kitchen, Alice hollered, "HEY, YOU GUYS WANT ANYTHING? I HAVE... MMM... POPCORN... I THINK," then the cupboard slammed and she popped open the fridge, the rubber seal making a slight smacking sound.

I yelled back, "SURE..."

Ruben hollered for another round of beers.

Alice, "ANABEL, YOU WANT ANYTHING?"

She replied, "NO, BUT THANKS, LOVE."

Ruben, "Hashtag: lesb-be-honest here..."

"Here," Alice stepped in and handed out three more beers, "Right now we'll have to go get some more."

Me, "Thank you."

Ruben, "*Enchanté.*"

Alice smiled at Anabel who looked a little lost, "You sure you don't want anything?"

Anabel held out her cup, "It was limeade."

Alice went back into the kitchen then came back and handed me a giant, white plastic bowl of popcorn. She then handed Ana her cup, then swiveled back and grabbed a handful of warm buttery goodness. She plopped herself back down on the Marley couch, "Do you guys think you'll ever go to war? Like actually get drafted and fight in one or something?" she leaned over to grab another handful.

I thought aloud, "Mmmm.... for awhile I was thinking about joining the army or some kind of military branch. My brother in-law was in the Air force. But I dunno."

Ruben daintily pinched two kernels from the bowl then, "My little brother's in the Army. I love him so much. He's just the cutest thing," I offered him some more, " No, no thanks. I just wanted a taste. Gotta watch my girlish figure," then he pushed away the popcorn.

Anabel chimed in, "I'd do it."

Alice to her, a bit surprised, "Really?"

Ruben pursed his lips, "Lesbian," then set his foot on the skateboard in the middle and began to rock it back and forth.

Anabel went on, "Yeah, why not?"

"Hashtag: greens not your color..."

I scratched the corner of my nose, "Well at least you'd get benefits. Well in America that's how it goes."

"SEE," Anabel went on, "I can get my nose fixed."

We all looked at her questioningly.

I said with a mouthful, "What's wrong with your nose?"

"It's too wide," she crossed her eyes and stared at her fingers as she dragged her thumb and middle finger along her nostrils.

Ruben snickered, "Hashtag: Body dysmorphia."

I sighed, "I should get Domi to join the army. Widows get pensions in Mexico, right?"

Alice laughed, tossed some more popcorn into her mouth then said, "Yeah, but I don't think they pay that much. But Domi would love that."

Ruben, "Hashtag: you can't possibly drop the soap that many times..."

We all laughed as the men tossed their hats up in the air, excited at the prospect of a good old adventurous war.

"Hola, *bebe*, how'd it go today with the girls?" Domi laughed and kissed me on the top of my head. I was sitting on the floor with my back to the mattress, trying to figure out what to write about.

"Fine," I bit my lower lip, "We had brunch then watched a movie at Alice's," I turned to face him. He was teetering, trying to take off his shoes and his shirt at the same time. I went on, "The place is hella messy."

He laughed, unbuckled his belt, "Yeah, I know. Alice is super unorganized. When I first saw her place, I imagined your apartment might've looked the same but with dogs and antique kind of things."

I sighed and tapped my pen against the lined paper of my moleskin. If I was going to be a writer, I figured I should invest in something flashy with a bit of panache, "I think Ana might move back in though."

"Why? She used to be the first to complain about the mess," he asked as he shimmied off his skintight pants near the dresser.

"I dunno. I think there's something wrong with Gilberto or something. Hey, how was dinner?"

"Fine," he grinned tensely then leaned over and kissed my forehead.

"Just fine? Did you talk to them about school?"

"Yea, my mom just sipped on her wine and my dad kept hitting on Elma."

"Well..."

He laughed, "I'm kidding. Elma's like a sister to me. I think they were more interested in what she was doing with her life than what I was doing with mine. But David took a friend and he was funny so that made things go by a little easier."

I tapped my pen against the page, a little bit harder this time. "Oh..."

"Oh? Oh what? Don't start. I know that look..."

I smiled in protest, "What look? And 'oh' nothing, I was just thinking about what Ruben said today. It was really funny he said..."

"Yeah, David's friend was really funny too. He actually works with me so it helped that he spoke well of what I'm doing at the firm. Apparently everyone says I'm an asshole but they respect me for getting my work done."

I smiled and looked away, then tried to go on, "That's nice. But, anyway, so Anabel had said something about never having..."

"You'd like him. He's nice."

"... Ahm," I smacked my lips, "I'm sure I would. So how long has David been dating him?"

He laughed then tussled my hair and pushed my head back playfully, "Oh, they're not dating. They're just friends. He just got back from *Nogales.* He used to live here but they moved him for a project."

"But he's gay, right?"

He laughed, "Yes, he was singing Beyoncé at one point."

"Oh," I stared out along the lines of my legs and then unto my shoes and then out towards the door that lay across. A part of me said, just one shot. Just one fucking drink and then we'll get back to work.

"What's wrong?"

My eyes dropped at the corners, "Nothing. I'm just tired. I haven't had a real drink all day."

He was folding some clothes into the drawer, "Don't start. What movie did you watch?"

"Gone with the Wind. Hey, so like if David took his gay friend why didn't you wanna..."

He sighed deeply, already vexed by what was coming, "Don't start! I told you. We already went over this. Why does it feel like I'm always talking to a wall with you? And anyways, I have no control over who David invites to dinner or not."

"Yea, I know but..."

He grabbed onto the edge of the open drawer as if he wanted to crush the wooden plank. For a second it was touch and go but he merely peered inside and started fidgeting with the loose screw that held on the handle, "Listen, my folks just aren't ready yet. My dad's sick and I don't want to stress him out anymore than he has to be. That's why they're on vacation."

I sank into myself. How selfish and stupid I sounded, "I'm sorry. It's just that they were saying..."

"Who was saying? Ruben? I told you that he's nothing but a fucking gossip. If you think it's so important what he says or any of your stupid friends say, who, I might mention, were originally MY friends, then why don't you go off with them? I'm sure they wouldn't mind putting up with the..."

I pulled myself up and walked towards him, tried to grab him comfortingly on the shoulder but he shrugged me off with a, "Why do you always have to do this?!"

"Do what?!"

"We were having a nice talk and you have to start with your shit!"

I threw my head back. I couldn't seem to do anything right, "Hey. I'm sorry. I just don't get why..."

"Listen, Marveen, when I'm ready, I'll tell my folks. You don't know them. I do. You don't get to decide. I do. When you get your life together, then maybe you can give me some advice. But until then, trust me, I know what I'm doing."

"Yeah, that's kind of the point: I don't know your parents," my face scrunched, "And what the fuck is that supposed to mean that I don't have my life together? Hello? Velcro shoes... Best investment ever..."

He turned to me, dropped his shoulders, rolled his eyes then said, "I'm going to take a shower. It's too cold in the morning."

I tossed my notebook on the bed, grinned sternly and said, "Fine." then walked out towards the kitchen and that bottle of mezcal Luis Raul had bought the day prior. While I was pouring a drink mixed with tang, I reprimanded myself for not having had said something like, "Yea! Well it's pretty chilly in here tonight too!"

But I hadn't. I just stood in the kitchen listening to the water start then stop in the shower. I chugged more mezcal than should be advised. Then before Domi got out, I buried my head in a pillow, fully clothed but never asleep. For hours it seemed, I lay there awake listening to the rhythm of his breaths. The stifling air. That fan that never really worked. I felt as if I could will the house into a burst of flames. If I had undressed, I'd be caught naked in the street.

The next morning, I awoke to Domi trying to pull off my shoes, "I told you not to sleep with your shoes on. Now you're going to have to change the sheets," first one shoe, then the next. He waved his hand in front of his face and continued, "You're kidding me, your feet smell so bad."

I tried lifting my head off of the pillow and forgetting the argument we had the night prior, "I've been hanging around Luis Raul."

"Mmmm... " he was pulling out a pair of gray jeans which he hung near the bed off a nail on the wall, "So what movie did you guys end up watching last night?"

I was lying on my belly, completely prostrate, but I had turned my head to watch his skinny ass squeeze into a size negative 20, "Gone with the wind."

"Ah, I've never seen it."

"That's what Ana said."

"Did she like it?"

"She fell asleep but then woke up. Said it was okay. She also said you're stupid."

He laughed, "I sincerely doubt that. She loves me. She was my friend before she started hanging around fatties."

"I know. You never let me forget that everybody and everything was yours before I got here. Also, Ruben's not that fat..."

He smirked.

I was so thirsty. Part of me wanted to run a bath and just soak there for an hour but we hadn't a tub. For a second I imagined myself wading in a pool of mud in that fountain out back.

"What are you laughing at?" he said as he parted his hair."

"Nothing. Why do you even comb your hair? You have like less hair than I have pubes."

"You have a lot of pubes." He laughed.

"Mmmm... it's glandular. Hey, why don't you join the army?"

He waxed his mustache with the remnants of his hair product, "Where'd that come from?"

I smiled reluctantly, "Just. Alice said they give widows pensions."

"No, *bebe,"* he hopped over to the bed and sat beside me, "Don't send me off to die in some god forsaken war," then he kissed me tenderly on the cheek.

"Fine. But you owe me a beer."

He rubbed my belly, "I'm surprised that you're not drunk already. It must be a new world record! Why don't you take off your shirt? It smells like nothing but cigarette."

"Right?! I wonder if there's still mezcal in the kitchen. Do you know how to make pancakes? No? Well, be a dear then and just fetch me the liquor..."

"Mmmm..."

"Mmmm... Come on... I didn't even get to get drunk last night. All they had was beer. I always get full before I get drunk on that shit."

He kissed me again, "Good. We'll have to start buying you more beer."

I laughed, "Best. Intervention. Ever."

"ARE YOU SURE THIS IS SAFE?!" he yelled down as I was shielding my eyes from the sun. Domi was on the roof, shirtless, cautiously tip toeing over the terra cotta shingles that lined the edge.

I yelled back, "Yes! But you probably should've worn a shirt! Some shoes would've come in handy too!"

"*NI MADRES!* FUCK THAT SHIT!"

About half an hour earlier, we were outside sharing a cigarette and talking about how he wanted to get the bullet holes fixed on his black Jetta because the cops were always stopping him at night, when all of a sudden, we saw this tiny black bird smack into the water heater. "Heater" was a term to be used loosely. As I've mentioned before, we had no hot water and now that spiteful thing was taking out Mother Nature's tiny creatures. I mean, I'd been known to fuck with the birds with the water hose but that damned boiler was just evil and useless as fuck. For ten minutes we heard it screeching like hell. Finally, I had convinced Domi that it'd be good karma for him to investigate.

I was nervous, well kind of, "Careful! Get me the bird before you fall! It's about damned time we had a pet!"

He laughed back, "Mmmm... *caldo.*"

"No 'soup'! Baby Bird Domi! We can send him off to the best finishing schools!"

"Mmmm... *caldo de Domi!"*

"Gross!"

Once back on the ground, Domi stood there examining the bottom of his feet, "Ouch, I think I cut myself...." I honestly couldn't care less. I was too busy coddling this tiny black thing. Clutching it to my chest as if I was nursing it with my teat. It had a light brown underbelly, beady little yellow eyes, and breathed hard with its beak open.

"Told you to at least put on shoes."

"Fuck that shit! *Tengo piel de Indio.*"

"*India Maria* maybe."

"*Callate!"*

"Shhhh!..." I covered the bird as if I were covering a child's ears, "You'll scare Baby Domi," we then walked inside and rustled up a shoebox and set it on the kitchen table. Poor thing was just scared and scratching and pooping all over the place. I got a cup of water, dipped my pinky in it, then drizzled drops of water into its beak. It just shook his head. Domi tried to do the same thing but it just bit him.

"Holy shit! That hurt!" he yelled and sucked at his index.

"Pfft, pussy... Ouch!" the damned thing bit me too, "Just like daddy! Always with the temper! Mom was right: I should've married that doctor."

Domi looked into the box lovingly, "Aww... Baby Domi *malcreado..."*

I angled my neck, surveying this new thing. This new something or other that had fallen from the sky perhaps deliberately, "Do you think he broke his wing?"

"No idea. He looks like a baby though. Maybe he just doesn't know how to fly yet.

I smiled, "Aww... retarded Baby Domi *malcreado."*

Domi laughed, "Maybe we should name him after you then. Baby Marvin *malcreado*."

I turned my head quickly to face him, suppressing a smile, "Shut up! I'm smart-ish..."

"Yes, baby," he kissed my temple, "You're a very smart girl. Whatever you say...."

"Smart girl?"

"Yes."

"Not even gonna ask..."

He smiled.

The bird eventually stopped chirping incessantly and remained starring up at us, hissing every so often. It was basically black but with a tuft of gray brown feathers on it's chest and a puff of fuzzy white below its belly.

"What should we name it?"

"I thought you said Domi?" he laughed and tried to pet it. It hissed and snapped at his finger again to which he scolded it with a, "NO! Bad Baby Domi!"

I pondered the question, "Mmmm.... How... about... Firetruck?"

Domi looked puzzled and tried to sound it out, "Fy-ay-troc?"

I smiled to myself proudly, "Yes. I like it. I used to want to be one when I grew up."

"*Que significa eso?"*

"You know, that thing that firemen ride."

"Ah '*streep-per-pols*' " he laughed and pretended to dance seductively.

I winced in affected disgust, "Ewoo... No, that truck that goes 'wee-oo-wee-oo-wee-oo'.""

He clapped his hands then came to a still, "*Si, ya se cual,*" and then went in to pet the bird again "Aww... baby FY-YO-TROC," then he let out another squeal of pain as it bit him again.

I shook my head, "Ay, Domi, *you're* the *smart girl..."*

He laughed and did a "sexy" moonwalk into the hallway.

"What on earth are you gonna do with a bird?!" Ruben had decided to take me shopping. He'd been bragging about taking spinning classes every day for the last few weeks. "Hashtag: New Years 'Sexolutions'," and had decided he'd lost enough weight to warrant a new wardrobe.

"What do you think about this?" he leaned a shirt on a hanger against his chest.

"Mmm,,, why does everything have triangles? Is it like an Aztec thing?" I asked.

"Mayan, bitch. Hashtag: know your roots."

I rolled my eyes, "Do they even have any regular sizes?" I held out another shirt with splatter neon paint designs, "This says, 'large' but it sure as hell doesn't look like one to me."

"Us Mexicans only wear Baby Gap. I heard that in America they changed the standards a few years back.

Medium became the new small. And extra large..." he smiled and motioned to me, "Became whatever it is that you're wearing," he laughed.

"I know! I've been hanging around Luis Raul too much. Didn't think that fat was contagious."

Ruben smiled, "I'm just kidding, gurl. Don't get your panties in a bunch. Besides, you do look thinner than when I first met you."

I looked down and grabbed my gut with both hands. Squeezed it. Felt like a loaf of meat, "Ugh, maybe I *should* start going to the gym with Domi."

"Hashtag: bitch needs a sandwich. Well, why don't you?"

"I refuse to get out of bed before noon. He goes at like six or something. Right before work. And I'm all like fuck... that.... shit."

"Hashtag: No pain, no gain. I go at like five."

"See, I could do that, Plus, they say it's better to exercise in the evening because your muscles are more relaxed."

"Pfft,... girl... I meant 5 a.m."

"What?!"

"I'm up by then so I just go."

"How is that even humanly possible? Ooo, that looks nice," I ran a finger across a simple striped shirt.

"You think? Mmmm.. I'm not sure if I'm ready for horizontal stripes yet."

"Looks like an old time-y prison outfit. Besides, aren't horizontal stripes supposed to make you look taller?"

"Hashtag: bitch that's what stilettos are for," he kicked up the heel of his left foot, exposing his new boots.

"Those are nice. Where'd you get them?"

"Aldo's. I know they're *cheap* but expensive BUT I get a mall discount. Hashtag: 10% off bitches!"

"Mmm... must be nice. I can't believe they have spinning classes so early."

“They don't. I wake up at four. Check my Grindr, then my Scruff. Have a cup of coffee with my parents..."

"They're awake at that time too?!"

"Honey, they were teachers. They have to be at school by 7."

"I thought your mom was a nurse or something..."

"Ugh, you never listen! She WAS a teacher. Now she does orders for a medical supply company. Hashtag: all the latex gloves a girl could want," he then half curtsied, "So she still has to get to the office by seven or so."

"Oh..."

"Whaddya think?”

"Mmm.. I don't like all that random geometric shit but the wolf's head looks kinda nice."

"Mmmm... I need a gym shirt anyway."

“SO, you were saying..." I continued.

"Oh, so coffee, then a shit. Hashtag: hemorrhoids ain't helping nobody," we both laughed, "Then I drive to the gym, do some stretches, watch some cuties do *their* stretches. Then, ten minutes on the treadmill. Half an hour on weights. Sext some more on Grindr. Do a walk around. Grindr. By six fifteen they have their first spinning class. By seven I'm off to school."

“Dayyyyuuummmm."

“No pain, No gain, momma.... I dunno how I feel about pleats."

I stared at the pants in his hands, “I personally never liked them. SO how many hours do you sleep then?"

"Like four or five."

"Fuck I used to be like that."

"Naps are a girls best friend. Mmmm but I like the color. Mustard brown is so in this year."

"Mmmm... guess so. I think pleats just don't work for big people."

"Girlfriend, the revolution starts today."

I sighed, "If you say so."

Two stores later, Ruben was holding four bags and I was holding an ice cream cone. One scoop pistachio, one scoop mint chocolate chip.

"Doesn't Anabel work around here?" I asked.

"Where do you think we're going?"

"Oh. Everyone here is so skinny and fit." I observed.

He laughed, "How's your ice cream?"

Past us walked svelte young pretty things done up in nice hair and with nice shoes. Everyone seemed posh. Pretty but nice and approachable. Most of the time they'd smile at you and it wasn't all too uncustomary for them to say good day or good-bye. I went on:

"And what kills me is that they're so nice! It's like everybody's so freaking beautiful that they think nothing of it! Back home, even if you were born with a harelip, you act as if you could be a model. But these people are freaking, real life, walking models!"

A bit annoyed, Ruben: "True, but that's just what you see because you choose to see that. There are plenty of ugly, short, brown people. You're just preoccupied by skinny jeans and tight asses."

"Shut up."

"Girlfriend, what you need is *thinspiration."*

"Meh. I'm practically married, I can let myself go. Sometimes I wish I had moved here single. David and Luis get so much play it's ridunkulous," I licked my cone, seeking succor in its icy embrace.

We walked into another store blaring obscure music that belonged in an iPod commercial.

"And how's that working for you? Where is this bitch?" he panned the store floor looking for Ana.

"Mmmm... fine," I ran my hand over a rack of clothes. The hangers rippled and the shirts undulated like multicolored cotton water. The little labels near the hooks all read "S", "Domi just works a lot, I guess."

He hunched in on himself to better scrutinize the designs on the shirts he perused, "Hashtag: *mantenido*",

"I hardly see him and when I do it's like every little thing pisses him off. Sometimes it feels like I'm dating more Elma than him. I think we'd make a cuter couple too."

"Gross. Vaginas," he dramatically cringed.

"I really need a job," I sighed.

"You DO. Do you think they have this in a medium?"

"*Hola guapos!*" Anabel came up from behind, arms outstretched.

"Hey baby," I smiled and hugged her, accidentally shoving my chin too hard into her cheek, as I was prone to do.

Ruben, "Bitch. Do you have this in a medium?"

She laughed and slapped his arm, "Let me check." then started surveying the rack, "What are you guys doing here anyway?"

"Hashtag: *dia de compras.* Hashtag: Shopping spree!!! Hashtag: Video montage later. You know, the usual."

She, furrowed her brows at the slew of clothing, "Ah. I just saw Alicia. She came in for lunch."

"How's that bitch doing?" he then put another shirt against his body, "Does this come in silver sequence? Gold sequence makes me look fat."

She mused aloud, "Mmm... doesn't look like we have any more mediums. There's a large and an extra large though."

"Girl, I don't need to be swimming in it! Sell it to Marveen. We can just have the tailor let it out a bit at the edges," he laughed.

I replied, "No thanks. T-shirts make my man boobs stick out."

Anabel laughed then tried twisting one of my nipples, "And Domi? What does he say? Did he lend you the credit card or what?"

I sighed, "Working. Hahahaha he doesn't trust me with money. I'm pretty sure he's afraid I'd come home with a lifetime supply of potato chips and a week's worth of *caguamas*."

"Hashtag: A girl needsta eat."

She patted me on the shoulder, smiled and said, "Well, maybe it's for the best. Oh," she gasped into her hand, "you'll never believe who I saw yesterday! David! And he was on a date or something with this short old dude!"

Ruben snorted out, "Girl, don't be discriminating. Sometimes the smallest packages pack the biggest umpf."

She turned to face him then caressed the side of his face lovingly, "Ah, babe, but you're adorable. It's different."

He raised an eyebrow, "Hashtag: petite is pretty."

I leaned in on the rack, "Where did you go out last night or what?"

She turned back to me, "Nowhere. They came in here." she laughed, "I think he was trying to avoid me though. I said hi but they left soon after."

"Hashtag: pretty woman. Hashtag: the life of a *puta*. Hashtag: no kissing on the mouth."

"I know!" she squealed and jumped around a bit then slapped Ruben on the arm, "I dunno why he's so secretive."

I shrugged, "Who knows? Domi says that that's just how David's always been. At least Luis Raul introduces his bitches."

Just then, one of the guys Luis had dated came into view at the perfume counter. We all ducked behind a corner, trying to stifle our giggles. A lady in a red blazer and black pencil skirt walked by the other end. She was around late forties but with a tight face under heavy make-up. She raised an eyebrow at us disapprovingly. Anabel, quick on her feet, snatched a shirt from Ruben and turned to the lady who was now about to pass us. She called out, "Hey, Maribel" and the lady curtly stopped, did a half turn, giving her the right side of her face but refusing to give the complete attention of a full body round about.

She grinned, almost uncomfortably, "Yes, Ana?" and eyed me and Ruben somewhat suspiciously.

Coyly Ana asked, "Do you know if we have this in a medium?"

Bluntly Maribel responded, "I don't know," she winced her eyes, "Do we? Have you checked?"

Anabel laughed nervously, "Yes, but there's none on the rack."

"Well, then there's none," Maribel began walking away then stopped, looked over her shoulder and said, "Have you checked the mannequins? I think I saw one there the other day," then she looked straight ahead and just went along her not so very merry way.

I leaned into the group and whispered, "What a bitch."

Anabel slapped me on the chest a bit harder than I think she even intended, "Shut up!" then she hushed out a laugh, "That's my boss! I hate that she calls me ANA. She knows I don't like it."

"Hashtag: devil wears the softer side of Sears."

We all laughed.

Ruben grabbed back the shirt, held it out, "Mmmm... I'm not convinced," then put it on the nearest rack carelessly.

Anabel immediately picked it up with a, "It doesn't go there," she smiled, "So what were you looking for?" she began walking us through the floor.

Ruben, "Mmmm... well I really wanted a full on mink coat but I said, I said to Marvin, NOT unless they have it in hot pink."

She laughed, "Shut up! You know we got some nice button ups in the other day."

"As long as they're not plaids," he said, pursed his lips then stared in my direction. I looked down at my shirt.

"Hey!" I feigned offense, "It's all that fits! Besides you can never tell if I have stains or if that's just part of the design."

He snickered, "Girlfriend, I count three and I don't even have my contacts on."

I looked down again, stretched out the front tails and examined the wretched mess I tried to pull off as an ensemble, "I'm waiting for Domi to do laundry."

Anabel laughed, "Why can't you do it?"

"He takes it to his aunt's. I only have like four shirts anyhow so we usually just wait until he goes through all his work stuff," I ran my hand over another rack of clothes, "I hate Ed Hardy."

"Yea, me too," Anabel nodded in agreement.

"Hashtag: globs of glitter and random cursive shit."

"Fist pump bay-bee," I followed suit in the mockery.

She laughed, "*Que nacos*. Here, this is what I was telling you about," she pulled a white short sleeve button up with ruffles running down the middle.

Ruben scrunched his face and, "Mmmm... I dunno if I can pull off 'Pirates of the Caribbean' yet."

I countered with a, "I think it's cool," musing more so aloud than anything.

"Fine. You buy it," he shoved the shirt towards me.

In the back of my mind I was thinking about how back home I might've found something like that in a thrift store. How back home, even if I had come across it in a department store, even though I never shopped in them, that I could certainly afford it. Here and now I was just living off of borrowed time. My money wouldn't last much longer. I wasn't as free as I'd come to expect by having had given up all of my belongings. If anything, I felt more trapped by the insecurity of not having a real job. But instead of saying all this I merely went on with, "Na, I'll probably just look like a fat man in a silly shirt."

Anabel placed the shirt against my chest and pulled out one of the sleeves, "I think it looks nice. Lots of details in the stitching."

It did look nice. The stitching made it stand out but the not in a flashy way. The details were what made it pop, not some showy excuse for a street pylon.

"Na, trust me. Besides I can't even make black look slimming," I admitted.

Ruben sighed, "Hashtag: *thinspiration.*"

I responded with, "Hashtag: Do they sell pretzels in this mall? Hashtag: Does that come with sprinkles?"

We chug a chugged out of the parking lot in Ruben's old blue minivan. The first row of back seats was piled high with bags and two shoeboxes. Behind that, various art supplies: Pieces of wood, Corners of frames, A roll of canvas tucked to the side. Outside, before us, lay a bunch of rolling hills. Living so close to the center of the city with all those reaching buildings and three story homes, I sometimes forgot about the mountains. I sometimes forgot about the horizon. These trips out were nice. Honestly I didn't even remember the ride from the airport all that long ago and as we passed the signs that pointed to its direction, I laughed to myself. I wondered how the fuck I even made it home that day.

Ruben broke my reverie, "What do you feel like listening to?"

"Ugh, anything but fucking deep-house. That's all Elma listens to."

"How's that bitch?"

"Fine. She got in another fight with her boyfriend. Her and Domi stayed up Saturday drinking Mezcal."

"And you?"

"My throat hurt. Think I'm allergic to Domi."

"Hashtag: the GAIDs"

"Heheh, something like that. I'm even breaking out in pimples. Look at this, my poor nose is all greasy and red."

"Momma always said, Change your pillow cases every three days."

“Na. It's from all the kissing. Used to happen with my ex too. It's like both of our faces’ oils and bacteria unite to throw Gross-fest 2014," I stared out the window.

"What are you smiling about?" he asked.

"Nothing. I was just remembering something..." In the midst of those hills and that forest and all these cars making their way home or out to the city, I remembered my first boyfriend and all the stupid shit we ever went through but this time fondly. I remember thinking, wow, if he could only see me now living my life internationally. Albeit, being an expatriate was about all I had going for me at the moment. But still, I felt as if I was making a move in the right direction. For chrissake, I think he still lived at home with his mom.

Ruben looked at me as he was signaling to change lanes. A giant passenger bus speeding right past us, "Aw, Hashtag: the Notebook"

“Ugh, that movie is so stupid. Ryan Gosling looks like a retarded baby with a flat shovel face."

"Whaaat??? Girlfriend, every woman's dream!" he shouted as if personally offended.

“Mmm... I liked his band, that Dead Man's Bones thingy. It ruined it for me when I found out he was in it though. Now every time I hear them, I see his stupid face squinting and shit."

He laughed, "Well, who do you think it was?”

"I dunno, some indie dude with a beard and a long mustache."

"Hashtag: Hannah Montana."

I laughed, "Something like that."

The sun was setting behind those tall buildings. The traffic was so horrible and we were stuck in this circular turn about. Felt like a merry go round and with each pass the sky got darker. Blue black. Hazy at the edges from all that smog or maybe it was just the weather and a few rain clouds looming. Those big puffy things miles away in the suburbs.

"What are you planning on doing later?" I asked.

Ruben was lighting a cig, "You mean if we ever get out of here?"

I laughed, "Yea."

"Homework. Grindr. I dunno. My parents are watching Breaking Bad. If they've caught up to the episode I'm on, maybe I'll just watch that with them."

"Never got into it but I heard it's good. Like crack candy, deep fried, and smothered in ranch, kind of good."

"Oh my gawd, Marvin, you have no idea..." he said emphatically, bringing a hand to his chest.

"Yea, yea, but honestly I don't need anymore distractions."

"You?"

"Mmmm... I dunno. Prob' just read. I'm trying to finish Breakfast at Tiffany's but Domi only has it in Spanish. Half the time I think all I'm reading is TACO, TACO, CHALUPA, TACO."

"No mames," he laughed, *"Chalupas* are an American invention, like Pizza."

"...or chop suey..."

"Mmm... I'm not sure about that one," he pursed his lips then honked his horn, itself almost like an effeminate squeal I would expect Ruben to produce at the sight of new shoes. Then he yelled at one car before cutting off another, "There now. Where to, princess?"

I looked at my watch, "Home, I guess." It was nearing 8:30 and I was wondering if Luis Raul had fed the bird or not. It felt nice to have something to come home to. These last few weeks sometimes felt as if one big static blur. Nothing to look forward to but an absent husband and a bottle of cheap mezcal with tang. I wasn't miserable, I just wasn't as happy as I had imagined I'd be. I merely summed it up to my perpetual state of being unimpressed. The idea or the fantasy is always a lot more appealing than the actual manifestation. Maybe that's why I had drank so much back then. Half the time I didn't think anybody noticed. Most of the time they would just ask if I had gone drinking the night prior. But no, that stench wasn't a hangover creeping, it was the booze I had just chugged to keep that hangover at bay. But now I had a mouth to feed. Now I had something that needed me. Now I wasn't merely a mooching, home invader.

Ruben walked me in, dangling his keys from his hand. There was nothing but screeching. Firetruck's shoebox was on the kitchen table and there was the faint whisper of wings flapping against thin cardboard, almost like some untuned instrument.

"Fuck!" I exclaimed.

"Where's Luis?" Ruben asked, eyeing the place with a bit of disdain as he ran a finger over the edge of the table. He wiped his hands in the air, one against the other, as if wiping off cow shit from inside the corral of a rodeo.

I sighed, "I dunno. Maybe still at work," I made my way towards the sink and pulled a mug that lay in the basin by a still wet dishrag.

Ruben inquired, "What are you feeding that *thing*?"

"Dogfood," I always smiled at his disdain for any other living creature. If he could, I'm sure he would've delighted in drowning bags of puppies or tossing boxes of kittens into a busy road, "I just soak it in water. Read it online."

He rolled his eyes, "You know, they sell parakeets downtown. I'm sure we could get you one if you really wanted," he then stared down into the box, Firetruck hissed at him and then he said in a high pitched coo voice, "Aw, who da' baby? You da' baby? You wanna get da' flushed?"

I laughed, "Aw but he's an orphan. Just look at that face." Firetruck sat there jabbing the air in Ruben's direction with his beak. I pinched off a piece of wet kibble I had left soaking before we had gone out for the day. Leaned over the box and hung my fingers above his head then turned my back to rinse my hand.

From behind me, "OUCH! Fucker just bit me!" Ruben yelled.

I laughed, "Aw, that means he likes you."

Ruben shook the box and the bird started screeching. I backhanded Ruben on the shoulder playfully, "Quit it! Bad Uncle!"

He nursed his finger then said contemptuously, "Hashtag: sky rat."

The door opened and Domi put down his briefcase and unwrapped a scarf from his neck by the entrance. He shivered, "Ugh, it's getting cold out there. I think the rain is coming."

"Hashtag: no such thing as global warming."

Domi said with raised eyebrows, "*Hola* Ruben," made his way to the kitchen and grabbed me from behind, kissed my ear, then put his arms around my waist and rested his head over my shoulder. Ruben rolled his eyes then began to get up off the table counter he was leaning on and said, "On that note..."

Domi smiled into the box that I surveyed, "How's Baby Domi doing?"

"Ugh, he was screeching bloody murder when we walked in."

Domi laughed through his nose, "Uy no, he must've missed his momma."

Ruben forced a laugh, "Well, I'll leave you three. Say hi to Elma for me."

I waved him goodbye and he jingled his keys as he walked through the living room and out the door.

Domi asked, "How did it go today, babe?"

"Fine. We went shopping."

"What did you buy?" we were swaying in front of those two beady yellow eyes.

"An ice cream and a pretzel."

He laughed, "Ay, my fat little baby."

"What?! I'm eating for two now. Also I saw this nice shirt but I didn't have enough money. Besides, I don't think I can afford a new wardrobe at the moment."

He tapped my belly, "You sure it's not twins? You can borrow some of my old ones."

I smiled, "Triplets. Definitely triplets. Also, I don't think one of your shirts will even fit across my arm."

He laughed, "We could probably start a freak show with your babies. They're going to come out all dark and malformed."

"That's if they take after *your* side of the family."

"*Uy si*, I'm so sure. And your side of the family?"

"A duh! Blonde hair, blue eyes, obviously."

He laughed, "Well, let me go change and take a poop," he kissed me then walked away into the room. From the distance he yelled, "And my dinner?!"

I stared at the bird who looked around nervously as if he still recalled Domi suggesting soup the day we rescued him.

I yelled back, "You're on a diet!"

He laughed, "No, baby! *Anda!* Make me some *colitas de pavo* with rice and greens!"

I pictured an unappetizing plate of a charred attempt then thought of a delicious *colitas de pavo torta* smothered in mayo, one we could've gotten down the street a few hours ago.

I yelled back, "We have crackers and Milk! But I think the milk's expired! You can have the milk!"

He laughed then shut the bathroom door just as Elma walked in through the front.

I smiled at her with a, "I thought you worked?"

"No," she trembled, "Shit!, it's cold outside," and begun to rub the length of her arms, "We were so slow that Marco told me to go home. *Que haces?"* she looked down at the bird and in falsetto asked, *"Hola Frederico, como e'ta mi bebe preciouso?"*

The bird hissed and flapped his wings. I translated, "He's had a long day. Frederico? Where'd you come up with that name?"

She laughed then walked to the cupboard and pulled out a mug, filled it with water from a jug we had inside the fridge and popped it in the micro, "So yea... I didn't really like the name you gave him. And Domi?"

"He's pooping."

From the restroom he yelled, "*Dejame en paz!* I'm painting my nails!"

We laughed.

She bit the bottom of her lip, "And Ruben? Was that him that just left?"

"Yea, we went to the mall."

"Which?"

"*Galleria Aztecatuan Chimmy Changa* or something. The one Anabel works in."

"Ah," she nodded her head up and down slowly as the bird screeched. She walked back over to the micro and pulled out the cup then walked to the counter and opened a small jar of Nescafe instant coffee. Back in America, I'd always buy the big one. I wasn't sure why we didn't just buy the big one here.

As she mixed in the crystals and some sugar she commented, "Ay, poor baby. He probably misses his friends."

I smiled down into the box again, "Poor Ben..."

"Ben? Who's Ben?" she looked a bit confused and blew over her cup in attempts to cool the hot liquid.

"This character from a book I read once about some young couple that had a bunch of kids but that the fifth one came out all wrong. He started hanging around these older kids and because they kept saying 'Poor Ben', that's what he thought his nick name was or something."

"What's it called?" she asked.

"The Fifth Child or something. Was supposed to be scary but it kind of just fizzled out at the end. Like some old lady warning you about the primal evils of children playing on your lawn or something."

"Ah," she pretended to be fascinated as she stirred her drink, a bit absent minded, then, "And your book?"

"So far I've finished two chapters. It's horrible though, this writing thing. It's like it lives with you. Like inside of you. Like you're carrying it with you all the time. I sleep and have nightmares about it. I mean, I liked the idea of being a writer. Actually being a writer, however, is horrifying. It's like carrying a miscarriage. It's like carrying something dead inside you that feels as if it's still alive or, at least, as if it should be. It's literally self-induced dementia. You are trying to get your mind to visualize one thing or relive something. But you can't jump in the pool and expect to come out dry as fuck. Why? Because you've been soaking in it. You're going to be sopping wet and dripping, you mother fucking idiot."

She raised a brow, a bit taken aback, "So... where does your mother end up going?"

"Oh, I scratched that idea and instead started on a fictional account of me and my friend going on vacation."

"Ah, You have a title yet?"

"On the Lam with Luis."

"*Que significa eso?*"

"Like when criminals run away."

"Ah..."

Domi walked in shirtless, a towel draped around his head like a turban and opened the fridge, "*Hola* Elma."

She smiled into her mug, "*Hola, palito.* You're not cold?"

For some reason that man simply refused to wear a shirt or socks.

He laughed, "Yes, that's why I put on my *chanclas,*" then he kicked up his heel to show us his sandals and laughed then shut the fridge and poked me in the side, "And my dinner?"

"Ugh..." I rolled my eyes.

"Don't you *ugh* me," he said sternly.

Elma smiled while sipping her hot coffee, the steam and aroma rising to tickle all our noses. The smell was inviting but I knew if I drank any I'd pass out in less than half an hour. If anything, it reminded me how empty my belly was but I really wanted to get some writing done. She had reminded me that I hadn't touched the story in about a week. It was so hard to get started and stay started.

I capitulated to Domi, "Fine, what do you want? I think I saw a ramen up there somewhere. And what's with the towel? I thought you said you had to poo?"

He said, determined, "Lobster," as he flipped open and shut the cabinets, "I just took a quick shower. No biggie."

Elma laughed, "*Lobster*, fucking *mamon."*

I replied, "Buuu, I hate lobster but fine. How many? And only if you don't fill up on caviar beforehand. Also, I'm pretty sure that's why the water bill's so high."

Domi mulled it over in his head like a child, "Mmm... six! And you better make enough so I can take to work tomorrow. Hey, and what happened with all the mugs?"

I tucked the one I had filled with soggy kibble behind my back and suggested, "Luis Raul probably has them in his room... filled with chocolate milk or something."

Elma laughed, "Well, boys, I'll leave you to yourselves."

Domi asked, "What are you going to do?"

Without thinking I offered, "*Tocarse la vagina."* She walked behind me and twisted my love handles.

"Ow."

"Perv! No, well, I have to figure out what I'm going to do tomorrow. We've been so slow at work and they've been cutting everyone's hours. I think I might have to look for a new job.

"Marry Beto," I said.

She laughed, "*Ni madres!* He's poorer than me. Well, then, goodnight fellas," she waved from the hallway.

"Wait!" Domi yelled out then ran over in his sandals. Flip flop flap, "Gimme a kiss!"

She smiled, "*Ay ternuda!"* and grabbed him by the face and they kissed each other on the cheeks goodnight. By the time he turned around, I was standing with two cups of ramen in either hand.

"Do you want Spicy Chicken or Chile lime with Shrimp?"

I don't think I've ever had a memorable Valentines. Well, I'm lying. The year before, Domi had broken up with me the day prior. So, obviously, I had to, the next day stumble into the pet store and buy my first pair of parakeets then name them after us. Obviously.

"So where are you taking me?" I was on my stomach in bed, kicking my feet back and forth like a kid. I had been eyeing him put on his tie before work.

He said, "It's a surprise.." and smiled as he straightened out the knot.

"McDonalds?"

"No," he laughed, "Wendy's"

"Oo la la..."

"Nothing but the best for my baby," he smiled and sat down beside me to slip on his shoes.

I rolled over, and stared at the ceiling fan."Mmmm..."

"Mmmm.. .what?"

"Nothing. "

He rubbed my belly, “You and your 'mmm's'," he laughed.

When I woke up a couple of hours later, Ruben was online so we chatted a bit.

Ruben: "So what's the plan, Sam?"

Me: "?"

Ruben is typing...

Ruben: "For V day"

Me: "Herpes?"

Ruben is typing...

Ruben: "LOL- the gift that keeps on giving."

Me: "I dunno. I was thinking of getting him a book but I forgot to buy one."

Ruben is typing...

Ruben: "#worstboyfriendever"

Me: "You?"

Ruben is typing...

Ruben: "Got a hot date with a cutie."

Me: "#LuisRaul"

Ruben is typing...

Ruben: "LMFAO He wishes."

Me: "Facebook?"

Ruben is typing...

Ruben: "He doesn't have one."

Me: "Oh, he's one of THOSE..."

Ruben is typing...

Ruben: "Yes."

Me: "Ain't no party like a hotel party cuz a hotel party don't stop."

Ruben is typing...

Ruben: "?"

Me: "I was singing."

"I still don't see why we couldn't have just stayed home and watched Parks and Rec'."

We were walking up some stairs and Domi scolded me: "Don't start," he said as he was fixing the cuffs of his sleeves and I was tugging at the collar of my shirt.

I moaned, "Feels like midget hands are strangling me."

He laughed, "You look nice."

I mimicked him sarcastically in a high-pitched voice, “Ohhhh… You look nice. Meh meh…”

He opened the door for me. These big glass wooden things. Inside the atmosphere was quaint and mellow. Red carpeted walls set in dark wood.

"For four?” the host asked.

“No, just two, by the window please. We reserved a seat under Hiberto… Hiberto Dominic Hernandez."

The host scrolled a finger down his book, "Let... me... see..." He was balding, a little shorter than me and with hazel eyes. Maybe in his early 50s. "Ah yes, this way please."

He pulled out Domi's chair as I was busy taking off my coat jacket.

Domi scooted up his chair and scolded me again, "Why are you taking it off?"

"It's hot in here. Besides, if I get ketchup on one more thing, Luis is gonna kill me."

He laughed, "*Bueno,* you have a point there."

Another waiter came by. He was a dark short man, maybe mid thirties. He had a full head of thick fuzzy hair, "To drink, *señores*?”

I flipped the menu over a few times, looking for a list of drinks, "What... kinda... beers... do you have?"

Domi laughed nervously to the waiter, "Wait, do you think you could give us a few minutes?"

The waiter half bowed and smiled politely, "Absolutely, *señor*. Whenever you are ready," then walked away.

I was still staring at the menu then said nonchalantly, "Don't you even try and tell me that I can't drink on my birthday."

He laughed, "It's not your birthday."

I leaned in, covered one side of my mouth and emphatically whispered, "Shhh! They don't know that!"

He laughed, “*Callate, baboso.* Hey, we should order a bottle of wine, no?"

"Mmmm..."

"Come on," he leaned back in his chair and rapped a finger on the table. tap tap tap, "It'll be romantic."

"Fine," I flipped a page, "But can I get two?"

"We'll see, but I don't really feel like drinking."

"No, I meant two for me. You, you can have water."

He laughed and kicked me under the table, "Let's see.." he flipped through his menu, "...how much... hmmm... okay, we can get two but no appetizer."

Feigning disappointment I let out an, "Ash"

He laughed, "I'm kidding. Order whatever your little heart desires, my love."

I smiled into the menu, "Lobster. Where is that damned lobster..."

"Lobster?! I thought you hated lobster."

I looked up and grinned mischievously, "What is this place? Like Italian?"

"Yes, David recommended it."

"Ah, and what has he been up to? Is calamari even Italian?"

"He said he was off to a cabin with some dude he's dating," he laughed, "He told some other guy that he had to take his mother out for dinner."

I pursed my lips, "Ah, my mom... miss her."

"You didn't call her?"

"No. I hate talking on the phone."

He gasped, "You shouldn't be like that, babe. She's your mother."

I shrugged, "A duh, I know that. But she knows I love her."

"I'm sure but you should tell her every now and then."

I rolled my eyes, "Don't start. I'm not holding your hand in public."

He laughed, "Come on, hand in hand... skipping through the city. *Look, there go the faggots!"*

"Like when Luis Raul struts down the street, sucking on a lollipop in big sunglasses, wearing pink lip gloss."

He laughed, "Leave my *amiga* alone!"

I bit my lip and continued to scrutinize the menu, "What about snails? Isn't that French though?"

"*Que son 'es-snalls?"* he asked, straining with the pronunciation.

"*Escargot*... those things... like we find smooshed in the pavement at the park."

"*Wacala!"*

The waiter returned and cordially, "Have you sirs given any thought on what to drink?"

"Yes," Domi flipped the menu over, "Can you please bring us a bottle of Lambrusco."

The waiter, "Good choice, sir, I'll be right back"

I rolled my eyes.

Domi asked, a bit perturbed, "What?"

"Nothing."

"You don't like Lambrusco? It's really good."

"Too sweet. But hey," I squeezed his hand, "You looked cute ordering it."

He laughed and tossed his head back to get a strand of hair from out his face.

"What about.. an order of buffalo wings. Now I know for sure THAT'S not Italian."

He laughed, "Whatever you want, *amor*."

"Meh. When's the last time you cut your hair?" I asked still undecided on what I could stomach.

"Mmm... this past week. But it's too long again."

"Looks nice. I like it longer. How... about... this?" I placed my menu over his and pointed to a line of tiny letters in gibberish.

"Whiskey? Whiskey isn't an appetizer!" he said histrionically.

I, flabbergasted, "Ah! Since when?!"

"I told you, don't start," he said, in the back of his mind likely already regretting not having taken me to a taco stand. He then sipped from a glass of water the first host had poured.

"Fine." I thought aloud and to myself, "Best Valentines Day NEVER."

After a brief silence he went on, "Hmm... should we order one of these specials?"

"What do they have?"

"They're on the back. There's three options."

"Mmm..."

"Look, they come with an appetizer, two entrees and a dessert."

"Dessert? You mean like Rumplemintz?"

"Wacala!" he spit out

"No dice then!" I countered.

"No?"

"Not really. Just kidding."

The server, "Here we are, sirs," he leaned the bottle forward so Domi could inspect the seal.

Domi replied with a, "Yes. That'll do just fine."

The waiter turned around and I whispered behind a hand, "I can't believe you like wine with a twist off cap."

Domi didn't hear me and related, "What?"

I laughed to myself and he kicked me from underneath again. The waiter rolled a small cart against the table. There was an ice bin and some glasses. He poured one out for Domi, then me, then set the bin down near the edge. By the window was a candle and a white flower in a tiny blue glass bottle.

I leaned up my chest against the table, clasped my hand under it and said, "Aw... how romantic.."

The waiter, "Have we decided, sirs?"

Domi, "Yes, Can you bring us the dinner for two?"

Waiter, "Excellent choice. Which would you care to try this evening?"

"Ahmmm..."

I turned to the waiter and asked, "Which do you recommend?"

The waiter, "The second comes with shrimp fettuccine and a 9 ounce cut of steak."

Me, “Mmmmm…”

Domi, "Ahmmm..."

I looked up from the menu and asked, "How about the third?"

The waiter smiled, likely annoyed, "Oh yes, that one is a very good choice too. You get lasagna and two breasts of parmesan chicken."

I leaned towards Domi, "Ooohh, that sounds good."

Domi, "*Bueno,* we'll take that one," he then folded his menu and began to hand it to the waiter.

The waiter, “Very well. Would you all care to have a soup or a salad to start off with?"

Domi pulled back the menu and flipped it open. By then I was already chugging the grape juice. He asked, "Does it come with the meal?"

The waiter said, "Yes, sir. Every dinner is accompanied by a soup or salad."

Domi, "Well then, for me, the salad."

The waiter, to me, "And you sir?"

I was pouring myself another glass, "Salad. Salad's fine," I smiled. He walked away.

Domi, to me, "Babe! You didn't even wait for me!"

Holding the rim of the glass to my lips I smiled, "What?"

He laughed then held out his glass, "*Salud!* Finally, we can share a Valentine's Day. Here's to sharing many, many more!"

I followed with, “Here's to hoping the wine keeps coming.”

Clink.

Clink.

In bed, later that night, lying naked in each other's arms. Legs intertwined, dicks touching. My lips stained purple, my bladder about to burst but my prick still hard from the Sarah McLachlan fucking. I cooed, "Domiiii... Domiiiii"

"Marveeeeen... Marveeeenn"

"You still awake?"

His eyes were closed but he answered, "Yes. Ouch, but I'm hurting."

I laughed, "*Pero bien que te gusto...*"

He kissed my forehead, "No, I just do it out of my love for you," then laughed and said ouch again.

"Oh please, for 'love' my ass. Hey, look at me, I'm Domi, I'm a little girl. Let's watch Twilight. Meh meh meh..."

He laughed, "*Wacala*, What a horrible movie."

"Don't lie, I know you liked it."

"No, better yet The Notebook."

I dramatically whispered, shaking my head side to side and pretending to cry, "She can't remember!!! She can't remember!!!"

"You liked that movie?" he asked.

"Nopes. But I know that much about it. I don't think I've ever actually seen it."

"All the gays like that guy."

"Who? Ryan Gosling? Gross."

He laughed, "Yes, he has a nice body."

"Maybe but he has this shovel face and tiny little beady eyes that are too close together. He looks like you need to pin notes to his mittens or something."

"*Que es eso?*"

"Forget it. Did you have fun tonight?"

"Yes. *Me lo pase muy feliz*. Even though the entire restaurant stayed staring at us."

I chuckled, "Everybody! Look at those faggots!"

He laughed, "Yes, but there was another table of fags. I recognized them. They were some of David's friends. He went out with the darker one."

"Which? The muscle guys?"

"Yes."

"They were cute. But from what I saw they hardly talked."

He sighed, "I know, they spent most of the time on their phones."

"Playing candy crush..."

"On their Grindr's. *No mames, que weba.* What a bore."

"Yup. Did you see that little old couple?"

"Yes. *Me dieron ternuda.*"

"Yea," I agreed dreamily, "until he started coughing and I swore I heard him fart."

He laughed, "Yea, but it was funny."

"The gays turned around and made faces."

"Fucking faggots. What did you do, spend the entire time eyeing them?"

"No, I just like people watching. Like our waiter kept texting too. And did you see the chef?"

"Which chef? the fat guy with the black hat?"

"Yeah, now HE was hot."

"Oh for sure. You're only interested in him because he knows how to cook."

"Hey, hey, hey... free breadsticks for the rest of my life...."

"No, bebe," he dug his head into my collar bone, "*No me dejas por pan gratis...*"

"*Pan-nocha...* Fine, but you at least better get me free crackers."

He laughed, "*Menso,* at least with that you can get a girl pregnant and then come back to me with a baby Marveen."

The bird screeched from the kitchen.

I smiled, "But we already HAVE a baby."

"No, no, I don't like him. *Esta bien prieto.*"

"Racist."

"Yes. I want pale babies or *morenos claros*. I'd even settle for caramel colored kids."

"I used to want 8; all from different races."

"Eight? Why so many?"

"Just. I thought it'd be funny. On holidays I'd get them all together and it'd look like we were having an UN Summit."

He laughed and tapped my nose, "*Bebe chino Marveen, Bebe italiano Marveen. Hehe hawayano Marveen...*"

"Baby Kenyan Marveen."

"Really? You'd like a black baby?"

"Yes. I always wanted to be black like Storm, from the X-Men, as a kid."

He laughed and kissed me on the cheek, right below the eye, "What a faggot. I wanted to be Cyclops."

"Cyclops? He's like the one nobody ever likes!"

"Yes, but he was very handsome and in the cartoons his voice was very *fresa*, like a yuppie's."

"Gross. He always seemed like such a pussy. Like such a fucking good-e-two-shoes."

"*Haci,*" he began to mimmick a snooty accent, "*Alejate de Jean, Logannnn..*"

I laughed, "Am I Jean then?"

"Yes," he kissed my nose.

"Can Luis Raul be Logan?"

"*Uy si! Wolverine come todo.*"

"Elma can be Nightcrawler."

"No, she's Mystique because she's always up to no good."

"David can be Professor X."

"Why?"

"Because he's the shortest."

"Nada que ver con eso!"

"Well Professor X is always sitting down."

"Ah, now I get it," he nestled his leg further in between mine, "You're still hard?"

"Yes," I sighed, "And I need to pee like really, really badly."

"No bebe, mejor lo hacemos otravez."

I tossed my elbow over my eyes and said, "No. I'm tired. I have a headache. The dog ate my homework."

"Ash! *Que chafa! Y eso que te compre dos botellas de vino."*

"I told you to go for a third bottle but nooo...."

"I thought you said you didn't like it?!"

"Baby, honestly, I'd drink anything. I'm an alcoholic. Like seriously you should've planned an intervention the minute I stepped off the plane."

"*Si lo eres.* I know..." he wedged his face between my head and the mattress then let out a muffled, "*Te quiero.*"

Me, "*Taquito* you too."

He then slapped my ass, "Why can't you ever be romantic?"

"Five dolla make ya holla."

I was still waiting for my boner to go down. I lay there staring at the luminescent curtains but my eyes got heavier and heavier. I thought about how nice the evening had been. I imagined a slew of many more nights like this to come but the room spun a bit. It spun a bit more when my eyes closed but not enough to keep me from drifting. Sometimes things just happen in spite of us or how we feel. Sometimes...

"What's up with you?"

It was Friday night, movie night. Ana, Alicia, Ruben, and I were sitting like sardines in Al's living room. I was sitting on the floor next to Ruben. Everyone had a couch but me, but I didn't mind.

"Nothing..." I sighed and poked at Firetruck with a finger. He screeched an, "I love you, daddy."

Alice asked, "And *why* did you bring THAT?!"

Ruben, "Hashtag: bitch get a baby sitter."

Anabel, to our defense, "Leave him alone!" she was in PJ's, hair wet from just getting out of the shower.

Alicia warned, "If that thing poops anywhere..." then motioned a slicing finger across the top of her neck.

I looked down, "Poor Ben..." this poor unlovable, malformed creature.

Domi and I had been fighting the last few days. February was barely ending and the honeymoon was already over.

Anabel, combing her wet hair, asked, "And Domi?" she assessed the ends of her tresses, looking for damage and split ends.

"Oh, he's at home. I think David was gonna take him out somewhere."

"*Y eso?* What's up with that ?" Ana went on.

Ruben and Alice stared from the corner of their eyes.

I said, "It's fine. They hardly see each other. I think Elma was gonna go too."

"Why didn't you go?" Ruben kicked me in the back. I was rocking the baby on the skateboard that seemed to forever serve as a tiny coffee table and weed dispensary.

Despondently I said, "Didn't really feel like it. Money's tight. Besides we spend too much time together. He needs a break. I need a break. We just need some space."

Ruben sucked his teeth, "Oooo, Hashtag: Trouble in paradise."

I shrugged, "Yea... kinda. We've just been fighting about stupid things. I really need to get a job. I'm like basically down to nothing."

Alice, "Well, maybe," she laughed, "This might sound crazy, but have you tried staying out of the bars?"

I laughed and took a swig from a *Tecate* can, "I have! I swear! Ah, I miss Francisco Javier... "

Sarcastically, she said, "Right..."

Anabel accidentally flicked some water from her comb onto Firetruck and he shook his head. His beak open, inside his mouth, his tongue pulsating up, in and out, as if out of breath.

Ruben: "Well, I told you Gil's hiring."

Alice, "Who's Gil? So what did we decide on?" she was flipping through the channels.

Ruben tried getting a bit more comfortable in his seat. He shifted a leg under his ass then said, "He's the owner of that new gay bar on *Libertad.* It's like a pub called 'Beard and Bush'. Hashtag: FABULOUS!!!! We just went there like last week. It's pretty cool. But they have like no bartenders."

I petted Firetruck, "Who'd you go with?"

"Hashtag: A lady never tells... No, but seriously, it's like the owner and a doorman. But the place is really neat. Was an old house or something. There's a patio out back with this giant twisting tree full of these thick old vines."

I interjected, "Pffft... you would like it thick."

"Hashtag: it's not all about the motion of the ocean."

Alice popped some Whoppers in her mouth, "So what movies did you bring, Rubes?"

He scooted up to the edge of his couch and leaned over into his backpack, "Let.. me... see... Easy A, Mean Girls... Pretty in Pink... Mrs. Doubtfire... Forest Gump and...."

"Hmmm..." I said as Firetruck screeched in protest. Anabel, sitting Indian style on the couch, stared out thoughtfully, "Mean Girls?" she eventually said.

"Pop it in," Alice threw a whopper at Ruben.

"I never did get that movie," I grabbed the whoppers, "Who bought these anyhow? They're like the worst candies ever..."

Alice, with a mouthful, "They were free!"

I said, "As a kid, these were the last candies you ever ate if you ever were so stupid as to eat them. I think once or twice I fooled myself into thinking that they'd be good. I mean, they're chocolate covered and shit but bleh! Weird crunchy crap inside!"

Ruben, exasperated, "Geezus woman! Put a cork in it!" he said as he maneuvered over me, and the skateboard, towards the DVD player. Firetruck screeched and flapped his wings. "Hashtag: Debbie Downer. Hashtag: flying monkey."

Anabel laughed, "Aw, he's just a little *bay-bee*," then she cooed to him, "Yes, yes you are. Yes you are. Little *bay-bee...*"

Firetruck ruffled his feathers then started to preen a little; enticed by the sudden show of affection. Ruben snaked himself over the small space, at one point pretending he was going to step on the shoe box. I punched him near the balls and he flinched then fell toward Alice.

"Sorry," I said, "Maternal instincts, you know..."

A little hurt he retorted, "Hashtag: you... should've... flushed... it...Ow."

Alice threw another candy at Ruben's face, "Down in front!"

"So wait, I still don't get this."

Ruben kicked my back again, "Don't get what? They're girls. They're mean. It's funny."

Alice chimed in, "A doy!"

I pushed back his leg, "No, not that. And it's not really that funny. I think Easy A is better."

He whined, " Eh....It's *okay* but it's not Mean Girls."

“Meh, Still don't get why faggots love this shit so much"

“BECAUSE,” he kicked me again.

"Stop it!" I groaned.

“Hashtag: SHUT DA FUCK UP!"

Firetruck hissed.

"NO! NO! NO! NO!"

We were watching "You're Next" some gore-fest about these assassins in animal masks. So good.

Ana screamed, *"Pendeja!"*

Alice spent half the time laughing nonchalantly and gnawed on a red Twizzler. She held out an arm, "Anyone want some?"

"Hashtag: Is butter a carb?"

I also declined. I had been trying to feed Firetruck but he was having none of it. I covered my eyes and we'd all screamed:

"NO! NO! NO! NO!" again as this girl ran straight into a piano wire, having her neck sliced practically in half.

Again, so good. Highly recommend. After that movie we turned on the lights, stretched, and took a break on the tiny balcony outside. There was this door to the right of the TV that led to this flimsy fire escape barely large enough to fit us four. I stood in the doorway. Ruben took the furthest corner and lit a cigarette. Behind him, the twilight of the city and a thousand bulbs from a thousand people twinkled as the trees waved in front of light posts, bags flew over house windows, and cars took lefts then rights. Every candescent nature, consumed in its own story and time. Like the cherries of our three cigarettes and from the lighter Alice used to spark her bowl. Each and every one oblivious to the other, for a second at least.

Ruben motioned to Anabel, "So how's the Gilbert Grapes thing going?"

She took a drag and exhaled, "Better. I think it was smart to move out. Now he actually seems excited to see me again."

"Hashtag: men be bitches," he then pointed his chin to me, "Maybe that's what you and Domi should do?"

Absent-minded, lost in a reverie and trying to figure out my next move, I realized that smoking wasn't really my thing. That I had used it far too long as a crutch to stifle my feelings, "What? Oh…maybe. I can't afford it anyhow."

Alice laughed, "Don't be stupid", she passed Ana the pipe, "Isn't THAT the whole reason you moved down here? To be together and shit?"

Anabel motioned to Alice to hand over the lighter.

Alice, "Oh sorry."

Anabel took a hit, nodded her head up and down as she held in the plume of euphoria, then choked out a cough and added, "Definitely," cough, cough, cough, "Besides, I don't think Domi would let you."

I looked east to the approaching gloom, "It's just that we had our own lives. Now it's like I feel I'm a house guest. Somebody that's outstayed his welcome."

Ruben, "Bitch please! No thank you," he waved away the bowl and Anabel passed the pipe and the lighter to me. He went on, "You put out. You moved cities. You gave up everything for the sunny shores of Mexico," lightning flashed from behind followed soon after by thunder, "Well," he said rolling his eyes, "You know what I mean."

"Yea..." I sucked air in through my teeth then exhaled, "But still. I really need to get a job. I think money's a big issue right now. Even Elma's having trouble making ends meet."

"Market sucks," Ruben said as he stared down at his feet, examining the tips of his new shoes.

We all nodded in unison as a streak of lightning sparked a mile away.

I laughed, "Did you just see that? Whoa, you sure we're safe up here?"

Anabel smiled and took another drag off her cigarette.

Alice, "The problem is that we're stuck in this extended period of adolescence. Our parents at this age had families, houses, etcetera. We're still going to school or living at home or living ten people in a house or some stupid shit like that."

Ruben, "Hashtag: *mantenido!* Whoop! Whoop!"

Alice went on, "And not having a good job is part of that. Do you think I wanna work as a waitress? Hells no! But it's good money. I get free food and they let me do whatever I want. Monday through Friday, I have to deal with a bunch of snot nosed squirts who couldn't care less about learning English. Like seriously, you know how hard it is to try and teach somebody who's immature and ashamed of their accent? And they don't care. They're not paying for it. But I work two jobs, no vacations, because I can't go back to living off of 200 dollars every two weeks."

I muttered out, "Been there," and reached for the pipe.

She motioned intensely with her hands, "What we gotta do guys is start our own business. Like maybe we can print shirts, or raise organic fruits, or like even just dog walking..."

We all stared at her quizzically.

Ruben put in his two cents, "Hashtag: that shit must be good."

Another roll of thunder. Ruben looked to the sky with a dainty palm held up, "Uh oh..." then just as quickly, a downpour, and we were rushing to get back in. I stood there though, still by the door, and just watched. Holding out the cigarette feeling this warm wet. The cherry singeing and hissing.

Ruben held up a copy of Halloween and Mrs. Doubtfire, "So, ladies, Terror or Trannies?"

It had been hours and the rain wouldn't let up. Nearly midnight and we had watched about four movies and an episode of Girls. It was like Sex and the City but with younger, less "fabulous" people, travailing the pitfalls of post grad life.

Ruben moaned, "Ugh, I'm not getting signal."

Alice tossed back three kernels of popcorn, "Ya, leave that Grindr shit alone!"

He cocked his head to the side and tucked his chin into his chest, “Hashtag: jealous much?"

Her rebuttal, “Hashtag: Whore much?"

Ruben rolled his eyes, "Well, chickadees, we really have to get going. Have to have Cinderella here home by one."

Alice, "Why don't you stay here? Looks horrible outside..."

He sighed and pointed his thumb to me, "Ask this bitch."

"I dunno. Domi might get mad or pee on my clothes or some shit."

Anabel, "Pfft, if he's with David, they won't get home till like three. If Elma's with them, then four. Here," she reached for her phone, "Let me text him."

A few seconds later, "He says fine and not to be a *puto* and to give baby Domi lots of kisses."

I sighed, "That's weird. He's weird. I hate that he pretends things are one way when in reality they're another."

Anabel, "What did you expect? Him to tell me, to tell you, to fuck off and die?"

Me, "Would've been more akin to the way our conversations have been going."

Alice chimed in, "So then... Forrest Gump?"

When I came to, Sergeant Dan was fighting off prostitutes on New Years. Everyone else was asleep. Well, Anabel must have gone to her room, but Ruben and Alice were passed out on their respective couches. I swore that there was a Twizzler stuck in her mouth. Firetruck seemed fine but was alarmed when I went to get up. He opened his eyes with the rustle of my feet but closed them with a chirp.

By only the light of the TV, I tried to make my way towards the kitchen. I wondered if there was anything to eat. The fridge was filled with take out boxes and condiments. Mustard, an all but empty mayo jar, a bottle of Sriracha, and a quart of beer with a piece of napkin stuck in at the top in lieu of a bottle cap. But there really wasn't much else. Not to mention that the green-black mold growing on the sides made me lose my appetite so I just grabbed a can beer, rinsed the top off and called it breakfast. I heard someone walking down the stairwell outside. I tried to peek through the little slit by the plants on the window but I couldn't tell if it was still raining or not. I opened the fridge again. Nope. Still didn't want to risk it. I grabbed another beer though and shuffled back to the living room and sprawled out on the couch Anabel had left empty. I stared into the TV, not really watching anything. Firetruck chirped and I reprimanded him softly, "Shhh... Poor baby...poor, poor, ugly baby...."

Beto, Elma's boyfriend had basically been living in the house now for a week. I wasn't sure if they were just fucking a lot or that he had lost his place downtown. Tensions were running high and I sometimes sat back and imagined myself as a fly on the wall watching my own move-in reenacted but with a lot of "artistic license" involved.

Domi became more and more on edge. Luis Raul spent most of his time at some guy's he was dating. Elma was not even home half the time. She picked up a second job at the sushi place on the corner of *Lopez Cotillas* and *Del Federalismo Sur*.

Beto kind of just walked around in the same clothes he'd been wearing for days. He was like me but a thinner, less agreeable version. One day I came back from the corner store to find him rummaging through Domi's top drawer. He pulled out a cigarette square and asked if I minded him bumming one. What was I to say? I never felt like I needed to hide my money up till then. I told Domi but made him promise not to make a big deal out of it. Another week went by and Elma and Domi were at each other's throats. Poor thing. She looked tired and stressed. She didn't even iron her hair anymore. Most days she'd just tie it up in a ponytail and rush off somewhere.

Week three and we all went out for my birthday to this seafood place down the street. It felt more as if we were going through the motions than anything. Beto would not shut the fuck up about being French and visiting Europe often as a child. Said you'd run into a lot of people from home just because everyone took the same flight over and back. When the bill came, Elma didn't have enough to pay their share so Domi lent her some. He later told me that he'd probably never see that money again, but what really irked him was that Beto kept asking me for cigarettes throughout dinner and making fun of the academy Luis Raul's boyfriend attended. It was just some kind of tech school but whereas we were all giving him props for having a life plan, Beto just kept trying to discourage him. Saying he wouldn't find a job anywhere and that he was wasting his money on a bunch of con artists who themselves couldn't find jobs so they ended up having to open that school.

Later that night, as we were getting ready for bed, I sighed to Domi, "Takes all kinds, I guess."

"No. It just really pisses me off."

I said, "I know. Ugh, and he kept talking about this fancy car I've never seen. Are you sure he doesn't have a little dick or something?"

Domi laughed, "No idea. You should ask."

"Ewoo. No. Then I'd get stuck having to talk to him about Italy or Bangladesh or some shit. I swear, at one point he was describing Six Flags as Paris."

"Well, ask Elma."

"Ay, poor thing. I hardly see her anymore. I think she's aged like ten years."

"Ooo, don't even think about mentioning that to her. *Pobre estupida*, she doesn't even put on make-up anymore."

The final straw came when one night, Beto and Elma came home drunk and were yelling at each other. At first I thought they were laughing. Me and Domi were laying in bed staring at the ceiling. Listening. He was shaking his leg and intermittently trying to keep his eyes shut tight but no dice. He just kept repeating, "Fuck, I have to go to work in the morning." I squeezed his hand and brought it to my chest.

All of a sudden we heard a thud and then Elma calling Beto a fucking faggot ass bastard. Domi shot up and out of bed then ran out the room. A few minutes later I followed. I just assumed he got so pissed off at the racket that he went out to tell them to shut the fuck up. I was sleepy, tired, same old shit every other day.

But when I stepped into the light of the kitchen from the shadows of the hallway, I came to find Domi sitting at the table and bleeding above his left eye. Elma was smoking a cigarette, staring out into nothing and leaning against the furthest kitchen wall. Luis Raul was standing by the front door. The rod iron one was closed but the wooden one was open. He was yelling at Beto to man the fuck up and get the hell lost. Something about "What a big man, hitting girls" and shit.

I rubbed Domi's back, "You okay?"

Elma rushed over to us and started hugging him like a mother who'd lost her child in a department store.

"Perdoname! Perdoname!" she cried and rocked him back and forth in her arms.

He just laughed, "Gimme a hit of that cigarette."

I looked at them both as Luis slammed the door. Poor disheveled things. One bleeding, one's mascara running, one, uhm, fat and stinky. I took a deep breath, "He didn't take the mezcal, did he?"

Our heads were tucked under the covers again. We sometimes only used bed sheets because it got so hot at night. His alarm clock had gone off twice and the morning bells from the church, along the way, had rung about four chimes. I laid on my side staring at his imperfections as he laid on his back. No chin, big nose, giant zit by his mouth. I reached over and he yelled, "Leave me alone!"

"Come on," I pleaded, "lemme pop it!"

"No. Your hands are dirty. I'll pop it right now."

"Oh please. How's Elma doing? She hasn't said much."

"She's fine. Let me sleep... Five more minutes at least."

"She's probably more embarrassed than anything."

"Yes. Five more minutes...."

"Maybe I should punch you so..."

"What pisses me off is that I'm know she's going to go back with that idiot."

"... You think? Still, at least let me push you around a bit and call you a..."

"Yes. She always does this."

"You've never been in an abusive relationship? They're fun. I swear. Just one punch. Com'n..." I smiled.

"Physically? No."

I punched him in the stomach.

"*Quedate quieto!*" he turned over and grabbed my hands and laid his belly over them so as to keep me from having any fun. He went on, "No, but with my ex we'd yell at each other. He'd always get mad when I'd wash the dishes because I'd sometimes break them. But now he wears dresses. I think only once did we ever end up pushing each other. You?"

I sighed and pulled my hands out from under, put an arm below my head, and stared up at the rays of sun creeping over the ceiling, "I wouldn't mind a kilt. Yeah, with my ex. I'd always end up punching him because it was like he was so stupid he couldn't understand what I was saying. I guess I was stupid for hitting him, but seriously, I thought the only way I could get the words that were coming out of my mouth to sink into his head was to shove my fist in his face."

Domi opened his eyes and looked at me, then smiled and closed them again. He frowned then his face went serious. He opened his eyes again and grabbed both my cheeks then smooshed them together, "No, *bebe*, that's not right to disrespect your partner like that."

"Pfft, fucker would always break my stuff, steal my stuff, or cheat on me. I think the whole punching him in the face came from the first time we broke up. I told him that if he ever went with somebody else that I wouldn't forgive him until I could punch him in the face."

"Well," he laughed then kissed me, "I guess that's fair..."

"Would you ever hit me? What size of kilt do you think I'd wear?"

His eyes rolled to the right, "Mmm... If you cheated on me, yes. And I don't think they make your size. Maybe we could just sew something out of one of the old bed sheets?" he laughed, "And you? I mean, would you hit me more than you already do," he started to tickle me and I fag tagged him in the balls. He moaned out painfully.

I mulled the idea over out loud, "Mmm... yes. I think so. But I dunno. I think it's different with boys. It's one of the few perks of dating a guy. You're both dudes and can take a swing at each other. But if you like beat on a girl, or a kid, or some kind of midget, then everyone thinks you should burn in hell."

He laughed, "No, *bebe, ya no me pegas.*"

"Fine.... BUT WHERE'S MY BREAKFAST?!!"

DING DING DING DING DONG DING DING DONGGG

I walked to the front door half expecting Beto to pop out of the bushes spewing some bullshit about how he'd forgotten something at the house.

Not by the hair of my chinny chin chin, I thought as I was telling myself "I sooo don't need this right now." Cautiously, I opened the door, hoping that Luis had left the rod iron locked.

It was Ruben. Sunglasses, lollipop, red polo and fitted khaki pants, "Hashtag: rude much? Open up, bitch. I'm your salvation."

I laughed and unlocked the rod iron door and grandiosely ushered him in.

“Hashtag: love what you've done with the place," he kicked a red disposable cup that had been lying on the floor. I leaned over to pick it up as he went on, "Oh no, don't put yourself out on my account. So where have you been, bitch? Been trying to reach you all week. It was either send smoke signals or knock on your door and right now I'm trying to stay away from carcinogens," he leaned in and whispered, "Bad for the complexion, ya know," then loudly, whilst snapping his fingers, "HASHTAG: GIRL'S GOTSTA STAY FABULOUS!!!”

I politely laughed, "Sorry, we haven't paid the internet."

"Yeah, I saw the gas disconnection notice on the gate. Thank baby geezus, I'm here to deliver you from the sins of poverty!"

"...." I looked at him questioningly.

"Trust me. You showered yet? And no, no, no, that simply will not do!" he pinched the shoulders of my plaid shirt.

"Showered? How do you spell that?"

"Ugh, god, bitch, I think the hobo down the street takes better care of himself than you do."

"It's called *Eau de Street People Pee Pee*."

He playfully slapped my cheek, "Hurry, the bar opens at three!"

I sighed, "Can't. No money. Domi says that I'm on a budget and that if I don’t quit drinking so much, he's gonna tell the corner store to stop selling me beer. Can he really do that? Besides, it's two-thirty."

Ruben laughed, "Child, momma's gonna take care of everything! Now, hurry! You have to look presentable!"

"Really can't, man. Maybe tomorrow. I've just gotten to a part in the book where..."

He walked around me and started pushing me towards the kitchen, "No! there's no tomorrow! Now get showered, get changed! We're getting you a job today!"

"Job? How do you spell that?"

"This?" I turned around in front of Ruben as he sat on the bed, one leg over the other knee and propping himself with one arm as with the other he texted.

"Ugh, Don't you have anything in solids?"

"Yes," I pulled out a black western short sleeve, "What about this?"

He sneered, "I guess it's fine if the first impression you want to make is 'Hi, My name's Marvin. I enjoy pit stains and grease marks.' Just go get in the shower. I'll pick something out."

I smiled a bit disheartened. "Fine."

BANG BANG BANG

"Geezus, woman! You're worst than my sister!" Ruben was standing outside the bathroom door, impatiently imagining me naked, I'm sure.

"Shuddap! I'm almost out!"

"Hurry your ass! It's already 3:15!"

I popped open the door wearing the same clothes I had on prior save for a new pair of underwear and no socks. He waved a hand in front of his face to dissipate the steam that assaulted him.

"God, woman, are you baking rice in their or something? OH, and take off those pants."

"I thought we agreed..."

"That was before I found these little gems," he smiled and held up a set of clothes, "Do you think Luis would mind?"

I furrowed my brow, "Were they from the right or the left of the closet?"

"Mmm..." his eyes shifted right then up mischievously, "Right."

"Then yes. That's the stuff he just bought."

"No no no. I meant Left. YES, definitely a left pair of pants."

"Ugh, I don't even think those will fit me. He bought a whole new wardrobe because he lost a few pounds."

"Bitch please, I was all over that closet and every thing's a size 38."

"That scoundrel," I said, feeling a little betrayed.

"See, he deserves what he's getting. Besides, you're going to get a job. You can repay him or buy him a family *flauta* pack or something."

I laughed, "Fine. But keep me away from ketchup."

He raised a brow questioningly.

"Never mind. Here, give it here."

Back in Domi's room, Ruben was trying to put the ensemble together. I was like his fat mannequin and he some contestant on Project Runway, "Now we cover your pit stains with this cardigan and VOILA! Respectable fine young gentleman!"

I stood in front of the mirror, "Not too shabby," I was wearing a tan cardigan with that black western shirt and a pair of rust colored khakis.

"I guess the closest thing to dress shoes you have are those ratty boots but they'll have to do. Actually looks kind of hipster-ish. But just in case, smile a lot and shake your head. Keep the boss man distracted from below the waist.

"Hey! I like these boots. I actually get a lot of compliments!" I said preening in the mirror.

He laughed, "Bless your little, retarded heart," then patted me on the head, "Now hurry. It's almost four already."

The Beards and Bush was on *Libertad*, an entire street dedicated to little pubs that tourists often visited. They were carved out of old homes. Most of them were beer bars with nice little patio fronts. Ruben said that this one used to be owned by this little old lady who died or got tired of the loud noise. For a year or two it had lain vacant. Not even boarded up. As we drove from the house down *Chapultepec* and towards the street, I looked out longingly at the bicyclists merrily going about their business. The weather had been nice and the sun was shinning. I was reminded of how little I ventured out during the days anymore. If I had been back at home with the pups, it would've been mandatory to walk them once I woke up, and at least once more before work. These days I didn't really have any incentive to leave the dark of the cave that we lived in. The museums didn't interest me much and, after a while, I got bored of just following the streetlights. I used to play a game in which I'd wander the city and at every stoplight, I'd follow the direction that the first pedestrian signal gave. It took me a while to realize that there weren't always birds singing. That it was some sort of device alerting the blind to a valid crosswalk although, I must say, I never did see a Ray Charles impersonator.

Ruben went on to say that after such a long stint of nobody willing to rent the property, in stepped Gil. Gil was part owner of a club called *Babel* but decided to venture out on his own. *Babel* was a notorious gay club. Like the big gay club in town. The scene was good though, so much so that more often than not, half, if not more, of the clientele was straight. Gil purchased the property, renovated, and reopened it as a posh bohemian bar. Something a bit more low key.

I interjected, "Bohemian? Ugh... I hate hookahs!"

"No child," he slapped my arm and took a quick left, "It has like pillows on the floor and shit. Mmmm... also like maybe one or two hookahs."

"Those things are gross. Read once that people were transmitting bronchitis or something through them."

"Bitch please, we lick assholes."

"Touché, " I acquiesced.

We found parking on a side street around *Moscu*. Ruben told the *parkero* that we'd tip him when we left and to take care of his ride.

He replied, "Sure, *señor,* anything you say. Hey, do you happen to have an extra smoke?"

We both reached for our ciggies but Ruben was quick draw McGraw. Lucky strikes. The *parkero* reached out a dark wrinkly hand. He was old. Like older than someone should be who's just standing in the shade all day. I imagined he spent a lot of time under those giant tropical trees. His palm, a light calloused pink, almost white. His teeth were straight as an arrow. Colgate commercial with a gray baseball hat. His outfit like a post man's: Dark blue trousers and a white button up—short sleeved and the fabric so thin you could see another shirt peeking through from underneath.

The street was full of people just lazily going about their business. Two lanes divided by a median full of greens. The people not at all unkind but a bit blasé in the midst of the late spring heat. The rain was coming. It seemed to always be coming in those days and my head swooned at the prospect of another migraine. I hadn't had them in years until I moved to that place. Domi used to just say I was always hung-over. I'd say to shut his stupid fucking face and pass the naproxen and mezcal.

As we walked along, most people met our gaze and smiled. I waved at a few and they waved back. There were two dark short men working on the front of a business demolishing a wall. They stood staring for a bit, one leaning on a shovel, the other with a sledgehammer in hand. It looked as if they were smashing pieces of concrete just for the hell of it. Seriously, those pieces were tiny. Like hand sized. I smiled and they raised their chins in acknowledgment. If we were back in Juarez, the streets would've still been full but everyone would've been averting each other's eyes. I remember one night meeting a college student from the University downtown. She was from Juarez and we both took some kind of sick pride in coming from a fucked up community. We felt and we acted and we walked and we talked hard. Well, that's what we agreed upon. That in this sort of big city, small town mentality haven, we weren't afraid of much. We'd lived through daily murders and the constant cloud of random violence. I smiled to myself. This is where I should be. Where I belonged. If only there was a shooting star, out there, somewhere above my head.

An old man shuffled by. Worn khaki fedora with a black stripe. Light tan jacket, in spite of the oppressing humidity, and trousers pulled up to near his rib cage. His shoes were shined but cracked black leather that grated against the pavement. The pants were so high I could see the white tube socks he wore instead of the dressier black standard.

We passed two taco trucks. My stomach rumbled. That heat. Those nerves. I could swoon if I didn't think it really so inappropriate to dirty another one of Luis Raul's clothes. In the back of my head I just kept remembering him in the mornings trying to scrub out red stains. Half of them weren't even blood related. He'd just sigh, scrub harder, then sigh harder as if to make sure I had heard him sighing. My only saving grace was that I always shared my beer and more often than not, I was the only one who cooked for him. I'd be lying if I said he hadn't grown on me. He wasn't particularly smart and although our conversations largely revolved around one-liners, it almost felt like having my Saint Bernard around again. Oh how I missed Hachi, that drooling big oaf. That adorable, lazy thing of a dog.

All this I was thinking as my boots tap tap tapped on the sidewalk. That sound always made me feel pretty, important or dignified. Like I was wearing stilettos in a couture outfit. Ruben fanned himself as kids ran by us and into us. A wave of white polo shirts and black pants with varying colored packs strapped to their backs. Laughing little things, taunting each other, oblivious to anything else. I couldn't remember ever being so young and carefree. I remembered being young, but my youth had always been marred by manic depression. I wondered if ever me and Domi would have a few runts of our own and sighed. I suppose we could always just adopt Luis. Lord knew he needed taking care of.

A large new bus passed us, leaving behind it a wake of exhaust and a cool breeze. In another part of the world, all we had were big old school yellow ones done up like rusty trollops. In Juarez they'd paint them flashy flag colors. Greens and whites and Reds. Each one had it's own name. Here they just had numbers and were clean. Boring, I know. This city had everything new and pretty, set in colonial scenery. In Juarez there'd be nothing but prostitutes and hustlers around here. Drag queens waving kerchiefs from second story windows. One brunette and the obvious blonde fantasy. *Cholos* would've accosted us for spare change or to use our phone. A ploy to scope out whether or not you were worthy of being mugged. Cars would've been honking and cutting each other off. But here, everything was orderly, almost idyllic. What a strange idiosyncrasy of a city to be so nice and friendly.

We hit a corner and a few people waited with us. I didn't know why but people had the tendency to stare at me. Ruben said I looked like a foreigner. That I walked like Lurch from the Addams Family. That I hadn't learned to take slow strides and enjoy the weather and the climate of the people who lazily lounged or took steady slow breaths. The trees that we passed, their trunks were so huge and round and with such character. These giant replicas of those tiny, waxed leafed things they sold at Wal-Mart in the summer and the spring.

Green.

The light turned green and that old familiar bird chirp sounded. Old man. Old woman. Kids and teenagers crossing. Each in their own merry little world. They carried with them this relaxed expression. A courteous relaxed expression. As if they could fart or you could fart in each other's presence and nobody would give a dam. For how big the city was, I was surprised that nobody pushed and that hardly anyone walked with a cigarette. Reminded, I lit another cigarette. I felt like a fat Mexican version of James Dean.

tap tap tap tap

We kept walking and the rhythm of my boots really pumped me up. This was me, on a new grand adventure. I was finally taking root in this big old city. I was finally going to have my own spending money. Strippers! That was the first thing that came to mind. I could finally buy some real pots and plants and maybe they'd not last very long but at least I could get back into the routine of earning my own keep. Pretty soon I'd be carrying tennis shoes and wearing fancy pencil skirts. Pretty soon I'd be a real go-getter and be hobnobbing with the social elite.

From above, that rhythm melded into the music that was booming, but muffled, from a three story. I had yet to learn the dates of these buildings. From what I understood, either Moses or a group of very determined Tyrannosaurus Rex's had cobbled them together. Maybe Betty White had something to do with it. I didn't know. There were these big black metal doors left wide open and a tough looking bald man about 6 feet. He wore a skintight black shirt and light blue jeans. Boots black and imposing with an inch or so sole. Arms crossed like Cerberus bending his necks. Ruben approached him and whipped out an id. I fumbled with getting out mine. Smiled and handed the angry fellow it then looked around on the ground to make certain I hadn't dropped anything of importance. I swear that's where all my money went. Everyone assured me that I just drank it all away.

Cake.

The big old grumpy bear then broke into a smile, patted our backs, and ushered us in. Why is everyone here so nice? I don't get it. How can you expect to be intimidating and so cordial at the same time? The place smelled like a weird combo of potpourri and piss, sprinkled with a touch of *Fabuloso* and incense.

We walked in and to the right there was a circular counter with a register. Behind it was wall of hookahs. Rich stained glass. Tall ones. Taller ones and a tiny little baby of a thing.

Ruben dragged a finger across the counter as a bee zig zagged an inch beyond my nose. I wondered if the bee had to show his ID. The counter was bar high and led to what looked like a little sitting room. A couch to the left. Victorian style done up nice with neon yellow upholstery. It was velvety and wearing at the sides but in an elegant way as if many an ass had sat there then had a brilliant idea and scooted to the edges to tell their friends a story. A set of thin rails ran under a glass coffee table that sat in front as a companion to the piece. On the opposite wall, two tall black round tables about two feet in diameter. Barely enough room to put your elbows on. Two bar chairs at each. The wooden slats that made up their backs were multicolored. Red, blacks, whites, and pinks. The ceiling was painted in a star scape over thick exposed beams. A smiling sun in the middle. A table lamp as elaborate as the hookahs, sat demurely on it much like a posh Swedish model might stand in the corner of a foreign country. Don't worry, little lamp, I don't know much of this language either.

I raised an eyebrow and we walked through where it opened up into a dance floor. There was a small table with two chairs tucked in the crevice of a wall to the right of the doorway. To the left, a cornered bar. About ten empty bar stools. The far right, a DJ Station.

A short man with thick black rimmed glasses leaned in from behind the bar, folding some card board box, breaking it down after having had stocked a few beers. He smiled and daintily waved as if he was trying to clap with one hand. He voiced out a hello in something caught between a tenor and a raspy falsetto.

"Come on in, fellas. Have a seat," he smiled, "What can I get ya?"

I smiled and waved politely like a retarded child. Quick rapid side to sides. I stared out behind him. He had a cooler with glass doors, the kind you see in convenient stores. There was a litany of Mexican beers. Sol, Dos Equis, Negra Modelo's, etc. I opted for the last. The shiny gold aluminum wrap catching my eye.

Ruben asked for a vodka tonic. Barkeep smiled. He was short, about 5'6", with broad shoulders. The physique of someone who must've done some kind of body building in their hay day, but since, the muscles had sagged. He had a kind face though. Big nose that bulged out at the end. We could've been twins in that department.

"Here you go, ladies," he set down the drinks. My beer bottle and Ruben's rocks glass with a thin, red, short straw, like a coffee stirrer resting on the rim, "That'll be 50 pesos," he smiled.

Rubes whipped out his piece of plastic and handed it to the fellow, saying, "Keep the tab open".

Ruben quipped, "Hashtag: *mantenido*."

The bartender smiled, "Sure thing, ladies."

Rubes took a sip, sucked the air through his teeth as if there was more vodka than tonic in his drink, "*SO*, Gil, how's business?"

A little taken aback, by the familiarity, or maybe at being recognized at all, Gil replied politely, "Oh fine. Just fine."

"Have you found any new bartenders?"

"Well," he twirled a white towel between two hands, "We've got one coming in today. Some others came in to apply but they had no experience and, sweet heart," he put a hand on Ruben's arm, "I've got way too much on my mind to be training some twink on how to open a beer."

Ruben laughed, "I know what you mean."

"Besides," Gil continued, "We're only really busy Fridays and Saturdays. And even then, you know, the word's barely getting out about us so there's not really much of a crowd yet."

Rubes, “Oh girl, just you wait!"

Gil laughed, "Honey, I like you,” he winked and smiled then waved the towel at Ruben as if he was a southern belle and it his handkerchief.

"Well," Rubes continued, "If you just so happen to need an *experienced* bartender, my friend here," he slapped my back, "just so happens to be one."

Gil leaned up with both arms against the bar, "Really? where have you worked? Sandoval's? Alive? La Huerta?"

"No," I laughed meekly and swiveled in my stool, "I used to bartend back home," which was slightly stretching the truth. Long ago it had been determined by my bosses that although I was quick and knew how to make drinks, I was not to be trusted with the spirits.

My accent must've betrayed me. Gil went on, "Oh, a *gabacho,*" he smiled,

I shrugged and smiled shyly, "Yea..."

He grinned, "Where are you from?" then leaned closer. Ruben pinched his straw and drank effeminately, smiling to himself as his plan unfolded before his eyes.

I answered, "El Paso."

Gil looked confused for a second.

"It's right near Juarez," I offered.

"Aw yes! Juarez! I have two cousins and an aunt who lived there. They're in Colorado now. But I visited once or twice. Gurl, that city is crazy! And the weather is so weird! I got off of the plane and I was freezing my nuts off! The next day, I couldn’t stop sweating!” he laughed and slapped my arm, "How long have you bartended?"

I lied, "Oh, you know, like 5-6 years."

"Gurl," he blinked coquettishly, "You're too young. Don't lie!"

I laughed nervously.

He went on, surmising me, "What's your favorite drink?"

"Mmmm... I'm a whiskey and beer kind of man," another lie. Vodka had always been my love. Mezcal, my new mistress.

"Ooo, gurl, nobody drinks those around here. Everybody wants a skinny girl this or a vodka cranberry that."

I laughed sarcastically, "Well, it's not hard to learn how to make a drink. It's all about knowing how to make a drink taste great."

Gil smiled, "Go on then."

I looked puzzled. He winked at me, "Make me a drink."

"I dunno..." my eyes shifted to the floor.

"Come on, you say you're a bartender. Show me!"

I reluctantly swiveled off of the stool. I couldn't seem to find the bar entrance. I walked a few steps left then a few right until Gil opened the lift up bar from the far left. I crouched beneath it as he was still lifting it and bumped my shoulder against a cooler. It was claustrophobic back there. Under the bar there was another cooler. Overhead, a shelf with a series of bottles and an array of upside down martini and wine glasses. There was a sink towards the corner edge and a well with ice just to it's right. More glasses arranged just above the sink and cooler. There was a rectangular metal basket hanging off of the ice bin. Cheap well liquors. The labels reminded me of being young and inexperienced. Back when you thought all alcohol was supposed to taste like jet fuel. I gagged.

From behind me, Gil, "Make... me...."

"How about a margarita?" I said quickly.

"Oh," he cooed," We don't have a blender."

I scoffed, "Blender?! Now THAT'S gringo!"

I would like to say that I started juggling bottles and back handedly pouring drinks but I didn't. I just measured out a decent tequila, triple sec, sweet'n'sour, squeezed out three slivers of lime, splashed some Sprite, and shook it up. Then all there was really left to do was salt the rim and there: Margarita.

I handed it to him with a, "Girls love this shit."

He took a straw, "Not bad", he smiled. Now make me one with Patron."

In my mind I imagined some friends back home screaming at the top of their lungs, in a dirty dark bar, "PAAAATTTRRRRRRRONNNNNN!!!!"

In bed that night, Domi's legs between mine, I stared at the window, the curtains glowing with the streetlight. I could feel his breath. I could smell the rain in my nostrils. I could taste the cigarette on my tongue. Stinky and sour and stale.

I whispered, "Are you awake?"

Curtly and like a spoiled child he replied, "No."

I bit him and he said, annoyed, "Don't start."

"What do you want to do for your birthday?"

"To go visit my mom. *Que me hace mole. Mole* and some potatoes with *chorizo."*

"Mmmm..."

"Mmmm... what?"

"Nothing," I said and sighed.

He hugged me tighter, "Elma told me she was going to throw a party for me. That we should make weed lollipops."

I turned slightly to him, "Where?"

He laughed, "No idea. I'm guessing here?"

"What if we go to a bar?"

He snickered, "*Wacala!"*

"Where'd that come from?"

stuck to this job, that would mean less time for me and Domi to do exactly these kinds of things. It would mean going back to living a life where everybody enjoyed a Saturday trip. I assuaged myself with the idea that all they ever did was want to drive to the beach. I didn't have the body and therefore no inclination to wade in the water next to svelte young hipsters. Already, in my head, I was trying to devise appropriate excuses for why I'd be getting home late. For why I wouldn't be able to make that bonfire party. For why I'd miss every big DJ that rolled into town. But I told myself, if anything, I should be coming up with excuses to why I'd be late for work. I've never been on time and that was just something I suppose that we had inherited from my father. Even my mother couldn't help it. But Gil seemed like a nice enough guy. Maybe if I just ran in panting and explained about not having a car or something about trying to balance out my carb intake with exercise... yeah, that was it. Gay guys love exercise! I tried telling Domi this and he just sucked air through his teeth and told me not to even think about being late. Work was work. You had to make a good impression. I recalled how my sister was horrible at being on time. I told him about how she could call you from the shower and tell you that she was just around the corner.

On that note, although he was reluctantly happy that I'd found a job, he'd hint at the disappointment concerning the exact nature of my employment. In his opinion, he'd imagined I'd apply at an art gallery or start teaching English or perhaps get an office job collating papers. Domi's imagination was never one to be admired. I think the time he spent in a coma was often reflected in his lack of romance and adventure. Sometimes I secretly wished he had drowned in his own spit just so he could shut up about being late in the mornings or about being unable to stay up past ten. Also, let's just say that he had his reservations about me working at a gay bar and half jokingly threatened to cut my dick off if I ever got into any funny business. Back home, Elma and Luis were more enthusiastic although both had their doubts as to whether or not it was such a good idea that I should be trusted around such readily available alcohol. The running joke was whether I'd run the place bankrupt or double their sales and come home without a *peso* to my name.

On Monday, Ruben came over and decided that I should invest in a new wardrobe. I asked about any thrift stores in the area. He said that we could go to *Chapultepec Trianguis,* some market where you could find just about anything. He warned, however, that if I was about to show up to work wearing tattered hand me downs, I might as well just stick with what I already had.

He finally convinced me that our best option was to go down to the mall. Clearance aisles would be my best friend and besides, he said, "I doubt you'll find anything in your size at the *mercado*. And remember, you're in a big city now. What you wear is who you are. Nobody's gonna take a *pocho* seriously who walks around in stinky tennis and shirts you bought at the grocery store."

With a sigh, I conceded and soon found myself back under unforgiving fluorescent lights in the midst of a throng of uber fashionable every bodies. The babies were even dressed better than me.

Our first stop was a shoe store. The music alone was intimidating. It felt as if I should be popping ecstasy and waving a glow stick. The salesperson was this petite pretty girl in a short pink dress. The collar of which ran straight across with a little "V" slit in the center. Around her waist she wore a black belt and her strawberry blonde hair was tied tight into a bun. I wasn't sure if I had stepped into a corporate office or what, but I was at least glad that I had decided to change my socks that day.

She approached, not altogether warmly, but with her chin a bit raised, almost menacingly. Wall to wall shoes with mostly pointed tips and intricate lace designs. There were a few standard men's dress shoes though. Their leather had been treated to look distressed and "vintage". On that wall were tennis in bright colors. On that wall, there were Tom's.

On that wall, there were Converse. I missed that old street near downtown that had nothing but shoes. I reminded Ruben again that we should've just stuck around there. All he said was, "Honey, out with the old, in with the new."

The salesgirl clasped her hands haughtily. She didn't look like she was from Guadalajara and she didn't act like the locals I had met. For a second I tried to place her accent then decided that she must be from where Domi was from, from Chihuahua. Those people, his friends, were usually snooty and self-important. I thought, "Geezus woman! You fucking sell shoes!"

She grinned contemptuously, "Can I help you?"

Ruben ran a finger over the toes of the closest display, "We're looking for something..." he looked at my worn red Converse then raised his eyebrows, "... *nice*..."

She raised her own eyebrow and looked away as she adjusted the shoes he had just soiled with his stubby fingers, "Well, we have plenty of *nice* shoes. Were you looking for something for a funeral or a wedding maybe? We have some nice Italian leather, basic, but affordable, on the other end of the wall over there."

We both leaned to the left, looking past her to see this middle aged man scrutinizing a black patent leather something. He wore a white polo, khaki member's only jacket, pleated pants, and white socks in penny loafers.

Ruben sucked his teeth then said, "Mmmm... no, no, no... something, mmmm, more fashionable....:"

She forced a smile then turned her back to us and said to follow her. The place was small, maybe about twenty feet wide and fifty feet deep. She led us towards the register and shifted her weight on one heel, clasped her hands again and pointed with the tip of her thin, well-bred nose to a wall of ankle boots. Distressed leather... everywhere.

She bit her lip then said, "This is our latest shipment." She wore a pale pink lip-gloss and I could notice the slightest of peach fuzz growing just below her nostrils. There were top name brands, I think. I've never been good with names but I assumed as much. My first instinct was to turn the shoe over to check the price but there wasn't any. Back home there was always a sticker. Either inside or on the sole.

"Which one's do you like?" Ruben asked me.

"Mmm... I guess these ones." I held out a mustard brown pair of ankle high lace ups. They reminded me of the 1920's or axe men boots. Flannels in red and blacks. He snatched the pair from my hand, handed them to our salesperson, then turned around and quickly inquired as to what size I wore.

I blurted out, "11, 12, or 13… American."

She pursed her lips, clutched the shoe to her chest, giant in comparison to her tiny breasts, then disappeared into back.

Ruben, "11, 12, or 13? What?! Does your foot expand in relation to your fat ass?"

Me, "I'm just glad that she didn't ask me to convert it into metric. Besides, different shoes fit differently. Universal measurements my ass."

So we waited for her to come back and made fun of the other styles. Some shoes looked straight out of Blade Runner or Tron. Other's were almost inauspicious but with nice florid stitching. I read the material on the inside of their tongues. Half of them weren't even real leather. Everything was man made and man made in China.

Ruben whispered to me, "You realize you're picking out a lesbian's shoe, right?"

"Shut up! They're nice. Plus I can wear them everywhere."

Ruben: "... building houses... cutting down forests... man hater's book club... fixing your Subaru..."

I laughed, "Watching my football... rebuilding the carburetor ..."

Suddenly he pulled me aside behind a rack of neon running shoes.

"Shhh!" he hissed then whispered, "Don't look now but that's Popeye!"

At work, Gil fired Hector's friend, Humberto, because he was pocketing money from beer sales. They hired two more "boys" who were more eye candy than anything else. They were nice but "Straight" although I swore that once or twice they left with one of those creepy old vultures which hung around the place. Gil kept trying to convince me to shave my head, but I informed him that my scalp had wrinkles like a shar pei. He'd just turn up his nose and tell me to do the restrooms again.

My life in Guadalajara began to become eerily similar to that which I had left behind. Instead of dogs to come home to, I came home to a lover, two roommates, and a retarded bird. My friends were also amazingly similar. I do suppose bar people never really differ.

For all the excitement and all of the novelty, I began to realize that after the initial rush, it all just plateaus. I began thinking a lot about home. The mother I rarely called, my dead dad, my dead grandma, my barely living other grandma. My friends. My old coworkers. The good times, the bad, and what did I have to show for it? I felt like a dog chasing its own tail. And then I remembered my dogs. Wondered if they were being treated so well. Whether they were lounging on a sofa or out chained in the cold or exposed to the desert heat.

I thought a lot. All I had left to do was think. The bar was never that busy and my friends seemed to go over the same damned things. Anabel was still on the fence with Gilberto. Rubes was dating two or three guys who all looked the same and were short. Domi worked all the time. Elma was always high. Luis Raul... well, he was fine. I at least didn't feel guilty sharing a family sized bag of chips with him. The only one I hardly ever saw was Alice. Apparently she was now some sort of lesbian.

Gross, I know.

All those lips, tool belts, Subarus and soft ball. Gag me with a spoon! In hindsight, the signs were all there. The lack of decorum. The picking of nose in public. Jeans, t-shirts and fedoras to fancy occasions. Her disappearing into the dark with random ladies. At first I merely assumed she had a drug problem. But now, it all made sense. I felt like Lois Lane staring at Superman behind his Clark Kent.

With my new position came the dilemma of just what to do with Firetruck, the bird we had rescued from the roof. He had for some time now been eating on his own but his life was largely spent in a big cardboard box, perforated with hundreds of tiny holes. He could still not fly so I would while away the early evenings watching him hop around the garden. Well, Luis Raul's garden and my patch of yellowing weeds. Sometimes I'd place the box over my head. It was like seeing stars at night. The smell however was not all that romantic, so with my first good sum of money, which came to about 60 dollars for a week's worth of work, I managed to find a used canary cage in the *mercado* for about 150 pesos. It was painted white with a few bars that had begun to rust. The bottom was this yellow plastic tray with a thin crack running the length of the left side wherein the thing had supposedly fallen on it's previous owner. The vendor, a 5 foot brown man, with stark white hair and a face like a wrinkled paper bag, mentioned that it had belonged to his wife before she died. He showed me where he had rigged a piece of bailing wire on the top so that they could still hang it by the window.

Although, at the end of the transaction, he mentioned another story in which the cage had actually belonged to his eldest daughter who moved away and became some kind of doctor or the inventor of peanuts or something. As I left, he waved goodbye with a toothless grin and puffed out a plume of smoke from a cheap cigar. Maybe he was a meth head. Working in the bar and hanging around all those hip young kids had made me paranoid about just how much drugs everybody in the city used.